HOTEL CUBA

a novel

AARON HAMBURGER

HARPER ● PERENNIAL

NEW YORK ● LONDON ● TORONTO ● SYDNEY ● NEW DELHI ● AUCKLAND

HARPER ● PERENNIAL

HarperCollins books may be purchased for educational, business, or sales promotional use. For information, please email the Special Markets Department at SPsales@harpercollins.com.

FIRST EDITION

Designed by Jamie Lynn Kerner

Library of Congress Cataloging-in-Publication Data has been applied for.

ISBN 978-0-06-322144-4 (pbk.)

23 24 25 26 27 LBC 5 4 3 2 1

Praise for Aaron Hamburger

Hotel Cuba

"Deeply moving, compulsively readable, *Hotel Cuba* chronicles the early twentieth century immigrant experience with a profound understanding and crackling urgency I've not previously encountered. I could not put it down and I could not stop thinking about it long after I'd reached its stunning conclusion. In short: You need to read this book. Right now."
   —Joanna Rakoff, bestselling author of *My Salinger Year*

"I cannot overstate my love for *Hotel Cuba*. With expert perception and a capacious heart, Aaron Hamburger weaves together the daring tale of Pearl and Frieda, refugees from Poland who journey to Havana to start a new life. Carrying little but their own unstoppable vitality, their discoveries in this strange land will dazzle readers on every page. Thrilling and magisterial, the twists and turns of their story will break your heart and fill it up again with light. With every sharp and generous line of this exquisite novel, Hamburger creates dazzling worlds within worlds that I'll be thinking about long after turning the final page."
   —Kristopher Jansma, author of *Why We Came to the City*

"Aaron Hamburger takes the reader on Pearl's circuitous journey through Cuba to the United States, keeping us close to the visceral feelings of hunger, displacement, and loneliness as well as the blossoming that Pearl undergoes in Cuba as she begins to assert her creative identity. Set between the two world wars, *Hotel Cuba* explicates the past while presaging the future in an excellent historically based novel."

—Breena Clarke, author of *River, Cross My Heart*

"With *Hotel Cuba*, Aaron Hamburger sees the poignant gravity behind the ongoing search for home and the battle that can ensue between family obligations and the weight of history. With great empathy, this rich, engrossing novel lets us see that no place is ever transitory and that even the briefest of stays forever affects us, no matter our last horizon."

—Manuel Muñoz, author of *The Consequences*

"Aaron Hamburger's deeply compelling new novel *Hotel Cuba* takes us to 1920s Havana, where it weaves a beautiful story of sister love and leave-taking. The book is syncopated by Hamburger's signature, perfectly timed humor, his generous storytelling and agile prose. What a wise, knowing, big-hearted story of belonging, and the lasting imprint of place, written by a writer at the height of his craft. There's a feast for the eyes and ears and tastebuds here, so find a very comfortable chair and settle in. You won't be able to put it down."

—Susan Conley, author of *Landslide*

"Aaron Hamburger's *Hotel Cuba* is a beautiful, gripping story of immigration, hope, and personal fulfillment. Pearl, its protagonist, is one of my favorite characters in any recent novel; she is complex, wounded, occasionally ferocious—and always engaging, as she follows a long, fraught path from Russia to America via a vividly rendered Prohibition-era Havana. Pearl seeks what we all do: safety, family, and, ultimately, a place in which she can be her best self. I loved this book."

—Christopher Coake, author of
You Would Have Told Me Not To

"*Hotel Cuba* is a stunning and captivating read. It can be easy to show a cast of characters crossing such great distances, can be easy to show an immigrant's story, but it is another thing entirely to make a reader feel that distance and the love, sadness, forgiveness, and triumphs these people experience. There is so much love and compassion in this neatly detailed and moving novel. *Hotel Cuba* joins the ranks of some of my favorites, like Geraldine Brooks's *Caleb's Crossing* and Anthony Doerr's *All the Light We Cannot See*."

—Morgan Talty, author of
Night of the Living Rez

"In this vibrant and engaging novel, we join Pearl—practical, adaptable, and constantly underestimated by those around her—as she turns her mind to the task of learning the baffling arithmetic of a new culture, a new language, and new freedoms. How do you tally the price of a mango or the price of a dock-worker's strategic silence? How far can the distance between two sisters stretch without breaking? And how do you calculate the most delicate variable of all: the value of Pearl's potential and future worth as she finds her place in a new, unknown world?"

—Carolyn Parkhurst, *New York Times* bestselling author of *The Nobodies Album* and *Harmony*

"*Hotel Cuba* is warm, witty, and mournful, a hopeful and clear-eyed chronicle of roads both taken and not. Aaron Hamburger has a wonderful ear for the tenderness and loneliness of memory, and though his book travels continents, its most potent territory is the impossible idea of home. Pearl is miraculous and unforgettable, and so is her story."

—Hilary Leichter, author of *Temporary*

"Pearl is a character who will keep you reading late into the night. You cannot help but place your hand in hers and go along for this unpredictable journey that moves between continents in the 1920s. Thick with the humid air of a Havana summer night, rich with mesmerizing detail, *Hotel Cuba* will grab you and not let you go."

—Dolen Perkins-Valdez, author of *Take My Hand*, *Balm*, and *Wench*

"*Hotel Cuba*, the story of two sisters—one a sociable beauty, the other an independent thinker—and their journey toward the American dream is terrific. From the harrowing opening voyage as sheltered Russian Jewish refugees on their way to 1920s Havana, to the final pages set in an up-and-coming Detroit, Aaron Hamburger vividly reveals all the places and choices the sisters must navigate as they forge their way in a rapidly changing world. This is historical fiction at its best."

—Jessica Francis Kane, author of *Rules for Visiting*

"In *Hotel Cuba*, Aaron Hamburger brings a humane intelligence to the story of two sisters searching for home following the devastations of the First World War. Every finely observed detail resonates with hope and loss."

—Rebecca Donner, *New York Times* bestselling author of *All the Frequent Troubles of Our Days*

Nirvana Is Here

"Hamburger is tender and provocative in his examinations of sexual abuse, racial strife in 1990s Detroit, and the way that discovering Nirvana changes everything about Ari's world. The complexities of this novel are deftly handled by Hamburger, whose sensitive and observant prose is a pure joy to read on every page."

—*Electric Literature*

The View from Stalin's Head

"The stuff of a Czech fairy tale."

—*New York Times Book Review*

"Reminiscent of David Sedaris's *Me Talk Pretty One Day*. Laugh-out-loud funny."

—*Los Angeles Times*

HOTEL CUBA

Also by Aaron Hamburger

The View from Stalin's Head
Faith for Beginners
Nirvana Is Here

For Ethel and Morris Fishman
and all immigrants

HOTEL CUBA

ONE

FISH AND ORANGES. A SALTY SEA OF SOUP DOTTED WITH ISlands of potato chunks that Pearl can mash flat with the back of a spoon. Bread so dry, when she dunks it into her lukewarm soup, the stubborn roll remains firm. But Pearl can be stubborn too. She continues dunking the roll until it softens and melts into a paste.

It's depressing, the food on this boat they call SS *Hudson*. Heavy on salt and light on pepper, parsley, or any herb to give it character, like the shaggy dill in her yard back in Russia—or what used to be Russia, because this year, 1922, their town belongs to Poland. After a good rain, those dill stalks grow so high they collapse under their own weight. Starving blue-eyed soldiers from the tsar's army used to pull them out by the roots, mistaking them for carrots, then fling them to the ground.

"Eat," says Pearl, offering an orange to her younger sister, Frieda, sitting with her eyes closed and squeezing her temples. "Or save it for later."

"Don't bother," says Frieda. "I won't eat it then either."

"You can't starve all the way to Cuba." Maybe Pearl sounds more like a nagging mother than a sister, but she quit worrying about her own vanity years ago when Mama died, after giving birth to Frieda. Though Pearl was only nine then, people already called her Old Lady, Housewife, Empress of the Kitchen, Madame Singer Sewing Machine.

What will they call her in Havana, where no one knows her and she has no history? She might be anything. It's a thrilling, terrifying thought.

Before the war, a girl from Turya who'd immigrated to America returned to visit—as a rich lady. Some women laughed behind her back, mimicked her proud walk, lifted their hair to imitate her short haircut, and called her New Woman, as an insult. But Pearl didn't laugh. Maybe someday she too would become a kind of New Woman, like this shtetl girl who'd transformed into a prosperous American lady who could afford to coolly ignore the others' jokes, as if she didn't hear. Now there was freedom.

Frieda, who's in one of her states, won't eat, no matter what Pearl says. Arguing with her is like trying to empty the ocean with a spoon, so Pearl returns to her own soup. Tomorrow she'll eat the next soup, and then the one after that, and the one after that. In this way, always looking forward, never back, she and this creaking boat will slowly cross the Atlantic, leaving Europe behind.

When Pearl finishes her bowl, she's still hungry. She has long been cursed with a healthy appetite. Her solid, sturdy figure bulges in the wrong places for a woman who loves dainty clothes, loves looking at them and making them. Before the Great War, when people cared what they looked like, Jews and Gentiles alike paid her to make dresses sewn with fine stitches you'd need a magnifying glass to see. For each dress she made, Pearl imagined a story, the potential to put on a new outfit and become a new person. But sadly, clothes never fit her as beautifully as they do slender Frieda, who even before the boat often forgot to eat.

Pearl has never forgotten to eat in her life. During the worst of the Great War and then the Revolution and war with Poland after, her hunger was so raw it addled her thoughts, gnawed at her stomach lining.

On the SS *Hudson*, many passengers are seasick, like Frieda. Pearl squeezes sideways between tables, casually skims stray peas and carrot knobs from abandoned bowls of soup, scrounges a section of orange, a scrap of pinkish-brown herring.

A willowy lady wearing a dusty-pink hat watches her at work—out of pity or disgust? She's a sophisticated city type. Jews are so desperate to leave Europe these days, they'd cross the ocean in a bathtub, so Pearl sees many grand people like her mixed with country folk in steerage. This lady has a long, lovely face, pale with a pointed chin, and shrewd gray-green eyes like a cat. Pearl noticed her when she came into the dining room on the arm of a young man who pulled out a chair for her. She stepped forward and sat, didn't even look behind her, confident the chair would be pushed in again, and it was.

Pearl imagines what it would be like to have that kind of confidence, to sit into air and know that a seat would appear below you. And that hat—it fires up her imagination. If Pearl could afford to wear a fancy pink hat like that, she could walk down the street with such a cold, blank stare that no one would dare bother her. She's known plenty of women who aren't strictly beautiful, but in the right hat or dress, they're magnificent. Their clothes teach the world to treat them with dignity.

The pink lady notices Pearl staring, gives her an inquisitive look, and Pearl, who feels a puzzling itch to capture this exquisite woman's attention, surprises herself by nervously extending a roll and asking, "Maybe you want half?"

In response, she averts her eyes.

"It's all right," says Pearl, fearing she's committed a blunder but unable to stop herself. "You can have the whole thing if you want."

"I'm afraid I'm not very hungry." Looking as if she's smelled something rotten, the woman rises and leaves the table, followed by her male companion.

Pearl returns meekly to her seat. What was she thinking, speaking out that way? "This food's awful," she tells her sister. "If they let me in the kitchen, I could do better."

"I heard you," says Frieda. "The way you talk, it's embarrassing."

"What did you hear?" Pearl suspects her sister's right but doesn't like to admit it. She lacks her sister's talent—if you can call it that—for small talk.

Frieda grabs a roll and shoves it rudely at Pearl's chest. "'Go on, have it.' That's not how someone with manners speaks. Didn't you see that expensive dress she had on? Didn't you hear her pretty accent? Imagine what she thinks of us."

The back of Pearl's neck prickles with shame. I've gotten it wrong again, she thinks. But what if the pink lady wasn't offended, just jealous? Because Pearl was brazen enough to do whatever she felt like. If that lady wasn't so polite, she'd pick up scraps too. Polite people don't survive in this world.

"We're from plenty good stock," says Pearl. "Father's from Lithuania."

"Where we're going, they've probably never heard of Lithuania," says Frieda, pushing back her chair. "I can't sit here anymore. My stomach's not at all well."

"I'd better come with you," says Pearl.

Clinging to the shaky, narrow railings, the two sisters descend three flights of metal stairs into the ship's belly. Day or night makes no difference in the enormous room where they sleep, three times the size of a synagogue, crammed with endless rows of iron berths stacked with lean mattresses. Kerosene lamps put up a feeble fight against the darkness. Pearl and Frieda have claimed two narrow beds by the wall. They take turns holding up a blanket while changing their clothes. Not everyone is so delicate, and Pearl's eye occasionally catches the white curve of a stranger's breast or rump. Once, Frieda wasn't paying attention to the blanket and exposed Pearl's body. "Raise it higher! Higher!" Pearl hissed, imagining everyone staring at her fleshy, hairy arms, her dark-toned skin, the color of rye bread. But she wouldn't allow herself to cry, not for all to see.

"Was it really so terrible how I spoke to that lady?" Pearl asks.

"Leave it be," says Frieda. She climbs into her bed, pulls her knees to her chin, and faces the wall to retreat into her sullen self, silent as a widow.

It's wearying, the engine's eternal clanking, strangers' anxious chatter, and days of seeing only sea and sky around their ship. Pearl's ears ache, filled with the constant roar of ocean. Focus on other things, she thinks. A warm, freshly laid egg, or yes, a dusty-pink hat. But then the ship hits a rolling wave, someone screams or tumbles to the floor, and she's back in the present, lost on an ocean.

Like Pearl and Frieda, many passengers are Jews fleeing the cluster of shtetls on the Polish-Russian border, which shifts east or west year to year, war to war, and sometimes disappears. The passengers from cities like Minsk or Warsaw stand out to Pearl because of their store-bought leather shoes or their gloriously impractical ladies' hats, tight as bathing caps. She's seen such hats in a fashion magazine she found during the short time she worked as a hotel chambermaid in Warsaw. Every day she smooths the pages, presses out the wrinkles. In America, she hopes to make dresses good enough for a magazine.

The washrooms are right outside where they sleep, easy to find: just follow the stench to its source, where five faucets dispense cold salt water into metal basins. Some of their fellow passengers can't quite make it to the washroom to relieve themselves or vomit, so to ward off the smell, people tie dried herbs or chains of garlic to the iron berths.

When they first left Danzig, Pearl tried to shield Frieda from the mess, but it's impossible, as if this journey were purposefully designed to make them feel like animals. Despite the efforts of the crew, who hose down the floors with ammonia every few days, a musky stink has settled in the cavernous space: a mix of body odor, various human secretions, tobacco, garlic sausage and onions, damp laundry hung to dry, though nothing ever dries.

"Frieda, let's go out on deck, get some air," Pearl urges her sister.

"I'm staying," Frieda says, her voice muffled in her bedsheet. She fears the churning waves that crash over the deck, leaving behind a lacy foam.

Pearl has yet to meet a wave that would dare try to frighten her. Until this journey, she'd never seen the sea, and she recalls her surprise when she first realized that it wasn't blue. More like a dirty gray, or when the sun shines, the color of steel.

So Pearl leaves her sister, climbs up on deck to watch the ocean—an ocean! Such sounds it makes, the rhythmic crashing of waves, or a loud moan like a mama bear protecting her cub. Some people only run up here to vomit into the sea. They're in such a hurry they don't check the wind, and their mess splatters back in their faces.

That's what you get, Pearl thinks, when you try to fight the ocean.

○

BY SOME MIRACLE Father had saved enough for their passage.

The way he told it, Father was born in an elegant quarter of Vilna, studying Talmud, Shakespeare, and Spinoza, only to end up slaughtering meat in some backwater Russian shtetl where his intellectual life consisted of advising people who'd found blood clots in chicken carcasses whether the meat was kosher.

He blamed politics for killing his dreams. As a young man in Vilna, he lived through terrible times: strikes, food riots, protests calling for the tsar's head. Most Jews his age were more likely to be beaten in the street while agitating for revolution than to attend synagogue. Father found a post as assistant cantor at a small but prestigious shul, where he was given thankless, unwanted duties like chanting the "Giver of Salvation" prayer for the health of the tsar and his family. One *Shabbes*, as he opened his mouth to sing the usual platitudes, a band of Zionists rushed the bimah and chanted revolutionary slogans, bringing the service to a humiliating halt. No one came to Father's aid or said a word in his defense as he slumped down from the bimah. In fact, as the story circulated in the days afterward, he was blamed for his passive response.

Disgraced and fed up, he quit the shul and moved his family to the backwater shtetl where his wife had been born. In Turya, there were politics, sure, but not so much to interfere with life. A small-town cantor's salary couldn't support a family, so Father joined his father-in-law's butcher shop, and this in time became his own misery. He'd come home from work exhausted, snapping at anyone who talked to him before he got food in his stomach. As a girl, Pearl dreaded both his sharp tongue and the strap dangling beside the peg where he hung his coat. Though he never actually used the strap, its threat was enough.

Father lived for Friday nights in shul. Jews traveled from the surrounding villages to hear the famous Cantor Kahn's tremulous, melancholy vibrato. From the women's section at the back of the sanctuary, Pearl listened to his tender, delicate voice and felt closer to him than when they shared the same table. He'd come home lit in the afterglow of his performance, bringing along for dinner half the choir, boys he'd prepared for their bar mitzvahs, now men with muscles, rough manners, and wisps of beards.

For Pearl, Friday nights were also a performance, a kitchen performance. After her mother died, Pearl took over the cooking. Who else could have done it? Her eldest sisters, Elka and Rivka, were married with their own families to take care of, living on farms with babies and animals for company. Basha spent all her time at the regional school where the non-Jewish girls called her louse and threw stones at her back. When the war ended, she left for New York, hoping to attend a ladies' college. For now, she worked making dresses. Avram was a boy. Frieda was the baby, and even when she grew older, Pearl continued to think of her as such.

Before the Great War, Pearl roasted chicken or stewed meat for a crowd of twenty, sometimes thirty. She set the table with a red felt cloth and brass candlesticks—castoffs from wealthier relatives in Vilna, yet finer than anything on their neighbors' tables.

But then the tsar declared war on the Kaiser, and then the Revolution declared war on the tsar. More often than not, the butcher shop was closed. Once, to raise money, Father went out to pawn their china and candlesticks and came home in his socks, his forehead bruised, his hands trembling. Two soldiers had knocked him down, stolen the boots off his feet. A priest stopped to intervene, asking, "Why bother this poor Jew?" So the soldiers shot him. As the priest crumpled into the snow, Father ran away.

For three years, their little town of Turya was invaded by bands of Reds, Whites, and Poles, each of whom accused the Jews of sympathizing with the wrong side. Pearl and her family hid in the dark, behind locked doors and shutters, listening for soldiers, bandits, Bolsheviks—all bastards with different names and causes, though their purpose was the same.

Pearl did the best she could to go on with her Friday night dinners, her small act of rebellion. The menu was now fish balls mixed with bread crumbs as filler, or a thin soup with potatoes, chopped cabbage leaves, and any kind of root that escaped the notice of wild Gentiles on fast horses. She relied on her brother, Avram, to gather herbs and vegetables from the yard and water from their well, and to watch for strangers before opening the front door. When she found mice droppings in a small bag of precious flour, she swallowed hard, then carefully skimmed them off and used the rest to make bread.

As Pearl served, passed, then cleared plates of food, invisible as a servant, Frieda basked in admiration. Frieda, a charming, chatty girl who outgrew her baby fat and childish curls to become a precocious teenage beauty. Frieda with her high-pitched voice, who even in wartime could make sparkling conversation about nothing: delightful when you heard it, and forgettable minutes later. Frieda, who when the talk inevitably turned to serious subjects like politics, abruptly withdrew into a corner to sulk. Watching her, Pearl felt little jealousy, maybe more of an odd pride in the young woman her baby sister was becoming. Anyway, none of these teasing, boorish boys were to Pearl's taste. The kind of man she'd want—dignified, smart, adult—good luck finding him in Turya.

During the sisters' last Friday night dinner before going to join their sister Basha in New York, a steady procession of neighbors and relatives came to visit. The men wanted to look at pretty Frieda one final time, while the women entrusted Pearl with messages for relatives who lived in various corners of America, as well as advice.

Don't eat what smells bad.

Poke a man in the chest and watch his reaction to see if he's lying.

To fight the seasickness, lick a few grains of salt off your wrist.

Trust one eye more than two ears.

Pearl listened, promised to bear it all in mind, while Frieda made faces at the women when they weren't looking.

Last to leave was old Tzeitel Feldsteyn, a well-known do-gooder, always doling out bowls of watery soup to the sick and old, though she herself was poor as dust. A soft-spoken woman, inside she was tough like old bread. Frieda found her pushy, thought she ought to take better care of herself before worrying so much about others, but Pearl supposed all that charity sustained Mrs. Feldsteyn, kept her mind off her loneliness.

Mrs. Feldsteyn gave Frieda a bag of musty-looking candy and greetings for her grandsons, Ben the Oak and Mendel, who'd gone to America two months earlier, to join an uncle in the city of Detroit. Ben and Mendel's parents died young, leaving Mrs. Feldsteyn to bring up two boys while caring for half the indigent in their town on an income of rags. And mostly she managed it. "Tell them don't forget me," she said, clutching Frieda's hand with her rough, worn fingers. "This time next year, you and Mendel should stand under a chuppah."

"Maybe he's forgotten his old friends in Turya," said Frieda with a charming laugh and passed the candy to Pearl to hold.

"Maybe he forgot some," said Mrs. Feldsteyn. "But not you."

"Excuse me," said Pearl, who preferred not to be reminded of her sister's regrettable attachment to Mendel, that schemer-dreamer. In the room they shared, she tucked the candy into their wicker suitcase, along with food for the journey, clothes, and their sponsor letter from Basha, who advised them not to bring too much. They'd find all they needed in New York.

Glad for a break from all their company, Pearl sat on the bed, staring at the water-stained wallpaper peeling in the corners. She'd never see this room again. People who crossed the ocean rarely returned. Good, Pearl decided. That's why I'm going, to leave this life behind.

Back in the front room, Mrs. Feldsteyn and Frieda were gone, and Father was sitting sullenly at the table, his eyes red and anxious. "Where's Frieda?" asked Pearl, gathering the ends of the tablecloth.

"She walked Mrs. Feldsteyn home. Avram went with them." He reached for her arm to interrupt her cleaning and said, "I hear in America, even the water isn't kosher."

"Nonsense," she said, recognizing Father's flair for the dramatic.

"When children are young, parents talk about how smart their children are. When parents are old, children talk about how stupid their parents are," he said. "In America, I suppose you girls will start smoking and stop going to shul. You'll cut your hair, change your names, go with strange men, become modern women. I don't know, I don't know."

Pearl dropped the tablecloth and sat down to think of a response. You can't go back on your word, she thought. Even if you do, I'm going. I won't spend another winter starving, hiding, freezing because we don't dare light a fire to catch the notice of soldiers. I won't dig myself a grave in this dying town. I need to make a different life.

"If you don't know, then why did you let Basha go before us?" Pearl asked, her voice rising. "Why let us go now?"

"Of course you must go. Here, there's nothing for you." Father picked at his chapped lips. "God takes away everything that's mine that I love. I should be used to it."

Pearl often heard him say this, but tonight his sadness both touched and irritated her. I know you'll be lonely for us, she thought, but I'm not a thing, and I'm not yours.

"Promise me you won't work in a factory," Father said. "They lock the girls inside and burn them to death."

"That's an old story," Pearl said in a harsher tone than she meant. "Before the war even." Daddy, she thought, it's our last night. Let us be gentle with each other. She searched his eyes, hoping for a kind look. He flinched.

"And promise me you won't let Frieda marry that peacock Mendel," he said.

"I don't like him either, but does it matter if we like him or not? In America, she'll be free to make her choice." Pearl didn't see why Frieda, still in her teens, should marry at all. In America, some girls waited until well in their twenties to settle down. The Yiddish papers said so, and Basha confirmed it. Not that Pearl believed everything Basha said, but on this point, she accepted her sister's word.

"Mendel's the type who looks in the mirror every five seconds to visit with his best friend." Father gripped Pearl's arm again, this time hard enough to hurt. "He isn't worthy of her. With him, she'll have a miserable life. Now promise me."

He had this awful look on his face, and his grip tightened even more. Pearl imagined herself a girl, being caught with her fingers in the honey pot. If she refused his demand, he could change his mind again about America, hold back the money he'd promised. A possibility, but not likely. Far more likely, she realized with a painful sense of sadness, was that this could be the last thing he'd ever ask of her face-to-face. When she left Turya tomorrow, she would probably never see him again.

"Yes, I promise," she said. After all, what did it cost her? He let go of her arm, and his face took on a more peaceful aspect. Then as she picked up the tablecloth again to shake out the crumbs, another thought came to mind: Why don't you care who I marry?

Maybe he didn't think she would.

As a child, Pearl used to watch on summer evenings as boys and girls strolled up Greyble Street. A few daring couples held hands openly. Pearl admired the girls in their summer dresses yet dreaded the prospect of holding some oily-faced boy's hand, making promises as a child to another child before knowing the man he'd become. And then the war and Revolution swept away the young men her age, not to mention several of the girls she'd played with in school, who were now in their graves. If she wanted to find a husband in Turya, all that were left were toothless old men, young wet-ears, or the few who returned from the war alive but with broken bodies, broken minds.

That was how she made it to twenty-seven unmarried.

○

A LITTLE AFTER dawn, Pearl and Frieda, dressed in gray like old women to ward off strange men's eyes, climbed aboard a horse cart crowded with fourteen passengers, all heading west across the scarred countryside. It hardly seemed real. No tearful partings. Even Frieda was unusually solemn. Just a wave to her father and brother, and then the jingling of a harness and the soft plop of horses' feet sinking into mud.

They passed the large black cross marking the edge of town, and the main road turned into a dirt track barely visible in the scarred, empty fields of sandy soil stretching out in all directions. All wasteland. Pearl felt like Moses crossing the desert. What the Germans didn't manage to bomb during the Great War, the Russians burned. Villages were flattened, replaced by snarls of barbed wire, piles of broken brick, and burnt trees skinny and black as whips. The few remaining buildings were sprayed with bullet holes, their windows cracked, their roofs fallen in, their doors stolen for fuel. On the side of the road stood rows of wooden crosses, some marked in charcoal, others carved neatly with the names, ranks, and ages of young men, or simply, "Here lie 3 German soldiers."

"Where are the people?" Frieda whispered. The man next to her overheard and pointed them out, poking their heads out of homes dug from the earth, mounds of sod, scrap metal, and stove bricks covered in green thatch. Peasant children nestled together for warmth, their cheeks and bare feet red as cow's blood. Frieda shut her eyes, but Pearl forced herself to look, to witness, and to guard herself from wanting to come back.

That night, they reached a half-destroyed train station where the Polish border used to be. Pearl and Frieda stretched out on the cold tile floor, staring at the stars through boards laid across the blackened walls for a ceiling. Men occupied the benches, while women sat on the floor with blank-faced children and babies in puddles of urine.

It's just for tonight, thought Pearl. Tomorrow the train comes to take me to America. She took off her coat to cover her sister, then removed her shoes and rubbed her feet. "I wouldn't do that," warned a woman next to her. "Look." She gestured to the other passengers' feet, clad in strips of rags or shoes made of birch bark tied with cords.

"Oh, I see," said Pearl, putting her shoes back on. "Thank you."

"You wouldn't have an extra bit of food to spare?"

Pearl tore off a hunk of her dark bread, and the woman pressed it into her mouth.

In the morning, Pearl's back was sore and her cheeks were chapped with cold. She and Frieda lined up to fill glasses with hot tea from a large brass samovar. A man tossed a cigarette butt on the ground, and two others rushed to grab it and suck a few puffs.

The ticket office, a shack made of whitewashed pine boards, remained closed until just after their train arrived. While Frieda watched the one suitcase they shared, Pearl joined the crowd pressing against the window to buy their tickets, bodies against bodies. "No, let me through! The train can't leave without me," she begged, but the crowd kept pushing. Finally, she pressed her lips into a tight line and pushed right back, rammed her shoulder into a stranger's arm.

When it was her turn, she learned that overnight the fares had risen; the Polish zloty had lost a tenth of its value. Luckily, Pearl's American dollars were still good.

As she rushed to rejoin Frieda, a man bumped into her roughly, nearly knocking her over. "Lousy she-Jew, watch where you're going!" he said and vanished into the crowd, taking with him her sense of triumph at getting the tickets. Then she checked her pockets and her heart seized. The change she'd received at the ticket window was gone.

She and Frieda passed the five-day journey to Warsaw in a third-class carriage without seats, just a wooden floor packed with passengers and stinking of garlic sausage, sweat, and dirty skin. They arrived hungry, exhausted, and nearly broke, only to discover the laws in America had changed. Previously a sibling in America could sponsor a visa, and for that they had their sister Basha in New York. Now immigrants from Eastern Europe needed a child or parent as a sponsor. Siblings like Basha were useless.

The line of would-be immigrants eager to plead their case at the American consulate extended for blocks. Smugglers, touts for travel agents, and peddlers roamed the line, plying their trade in bored singsong voices. Each day, Pearl went earlier, at six, five, then four in the morning. No use sleeping there all night; the police chased people away. One man who managed to get inside had his application refused, so he jumped out of a second-floor window. After that, the windows were locked and guarded.

In the afternoons, Pearl found work cleaning rooms at a hotel. Most of the guests were men or small families, though once, she saw a pair of elegantly dressed women coming out of a room together, their elbows just touching. One of the women, eyeing Pearl, whispered something into the ear of her companion, and Pearl longed to know what it was. She'd never had close friends, aside from her sisters. What might it be like to share such closeness with a girl who wasn't a blood relation?

Frieda also earned a few pennies, selling flowers outside a Russian Orthodox Church that was slated for destruction. For safety reasons, the government said, though Pearl knew the real reason: hatred. They hated Russians here, as well as Germans, Gypsies, and Jews. The Poles were a people of hatred, and she hated them right back. Their language, their hulking churches where priests preached Jew hatred to ugly men with tight, smirking faces that made her want to run away.

Pearl was beginning to despair of ever leaving Poland, when a Jewish couple in line at the consulate told her about Cuba.

Ever literal minded, Frieda opposed the idea. Their goal was America, not Cuba. "If we keep waiting at the consulate, someone's bound to hear us," she said as they ate gritty day-old bread in their rented room. They shared a single bed and woke up in the middle of the night scratching from bedbugs. "Your way of talking to people, it's so . . . direct. Try flattering a little. Or let me try."

"Doesn't matter, no one there will ever listen," Pearl argued.

"But why do the laws apply so specifically to *Eastern* Europe?" Frieda asked.

"Look who's lining up outside the consulate for visas," said Pearl, but Frieda shrugged. "Enough Jews to make a minyan a hundred times over." Frieda still didn't understand, so Pearl laid it out plainly. "Americans don't want Jews."

"Where in the world *do* they want Jews? I say let's wait to go to America. What's in Cuba? Who do we know in Cuba?"

"Cuba is next to America. You stay there a year, then you can go to America without a sponsor or affidavit or anything. That's what the travel agents say, and a Jewish couple I met told me the same."

And one more thing, Pearl thought. At least Cuba's not Poland.

She'd asked the travel agent to show her Cuba on the map, to prove he wasn't playing some Turkish trick. The claw-shaped island really did seem close to Florida, as if she could jump across the water from one coast to another. He showed her pictures of palm trees by the water and a lighthouse. So they did have proper buildings, thought Pearl. Cuba wasn't just a wilderness, like Sinai or Midian in the Torah.

"We should wait, to try for America," Frieda said. "What's the hurry?"

"We can't get stuck here. What if there's another war?" said Pearl, panic rising in her chest. "You're barely eighteen. How do you know what you want?"

"I just know," Frieda said. "Without Mendel, my life will be a desert. Please."

Frieda often talked that way, in the language of fairy tales and Bible legends that Pearl used to read to her when she was a child, as if they lived in the time of Moses instead of 1922. As if she's the heroine of a story, ennobled by suffering for love. A dreamer. Perhaps America might cure her sister of her silliest dreams.

While Frieda lived in dreams, Pearl handled money and documents. She paid ticket agents who counted money to the last kopek. She bribed their Polish landlady with knitted socks and earnest promises to pay the balance for their room. She kept strict accounts of their meager budget, refusing to indulge her sister's whims for penny candy or pretty stockings. And then Frieda accused her of having no heart.

"Promise me that Cuba is only temporary," said Frieda. "Just a stop, not the end. Our goal remains America."

"Of course," said Pearl, annoyed by all these promises she was being asked to make, first by Father, now Frieda. "Who wants to stay in Cuba? What's in Cuba?"

O

ON THE SS *HUDSON*, nights are the worst. As the boat rises and falls on the waves, Frieda lies in her berth, clutches one of Pearl's clean handkerchiefs over her face, and recites childhood prayers. In her berth above, Pearl listens to the others' crying, coughing, and retching. Periodically the ship's doctor tours their quarters, checking for measles or tuberculosis. The passengers beg for medicine for seasickness, but he has none to give. He suggests they rub their temples.

She sleeps in her clothes, as they did in Russia, in case they needed to jump out of bed and escape to the woods from whomever their enemies were—Cossacks, Poles, Reds—depending on the day. Her good wool dress with the lace collar, the one she'd worked on for weeks to make a good impression in America, is now hopelessly wrinkled.

Tonight is one of those stormy evenings when clothes, books, and tin cups go flying. Passengers roll out of their bunks, tumble onto the floor, cry, scream, or pray, terrified their boat will sink.

When the mood grabs her, Frieda kneels on the floor and prays, her lips moving dramatically, her face a pretty picture of solemnity. Pearl also wants to pray or, more accurately, wants to want to pray, but she can't make herself believe that saying a few words can force God to serve her will. She prayed plenty during the war and then again during the Revolution, and look what happened. Nothing.

In her berth, she lies awake, trying to shut out the noises, particularly the low yet distinctly savage sounds of men pushing into their women, who cry out, making horrifying sounds. Like they're being stabbed.

Even before what happened to her in Turya, Pearl disliked those funny-looking Poles, with their thin lips and eyelids, but there was nothing humorous about the anger they carried with them always. It wasn't only women they wanted. They liked boys too, to serve as personal valets, and other gruesome uses Pearl overheard Father mention to their neighbor. Pearl hated their clean-shaven Polish faces and their ugly nasal Polish language, those long, knife-straight noses, and those mocking blue eyes.

Since the Revolution, it wasn't safe for a chicken, a cow, or a woman to linger outside. The only animals in the streets were wolves, who'd lost their fear of humans and walked through the town single file, in daylight. Pearl and her sisters did the laundry and hung it to dry in the house. Rather than visit the public baths, they cleaned each other with damp rags. No more trips to the outhouse. They relieved themselves in a pot.

All during those days of fighting, she yearned for a proper bath. As a girl, Pearl used to go with her mother and sisters to the bathhouse in winter, or the women's bathing area in the river. She'd hold Mama's hand and splash beside the riverbank, while her sisters went in up to their necks, their nightdresses billowing under the water. Some girls swam naked, and Pearl admired their white limbs swaying like reeds in the river. Every man in town knew this was a private area for women and avoided it, yet once a stranger from another town appeared, stripped off his clothes, and dove in the water. The other women quickly chased him away, yelling and throwing rocks at his back, but Pearl got a good look at the firm, flat lines of his bare chest, in such contrast to the swelling breasts of the women. She felt marvelous and warm in the presence of so much beauty, in both kinds of bodies.

Staying cooped up at home for so long, Pearl felt as if she'd swallowed a nest of crickets. So she'd sneak over to the root cellar to satisfy her cravings for both privacy and food. She'd steal licks of apricot jam, chew a leathery ring of dried apple, crunch the meat of a walnut. She made a sugar cube between her teeth last for ten minutes, letting each grain of sugar melt on her tongue. Her palate was simple yet intense.

Coming out of the cellar one afternoon, Pearl saw a Polish soldier urinating on the side of her house.

He carried a long gun and wore mismatched pieces of different uniforms: the gray army jacket of a German, the peaked cap of a Pole with a dirty red rim, and the black leather boots of a well-to-do Russian peasant. Maybe he wasn't a soldier, just an opportunist. His face was shaved, so she knew he wasn't Jewish.

For years after she'd remember how she was too startled to speak or scream.

He could have taken her into the trees, or behind a shed, but he did it in the open.

One minute she was sucking raspberry jam from her fingers in the safety of their damp cellar, and the next, she was pinned to the ground by this man's body, heavy and smelly, like the underside of a horse. With one hand, he pressed his cold mud-stained fingers over her lips, and with the other he opened his pants. At the initial burst of pain—like a barbed spike ripping through her insides— her mind jumped to another place, like fainting but awake. It's not real, she told herself, like those horror stories grandma used to tell to scare us children so we'd stay out of the woods. Imagine it's already over. She shut her eyes and thought of the female animals squawking and bleating in the yard during mating season.

She's glad now for what she cannot remember. Pearl heard him buckle his belt but didn't see him run off. She lay there with her eyes shut, the cold earth chilling her back, the dirt clogging the tips of her fingernails. Her hair hurt. So did the insides of her thighs.

She still felt his weight pressing her down. She smelled him. Words came to her lips, a jumble of different prayers. "God, why?" she pleaded under her breath. "If I'm guilty, tell me how I've sinned. From the well of my distress, I call on you."

Since she was a girl, before she knew what the words of the prayers meant, she'd regularly addressed the Lord without expecting a response, but on this day the silence chilled her heart.

Pearl pulled herself up and hobbled back to the house. The garden gate squawked loudly in protest, sticking as usual, so she kicked it in, then continued to the front door, stiffening her neck before entering. Frieda and Avram were reading by the stove. Though it was unlit, the memory of its heat made them feel warmer.

"I slipped in the mud, big deal," Pearl said. "Stop staring."

"No one's staring," said Avram as Frieda averted her eyes. Pearl hurried to their room. After sponging herself with as much soap as her skin could stand and changing into fresh clothes, she slumped onto her bed, curling up tight and hugging her knees.

That night, she came out and made dinner and did the dishes too, scraped off every crumb. Did she eat? She must have eaten, or maybe she was too sick to eat.

In the following days, Pearl watched Frieda, studying her face for some flicker of recognition of what had happened. Her sister was a child in such matters. Better she should stay a child.

Now, clutching the sides of her berth on the SS *Hudson*, Pearl wishes she'd screamed. Or that she'd never gone outside, betrayed by her own body, her hunger. My fault, my fault. Someone, anyone, must be at fault besides the soldier, who can't help being what soldiers are: animals with uncontrollable appetites. As for the God that Frieda now prays to, perhaps it is easier to think that

He wasn't there than that He let this happen. In any case, she can't rely on Him to intervene to protect her. She must protect herself, figure out her own mistake to learn not to repeat it. Which leads her back to the thought that she shouldn't have gone outside.

But she was so hungry, with a hunger so fierce it led her as if bewitched toward danger. Even now on this boat carrying her far away, Pearl feels the soldier close by. She'd wanted to leave him behind, him as well as the old Pearl, yet apparently she'd brought them both along.

Somewhere, as always, a child is wailing.

At least she wasn't left with child, a child whose father's name she doesn't know.

Pearl desperately needs air, so she throws a blanket over her shoulders, shoves her feet into her boots, and fumbles through the shadows to the exit. She's learned to navigate their rocking ship in the dark.

She climbs up the three skinny metal ladders out of steerage and then goes out on deck, where the sky is clear, with a moon, just like the moon in Turya. The frigid, salty wind stings her neck, her earlobes, her nose, makes her feel clean, blank, like no one, nothing. It feels better. The ship's horn groans overhead, signaling their presence—to whom? Even in daylight, they're enveloped in fog as thick as beaten cream. All she sees are waves, swelling to impossible heights and then collapsing in a fury. Sometimes she's as angry as those crashing waves. She too wants to crash into someone or something.

Gripping a knotted rope along the outer wall of the cabin, Pearl wills herself into calm. She runs through her plans in her head, organizing her emotions the way she used to fold her father's laundry and put it away in the right drawers. Shirts here, pants and socks there. Anger tucked away like folded shirts. Fear buried beneath the bedsheets.

When Pearl's settled her soul, she'll return to bed. Tomorrow in the third-class dining room, she'll eat her ration of fish and oranges. She'll keep the peels to wave under her weary sister's nose and rub into their handkerchiefs like perfume.

TWO

THREE WEEKS INTO THEIR VOYAGE, THEY DRAW CLOSER TO the equator and the weather makes an abrupt shift—hardly an improvement, just torture by different means. The sun grows brighter, roasts them like chicken for *Shabbes* dinner. It's February, and if she were in Russia right now, Pearl would be shivering under a thatched roof crusted in snow and ice.

Three miserable weeks of storms, fog, and chill, and now this heat so thick Pearl is choking on it. Like living in a swamp. There's no escaping the heat, whether she hides in the shade of a smokestack or cowers in her narrow berth down below.

One morning, she's so sick of fighting the heat that she goes out on deck and puts her face to the sun. Go ahead and burn, do your worst! But within minutes, she can't take it anymore and retreats to the shady side of the boat.

She fears what this heat must mean about Cuba. Out of nervous habit, Pearl prays: *Dear God, send a cool wind, a hint of fresh breeze.*

No answer.

Her wool dress weighs her down like a blanket. No one's looking, so she unbuttons her collar and pushes up her sleeves. Her arms are hairy and sturdy from years of beating laundry by the river, lugging samovars, and dragging garden rakes. She has a scar on her arm from brushing against a hot iron and a mark on her left forefinger from a nasty slip of a kitchen knife. Her arms and hands are not delicate as a woman's arms and hands are supposed to be, but they serve her. These arms are for work. They're strong.

○

FRIEDA SITS UP in bed rereading Mendel's letters from America.

"Back to your old dreaming," says Pearl.

"You're jealous because I'm engaged before you," Frieda says.

Wrong, Pearl thinks. In ordinary times, a younger sister shouldn't marry before the older one, but lately, all rules are upside down, and Pearl is glad for this excuse.

"Find your own man," says Frieda. "In America, you'll have plenty of choices."

"You will also have choices," says Pearl. "Mendel will too."

"Pearl, what have you got against Mendel? Why are you so angry with him?"

"I'm just talking about his nature. Some people when they speak truth, other people call them angry."

"You're in a mood, so there's no use talking to you," says Frieda.

That's unfair, Pearl thinks. Even if Mendel was the sweetest angel, she'd wish for her sister to wait, to see what she's capable of in a new, free country. Why settle for an ass like Mendel, who like all asses enjoys hearing himself bray? His letters, written in a careless scribbled hand, are devoted to his favorite topic: himself and his plans to become a famous man of business. For now, he delivers groceries. With his last letter, he sent a picture of himself in a shiny new suit, with a useless straw hat. What's he dolling up for? Pearl thinks. They're going to America for work and peace, not lavish dress balls.

Mendel's living with his older brother, Ben the Oak, who is Mendel's exact opposite, hardworking and relentlessly dull. Once called Slow Ben, he earned the nickname of Oak after being drafted as an indentured servant during the Great War by the Russians, then the Germans, and yet he managed to come home with his intestines in his stomach and his head on his neck.

Mendel, meanwhile, was just young enough to avoid being conscripted. Father joked that he'd timed his own birth, hiding in his mother's womb a few extra months without a care for the suffering he'd caused her, to save his own skin.

Maybe in Turya, Mendel's wiles and reputation as a charmer made him a catch, but now Pearl and her sister have all of America to choose from. Frieda's pretty and enchanting enough to attract a real gentleman. Pearl hopes for her to find work in a shop, or to be a teacher. But no—like most women, Frieda wants what's not good for her.

Not me, Pearl thinks. I've got this chance and I will not ruin it.

o

FRIEDA'S SPIRITS IMPROVE now that they see the sun. She's eating again. She befriends some silly girls her own age, and they trade stories about American millionaires who marry pretty young women without dowries, just for love. Three weeks on this boat and Pearl hasn't made a single friend, while Frieda's Queen Esther in her court.

Those girls wouldn't be my kind of friends, Pearl thinks. In America, I'll meet serious women who fill their heads with ideas, not romantic nonsense.

One of Frieda's new friends has loaned her a Yiddish-Spanish textbook. At dinner, Frieda mouths the foreign words while Pearl watches the lady with the pink hat, imagines a conversation with her.

As the pink lady uses her own silverware to delicately pick at a piece of herring, Pearl bangs a roll on the table. Can they have grown more stale? The lady raises her head sharply, catches Pearl's eye, and frowns. Blushing, Pearl stops.

Frieda says something that Pearl, distracted by her thoughts, misses, so Frieda repeats it. "Buenas noches. That's 'good night' in Spanish. You try it."

Pearl frowns. "Buenas nachas," she says slowly, stretching her mouth to fit around the unfamiliar words.

The lady finishes her breakfast and leaves the room. Pearl watches her disappear.

"No, you goose." Frieda digs her knuckle into Pearl's shoulder. "You're hopeless."

Pearl shrugs, helps herself to dessert. The cook, who's in a good mood because the fog has lifted, has made steamed pudding studded with raisins. Not great, but something different. The spongy pudding warms her throat and fills the hollowness in her chest and belly. Pearl relishes each bite.

○

LYING IN HER berth that night, Pearl worries that her sister may be too delicate to face the hard times ahead of them on some strange island. I raised her too soft, Pearl thinks. I felt sorry for her because she should never have been born, but I ought to have been harder on her. Now her personality is my responsibility, my fault.

Before having Frieda, Pearl's mother gave birth to two stillborn children. Though the doctor warned her she might not survive another pregnancy, Mama once again was with child. Pearl, only nine years old, didn't understand why everyone was upset with Father, since it had been Mama who'd ignored the doctor's advice and become pregnant.

Pearl's mother decided that this time rather than rely on a midwife, she'd go to Pinsk to have the child, a city with a proper medical clinic. Basha went along.

Right before Rosh Hashanah, Basha sent a telegram. Mama had given birth to a girl, and they needed money. Father chose Pearl to bring it. A neighbor who was going to Pinsk for the High Holidays escorted her on the boat up the Polkva River.

Mama and Basha were staying in a poky, airless room at the back of a wooden tavern. Pearl briefly lost her breath seeing her mother lying at a crooked angle in bed. By the flickering light, her face looked moist and very pale, and her hair had thinned so her scalp was visible. Basha held her hand while a nurse filled an ice bag.

"Careful where you're stepping," Basha said, nodding at the floor.

Pearl was so nervous, she hadn't noticed the baby at Basha's feet kicking its tiny legs in a woven basket lined with soft blankets.

All that evening and into the next day, the nurse applied bags of ice to Mama's stomach to reduce the swelling. Meanwhile, the baby, a shriveled, red-faced fish and supposedly their new sister, kept crying because she was hungry or wet, or sometimes for no discernible reason. They took turns trying to soothe her, until they grew so frustrated they left her in the basket to cry herself to sleep.

In the morning, a doctor arrived and said their mother should go immediately to a hospital in Warsaw. Basha wired Father, then hurried with Mama to the train station, using the money Pearl had brought to buy the tickets. Pearl would have to take the baby home. By herself.

The nurse wrapped the baby in a towel and packed her in the basket, "Like Moses in the Torah," she said, hugging the basket all the way to the boat. The baby stayed eerily quiet. Her cheeks, usually red from crying, glowed a healthy pink in the crisp autumn air.

Before saying good-bye, the nurse gave Pearl three bottles of water mixed with a little sugar. "If she cries, give her a bottle," she said. "She'll probably sleep most of the way. You won't know she's there."

Terrified of dropping the baby, Pearl stepped carefully onto the boat, steadying the basket against her stomach until she found a seat on a bench. After a deep exhale, she set down her basket containing her funny raisin-faced sister, wrapped in cloth like a parcel of stinky cheese that someone was trying to pass off as fresh.

The other passengers stared and whispered. A girl alone, with a baby? All this attention, especially from big-city strangers, mortified Pearl. She was glad when the sailors loosened the ropes and pushed away from the docks. The air felt cooler out on the water, so Pearl drew her wool shawl around her shoulders, then checked her sister, who started to cry. Pearl tried the bottle, but the baby wouldn't take it, just cried harder.

A stout woman with blond hair wrapped in a dotted kerchief came over and took the baby from Pearl's arms. She unfastened the swaddling cloth, which was wet and soiled. This she tied in a tight knot, to wash out later. Next, she cleaned the baby and wrapped her in a fresh towel, showing Pearl how to do the same. Finally, she opened her bag, taking out a package of cookies. She gave one to Pearl, who bit it slowly, tasting the comfort of butter and sugar. The woman crushed another cookie, mixed it with water, and dipped a handkerchief into the sweet mash. The baby sucked it greedily, then fell asleep.

Pearl's brother, Avram, was waiting at the landing in Turya. "Father's halfway to Warsaw already," he said. "I'm alone at the house."

"This is our sister." She held up the basket. "She needs to be fed."

"How?" Avram took the basket with his skinny arms and tried to balance it in his wobbly grasp. The other boys called him Noodle Arms.

"I don't know," she said.

"You're a girl. Don't you know?"

"We have to find a woman," she said.

It was terrible timing for such an errand, the eve of Rosh Hashanah. Elka had gone to her husband's family in Luninec for the holiday, so Pearl and her brother took the baby to the home of Rivka's husband's uncle, where Rivka was helping prepare for the holiday. She suggested a wet nurse near Father's butcher shop. By then, Avram had to go to shul, leaving Pearl to rush to the nurse's home. Of course the baby was crying again.

At the wet nurse's cottage, the baby clamped onto the woman's breast immediately. "I can keep her tonight, but then you have to find someone else," said the woman in a sharp voice, swinging the baby as it was sucking on her breast.

The next day, while her brother was in shul, Pearl searched in vain for another nurse. She trudged back home and found Avram crying over the telegram from Warsaw, which she didn't need to read. Pearl was too stunned for tears. Mama—dead? Perhaps the telegram machine had mixed up the message.

It wasn't until they heard voices of people coming home from evening prayers that she remembered her sister and ran to the wet nurse's cottage.

"I can't help you anymore," said the woman, handing Pearl the baby across the threshold. "Try Simcha the goatherd. His wife might do it."

It was already dark, so Pearl waited until morning to make the long journey to Simcha's farm, heaving her sister on her hip. Simcha's wife had no more milk, but she had a friend a few farms away who could do it. Now the baby was furious, screaming her lungs out. "Keep calm," snapped Pearl, wanting to scream too. And then she did, hoping to scare the baby into shutting up. Though it didn't work, Pearl felt better.

The friend's farmhouse wasn't as large or nice as Simcha's, but the woman seemed friendly and took the baby. However, Pearl returned the next day to check on her sister and found the farmhouse empty, dark, and cold. The whole family had gone out, leaving Pearl's sister alone. The baby's face had turned an awful shade, almost blue.

Pearl muttered a curse on the family and grabbed her sister. Somehow she managed to carry her home, pressing the baby's face—her baby's face—to her chest, rubbing her little head, praying to God to spare her life.

At home, Pearl cut a slit in the finger of a cotton glove, filled it with cow's milk, and gave it to the baby, who drank and drank until she fell asleep with the finger in her mouth. Pearl removed the glove and rocked the baby until she fell asleep too.

In the morning, she felt a heavy hand moving through her hair. The baby was gone. The hand belonged to her father.

"It's all right," he said, but his voice sounded deep and far away. "I'm here now."

Hearing those words, Pearl burst into tears.

She's never told any of this history to Frieda. There seemed little point in making her feel guilt or shame for coming into the universe as she had. Now Pearl wonders if that was a mistake. A bit of guilt might have taught Frieda to be less free.

o

A SKINNY OLD man runs through steerage, bragging he's seen a bird. A real bird. Pearl rushes to join the passengers crowding on deck, hoping to see it also, and they cheer when they do: a white seagull swirling in the sky, followed by a flock of gulls. Pearl's cheering too, screaming until her throat hurts. She doesn't care who hears.

o

THE FIRST SIGN of Havana is the castle, a bulwark of brown stone with a watchtower topped by a funny little dome like a woman's bathing cap.

They sail alongside the heavy brown fortifications until their ship rounds a corner, and the land opens up like a mouth. The water turns a vibrant turquoise, and through the surface, they see masses of curled brown weeds swirling. This is Havana harbor, crowded with large ships like theirs and smaller fishing boats. All the passengers, first-class, second-class, and steerage, are on deck, pressed against the railings to see this new country, palm trees waving their fronds—and land! Gloriously firm land.

Beyond a thick retaining wall lies a tightly packed city with curlicued architecture and covered balconies, like the grand boulevards of Warsaw. Donkeys pull carts loaded with hay, coal, and fruit, while dark automobiles bump cheerfully past them. "They have automobiles," says Frieda. "Maybe it's a rich country."

"Possibly," says Pearl, preferring to wait before making judgments. She runs through plans in her head. They have to find a rooming house. And work of course, but first, a room. There must be places near the port. How will they find them? How will they make themselves understood in a strange language?

Down the shore, by the retaining wall, stands a man with the darkest skin Pearl has ever seen. The European passengers point and stare. Pearl has heard stories of such men in folktales, sinners whose skin the devil has burnt to black. But this man doesn't look like a sinner. He's just a man gazing at the water.

Frieda recites English names, trying to choose one . . . Francine, Florence, Flower. As if Cuba were America, and she can become a new person by simply taking a new name.

Pearl spots a yacht flying the American flag, wishes they could jump onto that boat.

○

PEARL AND FRIEDA pack their everyday suitcase, then go to the checked baggage room, filled with teetering piles of trunks and large cases. Some have burst open, spilling pictures, books, girdles, silver Kiddush cups, and dried mushrooms. Pearl, who's learned by now how to push through a crowd, waves their claim ticket and shouts for the porters' attention. She retrieves their heavy wicker case, which they lug up the ladders. The upper-deck passengers, whose papers were inspected on board, are ushered into town.

Pearl and Frieda follow the crowds from steerage toward immigration.

As she steps off the gangplank, the pressure in Pearl's shoulders and chest eases. For the first time since their weeks at sea, the noise of the water stops. The solid ground beneath her feet feels both reassuring and unfamiliar. She can walk in a straight line without bending her knees and planting her feet to keep her balance. Frieda also notices the difference and laughs.

The dockworkers speak rapidly in Spanish. Their voices—loud, rough, and male—scare Pearl at first, but she swallows her fear. She asks Frieda to teach her the word for "please," *por favor*, which Pearl keeps repeating. From the little book she borrowed, Frieda can already string together broken Spanish sentences.

They stand in a hot, crowded building, or not a building really, just a large tin roof balanced on a metal framework of poles. The sides are open. At the far end, officials slowly ask endless questions. The waiting passengers stand and whisper, trying to guess the right answers. The sophisticated city lady with the dusty-pink hat chews nervously on a fingernail. Not so grand now, are you? Pearl thinks.

"You keep staring at that woman like you're in love with her," Frieda says.

"Her I could take or leave," says Pearl. "It's her pretty hat I'm interested in." It sounds plausible enough to be true.

Frieda snorts. "You and your obsession with clothes."

There are no chairs or benches, so people sit on trunks or on the ground, but Pearl won't allow it. She and Frieda were brought up better than that. They remain standing. The air smells of oil and brackish water, and the heat feels more oppressive than at sea. Pearl fans herself with her hand. How will she understand the customs officers and their questions?

A bird swoops in, flies to the roof in confused circles, then flies away. Pearl sees no fence to pen them in, and the few guards look bored. Perhaps she could take Frieda's hand and march past them into town. Isn't that what a real adventurer would do, a New Woman? Evidently, Pearl has not yet become one.

A handsome woman in a cream-colored blouse and navy skirt walks by, saying in a gentle voice, "Yiddish? Anyone speak Yiddish?" The passengers watch her warily. But Pearl, glad to hear Yiddish in such a strange place, speaks up.

"Yes, Yiddish," she says, her voice choking.

"Welcome to Havana." The woman stretches forward to kiss Pearl's cheek. She's wearing a light floral perfume, and Pearl is embarrassed about her own smell and her wrinkled, sweat-stained clothes. The odor of the journey lingers in her pores. The woman presses some paper into Pearl's hand. Three American ten-dollar bills. "Show them to the man in the uniform."

"Is this a bribe?"

"No, no, he won't take it. It's just for show, to prove you're not indigent. Once you're through, you'll give it back to me on the other side, where I'll explain more." The woman lets go of her hand. "So good to see you again, dear," she says in a loud voice.

The woman resumes wandering through the crowd. Are all the women here like this, strong, assured, handsome? If so, Pearl hopes what they have is catching. But what will this woman expect in return for this loan? Is it some kind of scheme?

"Can we trust her?" Frieda asks. "Maybe she'll accuse us of stealing."

"She wouldn't," Pearl says, tired of being afraid. "She speaks Yiddish."

"It's so hot." Frieda leans on Pearl's shoulder as she used to when she was a girl. "I want some water."

"Just a bit longer," Pearl replies and strokes her hair, but she's worried. Maybe we'll wait here forever. Maybe we'll die here.

Another hour passes before it's their turn to approach the guard sitting at a little desk. He's a good-looking man with a thin mustache and a spotless white uniform. The guard accepts their papers, and Pearl draws herself to her full height, which is not so very tall. Frieda's left foot taps nervously, and Pearl slaps her leg.

The man asks them a question, not kindly or unkindly. Pearl's throat is dry, and she can barely say her Spanish word for please. Frieda says, "I speak little Spanish," and she smiles so sweetly that the man in the uniform smiles too. She tells him their names: Pearl and Frieda Kahn. Pearl shows him the money, wishes this handsome man would smile at her too. He looks at her palm, not at her, and miraculously does not touch the money.

The man stamps their papers and waves them through. Pearl gives him a last look—remarkably neat and trim in his clean uniform. She wonders what his name is.

Outside the shelter of the tin roof, the sun attacks their eyes. Where is the lady who gave them the money? Dear God, Pearl thinks, I'm thirsty. Across the road is a small square with tall palm trees and bright red flowers in strange dripping shapes, like fringes on a shawl. The shade is inviting, but they must return their borrowed money.

Frieda spots the lady, standing beside a woman wearing a stylish silk dress and glasses. If it's a plot, this could be their last chance to escape, but she and Frieda have to be honest.

"We are returning your money," says Pearl.

"Thank you, you good girls." She removes it gracefully from her hands. "We'll use it again." Her name is Milly, and she explains she belongs to a group called the Ezra Society. They meet the boats from Eastern Europe, to help young Jewish women. "We'll take you where you can rest. Would you like that?"

"How expensive is it?" asks Pearl.

"Oh, it's absolutely free. Don't worry."

How can it be free? Pearl thinks. Nothing is free.

"Could we get some water?" Frieda asks.

"Of course!" Milly stops a young Cuban boy who runs to a nearby café and brings back a pitcher of water and several glasses. Pearl tears up, feeling the weight of this journey. She wishes to say thank you in the boy's language, but she only knows "please."

A cluster of well-dressed ladies are discussing their situation in a mix of Spanish, English, and Yiddish. They are like no Jews that Pearl knows, so refined and proud, like aristocrats who expect service in a good hotel. Beside them, women from the ship, several with small children, have gathered on the sidewalk. The contrast is stark, and Pearl is embarrassed to note which group she fits in with.

"Don't worry," Milly tells Pearl and Frieda in Yiddish, beckoning them to follow. "We have for you a nice place to stay."

Frieda asks if Pearl is sure these women are Jewish. "Should we trust them?"

Pearl, relieved for someone else to be in charge, shrugs off the question. She grabs her wicker case and starts to follow Milly.

"That's all you have to wear?" Milly asks, taking in Pearl and Frieda's European-style wool dresses. Milly's blouse and skirt are made of a light material, like linen or cotton, thin and fine. Pearl imagines it must feel very free to move around in such garments. "We'll get you cooler clothes," says Milly. "You'll suffocate in those."

They leave the air and light of the harbor behind, moving into the city. Clutching Frieda's elbow, Pearl studies her surroundings to get her bearings. The streets are cobblestone like in Warsaw, but the buildings are painted in bright colors and decorated with wrought-iron balconies. The narrow space between the buildings traps the humid tropical air. A man with a heavy-looking box strapped to his neck sells chips of ice that people suck like candy, and two men in white outfits stop him to buy a few pieces.

"Those are Americans," says Milly. "Sailors."

The men are laughing in a way Pearl doesn't like, and she looks away. Soldiers are the same everywhere, even Americans.

The streets grow narrower and the women have to walk single file on the sidewalks to avoid the cars and bicycles. The Cubans are watching them. Several of the men have dark, dark skin, and Pearl sees a woman like that too. If I brushed against them, Pearl thinks, would the darkness rub off? The Cuban woman notices them staring and smiles defiantly, her white teeth stark against her face.

Frieda shrinks closer to her sister. "What kind of place is this?" she asks.

Pearl is too nervous to answer.

Mixed in with the locals are Jews, some with beards, others clean-shaven and without hats or yarmulkes yet recognizable to Pearl because of their pale skin and their European faces. It's all bewildering, as if they haven't left Europe.

The bakeries sell bread in strange shapes, none of it black like at home, and Pearl remembers she's starving.

"We're getting close," says Milly. "It's just down this street."

By "street" she means a tight alley where the sidewalk peters out and there's barely room for a carriage to pass. The woman pushes open a metal gate and then a wooden door. They move through a dark vestibule to a cobblestone courtyard with a drain in the middle. Across the courtyard is another door. Milly knocks, and Pearl and Frieda set down their cases and catch their breath. Pearl is exhausted from the heat, the walk, and mostly the strangeness of it all.

A woman answers. She has dark hair in wide curls and bright lipstick, which seems the fashion here. "This is Altagracia," says Milly. "She'll take care of you."

"Altagracia," Frieda repeats slowly, but Pearl can't quite pronounce this long name. Is it Christian? She, Frieda, and the others follow Altagracia upstairs to a peach-colored room with a window that has iron bars over the glass panes, like a jail. Maybe it is a jail. There are several beds with thin mattresses and rough gray blankets, and between the beds are short tables covered in black lace.

Altagracia says something, but no one understands, so she laughs and calls for Milly, who comes upstairs and explains, "She says she's sorry we don't have anywhere to put your clothes for now. We'll find you something by and by."

After washing up, Pearl feels calmer. The water for washing is fresh, not salt like on the boat, and she splashes it greedily on her hands and cheeks, behind her ears, even sips a bit from her palms. Then they go to a dining hall for black beans and bright yellow rice. How did the rice turn yellow? It looks as if someone painted it.

Milly has to leave, but tomorrow she'll return with new clothes, more suited to this climate. They'll learn a bit of Spanish, receive money to get them started and help searching for work, which will be hard to find. Times are tough here since the end of the Great War. They are now in Old Havana, an area with many Jews, and a synagogue, though not like in Europe. Kosher food is expensive and scarce. "Life here is very different from what you are used to," says Milly.

Tomorrow they'll hear more. For now, they can rest.

Some of the women are crying, they're so grateful. Frieda offers Milly one of her practiced pretty smiles. Pearl says thank you too, but she's waiting for bad news.

That night, as Frieda snores in the bed beside hers, Pearl dreams she's back in Turya and badly needs to urinate, but someone has hidden the chamber pot. Voices drift in from outside, speaking a language Pearl doesn't understand. A man grabs her elbow, rudely, roughly. He smiles, says not to be afraid. She wants to scream, yet nothing comes out. He's ripped out her vocal cords and holds them up, laughing. They look like raw pink lengths of rope. As she reaches for them, he holds them high over her head.

Something releases inside her chest, like a spring that's come loose. As Pearl opens her eyes and it slowly dawns on her where she is, safely across the ocean, in the custody of kind women, she loses control of her bladder. These women have promised to take care of her, and this is how she's paid them back, by wetting her bed.

"Frieda," she hisses, shaking her sister. "Wake up. You've got to help me."

○

THE NEXT MORNING, Pearl's head is throbbing. At least it's a new day. At breakfast, no one seems to know what she's done, or at least no one mentions it. She and Frieda soaked her sheet with soapy water and hung it to dry in the washroom while Pearl lay on the bare mattress until dawn.

The other women are either single girls like Frieda or mothers with children. Yet again I don't fit in, Pearl thinks. I'm not a girl or a mother, but something in between.

They are served bread and coffee. And white sugar, like snow. Heaping piles of waxy-skinned fruit sit untouched in the center of the table, like a ceremonial centerpiece; the newcomers are flummoxed as to what to do. One woman attempts to bite a piece of fruit through the peel, until another woman who's been here a few days shows her to remove it, exposing the sweet white flesh underneath.

Eventually Altagracia cuts another kind of fruit to pass around. It's called mango.

"Maaahn-go," says Frieda, practicing the word. Pearl insists on trying it first before letting her sister bite into it. She nervously accepts a slice, suspiciously golden. After mashing the soft flesh between her teeth, she makes a face. "Tastes like old eggs," she complains to Frieda.

"Hmm," says Frieda, chewing her slice slowly. "Different, but interesting."

"Like a peach too ripe and not ripe enough at the same time," Pearl says. There's something dishonest about the mango's soursweet taste. Why can't the fruit here taste like normal fruit? With the honest, simple sweetness and crisp bite of an apple, the subtle luscious tang of a fat strawberry?

After breakfast, the women go to a sitting room that's been converted into a classroom, where Milly greets them. A volunteer will teach them some Spanish. They each receive a new cotton dress, two dollars of pocket money, and postcards to write their families. Pearl composes a brief message in neat, careful handwriting, unchanged since childhood. She tells Father they've arrived safely, then passes the card to Frieda, who inscribes her name at the bottom and sketches a flower underneath. After that, she resumes working on her postcard, addressed to Mendel in Detroit, USA.

As Pearl hands Milly her postcard, she mentions that she and Frieda want to go to America. Milly gives her a sympathetic look, then explains, "It's not easy. The consulate, their ears are closed to people like you. You'll have to be determined. Or . . ." she pauses. "You'll have to make your America here in Hotel Cuba."

We were tricked, thinks Pearl, clenching her hands into fists. She recalls that weaselly, fast-talking travel agent in Warsaw, his crooked necktie and yelping voice. Easy to blame him, but he was just making a living, as weasels do to survive. It's my fault, Pearl thinks. I'm the one who believed him and got us stuck here.

"We should have waited in Warsaw for a proper visa," Frieda says later to Pearl.

"Well, we didn't," replies Pearl, her ears burning with shame for having trusted the travel agent. But she can never admit her fault to Frieda. "We got from Turya all the way here, didn't we? Now we'll get from here to America. We're so close."

"I'll ask Mendel," says Frieda. "He'll help us."

You might as well write to Elijah the Prophet, Pearl thinks.

○

OTHER WOMEN AT this place, the Women's Home, are so weary and dispirited from the journey they don't even pretend to make an effort at Spanish. They sulk in bed all day, complain of heat rashes, the food, the weather, the hard, bright Caribbean light of "Hotel Cuba."

Pearl refuses to be weak like these women, already nostalgic for Europe and its familiar miseries. Maybe as the world would define it, she's uneducated, but she knows a lot and she learns fast, not from books, but by opening her eyes and ears. She finds out there are small garment factories in Old Havana run by Jews who sometimes need seamstresses. Pearl tells Milly that she and Frieda are reliable, skilled, and eager. Someday she hopes to be like Milly, confident and handsome, a lady. For now she needs to work to survive. She labors at her Spanish, volunteers to help the servants with sweeping and dishes. She wears her simple new cotton dress and battles daily with her curly black hair.

On their sixth day in Cuba, Milly whispers to Pearl at breakfast: "You and your sister, come with me." They follow her into the corridor, where Milly says she's found them a unique situation, at a workshop that decorates ladies' hats. "You are two fortunate girls," she says, her bright red-beaded necklace swinging from her neck. "The Steinbergs are a genteel couple, in reduced circumstances."

Pearl and Frieda gather their few things in their worn suitcases. Frieda wants to say good-bye to a new acquaintance she's made, but Pearl, afraid they might lose their opportunity, says there's no time. "In America, we'll make real friends," she says, though she worries that when they get there, she'll have fallen out of the habit. Then again, she was never good at making friends to begin with.

○

THE HAT WORKSHOP is a few blocks from the Women's Home, on the ground floor of a gray building with sculpted cement walls.

They're greeted by Mrs. Steinberg, who rushes to clasp Pearl's hands and then Frieda's. "You poor things," she says. "You must have suffered terribly over there."

Her concern is frightening to Pearl. How can she feel so deeply about strangers?

Behind their steel-rimmed glasses, Mrs. Steinberg's eyes have a faraway, serious look, much like Father wears while studying a difficult verse of Talmud. She's a stoop-shouldered woman with gray-streaked hair parted down the middle and wound into a regal-looking chignon at the back of her head. Not as nice-looking as Milly, and not nearly as charming. But she will pay them and give them a place to live.

A rough tweed curtain down the middle of the room separates the work area from the living quarters, a corner with two narrow beds draped in mosquito nets, a gas plate, and wooden crates that serve as tables and shelves. Down the hall is a shared bath and water closet. Our new home, Pearl thinks, looking at the curved iron bars over the window.

Mr. Steinberg arrives, and his wife scolds him for being late. Something seems to have upset her permanently. Even her smiles appear grudging. By contrast, Pearl's impressed by Mr. Steinberg's supreme, confident good cheer, especially to a pair of strangers. She finds him dapper for a man his age, with dyed black hair slicked in brilliantine and healthy pink skin. When Pearl asks about the work they'll be doing, Mr. Steinberg waves off her question and hands them each an American nickel, for dinner. "Tomorrow we work," he says. "Today, make yourselves at home."

"I already feel at home. Thank you, kind sir," says Frieda, offering him her hand, palm down. To kiss or to shake? The choice is his. He gives it a light shake, then offers his hand to Pearl, whose hands are clammy with sweat. She tries to wipe them discreetly on her dress before shaking his hand.

"Yes, sir, thank you," says Pearl, but the words feel awkward, inadequate. This man and his wife are strangers. Yet she must trust them to keep her and Frieda alive.

THREE

PEARL OPENS THE WINDOW IN THE HAT WORKSHOP AND the sand flies swarm in. Now that she's been in Cuba for a month, she's learned to hear and feel the flies before seeing them. Their bellies turn red after they bite, and they leave small welts that burn the inside of her wrist or elbow. Their wings get caught in the birdcage-style veils she sews onto cocktail hats. Their bite is not in the style of the lazy mosquitoes who breed in Turya's swamps and puddles. It is bloodier, angrier, and makes a mark.

If only a breeze would drive the flies away, but there's no breeze to speak of in the crooked, dusty lanes of Old Havana, crowded with buildings that cut off light and wind. The bit of air that wafts through the curled-iron window grilles stinks of dung from donkeys drawing ice carts. Sometimes Pearl smells the acrid aroma of dark muddy coffee brewing—or if she's lucky, the sultry perfume of a freshly baked pineapple cake.

To fool her empty stomach, Pearl chews on a stick of sugarcane. Boys from the country, the dirt of the farm in their fingernails, sell the stalks, a penny per bundle. After the Great War, sugar prices are in free fall, from twenty cents per pound to two cents. It's a problem, Mr. Steinberg often complains, in a country whose chief industry is the growing of sugar for Americans to stir into their coffee.

Cheap sugar means fewer orders for the Steinbergs' fancy ladies' hats.

Pearl closes the window and turns on their rusty fan, on loan from the Steinbergs—like their lives. The fan buzzes louder than the nasty sand flies, and at random intervals screeches like the roosters in Turya attempting to impress the hens.

Pearl focuses on her sewing, imagines every stitch brings her a millimeter closer to New York. She tries to ignore the buzzing and her headache from this heat. But she can't ignore it when the fan's breeze scatters her neat piles of ribbons and feathers; beads, sequins, and rhinestones; artificial flowers and berries, into a mess of confetti.

Open the window, close the window. Turn on the fan, turn off the fan. Put back in order everything the fan put into disorder. It's like a dance. Cubans are so fond of dancing, Pearl might as well dance too. At this rate she'll be dancing in circles for a good long while—getting nowhere.

She douses a towel in a jug of water and pats the ever-present film of sweat from her flushed neck and cheeks. Then she steps into the courtyard for a minute to breathe, clear her mind. Pearl prefers the relative privacy of this place to the naked openness of the street, where peddlers hawk cheap undergarments or ice cream bars called Eskimo Pies, and old men argue over clattering ivory-colored domino tiles.

In the courtyard, women with plain faces and bold features scrub rich people's white underclothing with rough, thick hands. Two girls with tiny gold hoops in their ears huddle over a white cardboard box tied with string. Pearl has never seen earrings on anyone so young. Her own ears are unpierced.

Pearl breathes deeply, arches her shoulders, massages the ache out of her wrists and pinpricked fingers. At least they have fewer cuts than Frieda's—ironic, considering how little work Frieda does with the needle. Though she tries, her bows droop instead of standing smartly at attention. Her feathers come loose. Her ribbons are sewn on crooked. She can't be trusted to do an entire hat on her own, so Pearl does enough work for two and racks her brain for small jobs Frieda can do without getting in the way. Just like when Frieda was little, always anxious to help until she made a mess of things.

Same old Frieda, and same old Pearl looking after same old Frieda. For this, they crossed an ocean?

The Cuban girls fumble at the string around their box with tiny fingers. Pearl wonders what small treat they have inside. She used to sew leftover scraps into cloth-people for Frieda and then her nieces, Mitzi and Baile, Elka's two girls. Or she'd poke a hole in an egg, letting the yolk and white drain out, then glue feathers and draw a string through the ends so she could swing the decorated shell to make it fly. Those girls used to wear her down, to the point where she vowed never to have children of her own. But at night, they were so sweet with hugs and kisses, just as Frieda loved caresses as a child. Here in Cuba, Pearl has no one to touch—and no one to touch her.

Pearl smiles at the Cuban girls. Come here, she thinks, you're so pretty, I want to kiss you! But the girls give her a suspicious look and move to a corner of the courtyard, where they untie the string and open the box, filled with sand-colored shortbread cookies called *torticas de morón*. Pearl tasted them once. They're tough and gritty like sugar cookies, but flavored with lime and a hint of rum.

The girls fill their mouths with the cookies, a cheap indulgence for working-class Cubans. But Pearl can't afford to buy cookies herself. Most of her "pay" is eaten up by the cost of food and the rent the Steinbergs charge to live in the workshop. Pearl tucks the few leftover pennies into a pocket sewn inside her waistband, the coins tucked in a wisp of cotton so they don't jingle as she walks.

As the girls laugh, Pearl's stomach growls. She wants to rip those cookies out of their hands and stuff them into her own mouth.

Listen to yourself, Pearl thinks, shaking her head as hard as she can, as if to shake out that ugly voice that's invading her thoughts. The devil. Quiet, she tells the voice. But how do you quiet a voice in your head? It keeps whispering in her ear about God letting her down. She's tried reciting the Psalms, but here in Cuba, the words stick in her throat or slip away, leaving space for more wretched doubt.

If she were a boy, Father would have sent her to a proper school to learn the right arguments to bolster her faith. But as a girl, she'd merely learned to read and write her name and do simple arithmetic. Girls didn't need words or arguments to set a table or sweep floors or manage an oven. Pearl knew her oven like an old friend, the hot spots that burned her food and how to feed it fuel to keep a steady heat. She wishes she had an oven now, though she has nothing worth putting into it.

Time to return to the workshop and her hats. Pearl waves to the Cuban girls. They watch her warily, maybe sensing her hunger.

Back in the stuffy workshop, Pearl ties a scarf around her hair and resumes decorating hats with ribbons, swathes of lace, and beads that in the heat sometimes leave traces of dye on her fingers, like they're bleeding. Frieda used to amuse herself trying on all the different hats; now she's bored with that game. Pearl didn't care to risk ruining their work. Anyway, fancy hats only highlight her plainness. She prefers to imagine the wealthy women who'll wear these hats, perhaps to a party at a mansion with a walled garden, out in Vedado. A wealthy woman is free to live as she chooses, attend a concert, eat in a restaurant every night, or dance at one of those tall, elegant hotels where Americans come to get drunk because alcohol is forbidden in their country, which confuses Pearl, since America is meant to be the land of the free.

The Steinbergs are also Americans, but not wealthy and they certainly don't drink in hotels. They're a different kind of American.

Pearl clenches a silver pin between her teeth, stretches a gold turban over a wooden head, and places a faux diamond brooch dead center, above the eyes, like the model that Mr. Steinberg provided for her to copy. He himself is also a kind of model to copy. His good cheer is so infectious, she likes whatever he likes out of sympathy, and what he dislikes, she dislikes too.

Or maybe she's just lonesome and confuses his friendliness for friendship.

Pearl uses a ruler to check the spot. Once again, exactly right. It's a satisfying, powerful feeling. She might do this work in America, using her imagination to come up with her own designs for hats, maybe meet their future wearers and advise them on which style would be most flattering. Wearing the right hat at the right time could change a woman's life.

It's good that Pearl likes work, because in Havana, she works constantly, even on Saturdays. On Sundays too, though with the shutters closed, since working on Sunday is forbidden in this country. But it's the Saturdays that trouble her.

That first Saturday that she sat at her worktable, her fingers felt heavy, stiff. Work on the Sabbath? She might as well smear her lips with pigskin. Is this part of being a New Woman? But then also in Turya, Jews sometimes worked on *Shabbes*, especially lately during the desperate times. Father too. Once she spied him handling money on a Friday night, a dire sin. Pearl slowly picked up a needle and stared at it for a full minute. Finally, she quickly and expertly slipped a black thread through its narrow eye. In Cuba, she thought, this is what I must do. In America, I'll save my soul.

Finished with the turban, Pearl goes to open the window again and sees Frieda trotting up the street, her cheeks flushed, hat in hand, wavy black hair coming loose from its black ribbon. Is it one o'clock already? Pearl sent her to deliver a hat to a customer on Paseo Avenue, among a colony of wealthy American Jews.

Frieda brings a small sack of mangoes, which Mrs. Steinberg asked her to pick up on the way. She waves a mango under Pearl's nose to show how fresh and fragrant it is. Mangoes no longer remind Pearl of old eggs but of bright pink Cuban flowers dangling from tender vines, soaking up the sun. She wants to devour this mango right now, and for its flavor to linger on her hands and lips for hours.

"Hurry, please," says Pearl. She removes her headscarf and struggles to smooth her hair, which has turned permanently frizzy and plump in this humidity. Her locks snarl against her comb. When she first arrived in Havana, she'd tried doing her hair a slightly different way to mark this change in her life, but her hair resisted all changes. "And make sure you eat today at lunch. You look skinnier every day."

Frieda shrugs. "Mr. Steinberg should be happy. Señora Davis wants two more hats like the ones with the . . ." She mimes the rolled-up brim of a summer hat.

"The straw cloche with the ribbon flowers."

"Yes, I think that's it."

"No, I know it's the one. I just made it for her."

"Pearl, let me tell him the good news. Would you mind?"

"Go ahead." Pearl would rather eat than talk at lunchtime anyway.

"Look what else I've got," says Frieda, who brings back the oddest souvenirs from her travels through town, a purple flower or a rag doll. Once it was a deck of cards with pictures of the city's famous buildings, like that rumpled-looking church on Calle Obispo. Today it's a long, fresh, slightly sticky cigar.

"Señora Davis's gardener gave it to me," Frieda says. People are always giving her small gifts. Pearl tells her to decline them, but Frieda never listens. "They make such stinky smoke, you wouldn't think the cigars themselves could smell so nice, like wild grass or . . . or warm mud in spring."

To satisfy her sister, Pearl sniffs the cigar. Its pleasant earthy smell reminds her yet again that she's hungry. She's always hungry, not just for food. However, for now, food will do. "What would we do with it?" she asks. "We don't know any men."

Frieda's mouth curls upward. "I was thinking, we could light it."

"No thanks," Pearl says. "Give it to Mr. Steinberg." Though he's no doctor, Mr. Steinberg often extols the healthful virtues of cigars, as if simply saying something with authority gives him the power to make it true. However, Pearl likes him so much, she wants his outlandish claims to be true, like his theory that cigars clean out the lungs because no germ can survive on a tobacco leaf.

His proof? He says workers in cigar factories are immune to all diseases, even typhus.

Typhus, Pearl thinks skeptically, that's something. She's lived through too many waves of typhus, including the one that killed her grandmother, as well as the nasty outbreak after the Revolution, when there wasn't an aspirin to be had. Pearl nursed her oldest sister Elka, who'd fallen unconscious but thankfully woke up after two days; after three days, you were as good as dead. Yet like many survivors of typhus, Elka was never the same. She walked with a limp, and her speech was often slow and hard to understand.

Smoking cigars is vile, but maybe if Pearl licked the wrappers, she might achieve the same benefits.

"Why should I give it away?" says Frieda. "It's mine and I'm keeping it."

"Fine, keep it. By the way, your nose is red. Are you wearing your hat?"

"No, I'm not," says Frieda, toying with a silk flower that Pearl had been working on, so Pearl slaps her fingers away. "Wear it or not, I still burn. The only reason your skin remains fair is that you stay cooped up inside all day because you're afraid to go out."

Pearl goes behind the curtain to grab her hat, a lumpy, sour-olive-green derby that the Steinbergs couldn't sell. Good enough. On her, a fancier one would be a waste.

○

IT'S A NICE change to look at something besides the four walls of the workshop. Frieda easily navigates the irregularly laid-out streets of Old Town without a map. Pearl wishes she didn't have to rely on her sister, but for now she has to. She's tried keeping a paper with the street names in her pocket and repeating them fervently, the way she used to say the prayers, and she has asked Frieda to share her secret.

"I can't explain," says Frieda. "I just feel my way around."

The streets of the Jewish quarter have Christian names: Obispo, Jesús María, San Isidro. Pearl's ashamed to tell her father she lives on a street named for Jesus, with a church at the end of it. Cubans walking by make the sign of the cross on their chests as she and Frieda used to do as girls playing "Gentiles," crossing themselves over and over until they fell to the ground laughing. The church bells ring to mark the quarter hour, and as Pearl plugs her ears, she wonders what the priests tell their worshippers about Jews.

They pass the corner grocery, which is also a bar—everything in Havana is also a bar. The fat old man at the counter oils his cash register and chats garrulously with his customers. "That old windbag," says Frieda. "He's bragging about fighting with José Martí. He claims he killed two men. As if anyone believes him."

That's something to brag about? Pearl thinks. How had he killed them?

Frieda's Spanish has improved so much she can now barter at the market and chat with strangers. Pearl knows words like "water" or "please," but can't grasp the musicality of the language, the way native speakers open their mouths and launch the words from deep in their gut. In the workshop, Pearl is quick of mind and fingers, but in the city, she sounds like a baby. The other week, after failing to make herself understood in a bakery, she ran into the street and let out a savage scream. Though she's exhausted of being this person, this ignoramus, this working drudge, there's no point in mastering Spanish. It's English she needs. Hotel Cuba is just a stopover on her way to America.

Now she sends Frieda to buy their bread.

A hoarse-voiced Greek sailor is pestering a pair of young Jewish men. A neighborhood regular, he's always promising in broken Spanish that he can smuggle anyone to America for fifty U.S. dollars. Pearl and Frieda keep their distance. The women at the Ezra Society have warned them not to trust such scams.

Housewives carrying black string shopping bags wave to a plump prostitute dressed in a slip, who sits by her window all day and calls out to men in Spanish or broken Yiddish with a Spanish accent. Pearl switches places with Frieda to block her view. Such business is officially illegal, but as in Russia, laws mean nothing here. If you know who to bribe, you can get away with anything.

Everything and everyone in Havana is for sale.

Pearl recalls a *zonah* from Turya, named Rachel, who trafficked with soldiers. After the war, the Hebrew Burial Society— the closest thing left to a local government—ordered her head to be shaved in the marketplace, then splattered her front door with red paint. On Rosh Hashanah, Rachel came late to shul and stood at the back of the women's section, her shaved head covered in a dark hat. Shortly afterward, she left Turya.

Pearl once shared her town's attitude of indignation about Rachel. But lately, Pearl thinks often of her, imagines seeing her again and asking her advice. Rachel seems like the only person who might really understand Pearl and her troubles.

Did Rachel's hair ever grow back?

At the corner, a lean, tough-skinned man sells warm peanuts in brown paper cones from a pushcart. His name is Isidro, like the street. Or like the saint and the street, Pearl supposes. He's her one Spanish friend.

Isidro wishes her a good day, calls her *"mi querida polaca,"* which means "dear Polish girl," though she hates the Polish. For some reason, Cubans think all Jews are Polish. At least the Cubans aren't anti-Semitic, not according to Mr. Steinberg. He says Pearl and Frieda shouldn't worry about strangers knocking them into the dirt or calling them Christ killers. There's no Spanish word for "pogrom."

"They haven't learned to hate us yet like in Europe," Mr. Steinberg says. "They recognize we're different, but they don't mind. Maybe that's why so many Jews have gone secular here. Without anti-Semitism, Jews go secular."

"That's not the only reason," says Mrs. Steinberg. "Some of us are modern."

Pearl wants to believe Mr. Steinberg's promises of safety, though she fears they might be another example of his optimism. Her breathing quickens whenever she sees a policeman or a band of young men sauntering down the street. This place is too poor, too lawless. Only in America will she feel safe.

She and Frieda turn onto a street with a non-Christian name: Muralla, which Frieda says means "wall." (Are the streets in America also commonly named for Christians? Basha's address is a mess of numbers and letters.) This is where the Steinbergs live, in a four-story building painted bright yellow like a banana. Their ground-floor flat has two bedrooms, a kitchen, salon, and dining room, and their own washroom, no need to share with the neighbors. Pearl and Frieda enter the building through a hall, then cross a courtyard with a gardenia tree in the center. The ruffled white flowers are in bloom, filling the courtyard with an extravagant, soapy-sweet scent.

Mrs. Steinberg leaves the door unlocked as usual. They walk in without knocking, which makes Pearl nervous, as does the absence of a mezuzah on the doorpost. She checks herself in the hall mirror, touches her hair, and wipes away the sweat in the ridge above her top lip. Frieda sets her hat down casually on the hook by the door and flounces into the salon, making herself at home.

"Oh, mangoes! How nice!" Mrs. Steinberg says, as if she hadn't asked them to buy the fruit. She gives them nervous pecks on both cheeks, and Pearl, who dislikes kisses from strangers, tries not to wince. Then Mrs. Steinberg accepts the sack from Frieda and rejects her offer of change. "You keep it, for such prompt service. Please come into the dining room, won't you?"

Her brown dress resembles a uniform. Mrs. Steinberg generally wears severe gray, brown, and black dresses without any ornament except a cameo pin featuring the Greek goddess Athena, which Pearl fears is wicked.

In the dining room, the walls are covered in stiff paper patterned with fat, dark-pink peonies. It makes the room feel heavy and dark and Old World. Pearl would have chosen a subtler, handsome striped pattern or pale blue, like the open sky.

Pearl watches the Steinbergs closely, particularly affable Mr. Steinberg in his white summer suit, a master charmer. Right now, as he devours shredded beef stew, he gaily twirls his fork as if it's a trick he invented. She's surprised he isn't more successful in business. With his kind face and personality, she'd want to buy whatever he's selling. At all times, he keeps candy and cigars in his pockets to give a shop owner, customer, or the local police, who all seem to be his old chums. In Russia, if you tried to cozy up to a constable or Cossack, you'd be robbed or beaten.

"Howdy, señoritas," Mr. Steinberg says in his odd mix of English and Spanish.

"My husband, the cowboy," says Mrs. Steinberg. "Just say 'good afternoon.'"

Pearl smiles shyly. Howdy, she thinks, eager to hold on to the word. Howdy, howdy, howdy. Her future is in the land of howdy, in America.

Frieda tells Mr. Steinberg about Señora Davis ordering two hats and he rewards her with a lemon candy. Pearl's jealous. Also, the meaty smell of Mr. Steinberg's lunch makes her dizzy with hunger, but she lowers her head and says thank you for her usual rice and beans. Mrs. Steinberg ladles out generous scoops onto their plates with her same apologetic smile. "I'd offer you stew, but I know you won't eat nonkosher meat."

"Sadly," says Mr. Steinberg, "a poor businessman like me can't afford kosher."

Fine, but can't they have something besides mashed beans? When Mrs. Steinberg once served fish, Pearl giggled with joy. Give me a nickel, she thinks, and I'll buy my own lunch for less than what you spend on your beans and save a couple of pennies for my America. However, for Mrs. Steinberg it's a point of pride or some other emotion to feed the two sisters her bland cooking. And to give them odds and ends. Half of a salt-and-pepper-shaker set. A chipped ceramic tumbler. A roomy housedress with a rent down the side; surely Pearl with all her skill could whip it into something lovely. This thoughtfulness occasionally irks Pearl, as if Mrs. Steinberg is more interested in their predicament than in Pearl and her sister themselves.

Pearl works silently at her meal. Small talk bores and fatigues her. Meanwhile, Frieda tells an amusing story about a man she saw with a cage of birds for sale. One bird stretched its pink neck toward the bars and said in Spanish, "Let me out of here!"

The Steinbergs laugh and then Mr. Steinberg says in a loud

voice as if they're deaf: "Have I told you girls you're the best little workers we've ever had?"

Yes, you have, Pearl thinks. Three times this week. Twice last week. "Thank you, sir," she says. That's about all she says these days. Better than saying the wrong thing, putting her and Frieda at risk of losing their temporary shelter. Still, Pearl feels humiliated watching her silver-tongued sister and the Steinbergs chat away as if she weren't there. She'd rather eat alone in a different room.

"My wife makes the best stew in Havana, better than the natives," says Mr. Steinberg. Pearl doubts it. She wonders, is he saying that to impress his wife or us? Let me try my hand in the kitchen, and you'd taste good cooking. "I wish you could have a bite of this stew," Mr. Steinberg goes on, chasing the stew on his plate with Cuban bread, gummy and white. "Religion's fine in its way, but not if it interferes with my lunch." Though Pearl disagrees with what he's saying, she loves his cheerful, musical way of saying it, modern and lively like the Yiddish in Warsaw, in contrast to his wife's brittle old-fashioned Yiddish or the slow drawl of Turya.

"Ignore him," says Mrs. Steinberg, then gives his ear a playful tug. "He learned his manners from a pack of bears."

Mr. Steinberg grins, as if he enjoys her scolding. He and his sober do-gooding wife are an odd match, yet they seem to like each other. Or at least, he doesn't beat her, and she doesn't henpeck him. But are they happy? Would Pearl be happy in such a marriage?

She takes a piece of bread, checking for bits of palm leaf that sometimes stick to the tender brown crust. The bakers here place leaves on the raw dough while it's baking to keep it from spreading.

Frieda finds Cuban bread sumptuous because it's pale and soft inside, lovely as a snowfall, but Pearl wishes the bread had more color and flavor in the middle, more chew and bite to the crust. More personality.

"Our friends thought we'd lost our senses, hiring strangers with all these natives desperate for work," Mr. Steinberg goes on. "They don't know the meaning of charity."

Mrs. Steinberg nods in agreement. She divides her rice into equally proportioned mounds and eats them one at a time, chewing carefully. "If we'd been blessed with children, we'd want them to be as polite as you girls."

Pearl shoots Frieda a look. It's her turn to say "Thank you."

Pearl imagines that Mr. Steinberg would make a fine father, generous, affectionate. Mrs. Steinberg must have been the one who decided not to have them. Perhaps she prefers causes to children. Or maybe when they emigrated here from Czechoslovakia and Mrs. Steinberg had been of childbearing age, they were too busy starting their hat business. Or what if there's something wrong with Mrs. Steinberg, so she can't have children? What if Pearl is that way too?

Panicking, she thinks: Is that why I didn't get pregnant?

"More rice?" Mrs. Steinberg asks, offering the earthenware tureen. Pearl would rather have potatoes, but she must admit Mrs. Steinberg makes fine rice, fluffy and faintly buttery, and thankfully not yellow. Pearl takes a scoop and mixes it with her black beans. Frieda stirs her food absentmindedly, then catches Pearl's eye and quickly manages a few bites.

After lunch, they eat the mangoes. Also, they get coffee. Pearl prefers tea, but Cubans like coffee, thick, brown, and bitter, served in tiny cups. Pearl sweetens hers with sugar and plenty of milk. Frieda drinks it straight, like a shot of schnapps.

Soon Mr. Steinberg will walk them back to the workshop. In

the afternoons, he visits his six workshops, scattered around Old Havana. The other workers are not Jewish, and they do not come for meals at the Steinbergs' home. Pearl should feel grateful, but she finds it embarrassing to accept charity, all these forced expressions of gratitude. She yearns for the day when she can say exactly what she means all the time.

Mrs. Steinberg collects their coffee cups. Though Pearl's palate may be bored, at least her stomach is full. She offers to help clear, but Mrs. Steinberg says, "Not today. We have something for you girls."

Another broken tchotchke? No, something valuable for a change: mail. Mr. Steinberg hands them two letters, forwarded from the Women's Home. One is from Father. The other, addressed to Frieda, comes from America with a blue-and-red stripe across the envelope. Pearl can guess who the sender is.

"Take a minute. Sit and read before you go back," says Mrs. Steinberg.

"Yes, of course," says Mr. Steinberg. "I'll go ahead to the shop. You two señoritas take all the time you need." He waves his hand in a grand gesture, the way Pearl's father used to lead the choir in shul. "Ten minutes. Fifteen, if you want."

"I'll clear the dishes," says Mrs. Steinberg. "Sit, read. You girls work so hard."

Frieda tears her letter open, while Pearl runs her finger inside the sealed flap of Father's envelope, then gently removes the folded letter inside like a lady's delicate veil. Paper's been at such a premium for months in the Old Country. Where did he get it? Then she sees printing on the back—he must have torn the frontispiece out of one of his secular books. She puts the paper to her nose to inhale a bit of Turya, but there's nothing.

She opens the letter and reads:

How are you, my dears, with nostalgia and affection, we your loving family think of you Friday nights, how different the table looks without you. With tears in our eyes and sorrow in our hearts, we wish and hope someday maybe we will see you again with our own eyes. We cannot imagine where you are, what you are doing or where is Cuba exactly? Avram says it's between North and South America. It hardly sounds like a real country. What language are they speaking there? What do they know about God? Better to get to America as soon as you can. Maniek and Elka were here with all the dear children. Mitzi helps light the candles. She's a good girl. And Yossi sings beautifully. I am teaching him early so when it's time for his bar mitzvah he'll be ready. The river has flooded again. Anything not fixed to the ground is washed away. I saw with my own eyes grave markers from the cemetery floating by. Soon it will be the bones from the graves too. Avram still talks about traveling to Palestine. Maybe to cure him of it, I'll take him to visit Uncle Mayer. Write to your sisters too. Dear daughters, there is much more to write, but I hardly know where to start, so I'll keep this letter short. How the days are passing by. We should all live next year in Jerusalem. From your father, brother, and sisters and all the family, who wish you all prosperity.

Gripping the fragile paper and reading her father's vigorous slanted handwriting, Pearl feels as if she's back in Russia, hiding from ice storms and stray soldiers. She plants her feet firmly to the floor, anchoring herself.

Such a stiff and formal letter. That line "with nostalgia and affection"—like something from a book. And the hints of genteel sarcasm—"It hardly sounds like a real country." What would dear Mama have written if she were alive? Mama could write, but never liked to. She worked with her hands. Father was the big thinker.

Pearl imagines him now, coming home from the butcher shop, scrubbing the fat, flesh, and blood from his hands and wrists, wiping them dry on whatever was nearby, even the tablecloth and curtains, then gobbling down dinner and running back out to shul to lead the boys in choir practice.

Though Father once hoped Avram might join the singing, the boy had a voice like a sick mule. Poor Avram, always trying to please Papa and coming up short. But then it was hard to please a man who forgot to notice his own children.

Perhaps if he'd paid more attention, he'd have noticed Pearl's visits to the root cellar, would have stopped them sooner.

Here it comes, the devil's voice, slyly attacking her thoughts, hardening her heart, inspiring anger, hate, bad feeling. Lately, he's always close at hand. But she can refuse to listen. She squeezes her eyes shut, struggles to slow her breath, pulls at her collar, and whispers, "Hear O Israel. The Lord is God. The Lord is One."

The devil's voice recedes. Her shoulders settle. Her breathing slows. She's back in Cuba. Back in the Steinbergs' cramped, safe dining room.

Frieda sags in her chair, chin pinned to her chest, her letter crushed in her fist. "Don't you want to read Father's letter?" Pearl asks.

Frieda shakes her head.

"What is it, sister?" Pearl touches her arm. "What does Mendel say?"

"He doesn't understand," says Frieda.

"What doesn't he understand?"

Frieda says nothing. More and more, she inhabits a different world and won't let Pearl in, favoring Mendel over her sister, her flesh and blood.

"Frieda, stop making a scene and tell me exactly what's wrong."

Frieda finally speaks up. "He's trying to break off our engagement."

That's news? thinks Pearl, who reads Mendel's letters when Frieda's done with them, sees him trying to wriggle his way out of old promises. Frieda has always seen something different in those words. But today she sees what Pearl sees: the truth.

"He doesn't want to wait anymore, not without some hope that we'll be together again. And who can say when that will be? Being stuck here, we might as well be back in Poland." Frieda stamps a foot on the carpet. "We should have stayed in Poland. We should have waited to find a way to America."

Mrs. Steinberg gently opens the door. "Upsetting news from home?" she asks, almost hopefully. So eager to involve herself in our affairs, Pearl thinks. That kind of help, we don't need. I'm responsible for her, not you. I am her sister.

"It's nothing, ma'am," says Pearl.

"Your face is flushed," says Mrs. Steinberg, patting Frieda's shoulder.

"She has a naturally pale complexion," says Pearl. "I tell her to wear a hat so she won't get burned, but sometimes she forgets. The sun isn't good for her. And she doesn't eat enough. I keep telling her, but she doesn't listen."

"I am a bit sleepy," Frieda says, and as if to offer proof, yawns.

"Certainly you are," says Mrs. Steinberg. "You come into the drawing room and relax on the divan. I'll shut the draperies and close the door. Pearl can go ahead to the shop, and when you're feeling better, you can join her there."

"I'll wait," says Pearl, embarrassed, and maybe too proud, to admit she's unsure of the way. "She'll soon feel better." Back in the workshop, she'll give her sister a proper talking-to.

"No," says Mrs. Steinberg. "You go to the shop, Pearl. Your sister needs time to collect herself. I'll look after her. You'll do her no good here. Come with me." She raises Frieda by her elbows, guides her to the drawing room.

And that's that. Pearl goes into the hall, fixes her hat on her head. She waits a minute, in case Frieda's suddenly feeling better, then steps outside.

The full sun is hitting the courtyard, wilting the gardenia blossoms ever so slightly. In the heat, their lovely scent turns putrid. She passes through to the outer building, reaches the doorway, framed by two swans carved into the facade.

The streets and sidewalks are noisier than ever and filled with men. Not one woman anywhere. A man with a basket of rolls on his head calls out for customers in a throaty wail. He eyes Pearl, and she shrinks against the doorframe.

Stop being so afraid, she tells herself. You want your life to be different in America. Start acting the part now, in Cuba.

Mrs. Steinberg says that in Havana, men consider respect for women a point of honor. To force one into your bed is shameful, a sign a woman wouldn't come willingly. Even at night, women can walk alone, but they shouldn't make it a habit.

Don't worry, Pearl thought, I wouldn't make it a habit.

She has to move. Mr. Steinberg will wonder what she's doing. Turn right or left? Both seem equally plausible. Pearl chooses left and happily sees a familiar-looking awning with green and white stripes and a sign saying SASTRERIA, which she knows means "tailor shop." Should she ever lose her place with the Steinbergs, she can seek work in any shop with such a sign.

Okay so far. But at the next corner, she must choose again whether to turn. As she steps into the road to squint at a street sign, an automobile blares its horn at her, and she jumps back on the sidewalk, feels the car's exhaust burn her ankles.

She wishes she were back in Turya, where she could use the sun to tell where she is. But in Old Havana, the buildings, awnings, advertisements get in the way; though she always feels the sun, she rarely sees it. Two men standing in a doorway are watching her, and she feels penned, so lost she wouldn't know where to run if she had to.

Pearl is about to give up all hope when she hears the hoarse voice of an old man. "*Mi polaca hermosa!*"

It's Isidro the peanut vendor, pushing his wooden cart, his face webbed with scars from an old bout with malaria. "Yes, yes," she says, so moved that she briefly loses her breath. "*Sí, sí, quiero . . .*" Then she remembers the note in her pocket with the street names and shows it to him, pointing to her street. He laughs and shakes his head; she realizes he can't read. Isidro says something else and starts wheeling his cart, giving it an extra push to get over a divot in the cobblestones. Turns to look at her, tilts his head in the direction he's headed, so she follows.

He walks so slowly! Mr. Steinberg will think she's dawdling

on purpose and she'll lose her job. Cubans are rarely in any hurry, though the thought of being late makes Pearl anxious to the point of nausea.

Though there's no purpose in trying to converse, Isidro does it anyway, punctuating each run of sentences with an "*Entiendes?*" Understand? She shakes her head, but he laughs and goes on talking. She's increasingly antsy each time he stops to sell a few cones of peanuts, first to a woman with bright makeup smeared on her face Cuban style, then to two men in white shirts and pants. "*Son americanos,*" Isidro says. She knows. The city is filled with Americans, all wondrously clean, coming and going from their country as they please. She wishes she could pin herself to their uniforms like a medal and float back to America. On a whim, Pearl says, "Howdy."

The men look confused.

"Howdy," she repeats.

They talk to each other in their language. What did she do wrong? She said the word just as Mr. Steinberg always says it. They salute her and keep on walking, taking America away with them.

When Isidro and Pearl turn a corner, she recognizes the street. "Gracias, gracias," she says, so grateful she's crying. Isidro waves away her thanks, and she dashes to the workshop, pushing the door open with her shoulder. She's here, safe.

"Howdy, Pearl," says Mr. Steinberg, perched on a stool and making a note in the little brown book he carries with him all the time.

Howdy, she repeats to herself. Isn't that what I said earlier?

He gestures to the gold-and-black turban she'd been working on. "This is exceptional. Such talent. And to think it's being wasted on me."

No talent, she thinks. I'm just copying from a model. Even a monkey can do it.

"Thank you, sir." She steals a glance at the clock. She's not so very late, and he's not mad. Don't they say in English "Time is money"? But maybe that's only a rule in America, not in hot countries like this one. Maybe here, a little late is okay.

Mr. Steinberg is preparing to leave. He's got more workshops to visit. "Pearl, you've got magic in your hands," he says.

"Yes, sir," she says, but it's a lie. Magic, she thinks. No such thing. It's just me.

FOUR

AFTER LUNCH ONE APRIL AFTERNOON, MRS. STEINBERG pulls Pearl aside with a strange request: to make her a pair of pants. "For me, not my husband."

"For you, ma'am?" Pearl asks.

"Yes," says Mrs. Steinberg. "To wear at my next suffragist meeting. All the suffragists in America wear them." Pearl doesn't know this term, so Mrs. Steinberg defines it. "Cuban ladies must have the right to vote like American ladies now have."

Pearl has never met a woman like Mrs. Steinberg, always so concerned with abstractions like justice, fixing the world, causes unrelated to her own life. The idea that any person, and a woman no less, would demand a say in choosing her ruler feels insolent to Pearl. Still, she listens as Mrs. Steinberg explains that to be truly free, women must have the vote. Pearl disagrees. For her, freedom is being able to live and work in peace.

What interests Pearl more than voting for men she's never met is the technical problem of designing pants for a woman that don't look like a workman's uniform. She used to make simple boxy trousers for her father and brother, cut with straight lines. They'd lie on brown paper on the floor, and she'd pencil out the shape around their legs. But Mrs. Steinberg is not the type to lie on the floor. Also, her pants would need to accommodate a woman's curves, and she wants them to have absurdly wide legs. She's chosen an expensive black silk crepe de chine that would sway loose at her ankles like a dress. Oh, and a blouse to match.

"That's not too hard, is it?" she asked Pearl. "Of course I'll pay you."

Flattered that Mrs. Steinberg recognizes her skill despite her general preference for Frieda in most things, Pearl says, "Not hard at all." Mrs. Steinberg doesn't sew much because of her eyes, though Pearl has seen some of the impressive dresses she'd made in her youth. Mrs. Steinberg did fine work in her day. She knows what good is.

Pearl visits Mrs. Steinberg several times for fittings. Always while her husband is out. "He'd poke fun at me," says Mrs. Steinberg. "Then I'd lose the nerve to wear them."

The idea of Mrs. Steinberg losing her nerve to do anything makes Pearl smile. She's enjoying their fitting sessions. Now, after two months in Havana, she doesn't mind going to the Steinbergs' alone, since it's not far. Also, she knows a few useful Spanish and English phrases to ask for help if she gets lost, even if her Yiddish accent is heavy and plodding. She's mastered the art of walking right past strange men, avoiding their gaze. For further protection, she wears dowdy, roomy clothes that hide her figure.

Before each session, Frieda teases Pearl, saying, "Going to meet your boyfriend?"

"You know where I'm going," says Pearl. "What boyfriend? This is Cuba."

"The heart beats in Cuba just as it does anywhere," says Frieda.

"Please," says Pearl. "Stop teasing."

She works in Mrs. Steinberg's bedroom, which has a red carpet and pretty landscape pictures on the wall. To Pearl, the room always smells sweet, like orange blossoms. One afternoon, Mrs. Steinberg plays an album of opera arias on her phonograph, so exquisite that Pearl fights the urge to drop her pins and chalk to listen more fully to those surging voices. Father sometimes gave opera recitals with the choir, singing famous arias with such a tender, genuine, even vulnerable expression on his face, as if the song came from deep inside. He often said that in this life, you could rarely trust people, but you could always trust music. However, Pearl wants to trust people too.

Mostly, there's no music, just the strange new intimacy of plucking material around Mrs. Steinberg's body, which Pearl now knows with the familiarity of a lover: the thin shoulders, sharp elbows, and tiny calves. Was Mrs. Steinberg always this slender, or did something transform her body? Once Pearl caught Mrs. Steinberg with her hair down, loose from its usual chignon. It was lovely and wavy, with a silky texture. Pearl could imagine it turning Mr. Steinberg's head as a young man.

At their last fitting, Mrs. Steinberg peers down at Pearl, kneeling and pinning up the cuffs. She asks, "What's that tune you're humming?"

"I was humming?" asks Pearl. She thinks for a second, then hums a few more bars. It's a nursery rhyme she sang as a girl. She recites the words:

Bride, bride, beautiful bride, why are you crying?
Crying bitter tears, and already at the chuppah!
No one forced you to get married, to bury yourself alive.
Dry your tears, you chose this madness for yourself.

Mrs. Steinberg has a good long laugh, a rare sound from her. Usually she's nervous and wound up, such a contrast to Cuban women in their bright dresses and costume jewelry, with their wide, painted mouths. There's something mysterious and contradictory about her, Pearl can't put her finger on it.

"May I ask," says Pearl, "what is your first name?"

"Adela," she says. A strange combination of sounds.

"One more question? What is it really like, to be married?" Pearl asks.

Mrs. Steinberg lowers her chin. "Tiring," she says. "Husbands have to be trained at first, like dogs. Otherwise they're forever and hopelessly spoiled." Pearl thinks this over. Dogs are vicious, and Pearl hasn't the faintest clue how to train one. "Why, Pearl?" Mrs. Steinberg asks. "Do you have some special beau?"

"Me? No, no."

"Why not?" Mrs. Steinberg pours herself a glass of water. "You're a bright, capable young woman. And nice-looking."

Pearl notes the obligatory add-on of "nice-looking." It's the first thing people notice about Frieda, though they don't use that word, "nice-looking." They say pretty, charming, exquisite. "I've had bad luck," Pearl says.

Mrs. Steinberg takes a long drink of water. Pearl would like some too, but she wants to be asked.

"Bad luck can't last forever," says Mrs. Steinberg.

Pearl snorts before she can stop herself. What can someone like Mrs. Steinberg know about bad luck?

"Would you tell me about Frieda's young man?" Mrs. Steinberg asks.

"When we left Poland, they had an understanding," says Pearl. "Today not. Tomorrow, it'll be different. If his word was a bridge, I'd hesitate to cross it."

"That's an odd state of affairs."

Pearl's tempted to confide in Mrs. Steinberg. She seems to really understand, like a kindred spirit. Maybe if they'd met some other way, they'd be friends.

"You look as though you have something to say about it," says Mrs. Steinberg.

"I want more for her than to marry her schoolgirl crush. But she won't listen."

"I see," says Mrs. Steinberg, and Pearl believes that she does. "But what about you? What do you hope for, for yourself, if not marriage?"

Pearl has no answer. Her brother, Avram, and his friends used to sing Zionist anthems about hope and immigrating to Palestine. Pearl's too busy trying to make it through her day to waste time hoping and dreaming. But if she did allow herself to hope, there might be one thing: Whatever her fate, single or married, she'd like to be her own boss, in charge. With no one to give her orders.

When the work is finished, Pearl's sorry. Mrs. Steinberg tries on the finished pants. Though they're well-made and fit her body, Pearl thinks they look wrong on Mrs. Steinberg, whose old-fashioned bearing doesn't go with this modern outfit. Mrs. Steinberg, however, seems pleased.

A few meters of the black silk are left over, and Pearl asks for it. "Of course," says Mrs. Steinberg, continuing to admire her new outfit. "Lovely work, Pearl. I'm not surprised."

She pays Pearl, who hears the satisfying clink of the coins first in her palm, and then later in her pocket as she walks home, her cheeks sparkling with sweat.

○

AT NIGHT, PEARL uses the leftover silk to make herself a pair of pants too, for her private amusement. She loves this work, the feeling of the fabric, the way her thoughts disappear in the repetitive simplicity of hiding all traces of the human hand, the illusion of inevitability in a cuff or seam that are the result of hours of toil.

Pearl finishes the pants in two evenings. She thought she'd wear them around the workshop, or as pajamas, but they turn out too nice for wearing to bed. Imagine wearing these in public, Pearl thinks. I'd have to be a different person.

It's Frieda's idea for Pearl to wear the pants for a Sunday afternoon outing.

Pearl says it's an outrageous idea, and the Torah forbids women from wearing men's clothing, but Frieda argues that the pants are not in the least mannish. "They're made by a woman for a woman, right? So it's a sin for a man to wear them, not you," she says.

"I'll look like a fool," Pearl objects. "Or worse."

"If you walked about in Havana as I have, you'd see plenty of women in pants," says Frieda. "We're living in the modern age." She pushes Pearl and her pants behind the frayed curtain. "Go on," Frieda calls out. "Don't be afraid."

Pearl feels strange, stepping into one leg and then the other. Pants are for wealthy ladies wanting to make a sensation, not poor women like herself.

After putting them on, she sits upright on her bed, fingers laced, knees locked, eyes fixed on the wall facing east, toward Jerusalem. She's hung an amulet there, a prayer saying: GOD DESTROYS SATAN, A WITCH SHALL NOT LIVE! For now, it works. Those evil voices have faded to a faint hum. Not silence, but close enough.

"Aren't you ready yet? You know I'm no good at waiting," Frieda calls out.

"Almost," says Pearl, already deeply embarrassed.

"Let me see," says Frieda. She pulls back the curtain and freezes, her eyes wide, the rough fabric of the curtain in her fist.

"I look ridiculous," says Pearl. "I'll put on a dress."

"You don't look ridiculous at all," says Frieda. "Really."

"No? How do I look?"

Frieda tilts her head. "Like you were meant to look. Pearl, you're beautiful." And Frieda's tone is so sincere, Pearl knows she means it.

Pearl checks the mirror again. She can't get used to what she sees there. You wanted to be a New Woman, she reminds herself. Here's the result. The old proverb comes to mind: Stare in a mirror too much by day, and the image returns to choke you at night. "People will laugh. Like I'm Charlie Chaplin."

"False modesty is a sin. That's what you always taught me."

Pearl looks again, sees how flattering these black silk pants are to her, much more natural than they looked on Mrs. Steinberg. They're right for her. They make her body look different, feel different. It seems a lie to call them pants, because Frieda's right: no man could ever wear them. The pants swell around her hips, then unfurl outward from her thighs to her calves, almost swallowing her decidedly feminine shoes, black ankle boots with chunky heels.

With the fabric around her legs, Pearl feels supported, strong.

She's the same inside, but by changing her outside, it's affected what's inside. The pants give her a freedom of movement she'd never have in a clumsy dress. It's a strange, wonderful, uneasy sensation. Like when they first heard about the abdication of the tsar. No one could be sure the news was true until the next market day, when the constable appeared in the town square and ripped the badges off his uniform, throwing them in the mud.

Frieda tiptoes behind Pearl, fidgety, pretty, and fragile. In the streaked mirror, wearing her pale cream dress, she could be Pearl's ghost.

"Don't wear your ugly green hat, not today," says Frieda. "Here." She holds out a jaunty blue three-corner cavalier hat with an upturned brim. Its bold contour complements the shape of her head. Maybe I could be a hat person, Pearl thinks, in the right hat.

"Mr. Steinberg would be furious," says Pearl, admiring it in the mirror. The hat is destined for a high-end ladies' shop on Calle Obispo.

"He's never furious," says Frieda. "Not even after I spilled coffee on that velvet toque with the fur inside."

"I won't drink any coffee, then," says Pearl, as if that solves everything. "We might as well go, get this over with."

They lock up the workshop, then head west toward the open expanse of Paseo Boulevard, which is only occasionally visible through gaps in the striped awnings of shops or the pink and yellow arches of street arcades. She and Frieda step carefully over beggars and wicker baskets of dark-skinned dolls with exaggerated toothy smiles, a popular souvenir for American tourists that Pearl finds grotesque. Also popular are pawn shops promising DINERO in big letters, luring foreigners who've wasted their money drinking or gambling on horses.

Wearing her pants out on the street, Pearl feels exposed. She expects passersby to point at her pants and stare, but they're more interested in the shouting men on every corner selling lottery tickets, waving signs posted with numbers. Though Pearl has ordered Frieda not to waste her money on the tickets, she isn't sure Frieda has listened.

A short man with dark curls ambles alongside Pearl and Frieda, muttering, "What do you need?" in Spanish, English, and Yiddish. Pearl once mistook men like him for handymen offering their services. Now she recognizes them as dope peddlers.

"*Te voy a pagar!*" Pearl barks, and he moves on.

"Where did you learn that?" Frieda says, laughing.

"It means 'Go away or I'll slap you,'" says Pearl. "Isidro taught me."

"That's *voy a pegar*! You said *pagar*. That means 'I'll pay you.'"

Pearl resents being corrected, especially when she's wrong. "Anyway, he's gone, isn't he?" Suddenly she feels self-conscious in her new pants. "I look like a man," she says, stretching the material around her legs as if to transform it into a dress. "You shouldn't have allowed me to leave the workshop in these," she complains.

"Why, Pearl, I never knew you were capable of vanity," Frieda says.

Across the trolley tracks is a bar filled with American tourists in sunglasses and newly bought cheap straw Panama hats, packed together like herring in a barrel. Desperate for alcohol, Americans stop here on their way into town from their ships. Some are still carrying their luggage. Peddlers offer them tiny bottles of liquor, trophies to smuggle back home. Pearl once witnessed an American drop a bottle of whiskey on the floor and get down on all fours to lap up the liquid like a dog.

They reach the wide boulevard of Paseo del Prado, paved with crushed stones and bits of hard pink coral. Like many other ladies in Havana on a Sunday, Pearl and Frieda stroll along and peep at fashions they cannot afford in the window displays of the finer department stores: the English Bazaar, La Belle France, El Encanto, and La New York, stores that Mr. Steinberg wishes would carry his hats.

The Cuban ladies wear thin, boldly printed dresses that expose shoulders and legs, and their nails are painted a slick, glossy red. Pearl smells their sweet perfume mixed with sweat. They laugh and whistle back at the boys who whistle at them. Pearl watches curiously, tries to imagine herself whistling at some insolent man.

She's relieved to see several other young women wearing pants. Some women tuck their hair in boyish berets or wear neckties. One has cut her hair short, just below her chin, so it frames her face like a helmet. She walks arm in arm with a female friend in a dress. How confusing for the men, Pearl thinks. Well, good, let them be confused.

Several pairs of ladies' pants are displayed in the shop windows, but not one pair is as fetching as Pearl's. Noting that fact, she stands a little taller, allows a smile to creep into the corners of her lips. There are also dresses in silk and shirred chiffon, with beaded fringes and plunging necklines. Her eyes well up as she admires the workmanship. She'd love to run her fingers beneath the filmy material, inspect the subtle stitching, handle the gentle folds of the hems. Behind the dresses hang gauzy curtains in pinks and blues, and the floor is covered in a soft carpet. Imagine stepping behind the glass, feeling that carpet caress the soles of your bare feet.

A world capable of producing such beauty can't be all bad.

Frieda likes the furs. She says Mendel has pledged to buy her one someday—another of Mendel's matzo promises: quick to make and easy to break.

"Sure, sure," says Pearl. "He's a regular prince, that one."

"You'll see," Frieda keeps saying, "when you have a beau of your own."

"I doubt it," says Pearl. Even if she found an admirer, perhaps some man with an odd taste for expired milk, she cannot tell any man what happened to her, and she cannot marry any man who doesn't know what happened to her. But for now, standing beside these store windows, dressed in these pants that swish elegantly around her ankles, Pearl couldn't care less about husbands or old maids.

They walk under the lacy arcades of the Hotel Inglaterra, guarded by uniformed doormen and stiff potted palms, where wealthy tourists waste money on overpriced coffee in outdoor cafés. Pearl is fascinated by their lightweight summer suits in impossibly pale shades of ivory, tan, and pink, frivolous colors, so easy to stain. How lucky they are to be able to waste away the afternoon, just as Pearl's doing now on this walk. This thought stabs her with guilt—as if a moment's pleasure during her stay in Hotel Cuba is a betrayal, or means she'll be stuck here forever. But it does feel wonderful to wear an elegant outfit and walk idly along the Paseo, past bronze lion statues, marble benches, and black lampposts with electric lights that come alive at night.

I've been working here two months with no break, Pearl thinks. For one afternoon I can enjoy myself.

"My feet hurt," says Frieda. "Can't we stop?" So they retreat to the Parque Central, with its alarmingly tall palms. Their wrinkled gray trunks and wide fronds snap in the wind, as sunlight flickers through their spiky leaves. No tree has the right to stand so tall, thinks Pearl. In a flash, it might snap in half and crush her head.

Their heels dig into paths of gravel; bits of it get caught in Pearl's shoes. Jewish immigrants congregate in the park's shady northeast corner. So many Jews arrive in Havana each day, the city has no room. Several newcomers sleep on park benches.

She and Frieda settle on an empty bench, and Pearl spreads out the material of her pants to look like a dress. It's one thing to parade in pants before strangers, but these are her people. Pearl keeps an eye out for landsmen, other Jews from their town, and doesn't find any. Still, it's nice to sit under a finca tree and hear Yiddish spoken, or steal a peek at a Yiddish newspaper from America.

An amateur theater group is practicing scenes from a play based on *Les Misérables*, a French book that Pearl hasn't read. She watches a scene taking place during one of their revolutions—they have those too in France. But France is a rich country. What do they need revolutions for?

A slim man dressed in a wrinkled brown suit is staring at them. Pearl crosses her arms and frowns. What the hell does he want? To mock her pants? But he asks in Yiddish if they have any cigarettes to spare. That's all right. She nods at Frieda, who fishes one out of her handbag. Sometimes Mr. Steinberg treats them to cigarettes in addition to their pay, though neither she nor Frieda are big smokers.

"Where are you girls from?" the man asks, shoving the cigarette into his mouth. As Pearl tells him, he inhales a deep breath of smoke. "I used to run a barge on the Horin River, hauling barley," he says. "You know Elia the Bastard?"

"Sure, I knew him," she says coolly. Who could forget the story? Elia, owner of a dry goods store, lived in the largest house on Greyble Street. A band of Whites barged into his home, forcing the family out at gunpoint without giving them time to take with them even an egg. That evening, despite his wife's protests, Elia returned to have a look. "I'm entitled to come and go as I please to my own house," he argued. So he walked over, opened the door, and gaped in horror at the drunk goyim trashing his house, devouring his food, hurling glasses and dishes at the walls. One of the Whites saw him standing there and shot him in the head.

So began the new order of things.

"How many in your family died?" asks the man. Judging from the fashionable cut of his suit, Pearl guesses he used to be a something, whatever his origin. The man stubs out his cigarette and tucks it in his jacket for later. He wipes off the end of their bench with a handkerchief and sits down.

Pearl shrinks a palm's width away. "In our house, no one," she says. "But we're a small family. Only six survived childbirth." She nods at Frieda, who's removed her shoe to shake out a pebble. "She's the youngest." She almost said, "She's *my* youngest."

"You're lucky," he says. "I have five brothers, three sisters, and I don't know where they are, or if any of them are alive."

Being alive is a matter of chance, not luck, Pearl thinks. Even the sand flies biting her arms feel the impulse to survive.

"We're waiting to go to America," says Frieda, smiling brightly.

"Maybe you'll wait forever." The man runs a broken comb through his dark hair, which has a startling white streak across the front.

Frieda sits up. "Why?"

"You didn't hear? They're changing the laws. No more Jews this year."

"What nonsense are you talking?" says Frieda, angrily fanning herself with her wilting hat. "If you wait in Cuba for a year, you can go to America. Those are the rules."

"Not anymore," says the man. "I'm telling you, they're changing the law." He seems delighted to spread his bad news, eager to depress them all.

"Don't believe it," Pearl tells Frieda, who appears panicked. Pearl feels uneasy herself, but she's heard too many rumors to let this one upset her plans. She'll check with Mr. Steinberg, or maybe the women at the Ezra Society. She needs facts.

"Of course I don't believe it," says Frieda. "I don't take legal advice from a man who needs a good wash and shave."

"Believe or don't believe," the man says. "But I'm going to America anyway."

"How?" asks Pearl. "You're going to smuggle with the Greek?"

"I know someone who went that way. They stuffed him with ten others into a fishing boat, then dumped them in a swamp. When they reached the town of Key West, covered in mud and mosquito bites, clothes in tatters, the police caught them and sent them back to Hotel Cuba, twenty bucks poorer." He shakes his head. "Key West is an island, and you have to get off the island. But the police watch all the ships and the train station. So you have to look like an American. With ready-made clothes from a store, not made by hand. And talk English. At least enough so they think okay, this one's an immigrant, but he's been here awhile."

"I don't understand. What's your plan?" Pearl asks.

The man looks both ways, then slides closer to Pearl and Frieda on the bench. "I met a rum smuggler. He sails on moonless nights, turns off the motor so no one hears him in the water. He knows the coast, all the corners and rivers to hide. And if the

Coast Guard stops him, he bribes them with a bottle of rum. I'm going to be his assistant, help him smuggle rum, and in exchange he'll smuggle me too."

"That sounds thrilling," says Frieda. "I'd be willing to try it."

"It's no job for a woman."

"Why not?" asks Frieda. "Just let me try."

"Frieda, calm yourself," Pearl says.

"I paid a smuggler fifty dollars," says a young man, butting in. "We sailed around a few hours, then they put us on a beach saying it was Florida already, but it was just Cuba, several versts east of here. We had to walk all the way back to Havana."

Another man and then a woman nearby chime in with their stories. Slowly a small crowd gathers to trade rumors. How to fake papers, accents, and hair color. Hide with the rum or the pineapples. Bribe a sailor to take his place. Visit the "fast houses" of prostitutes by the harbor. They know how to cross. A Jewish guy at the American consulate sells visas for twenty dollars—yeah, but at Key West, they know they're fakes. Watch for a man in a white suit, white hat, white tie, and white shoes, he can fix things. Cubans aren't subject to the quotas and some Jews are dark enough to pass.

"Like you," says one man, pointing at Pearl.

Me? Pearl thinks. I look like a Cuban? Why not an American? All this talk makes her dizzy. "Let's go eat," she tells Frieda.

Feeling defeated, they head east out of the park, back to Old Havana. I was an idiot to bring us to Cuba, Pearl thinks. If what this man says is true, we're in a real mess.

"I could hide in some rich man's yacht," says Frieda. "When we land in Florida, he'll get off the boat, and I'll walk up the dock like a grand American lady."

"Without papers, even fake ones? What if a policeman stops you?" says Pearl.

Frieda says, "Pearl, if you worry about technicalities, you'll never get to America. Or maybe you want to stay here with your precious Steinbergs."

Pearl recognizes her sister's habit of taking out her feelings on whoever's nearby when she feels upset. And it's Pearl's misfortune to often be nearby.

"*My* precious Steinbergs?" says Pearl. "You're their darling."

"If you say so. In the meantime, we're both stuck here."

"And you blame me?" Pearl says. "Yes, you do. If you think so, say it openly."

"Who said anything about blame? Why is everything so extreme for you? All one way or the other? If someone dares to question your opinion, you take it so personally. And what if you were wrong? Pearl, you don't have to be right all the time."

"I don't understand. Speak clearly. Do you blame me or don't you?"

"No, I don't blame you. I never have. It's you who blame yourself. So if it's forgiveness you want, you'll have to give it to yourself. Even if I said I forgive you for whatever sin you think you've committed, you wouldn't believe me. Or you'd say, oh, she's so young, she can't possibly understand."

Her voice has a sharpened, mature edge that Pearl doesn't recognize.

"I'm just saying," Frieda goes on, "sometimes it's wrong to obey the rules, especially when the rules are unfair."

"And who's to judge fair or not fair? You? You haven't finished school even."

"A person doesn't need school to understand that it's unfair to be separated from someone she loves, someone who's waited patiently for almost a year . . ." Her voice trails off.

So it's back to Mendel again, is it? Pearl laughs. "Your Mendel must be a sorcerer, to have such a hold on you."

"I know he has flaws," says Frieda. "Like any man. But he's the man I'm going to marry. And when you insult him, you're insulting my taste, so you're insulting me."

That guy's hold on her really is magic, Pearl thinks. Nothing I say against him sticks. "Frieda, why do you choose to be on his side over mine? Why won't you listen to me?"

"How can you expect me to listen to you when you won't listen to me?"

"I am listening to you, but what I'm hearing makes no sense."

"Forget sense. I'm talking about how I feel. I should know my own heart. Right, Pearl?"

"I'm thinking." She's struggling to see Frieda's point of view. A girl in love who wants love. Why is that hard to accept? Don't I want love too like any other person?—however painful I find this to admit.

They walk in silence back to Old Havana, and the narrow streets close in on them like a human gullet around a morsel of food. The walls of the buildings trap the echoes of their footsteps and, of course, the heat. A pair of wild cats saunter lazily across their path; it's so hot, even cats can't be bothered to run when they chase each other.

"You really think it's true, they changed the laws in America?" Frieda asks.

"I don't believe it," says Pearl in a soft voice, her way of apologizing for her earlier sniping. Yet saying she doesn't believe it fills her with more doubt. For too long, she's told Frieda so many untrue things to reassure her.

They approach a church, and Pearl holds her breath until they're past it. In the plaza on the other side, vendors sell embroidered Spanish shawls, pornographic postcards, rosaries, and other toys of the Christian religion. Several doughy-faced Americans, including one of those Ask Mr. Foster tour groups, watch a quartet of musicians while Cuban couples in ruffled costumes dance.

"Observe," says their guide, "the Latin Lover in his native habitat."

Pearl and Frieda take a break from worrying to stare at the pink, green, and blue costumes, the dancers' strange, jerking movements, the swaying hips, the sharp angles of arms shaking to music. They smell the sweat from the dancers' bodies.

The Cuban women Pearl knows do not dance or dress this way, but these Cubans and their dancing amuse the Americans, who set up cameras on tripods to take pictures. The tourists laugh and try to dance too, awkwardly. Occasionally, a Cuban pulls them in to participate in the dancing, for tips.

Americans are friendly, maybe to excess. Too kind and trusting of strangers, maybe because in their land no one hunts you like an animal. It's soft living.

Next to Pearl is a woman in a little jacket like a cape and a polka-dot headscarf with a fake bird riding on top. She's chatting with two men in tight black pants. Also, she smokes a fat cigar, taking long puffs with a contented expression on her handsome, dusky face. Pearl is tempted to say hello or do something to get this woman to look her way.

A man talks to Frieda in Spanish, coaxing her to dance. She shakes her head no, though she's smiling. "Just one dance?" he says. "For half a song?"

"No, no," she says, her voice delicate like a tiny bell. He pulls playfully on her hand, and she yanks it back, wags her finger, but she's laughing.

Pearl steps forward between them. "Leave her," she says.

The man turns to Pearl. "Okay, why not you?" he asks in Spanish.

"I have no money," says Pearl, who dislikes being the consolation prize, as often happens in Frieda's company. But it's not Frieda's fault. She shouldn't resent her for it.

"Forget money. Just for dancing," he says, smirking.

"I can't, I don't know . . ." she says in her faltering Spanish.

"You don't know? Then we'll teach you." He grabs her hand. She tries to pull away, ready to fight if she has to. But he quickly hands her off to the Cuban woman with the cigar. Frieda giggles and claps in delight.

"Follow my instructions," the woman says, handing her cigar to Frieda, who holds it delicately between two fingers. "Put your right hand here, your left there."

"*No puedo*," says Pearl, reaching for the right words. "*Mi español malo*."

"You don't need words to dance, dear heart. I'll teach you without words." The Cuban woman is wiry but she's surprisingly strong. She grips Pearl, pulls her close to her own body. It all happens quickly. "It's not school, you don't need words to learn. Learn with the body. Understand?" She says more things Pearl doesn't understand. She nods anyway, hoping if she goes along, she can get this over with quickly.

The woman's perfume is dizzyingly sweet and her hands feel

soft. Up close, Pearl notices that her lipstick and face powder are smeared. Her pink polka-dot dress feels slippery, and the artificial bird on her headscarf trembles as if it wants to fly away. "Like this, learn with the body," the woman keeps saying, gripping Pearl's hips to make them sway. Pearl struggles to make her body do these things, but it won't obey her mind. Maybe in this situation, her head doesn't help. Her body has to feel what to do.

The woman says something else. Pearl doesn't understand, so she calls out to Frieda for a translation. "She says just because you are wearing pants, don't move like a man," Frieda says between peals of laughter. "Oh, Pearl, you're too funny."

"Be like a woman," the woman directs Pearl in Spanish. "Softly, slowly. Not like this." She moves her hand up and down in a straight line. "Like this." Now she moves her hand in a sinuous wave, curving inward and then out, in and out again.

Pearl has danced with women at weddings in Turya, where the dancing is buoyant, free form, and a bit clumsy. This style is different: serious yet teasing, dark and studied, precise as ballet. Though she's trying as hard as she can, she senses she's missing the whole point, failing to enjoy it the way these Cubans are. The men watch and laugh, as does Frieda. They're in league against her.

"Like this," says the Cuban woman. "Like this." Her eyes and her hands are so distracting, Pearl can't possibly follow her orders.

"I don't know how." How did she let this happen? She's on the verge of tears. If only she had more Spanish to explain her confusion. Usually she doesn't focus this intently on her body, except when it feels painful, hungry, or full.

Her back is stiff, and her shoulders sore from hunching over her stitches at work, and from hunching over in public too—if she's being completely honest—to hide her breasts from men's eyes.

The woman presses Pearl's hips into position and grips the small of her back. She's touching places no other human has touched, not even the Polish beast, whom Pearl shuts out of her mind. He's not here, and this woman is here, terrifyingly here, with warm skin and a firm touch. Pearl resists, but the woman grips her more strongly, says she's ruining the dance, just relax. Music thrums through Pearl's empty stomach and tiny drops of perspiration run down her temples.

It could be that no one is conspiring against her. What if they're just having fun? Something loosens inside. Her shoulders drop and she relaxes a little, feels a fluttering in her chest. It reminds her of when she'd go to the town bathhouse as an adolescent, where the naked women would pause their washing to play and shout and splash each other and laugh. One of the girls was so lovely, they called her Leah the Flower. She had a tall, willowy figure that drove young, plump Pearl mad with envy, or some other emotion.

The song ends abruptly, setting Pearl free. Oddly, she's disappointed. The Americans applaud and open their wallets and purses. Pearl lets go of the woman, offers a short bow. Frieda returns the woman's cigar, then says as they walk away, "You were marvelous, Pearl! At first I thought you were going to faint, but then you settled down nicely. I wish she'd asked me. I'd never dance with a strange man, but with a woman, why not? What harm could it do?"

Quite a lot, thinks Pearl, panting and dabbing the sweat from her forehead. She looks over her shoulder at the woman, already dancing with a new partner, an American man with extraordinarily bright teeth. Pearl hates him immediately. She still feels the pressure of the Cuban woman's hands. An unusual sensation, not altogether unwelcome.

○

THEY TAKE THEIR dinner on Compostela Street, at a cheap dairy restaurant that has Lenin's picture on the door, with his terrifyingly sharp chin and fierce glare.

When the Bolsheviks came to Turya, the Jews were glad to see them drive out their former tormentors, the Whites. But the Reds proved as bloody as their name, hunting "counterrevolutionaries," meaning anyone who owned a store or was thought to be a Zionist, even though the Zionists were socialists. After one of their forays into Turya, the townspeople found the wall of the main synagogue splattered with blood. Two dozen "counterrevolutionaries" had been lined up there and shot.

Cuban Bolsheviks, however, are harmless, barely able to run their European-style restaurant, with erratic service yet homey, satisfying food. And after the dancing, Pearl feels hungrier than ever. She and Frieda order two seltzer waters, or "Polish water," as it's called here, black bread with sour cream, herring, and roasted potatoes with burned skin.

The waiter who brings their dinner is striking looking, with a sharp nose like Lenin's and dark eyes with long, almost feminine lashes. He invites them to enjoy their meal in a soft, kind voice, and Pearl wants to take his hand, squeeze it in hers to thank him. She digs into the familiar, starchy food, the roasted potato, the sour herring, the rich tang of the sour cream. Also, there's hot tea, real tea, which in Havana is sold only in pharmacies—Cubans take it as a cure for upset stomachs. She drinks her fill, then turns her glass upside down to indicate she doesn't want anymore.

Afterward, she and Frieda walk slowly along the Malecon seawall, where half of Havana, rich, poor, and in between, come to feel the breeze and enjoy the spray of waves shooting up in the air, crashing against rock and cement. As they look at the diamond necklace of lights along the curved coastline, Pearl recalls dancing with that woman, her firm grip on Pearl's waist, and then that kind waiter in the restaurant, his gentle voice. Maybe Frieda thinks this way about Mendel. It's human. What's so wrong?

So much of my life wasted, Pearl thinks. I don't want to waste anymore. I want to be held, touched. I want to feel deeply. . . .

"Pearl," says Frieda, touching her shoulder. "You're crying."

"I don't know what's come over me," says Pearl. "Let's go back."

She feels better once they start walking home. They cross the Plaza de Armas, where the American consulate is located. All day, immigrants wait under its arcades. In the *Havana Post*, the consul complains they're becoming a nuisance.

Pearl and Frieda stop near an old tree that's holy to the locals, who leave coins, fruit, and bread at its roots and make wishes. Pearl is tempted to take some of the coins. All that money wasted on wishes, when it could do so much real good elsewhere.

What a country, where women smoke cigars and people worship trees.

She hears that old churlish devil's voice in her mind, asking what's wrong with worshipping trees? Is that any more bizarre than worshipping a pair of scrolls?

We don't worship the scrolls, she replies, but the words they contain.

Fine, so you worship words and they worship trees. In the end, it's the same. No one hears you. In the end, you wind up in the mud, with mud in your hair, in your skirts, on the backs of your bare legs.

My legs aren't bare any longer, Pearl thinks. I'm wearing pants.

"I'm writing to Mendel," says Frieda. "Pearl, did you hear me?"

"So?" says Pearl, seizing up as usual when she hears that name. "You're always writing to Mendel. News would be if he wrote you back as often as you write him." She doesn't mean to sound so harsh, but she's had too many years of practice of talking to Frieda this way. She's got to try to speak more gently.

"This is a different kind of letter. I'm going to ask for money." Frieda lowers her voice. "So I can smuggle to America."

"Good luck to you." Idle talk, thinks Pearl. Tomorrow it'll be another idea.

"I'm serious, Pearl. What if that man in the park is right, the laws have changed, and we're stuck here? There are people in Havana who can help us go to America now."

"If you get caught, they could put you in jail, or send you back to Europe."

"What if I wait too long? What if Mendel won't wait?" Frieda blurts out.

Pearl could say, he loves you, of course he'll wait. Or she could say, who cares if he waits. Neither option would change Frieda's mind. Finally, she says, "If he doesn't wait, then you know what kind of man he is."

They watch a woman kneeling at the roots of the magic tree. She lights a candle, then rocks on her heels, moving her lips with fervor and clutching her stomach. Maybe she's hoping to have a baby.

Pearl's had a long, dizzying day, and she's craving a break from her thoughts.

"I'm going to America. Nothing you say will change my decision," says Frieda. "I can be just as stubborn as you are."

She sounds serious, like she really means it. But why Mendel?

This is the point Pearl keeps coming back to. Here's Frieda, the daughter of a cantor, from Lithuania, young and strong and bright, and she's throwing away her life on a fool, so she can keep house like an old-fashioned *balabusta*. And she'd leave me here alone to do it.

Frieda, don't you want something more?

Or is that only my desire, my story?

Okay, fine, Pearl decides. Leave me, go to America. Join your precious boyfriend.

But this could be the solution to all Pearl's problems. Mendel might enjoy exchanging love letters from afar, but once Frieda's in the States and marriage becomes a real possibility, he might tire of their childish romance and break it off for good this time. Or maybe Frieda, seeing Mendel up close, will wake up to his true nature. For people like her, the only way to know a shoe doesn't fit is to try it on and feel it pinching her foot. And all the while, Frieda will believe that Pearl's really changed her mind, that she's open to the idea of marrying Mendel. Yes, it could be brilliant.

Pearl takes a deep breath. "If you're so determined to go to America, I can't stop you. But don't ask him for money." At the very least she can prevent Frieda from groveling to Mendel. "I'll earn it somehow." She doesn't know how, but she'll figure out something. "It's all I ask. Is that so unreasonable?"

"I suppose not." Frieda slips her arm through Pearl's arm. "Thank you."

"You're welcome." Pearl's voice is barely audible because it's breaking.

FIVE

PEARL APPROACHES MRS. STEINBERG. DOES SHE KNOW OF any ladies in need of some tailoring?

"Funny you should ask!" she says.

The pants Pearl made caused a sensation at the suffragist meeting. Several of the attendees expressed interest in acquiring a pair. Mrs. Steinberg makes the connection, and the women invite Pearl to fit them for slacks. Those women share her name with their friends, and soon business becomes so brisk, Pearl acquires an English nickname: Pearl the Pants Lady.

As spring turns to summer, it becomes Pearl's Sunday routine to pack up a sewing basket and hike west to the mansions in the Vedado district. At first she requested that the women be responsible for ordering their own material, but now she does it herself. They don't have Pearl's eye, let alone her sense of quality. The fabric stores and tailors sell them the coarsest, densest fabrics at the highest prices. Also, if Pearl picks out the material, she can make a modest profit on the upcharge. Sometimes the women give her additional small work like alterations, which is good money too.

Pearl's so busy now with work, she scarcely knows her own mind. Vedado's a far way to go, but Pearl likes the change of scenery, the airy rooms and peaceful gated gardens. Usually, she's rewarded with a plate of something to eat, shortbread cookies, peeled slices of fruit. Once she gets a whole wedge of cheese.

Most of the women are Jewish and speak Yiddish, though generally not well. Pearl communicates with them in a mishmash of Yiddish, Spanish, and a few English phrases she's picked up in addition to her Spanish. Imagine me, she thinks, speaking all these foreign tongues.

As Pearl works at their feet, she listens to the women discussing people she doesn't know, or politics. In this way, she hopes to improve her language skills. However, they speak together very quickly and mostly in English, so it's tough going.

In addition to their English, Pearl also studies the lives of these women, who have real money, real status, with servants and teas and largely absent husbands. Their lives are completely different from hers, and she has trouble truly understanding them. Sometimes their manners strike her as cold, even mean. At one afternoon fitting party, Pearl observes how they shun one of their guests, a dark-haired, dark-eyed woman wearing gold earrings, several gold necklaces, and a fox fur stole, which she keeps around her neck inside the house, though she's sweating. In response to this dark woman's valiant efforts to join their conversations, they nod coolly, talk over her, or look the other way.

While Pearl is taking a break, sipping tea in a corner, the woman comes over and introduces herself. Her name is Señora Sassoon and she's a Sephardic Jew, or a *turco*, as they say here, though she's from Greece, not Turkey. She'd like Pearl to come to her home on Thursday for a fitting. Pearl asks to come Sunday instead, when she's not working for Mr. Steinberg, but Señora Sassoon is very particular. She insists that Pearl come this Thursday, and by no means Sunday, which is bad luck. She'll pay extra.

So Pearl leaves Frieda in charge of the workshop and makes the trek out to Vedado, spending a whole nickel to take a streetcar partway, because Señora Sassoon lives further out than the other ladies. Hers is a new mansion, painted blue-green like the scales of a fish. It's set apart from its neighbors, with a large garden around the house and a high wall and gate to protect it from the street.

A gardener in blue overalls and a cap opens the gate with a friendly grunt and leads Pearl across a newly dug path through the grass to the patio, where piles of moving boxes wait to be unpacked. The doors to the house are open, and on one side a curtain billows in the draft. The other, its mate, is draped over a chair, waiting to be hung.

"*Hola?* Hello?" Pearl calls out. She wanders into the receiving room. Its tall ceiling is lined in brown wooden beams. The marble tile floors must feel cool if you're walking barefoot. The air, smelling of fresh paint, is flecked with sawdust.

A servant appears. He's bald and thin, with a long nose and hollow cheeks, and he wears a formal butler's uniform that looks silly in these tropical surroundings. Pearl pegs him immediately as a Jew even before he speaks to her in Yiddish. He regrets to inform her that Señora Sassoon will not be available after all.

"But I've come all this way!" Pearl protests.

"The señora says the hostile moon in the sky has arrived earlier than expected, and she will see no one until it passes. Of course she will pay you for your time."

Pearl pauses to consider this information. Someone can be paid for their time, without doing work? How much is time worth?

Apparently quite a lot, as the butler opens a leather wallet and pays her just the same as what she expected for the fitting. "The señora hopes you will return next week, when skies are more favorable." He then beckons Pearl to lean in closer. "They're all crazy about the stars, those Sephardim," he whispers.

"Can I rest a minute before I go?" asks Pearl. "It's a long walk."

"Of course!" He directs her back out to the garden, under a tree, so she'll be safe from the sun. There's a special kind of chair, a metal frame with a long extension where you can put up your legs. "I'm sorry," he says, "the cushions haven't arrived yet."

"I'm fine," says Pearl, sitting sidesaddle on the chair.

"Please," he says, "put up your feet. It's how you sit in such a chair."

She's not sure about it, but she sets her sewing basket on the grass, slides back in the chair, then swings up her legs. It really is comfortable to sit this way.

"You see?" he says. "I'll return in a minute."

She lies back, squinting in the sunlight. A fresh breeze tickles her hair, and she lets her body go limp. For a change, her hands are empty. The butler returns with a glass of crushed pineapple with ice and a straw. She drinks too fast at first, which hurts her head. Then she takes it slowly, and the drink tastes cool and sour-sweet. Why not rest for a minute? No one's asking her to leave, and she's being paid for her time.

The gardener reappears with a wheelbarrow of dirt and a tray of brilliant pink flowers, like little trumpets, with streaks of red and yellow stamens inside the blossoms. As he plants a heavy, pointed shovel into the earth, Pearl recalls her garden in Turya, probably a mass of weeds now. The gardener begins singing in a high, clear voice, and Pearl realizes this gardener is a woman. It's a lovely song, and though Pearl can't understand the words, she's moved by the sad melody. We poor people all the world over depend on music, Pearl thinks, like a folk medicine. The notes soar up, even as we stay down. The song ends, and she applauds. The gardener smiles and bows, then starts a new tune.

In Turya now, there'd be a late spring breeze. The air would smell of warm manure, yellowing hayfields, and late-blooming flowers, poppies and daisies. As a girl in springtime, she used to hide in the tall grasses by the river and crack flower seeds between her teeth, eating the meat inside and spitting out the shells in the dirt. What was the word for the flower? A simple Yiddish word, and she can't recall it now.

Sunflower! Yes, of course, sunflower seeds. She sees rows of them growing in the fields, turning their heads toward the sky.

Pearl opens her eyes and the sun is much lower now, hitting her in the face. The flowers are all planted and the gardener is gone. Pearl's cheeks, forearms, and calves are hot pink and tingling. She checks for her money; it's there.

How long have I been sleeping? I've wasted the day away. She grabs her basket and runs out the gate before someone chases her off.

During her long walk home, Pearl moves in a slow daze. Too much sun. She keeps massaging her head and rubbing her eyes, trying to shake it off. To think that some women, like Señora Sassoon, live like this always, sipping drinks brought on a tray, napping away the afternoon. But God hasn't willed this to be Pearl's fate.

Pearl crosses the Paseo into Old Havana, along with several

Cuban men wearing slim black ties, all walking home from work. The tourists are loitering outside the bars and peddlers run up to them offering souvenirs: beads made in America. Children approach them too, yelling, "Gimme one cent!"

Gimme one cent, Pearl mutters. It's like a song. Gimme a cent, gimme a cent.

Pearl turns onto Calle Obispo and sees a young Cuban woman with a young man, an admirer, walking slightly behind her. The woman yells insults over her shoulder as the man calls her pet names: *my love, my darling.* He comes closer, and she keeps insulting him. *You idiot! You ugly bastard!* But he is undeterred. Pearl's nervous, fears violence.

The woman spins around and lands such a slap on the young man's cheek it makes a noise, like a whip cracking. The man falters, cradling his cheek, and Pearl is startled too. The woman continues on her way, while the man leans against a wall and rubs his cheek. Pearl watches the pair in awe.

How did she do that? And he doesn't run after her. He respects her will. Maybe that's what Mrs. Steinberg means about training husbands like dogs. The women here have such a powerful way about them, and they are none the less beautiful for it.

The sound of that smack lingers with Pearl when she reaches her street, where Frieda is standing beside an iron window grille and laughing, talking to three men from Latvia who earn their living making purses in a home workshop. She waves to Pearl. "You look like you were working in the sugarcane fields all afternoon. Your skin's as red as a beet!"

Frieda offers to introduce the men to Pearl, who says she doesn't have time and drags Frieda back to the workshop.

"You were supposed to cover for me, finish those straw hats with the orange rosettes and the striped ribbon."

"I did," says Frieda. "I did them all, just as you told me to."

"Let me see," says Pearl. Frieda's telling the truth. The hats are done, and the ribbons along the brim are on straight, so the stripes line up where the two ends meet. The rosettes are centered perfectly too. "Well now," says Pearl, "that's fine."

"And I made dinner," says Frieda. Just bread and cheese, but it does the trick. Also, Frieda says she knows of something to help the sunburn. She goes out and returns with a spiky green stalk that she breaks in half. It oozes a thick, sticky liquid that smells like cucumber. Frieda massages the liquid on the burned places on Pearl's skin, and it soothes. Just as nice is the touch of healing fingers pressing Pearl's sore limbs. It's been awhile since Pearl has felt this close to her sister, who tonight seems more than a sister, like a friend. It's a shame to realize it just as Frieda wants to leave for America.

"Where did you learn about this leaf?" Pearl asks.

"If I tell you, you won't be angry?" asks Frieda.

"I promise I won't," says Pearl.

"Very well. It was from that *zonah* who sits in the window, looking for men," says Frieda. "Once she saw I was sunburned, and she told me about this plant and let me try it myself. She's a nice girl, if you forget that she's a *zonah*."

In Turya, Pearl thinks, such a conversation would be astonishing. But here in Havana, you can't be too picky about your friends.

"I'll have to thank her," says Pearl, "the next time I pass her window."

Later, while Frieda's not looking, Pearl adds the money from *Señora* Sassoon to her hiding place, a pin cushion she's emptied and filled with bills and coins. The cushion is growing fatter every week.

Pearl gives it a squeeze, then looks sadly back at Frieda, absorbed in her own labors, studying English phrases in a fashion magazine.

SIX

As Frieda sleeps, her hair falling in loose waves around her face, Pearl kneels by the bed. Because of the heat, they lie in bed without blankets. Frieda, always a blissful sleeper, snores gently, like the sound of pages ruffling in a book. She never wakes at dawn, haunted by nightmares.

Pearl hates to rouse her.

"Friedele," she whispers, using her sister's childhood name. "It's time."

Frieda wrinkles her nose. "I'm awake," she says, her eyes closed.

"Then act like it. I put out your pink dress." Pearl is already wearing her gray cotton dress that buttons up to the neck. "I'll make coffee."

"Not coffee," Frieda groans into her pillow. "Too hot."

"Fine. I'll drink yours," says Pearl and goes into the workshop.

"I want a pastry," Frieda calls after her. Her voice sounds feeble in the dark.

"We haven't got any." Not true. Yesterday, as an extravagance, Pearl bought Frieda's favorite, a flaky roll with vanilla cream inside.

After this morning, they'll be apart for the first time since Frieda's birth.

Pearl unwraps the pastry from its wax paper and sets it on their best plate, a blue china saucer with a crack on one side, one of Mrs. Steinberg's gifts. The pastry sheds a few buttery flakes, so Pearl wets her forefinger, taps them, and licks her finger clean. She's so miserable she wants to eat the pastry herself. Instead, she opens the window to the stuffy room. Outside, a girl sits on the sidewalk and cries, until her mother drags her along by the wrist. The girl dangles and twists in her mother's grasp, kicking up dirt and gravel. It's okay, Pearl thinks, go ahead and cry.

Frieda emerges from their sleeping corner, dressed, hair mussed. She bites hungrily into the pastry, drinks the coffee too, without a thank-you. Her manners can be rough since she's only had whatever lessons Pearl could give when she wasn't busy. I spoiled you, Pearl thinks. I made a poor substitute for our mother.

"We might as well go," says Pearl. "We'll be a little early, which is good."

"You're in such a rush to be rid of me?" Frieda remains seated on her stool, stretches and yawns. "When I get to America, I want to relax. All this moving from place to place and all this work, it wears me out."

"Me too," Pearl admits sadly.

Frieda looks around the room. "Have we really been here half a year? And now I suppose I'll never see this place again. What will I remember about it?"

"Here." Pearl hands Frieda a sachet of salt and pepper for luck and a small photo of Father, his yellowing beard glowing white, eyes velvety black. It's their only picture of him. "Hide it in your dress or shoe. No one will know."

"You don't want to keep it?" Frieda asks. "I'll have Basha and Mendel in America, but you'll be alone. You might want to look at Father sometimes."

"Take it," Pearl says. Frieda, so lavish with her affection in person, has trouble remembering people when they disappear from her sight. On her own, she might forget she has a family. "We should go."

In summer, the streets are filled with people early in the morning, doing their business before the hottest part of the day. Isidro is already pushing his peanut cart.

Just when Pearl didn't think the weather could get hotter, July blazed in. Her first few months in Cuba, Pearl thought the locals were exaggerating about the summer heat, but she quickly learned otherwise. Summers in Russia were hot too, but here, the very moisture in the air is scalded by the sun. People trudge along. Speech grows sluggish. By noon, the streets empty out as Cubans take refuge anywhere they can find shade. The Americans hide in bars.

The two sisters head toward the docks, where it's rumored that Syrians and Turks deal in morphine, opium, cocaine, and stolen gems of dubious authenticity. Chinese loiter near the water, looking wistfully out to sea. Unemployed day laborers gamble over dice and dominoes or curse losing lottery tickets.

The men stare hungrily at Frieda—until they meet Pearl's glowering eye. One man laughs and shouts something, slang Pearl doesn't know.

"Keep moving," Frieda says in a low voice. "Ignore them."

"Why? What did he say?" Pearl asks.

"Rude things. They think you are my . . . protector."

"Because I am your protector," says Pearl, so angry she can hardly see. She shouts back at the man in Yiddish, "I am her protector!"

"Pearl, don't!" Frieda says, pulling her forward as the men laugh.

The Hotel Louisiana slumps next to a fast house painted dirty red, with frayed pink curtains patterned with little red hearts. Pearl tries not to think about the business going on inside. As she and Frieda approach the hotel, their clothes and skin are drenched in sweat. Inside, the lobby is so humid, the walls appear to be sweating too. Pearl feels a prickling under her arm, a heat rash she thought had healed. The only person sitting there, a Cuban woman surrounded by bags of fruit, offers to sell them a used lottery ticket.

"I thought everyone in America was rich," says Frieda in an awed voice, her bottom lip trembling. "Two Americans would stay in this pigpen?"

Pearl can't think of a reassuring excuse. The front desk is attended by a stocky woman with dyed curly black hair piled high on top of her head and a beauty mark penciled on her right cheek. She puts down the comic she's been reading and in a high-pitched voice declares that she is at their service.

"We look for two people, the family name is Meyer," says Pearl in Spanish. She's practiced these sentences for a week.

"The second floor, room six." The woman gestures up the stairs. "Enjoy your stay in Havana." She picks up her comic and resumes reading.

As they climb the stairs, Pearl indulges in a long yawn. She could use more sleep, even a half hour. There's a long day of work ahead after this. She sees some unknown Spanish words scrawled on the wallpaper, beside a crude drawing of an angry-looking erect penis. "We can go back," Pearl says, flinching. "You haven't paid them yet."

"No," whispers Frieda, then clears her throat. "I'm going."

Room 6 is just off the staircase, near the shared toilet, whose stink wafts down the hall. Before they knock, the door opens a crack, and a haggard brown eye peers at them. The door opens wider; the eye belongs to Mrs. Meyer.

She pulls them inside and closes the door quickly. "You said in the café it was only one of you going."

"That's right," says Pearl. "I'm here to see her off, if it's permitted."

"It is not. We're trying to pass this young lady off as an American, not a Polish refugee with a teary-eyed sister waving good-bye."

"I'll be quiet," Pearl says. "No one has to know I'm there."

"Let her stay while we're getting ready," Mr. Meyer says in a thin, sleepy voice. He's sprawled out on the bed with his shoes on. There's nowhere else to sit in the tight room. The man needs a shave, Pearl thinks, and a few hours to sleep off the effects of whatever used to reside in the empty brown bottle by the bed.

"I think she should say her good-byes now," says Mrs. Meyer. Her voice sounded younger when they first met. This morning it sounds hoarse, as if she has a cold.

"Dry up, would you? It's okay," says her husband. "Let's see the money."

The Meyers seem smaller, sweatier, and grubbier since their previous and only meeting in the Café Suiza, where that good-looking Polish man—too good-looking, Pearl thinks in retrospect—from the Parque Central introduced them. Their Yiddish is interspersed with American slang. Mr. Meyer's shiny tie has grease spots, and his teeth are coffee stained. The powder that's settled into the pit marks and creases of Mrs. Meyer's cheeks exudes a metallic smell.

Imagine if Father saw Pearl and Frieda in such company. But to smuggle, you need people like these, not yeshiva *bochers*.

"We agreed she'll give half now, and the other half in Key West," says Pearl.

"If that's how you want it," he says.

Frieda smiles nervously, but Pearl steps closer to the bed and says, "She may look small, but she's strong, and I've taught her to slap and pinch and scream if she's in trouble, which would put you all in trouble."

"My dear, we're not criminals."

Pearl directs Frieda to take out the money. Twenty-five American bucks, mostly singles. As she deals out the bills on the mattress, Pearl sees the hours it took to earn those pieces of paper, each careful stitch, each accidental needle prick.

Mr. Meyer watches his wife count the money once, then a second time. "That's okay. Let's see the other half," he says.

"Show him," says Pearl. Frieda holds it up but does not put it on the bed.

Mr. Meyer smiles like an innocent child. Pearl watches him, in case he pulls a Turkish trick, like grabbing the money and running away. "Fine, fine," says Mr. Meyer, crossing his legs. The shiny crackled leather of his shoes toys with the light. "By the by, I have friends, here and in Florida, doctors who treat syphilis or other diseases."

Frieda blushes.

"No thanks," says Pearl firmly. "She's going to America, that's all."

"Just offering," says Mr. Meyer. "Also, I'm studying law by correspondence. I'll be finished in a year or so. I mention it in case you're needing any legal advice."

"We're not," says Pearl. She's tempted to drag Frieda out of here.

"Very good," says Mr. Meyer. "They're good girls, aren't they?"

"Wonderfully good. Let's get this girl dressed properly," says Mrs. Meyer, plucking Frieda's damp sleeves. "You're as sweaty as a kitchen maid who's been washing dishes all day. We want you to be a sweet little tomato." She nods at Pearl. "You'll help."

The three women crowd into the shared washroom in the hall, where Mrs. Meyer orders Frieda out of her dress, then rubs her cheeks, hands, arms, and legs with scented soap as if Frieda couldn't do it for herself. Mrs. Meyer's hands are trembling and occasionally she has to pause to massage her fingers.

Next, she directs Pearl to undo Frieda's braids—too Old World. There's no time to wash her hair, so Mrs. Meyer winds it up in back, pulls out a few locks in front, and curls them. Despite the moment, Pearl is fascinated. She wonders if such a style might solve the problem of her own hair.

Mrs. Meyer gives Frieda a dress. Without sleeves.

Frieda holds it up. "Is it finished?" she asks.

"Don't be daffy," says Mrs. Meyer, pressing it to Frieda's body. "Every smart American girl dresses like this in the tropics."

"People will see her knees when she walks," Pearl says. "Maybe more."

"Be glad she has nice knees," says Mrs. Meyer. "Mine used to drive men mad. Now they're a pair of wrinkled potatoes."

"I'll try it," says Frieda, but when she puts on the dress, she tugs at the hemline, then tries to cover her shoulders with her hands. "Sorry," she says. "I feel so . . . naked."

"I'll give you a shawl," says Mrs. Meyer. "Just the thing. I bought one of those Spanish shawls for my sister. Cheer up, you're a tourist returning home from an amusing holiday. You're going home to America!"

They return to the room, Frieda with arms crossed and her hands on her shoulders. While Mrs. Meyer searches her suitcase for the shawl, Mr. Meyer instructs Frieda how to act so she doesn't seem like such a Jew. The way he says "Jew" sounds unnerving, like an insult.

"Never use your hands while talking," he says, pointing at her with his cigarette-stained fingers. "Stuff them in your pockets if you're tempted. If you must speak, do it in a light, quiet voice. Say 'hi' or 'yeah,' not 'yes.' Or don't talk. Pretend you're shy. And for Pete's sake, smile all you can. Americans are always smiling. They haven't a care in the world, Americans." He sounds sad to say it, though he is an American.

"Here you are," says Mrs. Meyer, stepping between them to drape the shawl over Frieda's shoulders. It's sea blue, edged with white fringe, like Father's prayer shawl.

"I feel better," says Frieda, and Pearl does too.

"Good girl," says Mrs. Meyer. "And you'll carry this magazine and pretend to read it." She hands her the magazine. "Hold it this way."

"I can read English letters," says Frieda.

"Of course she can," says Mr. Meyer, slapping his thigh. "She's a real peach."

"She is pretty all right." Mrs. Meyer hands her a blond leather suitcase decorated with stickers, one saying "Miami," and another with a picture of the American White House. The inside, lined in plaid silk, is packed with ready-made American clothes and cheap souvenirs: maracas, a paper fan, a box of almond candy.

"You have documents for her?" Pearl asks.

"I've added her to our family passport," Mr. Meyer shows her the pale-blue paper with the American eagle at the top. In the bottom right corner is a photo of Mr. Meyer in a suit and necktie, looking grim. Several lines above, his full name is printed, plus: "accompanied by his wife Betty." Next to that, Mr. Meyer has carefully inscribed the words "& child Ann" in a similar handwriting.

Frieda belongs to another family now, with modern parents, though despite Mr. Meyer's up-to-date clothes and slang, Pearl finds his manner toward his wife old-fashioned. He talks to her like a servant.

"A good name, Ann," he tells Frieda. "Easy to remember, short enough to fit on this line here. I have a friend who knows what's what about forgery, and he showed me how." He pats "Ann's" cheek. "Don't worry. Those saps at Key West are too busy searching for rum to look closely at these things, especially if you're with a good American couple speaking English without an accent."

"I am Ann," says Frieda in English.

"Not like that," says Mrs. Meyer. "Listen to me say it. 'Ann.'" Pearl can't hear the difference and neither can Frieda. "You're not getting it," Mrs. Meyer warns her. "You sound like you're saying 'end.' This will never work."

If Frieda with her talent for languages can't pull this off, Pearl thinks, how will I manage when it's my turn?

"Of course it'll work," says Mr. Meyer. "She doesn't have to open her pretty mouth. Just smile, smile. Well, ladies, it's time." He looks at Pearl. "We'll wait for a bit in the hall, give you some privacy. Stay here five minutes after your sister leaves." He extends a hand for her to shake. "Good luck to you, my dear. May it be God's will."

Pearl finds the latter an odd expression coming from him,

though he sounds earnest. She touches his hand briefly, then wipes it on her dress.

When the Meyers leave, Pearl turns to her sister, and all the air rushes out of her lungs. She concentrates on Frieda's face, as if to memorize it, though she already knows that face too well. "Write from America." Pearl's lips are trembling. She's been so busy working and planning for this day, she's surprised that it has now come, much more quickly than she'd expected.

"I will." Frieda kisses her on both cheeks.

"Be safe. That above everything. And I'll follow soon. In the meantime..." She pauses. "Just don't do anything permanent until I arrive. Promise?"

"Of course." Frieda nods quickly. They hold each other by their forearms. "Pearl, in case we don't see each other again . . . I know we will, but just in case . . ."

"What is it?" Pearl asks.

"I know I tease you plenty, but—"

"Don't worry about that now," says Pearl, hugging her sister again.

"Please don't interrupt, or I'll never finish," Frieda says. "Terrible things happened to us in the Old Country. To us, and to many people. And to you. But they weren't our fault. It was just the situation."

Pearl lets go of her sister. Don't say more, Pearl thinks. Not here. Her ears and neck are bristling, and she senses keenly the Meyers' presence in the hall. Who else is there? Who else is listening? She feels the shadow of the Polish soldier here, in this room.

"Let's leave the Old Country in the Old Country," says Frieda.

"No one here has to know about what happened there. I certainly won't dwell on it."

Pearl has trouble focusing on the words, as if she's forgotten Yiddish and her sister's voice is just noise. What do you think you know about me? Pearl thinks. What is it you thought you saw? You were so young—but maybe not as young as I imagine.

"Pearl, speak," Frieda says.

Her mouth and throat feel too dry for speech. The Meyers are waiting. This isn't the time. Though when would be the time for such a conversation?

"Sure, just as you say," says Pearl. "Smile, remember? You're coming home from a lovely vacation. You'd better leave now, or you'll miss your boat."

Frieda looks confused as Pearl says a hurried good-bye, ushers her out of the room, and closes the door. Pearl has a terrible thought, but it's the one that comes to mind at that moment: She's glad her sister is leaving.

She sits on the bed among the mussed bedcovers, which smell of Mrs. Meyer's perfume and Mr. Meyer's aftershave. A bold red necktie hangs over the mirror. In their haste, they've left their room key on the desk instead of depositing it at the reception. Beside it lies a precious half-finished American chocolate bar. Pearl could take advantage, but she feels nauseous.

Those words Frieda said hardly seem real. Pearl tries to recall them exactly. How much could Frieda know about what happened? She was just a girl back then. How much would she have understood?

Pearl spots the sachet of salt and pepper she gave her sister for luck now lying on the floor. She puts it in her pocket. After counting off one more minute silently in her head, she turns the door knob and trots downstairs.

"Señora, señora," the woman at the desk calls out. "When are they returning?"

"Please? Again?" says Pearl in Spanish.

"The customers in room six. Are they going out for the day or coming right back? Can I send the maid up to their room? For cleaning?"

"Yes," says Pearl, realizing the Meyers have decided to forgo the formality of paying their bill. "Send the maid."

The woman says several sentences in rapid-fire Spanish. Something to the effect of this hotel may have its small problems, but it's famous for hospitality.

Dashing outside, Pearl sees the Meyers and her sister walking to the port. She follows at a distance. Mrs. Meyer has her arm over Frieda's shoulders and laughs loudly. They each carry a light suitcase. Mr. Meyer's case is brown, and Mrs. Meyer's is blond like Frieda's. They really look like a family, Pearl thinks. Frieda fits with them.

Closer to the port, Mr. Meyer hails a donkey-drawn carriage, the kind tourists engage for a lark. The three of them ride the rest of the way, moving slowly in the traffic that gets clogged in the narrow streets near the water.

At the harbor, they join a line of Americans about to board a tall white steamer with a black hull. Americans wait so patiently and neatly in lines. Mr. Meyer stands ahead of his wife and Frieda, who walk arm in arm. Nearby, a man finishes his last bottle of beer out in the open. Frieda, Pearl thinks, don't leave yet. I've changed my mind, I'm ready to speak, and I have more to say—I couldn't before, but now I can.

Mr. Meyer presents their tickets to a man in uniform, who waves them ahead. They file up the gangplank onto the boat, up and away to America. Frieda in her blue shawl disappears. Pearl has coached Frieda to scream if they try to shove her into the water or take her money prematurely. There will be witnesses everywhere. She will fight and scream as no woman has screamed before.

Pearl stands there sweating as the sun grows higher in the sky. Her head spins and her stomach growls, but she waits until ten o'clock, when the boat edges into the harbor. It slowly crosses the bay, floats out past the castle, all the way out to sea.

She's left me here, Pearl thinks. Now we're both on our own.

"Frieda," Pearl says, to no one. "May God bless and protect you as in the time of Sarah. May God show you favor and grace as in the time of Rebecca. May God deal with you kindly and grant peace as in the time of Rachel and Leah."

Father would recite this blessing on Friday nights while placing his hands on their heads. He continued performing this ritual as the girls grew older, and taller than their father. Pearl used to imagine the blessing extending from his fingers over her head and body like a tissue-thin bridal veil. Now Pearl sees what it really was, a moment for a busy and sometimes brusque man to give and receive an expression of love.

Busy and sometimes brusque—maybe that's how Frieda thinks of me.

She might not have known about the Polish soldier. It's possible that wasn't what she meant at all. What were her precise words? Pearl can only recall vague phrases that could apply to any number of the horrors of their old life.

The people at the dock move on, to other jobs, other ships. The cabs head into town to find passengers at the hotels. Pearl should go too. She has hats in need of trimming, and the news of her sister's departure to share with the Steinbergs.

The boat sails out of sight, and Frieda is gone. No longer a protective bigger sister, she's just Pearl, a funny little Jewish woman standing alone, scratching the heat rash on her arm on a street corner in Havana.

SEVEN

For one, two, then four weeks, Pearl waits to hear from her sister, at least to know that Frieda hasn't been dumped overboard in the Florida straits, or bitten by an alligator in Key West, or robbed blind by those grubby Meyers.

She's punishing me with her silence, Pearl decides. When we parted, she must have been terrified to speak out as she did. Our last words together were awful, frigid. But her outburst, or whatever that was she thought she was saying, caught me by surprise. What did she expect me to say?

Sick with worry, Pearl sews the lining of one of her hats inside out and has to rip out the uneven stitching on another hatband and start over. It's the kind of mistake Frieda would have made, but now Pearl has only herself to scold. She gives up fighting her frizzy hair, lets it grow where it will, and wears pants full-time. At mealtimes, she chews her food sullenly, hardly recognizes what she puts in her mouth. At night, she cries silently in her unmade bed. If she's lucky, she sleeps without dreams.

She misses Frieda simply for being Frieda, sweet and curious, brimming with idle fantasies and charmingly clumsy errors. Frieda, who advised her to leave the Old Country behind. Easy advice to give, hard to take. A thing or a person Pearl could leave behind. But memories, those tiny stabs of fear and shame, they remain stubborn companions.

The Steinbergs have hired a new seamstress to replace Frieda, and she's a talker. Though her real name is Hodele, she goes by "Julieta" and speaks Yiddish with an affected Spanish accent. She's a good worker, though a silly thinker who's obsessed with moving pictures. Pictures of her favorite stars, like Mary Pickford and Tom Mix, hang over her bed like family photos.

Julieta suggests Pearl consult Madame Wonderful, a soothsayer on O'Reilly Street, to learn about Frieda's fate. "She can predict tomorrow's weather to the hour," Julieta marvels. "She says in two years, I'll be married with a baby."

"Mazel tov in advance," says Pearl, which sets Julieta to laughing.

Maybe it comforts Julieta to think she can control her fate by predicting the future. Save your money, Pearl thinks. You want to predict your future? Look to the past. Mostly, life stays the same, just changes forms. Here I am, still stuck here making hats, still waking in a sweat at dawn, worried and alone.

However, in many ways Pearl's life has changed quite a lot since she first set foot on Cuban soil. She capably peels bananas and mangoes as easily as she would a potato. She recognizes the scent of the local white ginger flowers, which women carry on their wedding days or to offer their saints. The streets of Old Havana are familiar now. She can spot packs of drunken American tourists from blocks away, and she also knows the best strategies to avoid them. She has danced salsa with a woman smoking a cigar. She has worn pants in public. She's done and seen so many things that in Turya she couldn't have conceived doing and seeing, and going forward she cannot undo or unsee them.

At the end of August, more than a month since Frieda's departure, Mr. Steinberg visits the workshop, and instead of making his usual jokes, heads straight to Pearl's worktable with a letter. "For you," he says softly. Julieta claps, stretches her neck to see.

Pearl accepts the letter calmly, nods, says, "Would you excuse me?" and runs out to the courtyard. The postmark on the envelope is from New York. The energetic, looping handwriting is Frieda's. Go ahead, Pearl tells herself. Read.

From the first, she hears Frieda's voice, the impetuous head-long rush of sentences, the charmingly sincere apologies for not having written earlier.

> *. . . the trip from Florida to New York was frightfully long. At least I had the Meyers for company on the boat from Havana. The Meyers aren't bad once you get to know them, and Mrs. Meyer treated me to sandwiches on the ship. Is that all they eat here in America? Basha says no, but Basha doesn't know everything, though she thinks so because she's got her nose in a book all the time. Life isn't only in books. Basha sends love. She's given me a good tongue-lashing for not writing sooner. I prefer your style of scolding. Sharper, but efficient. I hope you'll join us soon . . .*

It's Frieda, alive, thank God. Alive. And she's not angry with me. For so long they wondered how New York would be. Now

Frieda knows. She's says it's dirty and crowded, and the weather's freezing. But she's safe. Mendel promises to send for her in the future. Once he's more settled.

As I suspected, Pearl thinks. She'll wait awhile yet.

Frieda doesn't mention their last conversation, but offers another apology:

> *Again I'm sorry I didn't write sooner, but it's so*
> *hectic here, I'm exhausted all the time. I hope I won't*
> *have to stay here too long before Mendel sends for me.*

Pearl's frizzy black curls keep falling in her eyes, so she ties them back with a kerchief. How my mind loves trouble, she thinks. Frieda forgets to write, and I twist her thoughtlessness into a feud. Don't I know my own sister? Frieda and her same old dreams . . .

Well, good. After everything, it's a miracle Frieda has any dreams left.

○

FALL IS THE wet season in Havana. Storms erupt in sharp, unpredictable bursts. In the streets outside the workshop, the rain and wind start again and the shutters pound against the wall like a drunken soldier trying to get in.

Today there's no work. Julieta lounges on a stool, reading a magazine about her beloved film stars. Can't she get up off her behind and close the shutters? Doesn't she hear the rain, the banging? Or does she like the noise? Maybe it fools her into feeling less alone.

"I'm closing the window," says Pearl, running over to the shutters.

"*Sí, sí*, okay." Julieta's eyes are fixed on her cheap movie magazine. She loves stories of whirlwind romances between handsome movie stars and earnest, pretty waitresses. If the Messiah himself came down from Heaven to open the gates to America personally and Julieta was reading a magazine, she'd make him wait until she finished.

Outside, a Cuban boy cradling a baseball darts between doorways. A bird pecks the puddles for insects. Otherwise, the road is empty. Even Pearl's friend Isidro the peanut vendor is gone. Isidro has a sixth sense for rain and disappears before the first drop, then returns as soon as the skies clear. The other peddlers, most of them Jewish, will remain off the street. Today is Rosh Hashanah.

A New Year, Pearl thinks. What trouble will this one bring?

Frieda has now been in New York for two months, long enough to choose a decent shul. In New York, they have all kinds: German style, Lithuanian style, one for socialists, also one for Jews who don't believe in God. Basha has written Pearl about it. Imagine it, a shul for nonbelievers, of whom Pearl is not one. She knows God is real, just as she knows He is not on her side.

"I can be on your side," the devil used to whisper. Pearl recognizes his phony promises. The devil's a gangster, on no one's side but his own. Let him give up trying to win her confidence. Go torment someone else.

Pearl fastens the shutters, then blots the windowsill with newspaper, which melts in the dampness that soaks everything. The ostrich feathers on the hats shrivel and droop in their protective boxes. Pearl's clothes feel cool and clammy and smell of mildew. Her hands are wrinkled and raw, as if she's constantly just stepped out of a bath. Her frizzy curls resist all combing. She can't remember what it's like to feel dry.

At least it doesn't flood here as in Turya during the spring, when jagged cracks start cutting through the thick blanket of ice on the Polkva River until the whole surface shatters and heavy slabs of ice float off with the current, sweeping away dirt, leaves, even wooden planks from house foundations. The river swells, overflows its banks, drowns orchards belonging to wealthy families, gouging out their rich brown mud and dumping it onto their poorer neighbors' fields of clay. As if nature's a Bolshevik, Pearl thinks with a snort. Why not? It's a crazy world.

Julieta might at least thank Pearl for closing the window, but she says nothing until Pearl turns on the fan, which rattles the pages of the movie magazine.

"Well, well," says Julieta. "Pearl in a dress. God will be most impressed."

"I doubt God is interested in my outfit," says Pearl, who dislikes the unfamiliar rush of air between her calves and inside her thighs.

"You're right," says Julieta. "He's probably much more interested in my outfit." She straightens her shoulders to show off her blue drop-waist dress with black polka dots, a ready-made one from a store. Julieta regularly wastes money on clothes, movies, candy, tortoiseshell combs, costume jewelry, even a genuine alligator belt. She says if she can't get to America, maybe she'll find a Cuban husband and settle here, citing that old Yiddish proverb, "If you cannot shit, a fart is also good."

No thanks, thinks Pearl. I'm checking out of this Hotel Cuba.

Julieta lets the fabric fall through her fingers. "Pearl, about all this God stuff, what exactly is your opinion?"

"God stuff?" Pearl asks. "I don't understand."

"You hang that good luck charm on the wall, and you never

touch a shred of meat for fear it might be *treyf*. But you work on Saturday, and today will be your first day in synagogue since I've known you. So do you believe or not?"

"It's not for me to say." God isn't a matter of opinion. God is like breathing, the ocean, the sky. A law of the universe. You think the ocean cares about your opinion when you're trying to cross it?

But that's Julieta for you. Always interested in opinions.

"So why go to shul, if, as you pretend, you don't believe?" she asks.

"Are you trying to trap me into some kind of confession?" says Pearl.

"No, *querida*, I'm trying to get to know you."

"Am I so interesting?" Pearl asks, though not to be sarcastic. I'm not complicated, she thinks. You want to know something, just ask.

Julieta shrugs. "Maybe I'm just selfish. Knowing what you think might help me to understand what I think too."

There's a knock at the door. Julieta answers it, calling out "Buenos días!" Her Spanish is even better than Frieda's, and Julieta claims she's often taken for Cuban on the street. Maybe so, though Pearl hasn't witnessed it herself.

The Steinbergs are here to escort them to shul. Mrs. Steinberg says a curt hello, while Mr. Steinberg's "howdy" lacks its usual twinkle as he shakes the rain off his umbrella. It's as if they've confused cheerful Rosh Hashanah for solemn Yom Kippur.

Don't be so bitter, Pearl tells herself, cheer up. But being cheerful is one of Frieda's skills, like her facility with foreign languages or her sense of direction. Increasingly, Pearl fears these things can't be learned, but are God given.

Mr. Steinberg wears a gray suit, a dark tie, and a felt fedora, in contrast with his shiny cheeks and nose, ruddy like a freshly burnished bronze doorknob. Mrs. Steinberg has on one of her black dresses, pinned shut at the neck by the cameo with the Greek goddess. To shul? Pearl will never understand the people here.

Mrs. Steinberg, always eager to sympathize with the down-trodden, tells Pearl, "You must miss your sister today. She's a delightful girl."

What will they say when I go to America? Pearl thinks. No one would accuse me of being a delight. Frieda, however, brings out people's sympathy. Since her departure, there have been no more lunches at the Steinbergs' home. Mrs. Steinberg's excuse is that it's too rainy for Pearl to walk back and forth. Too bad her wages haven't increased to cover the new expense of buying her own lunch. Also, to her surprise, she misses the Steinbergs' company.

"A good year, a lucky new year to everyone," says Mr. Steinberg, sounding unusually melancholy. He hands the three women pieces of soft coconut candy wrapped in wax paper. Pearl likes coconut, yet today, she finds the cloying tropical smell unappealing. She notices Mrs. Steinberg leaves hers on a table. "Every Rosh Hashanah, my parents gave me candy for a sweet new year," Mr. Steinberg says. "These days, we could use it. Bad times, bad times. Right, girls?"

"Back in Lithuania, we had a new dress every Rosh Hashanah," says Julieta. "When I was ten, I had a pink one with a blue sash. And a lace collar that my grandmother knitted. I looked like a china doll!"

"My parents used to dress me like a sailor, with the white cap and the kerchief around my neck," Mr. Steinberg says. "I was an adorable boy. Everyone used to pinch my cheeks. And now look at me. What happened?" He wears an expression of mock horror, or maybe he's serious.

"Yes, yes," Julieta cries out, laughing.

In a small-talk competition, those two could endure for hours, Pearl thinks. Maybe that's being a "delight." Mrs. Steinberg doesn't seem to think so. She gives Pearl a knowing, tired look, as if they're old friends. Maybe they are? Does she ever recall those friendly afternoons they spent making the pants?

"Appears the rain's letting up," Mr. Steinberg says. "Shall we go?" He offers Mrs. Steinberg his arm. She doesn't want it, so he tries Julieta, who accepts, and then he leads them to shul with his usual confidence, as if he can bend the weather to his will. Even if not, being wrong never bothers him as it does Pearl. What do I gain, Pearl wonders, for being right so often about bad luck? A little hope isn't so costly.

On their way, Pearl skirts a patch of bright red mud. In Turya after such a rain, the streets turned completely to mud, not red like here, but an ugly brown. Father used to carry Frieda over it on the way to shul, leaving Pearl to wade through the muck.

She imagines that today Frieda's at shul in New York with Basha. Unless she's already in Detroit with Mendel. Maybe they're married and she's forgotten to write.

Mrs. Steinberg talks to Pearl and Julieta as if her husband were not there: "He's only going to synagogue to attract business."

"Probably a good plan," says Julieta. "Shul will be full of Jews today."

"On the New Year, Jews go to shul," says Pearl.

"Sure, sure," chimes in Mr. Steinberg. "All around the world, all Jews go to shul today. It gives you a special feeling of connection. Right, Pearl?"

What does he want, applause? "On the New Year, Jews go to shul," Pearl says simply. "That's all."

"And as usual, the women will be tucked away in the back," Mrs. Steinberg says. "Safely out of sight. Who'll know if I'm there or not?"

"I'll know." Mr. Steinberg's voice sounds thin.

"What should I do while you're schmoozing with your buddies?" she asks.

"Pray," he says.

"With all the troubles in the world, what good is prayer?"

"Pray or don't pray. Think or dream or do whatever the hell you please to pass the time. But I will not be seen going to shul without my goddamned wife."

Mrs. Steinberg, fuming, goes on walking. Julieta fidgets with her umbrella, while Pearl lowers her eyes. She's never heard the Steinbergs speak with such bitterness. And what about Mrs. Steinberg's words? On one of the holiest days of the year, she'd stay home from shul because she dislikes where she's going to stand?

Mr. Steinberg, who hates any unpleasantness, looks around for something to divert his attention. He finds relief in an acquaintance also heading to shul. Mr. Steinberg slaps his back, offers him candy, and instantly they're like brothers. Someday, Pearl thinks, I'll learn how he performs such magic tricks.

Together the two men walk ahead toward the synagogue, sandwiched between a grocery and a residential building. The men going in are beardless and wear white or light gray suits with striped ties. The women wear floral print dresses and carry yellow or green umbrellas. Cubans passing by look on curiously or smile. Pearl watches closely to see if they say something hateful or spit, but there's nothing.

Inside, it looks like a proper shul, with a Jewish star painted in blue on the ceiling, a wooden menorah, and a wooden Ten Commandments crowning the ark. Pearl feels guilty for not having come here before. The crowd is mostly American, men who came with their families to work in the sugar business or who dodged the draft in the Great War and then stayed on. There are also a few Sephardic Jews, both men and women, dark as Arabs, dressed in rich fabrics, their fingers covered in gold rings. Whatever their background, these Jews seem proud, happy, and without fear.

The service starts late. The women linger at the sides of the room while the men compete for the best spots on the central benches, closer to the altar. It's a modern-style service, with many prayers cut out, cut short, or recited in English.

Does God want to be spoken to in English?

Perhaps to hedge their bets on this question, the congregation has imported an old cantor from Budapest to sing a few prayers in Hebrew. He's lost much of his voice and keeps clearing his throat to find it again. Pearl misses Father's honeyed baritone, backed by the soft treble voices of the boys' choir. She used to wish his personality could be like his delicate falsetto, tender and fragile.

She and Julieta are hidden behind a portico with the other women, and the balls of their feet ache from standing on tiptoe to see what's happening in the main part of the sanctuary. Mrs. Steinberg, still miffed from their morning walk, stands at the edge of the women's section. Pearl is glad to keep a healthy distance from her fuming.

Several of the women who hired Pearl to make pairs of slacks are there. Mrs. Steinberg used to tease her, "With all your pants money, you must be rich."

But the pants money is gone, sailed away on a boat to Florida, and for whatever reason, when the rains came, demand for women's pants disappeared. Plus, there were only so many Jewish merchants' wives Pearl could serve. The market has dried up.

Julieta keeps whispering silliness. Doesn't that man's mustache remind her of Douglas Fairbanks? Doesn't that woman look like Clara Bow? Pearl wouldn't recognize Miss Bow, though she admires the woman's peach-colored silk dress swaying from her shoulders, with its daring low neckline. Just looking at the material makes Pearl feel free.

Stop thinking of nonsense, Pearl scolds herself, on Rosh Hashanah of all days. Yet don't women do that in shul, let their attention wander? Men do the serious work of talking to God. Women put their trust in the men, then run home to pull pots of stew from the oven or set extra places at the table for unexpected guests.

But here is different, Pearl thinks. Here I've got no table to set or guests to serve, no man to speak for me.

Time for the shofar. The men gather their boys around them. Mr. Steinberg grips a friend's arm. The women hold their daughters tight. Mrs. Steinberg ducks out of the room. Pearl recalls an old wives' story: If you're alone in shul when the shofar sounds, you'll die the next year. A stupid story invented by men, Pearl thinks. I refuse to believe it.

The packed sanctuary falls silent as the ancient cantor from Vienna puts a curled pink-streaked ram's horn to his lips. It's so quiet, Pearl hears the raindrops tapping the windows. The strain in the old man's face moves her heart. Maybe he lacks enough breath in his body? But he plays the first *tekiah* note with firmness and clarity. This sound is followed by three curling blasts of *shevarim*, and the syncopated stutter of the *teruah*. All this is meant to summon God into the room, or godliness, anyway. In Turya,

Father is also blowing the shofar. In New York, her sisters must be listening to it too.

Pearl shuts her eyes. Her lips move as if of their own will. "I know I've disappointed you," she says under her breath. "I promise to do better if you'll let me follow my sister to America."

Even if God does not answer or hear, she thinks, I hear.

The final note, a *tekiah gedolah*, is sounded, and Pearl turns to Julieta, whose face has gone pale. A tear courses down her rouged cheek. The tear of a modest Jewish girl named Hodele who returns Pearl's gaze, then squeezes her hand. She's not so bad, Pearl thinks. I should be friendlier to her.

Listening to final blast of the shofar, Pearl has no pressing duties, no pants to sew or hats to adorn. She's simply listening, watching, and breathing. Through the windows, the bougainvillea looks especially bright in the rain.

◯

JULIETA LIKES TO stay up late chatting. Often Pearl pretends to sleep, but tonight, she's glad for the companionship. As they lie in their beds, Julieta says, "I miss the cold. I miss eating a steaming bowl of borscht in winter."

Pearl says, "I used to dip a spoon of sour cream into it and stir and stir." She can taste it now. Talking this way, simply, openly, it's refreshing. Even the room feels bigger.

"We had a shiksa neighbor who teased me," Julieta says. "'Eating that soup, you look like you're drinking Christ's blood.' I wanted to slap her but I didn't dare."

Christians, Pearl thinks with disgust. The Christian children in Turya used to hug themselves if a Jew walked by, fearing that greedy Jews might steal the buttons off their shirts. Greedy Jews indeed, she thinks. If we were greedy, it's because you never let us earn anything. She remembers Christian soldiers riding through town, singing, "Greedy Jews, your time is past!" Soldiers with clean-shaven cheeks, dirty grasping hands . . .

"I will never go back there," says Pearl. "Never."

Julieta rolls over to face Pearl. "Your sister's in America, right?"

"I have two sisters in New York," says Pearl.

"I wanted to go to Nueva York, but there were the quotas," says Julieta. "That first night in Havana, I got stuck in Tiscornia because I didn't have the money to get out, and I cried plenty, stuck in that damn refugee camp, not even in America. A nice old man lent me some money."

"Why? What did he want from you? He didn't bother you?"

"No, he was just nice." Julieta props herself up on an elbow. "Why do you ask?"

I shouldn't have said that, Pearl thinks. I shouldn't give myself away so plainly to a stranger, an outsider. "No reason," she says. Such things, you only tell a sister. No, not even then.

Julieta says, "It's nice here, just us two. I used to live in a workshop with four girls, making purses. We slept on the wooden worktables. My back was so sore. I'm sorry your sister's gone, but at least she made room for me." She sighs. "*La Habana* isn't so bad, right? Better than home anyway. No one bothers us here."

"No, no, I have to get to America."

"Why?"

Many reasons. Because I can't sleep for worrying over Frieda. Because I didn't cross an ocean to speak Spanish and live in a sweatshop on a poor island with no future, no proper shul, no kosher meat. Will I never again taste chicken?

"Here it's poor," explains Pearl. "And in poor countries, they always learn to hate Jews. They'll turn on us."

"No, no," says Julieta. "*Los cubanos* are very friendly. They don't know how to hate. But if you want to get to America very badly, you can smuggle."

Yes, she could smuggle. Where Frieda had succeeded, so could Pearl. "But to smuggle, you need money."

"Then make more of your famous pants."

"Not too many customers lately."

"Ask your sister in America to help. You helped her, now she can help you."

"I couldn't take her money."

Julieta reaches across the gap between their beds to touch Pearl's arm. "Why won't you let anyone help you?"

Pearl draws her clammy bedsheet over her neck. Nosy, nosy, she thinks, her insides twisting up tight. Why are you so interested in other people's business?

"What's wrong, Pearl? You can tell me. You might feel better."

Pearl is suddenly and wildly desperate to get outside. She feels Julieta's eyes on her, even through this darkness. Of course something is wrong, she thinks. Do I have to paint you a sign?

Now I'm being like Frieda, blaming whoever's nearby for my troubles. I suppose I shouldn't be angry at Julieta. It's not her fault.

Pearl turns over on her back, faces the ceiling.

Maybe if I shared some small piece of this weight with someone—a bit, not all—my heart might feel that much lighter.

But if I put these memories into words, they are no longer memories. They'd print themselves on my life here.

The word for it is so ugly, so judicial. So final.

In the end, the temptation to speak proves too great. "Something happened to me," Pearl says in a low voice. "Not here. In the Old Country." Does Julieta understand? It's hard to tell in the dark. To clarify, Pearl adds, "A soldier."

There, she's done it. What will Julieta say now? What will she think?

After a few painful seconds, Julieta replies, "It isn't your fault. He did this, not you. Don't you see?"

No, Pearl doesn't see. There were two of us there, she thinks. Don't I bear some responsibility? Don't I?

Julieta says, "You're not ashamed, are you? Pearl, he's a louse. A total louse."

"For me, he doesn't exist," says Pearl. "He might as well be dead. Let's not talk about him."

"Take my advice," says Julieta. "Forget him, forget the Old Country. And forget America too. Stay here in La Habana with me, Pearl. What, you think they don't fool around with women in America?"

"Good night," says Pearl. "I'm going to sleep."

But long after Julieta's snoring away, Pearl lies awake, wishing she could erase the words she carelessly let escape and have changed the shape of the air in this room. She should have kept quiet, followed Frieda's advice and left the Old Country in the Old Country. Now Pearl can't sleep for thinking. She imagines she hears a leak and the rain is dripping on her pillow, flooding their room. Air, air, I need fresh air. Pearl gets out of bed and tiptoes across the floor, which is damp on her bare feet. She steps lightly, trying to avoid landing on a stray bead or pin.

In the workshop, her fingers search her worktable for the tin where she keeps Frieda's knickknacks. Pearl wants to hold them now, close to her chest. I've got to join her, Pearl thinks. I've got to get away.

Opening the box, Pearl inhales the earthy scent of tobacco. She sets aside a swatch of pink silk, a ceramic flute shaped like a bird, a pillbox painted with an image of Morro Castle. Under these trinkets is a cigar, the one they'd joked about smoking. Frieda kept it all this time. I could sell it to a tourist, Pearl thinks. How much would he give me?

She closes the box, steps into her house slippers, and goes out into the hall. It's raining again, so she stands in the building doorway as water drips from the wrought-iron balconies. She listens to the tap, tap, tap of water on stone. Somewhere, a cat is crying. It's not your fault, Julieta says. Maybe tomorrow she'll change her mind, say it is my fault, or no one's fault. Maybe no one is responsible for anything anymore.

Pearl's head hurts. She breathes deeply for several seconds to slow her heart. The wet air is fresh and soothing. She looks at Frieda's cigar, then puts it to her mouth.

What if I were to light it? To taste it?

Pearl runs back in for matches and comes out again. Before lighting the cigar, she has to clip off the tip. That's how she's seen it done. She takes a savage bite off the end and spits the tip into the street. Then she strikes a match. The cigar takes longer to catch flame than a cigarette, so the match goes out. It happens with the second match, and the third. The fourth does the trick.

"To Frieda," she says, holding up the cigar like a glass of wine on Friday night.

A plume of smoke travels into her lungs and sets her coughing.

Finally, she manages to puff cleanly, letting the smoke float out into the rain. It tastes spicy, like cinnamon or cloves, and a trace of oak. She remembers what Mr. Steinberg said about cigars curing the typhus. Maybe it cures other things.

Dear God, she thinks, maybe I really am becoming a man. First pants, now a cigar. Why don't I feel powerful?

EIGHT

THE ANGLO-AMERICAN OPTICAL COMPANY ON OBISPO Street is a five-minute walk from the workshop. The smuggler at the Parque Central told Pearl to arrive at noon with her hundred dollars. She's bringing fifty.

A notice in the shop window claims that Anglo-American Optical sells the highest quality glasses in Havana. The sign over the door features a giant black eye, like a *keina hora*, an evil eye. Pearl avoids looking directly into its dark pupil. For luck, she tugs on her ear and sneezes before going in.

Inside, the stifling air smells of overripe melons, and a fine layer of sawdust has settled on the floor. The walls are lined with small wooden drawers.

The eye doctor lowers the shades and locks the door as if for the siesta. He's a short, slim American with a receding hairline. Behind his black horn-rimmed glasses are a pair of deeply set dark eyes—like the one on the sign outside. In fluid Yiddish, he presses

Pearl for the other fifty dollars, his breath smelling of fish, rum, and coffee.

Clearing her throat to bring her trembling voice under control, Pearl stands firm: "Not a penny more until I arrive in Florida."

The doctor's assistant, a dark-skinned Cuban in a black shirt, watches their conversation, as does the hollow-cheeked old woman from America who'll play Pearl's mother. Sitting in a wooden desk chair, she devours three of the sweet biscuits that the doctor has set before her. She eats a fourth more slowly, as if in apology for her earlier gluttony. Her hair is dyed a shimmering gray that looks blue in the low light of the store.

"Please, I'm not a rich man," the eye doctor says in the voice of a bleating goat. "I haven't sold a thing in weeks. These days, no one except tourists can afford a decent pair of glasses. And tourists don't come to Havana to buy glasses."

Pearl isn't falling for his shtick, but in the end, she compromises. She'll return that afternoon with ten more dollars. The rest she'll pay the old woman in Florida.

The Cuban assistant goes to the P & O office to book their boat tickets to Key West with train tickets to Miami attached. Pearl listens carefully to the eye doctor's instructions. She and the old woman will leave Havana tomorrow morning. Later that afternoon, their boat will anchor in Key West, across the pier from the train tracks. Foreigners get off from the back, to show their documents. As an American, Pearl will disembark from the front with her "mother" and cross the dock to the train. No need to stop or say a word to anyone. Understand?

"Yes," says Pearl. It's all arranged, she thinks. I've saved myself. After nine months, I'm leaving this island.

They help the old woman rise from her chair. She manages

it with labored breathing and squinting eyes, like Pearl's grand-mother in her declining days. "By day, I see fine," she insists, taking tiny steps toward the door. "But it's so dark in this shop."

"I don't like to keep the lights on in this heat," says the doctor.

He doesn't like to pay to keep the lights on, Pearl thinks. You're both liars.

"Many thanks, gentlemen," says the woman, as if Pearl is a man.

Pearl, swallowing the hurt of this remark, offers to accompany the old woman to her boardinghouse. It's located on a cheap block close to the Paseo, where the old buildings are crowded together like a mouthful of bad teeth. They shed flakes of paint or bits of stone facade onto the streets. Beggars stretch out halfhearted hands in their direction, then quickly recognize how poor these women are—not worth the effort. A peddler hawks Eskimo Pies out of a box on his back. Pearl's stomach growls, but she has stale bread at the workshop, and she'd rather save the money for America.

"You're too kind," says the woman, also staring hungrily at the peddler's box. In the light, her hair really looks blue. "Your parents gave you a good education."

No, Pearl thinks. I educated myself. I was my own parent.

The woman's name is Ella Friedman, and she and her husband are victims of a failed business venture that she declines to specify. "I'm relieved to see the class of person you are," she says. "I'm not like the man in that store. I was born in Atlanta." Mrs. Friedman pauses as if that means something. "You're Polish, aren't you? I hear it's all right if you're Polish. The quotas for Polish are still open."

"Yes, I'm Polish," says Pearl, which feels like yet another lie. She's told so many lately. She steers the old lady around a dog sleeping in the street, flies swarming around its face. Pearl used to fear dogs; now she tolerates them, at a distance.

"Things may change," Mrs. Friedman says. "The Republicans hate the immigrants. They're afraid of you. That's why anyone hates, because of fear. But there's an election next month, in November, and perhaps they'll lose, be out of power. You see?"

"Yes." Though she doesn't see, she lets Mrs. Friedman talk. Her birdlike voice reminds Pearl of her grandmother. It could be nice pretending they're related, for Pearl to borrow a bit of family instead of always being on her own.

"I've caught this awful tropical lung ailment. I want to go home, to consult an American doctor, but my husband and I are short of funds, and we have no family to help except my brother, with whom I'm on bad terms." She says this casually, as if it's normal for a brother to leave a sister stranded.

"No children?" Pearl asks.

"We had a daughter," Mrs. Friedman replies. "She died of typhus when she was young. She'd be older than you if she'd lived."

"I'm sorry. I know what it is, typhus."

"It isn't you who needs to apologize," says Mrs. Friedman, "it's God."

Pearl sucks in her breath. This old woman's blasphemy can't be a good omen.

In front of Mrs. Friedman's boardinghouse, a man with a gleaming ring in his ear squats in the street, lowers his pants, and relieves his bowels.

"This city is terrible. We must help each other escape," says Mrs. Friedman and hurries to the door. "Please go," she calls out over her shoulder. "Leave this street as quickly as you can."

○

BEFORE RETURNING TO the workshop, Pearl visits Mrs. Steinberg to request an advance on her wages. "For Frieda's wedding. For a gift," she says. Not exactly a lie. What greater gift can she give her sister than to be reunited?

I've become a good liar, Pearl thinks. A nasty habit. In America, I must break it.

"She's really going to marry that man, after all his crazy letters," says Mrs. Steinberg, opening her pocketbook. "She's what, seventeen?"

"Eighteen now." At least she's telling the truth about something.

"Modern girls often wait until twenty-five to get married. Even twenty-six."

"I've told her so," says Pearl, who is now nearly twenty-eight with no husband in sight. How near, she doesn't know precisely. She was born sometime around Hanukkah, but no one recorded the exact date. At the time, such information wasn't important.

"Don't blame yourself," says Mrs. Steinberg. "No one can give advice to young people. They do what they want." She looks Pearl in the eye, searching, then hands her the advance and five dollars extra.

"Thank you," says Pearl, her throat catching as she accepts the money. The generosity, it's too much. Somehow she'll pay them back. "Please excuse me." She rushes out of Mrs. Steinberg's salon. Once safely on the street, she allows herself to cry, although she's unsure whether it's from gratitude or shame.

o

THE NEXT MORNING, Pearl and the Friedmans wait to board the SS *Cobb*, just as her sister did with the Meyers back in July.

Mr. Friedman tells the ship's clerk that he's staying on, to conduct some business, but his wife and daughter are anxious to return home. The clerk says nothing about the fact that their daughter's name, "Ann," is not on the passport.

Frieda had easily carried off this show. Where is she now to teach Pearl how to act, what to say?

Pearl wears a dress she made, copying a garment on the cover of *McCall Quarterly*, one of Julieta's magazines. In the magazine version, the salmon-colored fabric hangs loosely off the frame of a long-faced, wispy woman whose waist is as skinny as a stalk of sugarcane. The woman in the picture—not really a woman but only a drawing of one—assumes an insouciant stance, legs crossed, hands on straight, boyish hips, a bored expression on her attenuated face. The dress is topped by what the magazine calls a Peter Pan collar, and a sash bow wilting from the plunging neckline.

Pearl's dress is a frilly raspberry-colored frock printed with black lilies. The material, a Canton crepe left over from a line of hats Mr. Steinberg couldn't sell, has a slippery sheen that refuses to breathe; it pinches her chest and stomach. Unlike the dress the Meyers gave Frieda, this dress has sleeves, and they squeeze her arms into sausages. She's found a rip under her left arm, so she keeps her elbow pinned to her side to hide it.

If a friend with her figure had asked for such a thing, Pearl would have gently, firmly steered her another way. A big-boned girl doesn't go for bright colors and snug fits. Pearl hoped this dress might make her appear more American, fashionably androgynous, a languid lady, unimpressed by fine things or fine people.

She planned to lose weight before the trip, but instead she's gained. Also, she tried bleaching her hair. It turned an unnatural olive-blonde, so she dyed it black again. The morning of Pearl's departure, Julieta helped her comb her bangs into a fringe of curls, apply layers of paint and shadow around her eyes and on her cheeks, and pluck her eyebrows. Pearl feels the sting of each hair ripped from its follicle.

When the operation was finished, Julieta stepped back, then frowned. "Well, my friend," she said, "the Americans probably won't look at you so closely."

My friend, thinks Pearl. She always considered a friend someone she'd known a lifetime. Lately, so many of her fixed ideas have turned out false.

Mr. Friedman, a stocky man with a swirl of brown hair streaked with gray, plants a sloppy kiss on Pearl's cheek as if to say good-bye, then squeezes her arms and sides like he's shaping a lump of bread dough into a loaf. The bastard.

Pearl pulls away, takes his wife's hand. "Step careful, Ma," she says in English.

Hearing her speak, the ship's clerk turns sharply and stares at Pearl, but he continues to greet the next passengers in line and lets her proceed.

○

PEARL STANDS ON the starboard deck of the SS *Cobb*. Fearful that her hat might blow away, Pearl has removed it, and the wind whips her dark curls into a froth. She's feeling worn out from trying to appear like a gay, carefree American returning from an island holiday. "I am a dressmaker," she says, practicing a phrase she learned from the Yiddish-English text she borrowed from the lending library in the Hebrew Cooperativa. At night in the workshop, she copied new words onto tissue paper.

Her insides are roiling like the white sheets of water spraying up the sides of the boat, though all she ate for breakfast was half a roll. Pearl visited the toilet, but nothing moved. Only gas. Also, she didn't lock the door properly, and an American walked in on her. The American woman said several sharp words in English, though Pearl was the one caught with her dress hiked up over her hips.

Pearl longs to belt out a deep-throated burp, which wouldn't fit the ladylike image she's been laboring to portray. There seems to be no audience nearby. . . . She checks again, making sure. Okay, let it go.

A long, loud croak. Like a swamp frog with bronchitis.

Pearl reaches over the ship's railing to feel the breeze. Then she puts her hat back on and returns to the cabin. I feel like a clown, she thinks, but it's worth looking foolish to reach America. She tries teasing out her bangs, but her hair refuses to be tamed, so she pushes her hat down more firmly.

Pearl: a country girl from a landlocked village, yet so many of her life's milestones have occurred on boats. Is this God's sense of humor?

Signs on the wall read: "CUBA LIBRE!" "SO NEAR, YET SO FOREIGN: HAVANA, ONLY 90 MILES FROM KEY WEST." *Libre*, Pearl thinks. That means free.

Passengers chat loudly about horse races, sneak sips of alcohol from tiny bottles smuggled from Havana, or guzzle watery American coffee, complaining about that mud Cubans drink. Pearl joins Mrs. Friedman, who's reading a novel called *The Sheik*. On its cover, a hook-nosed bearded man in a white headdress leers at a seductive blonde.

Mrs. Friedman wears an outmoded white jacket and a rumpled white hat, tilted diagonally toward her left eye. A black-and-white striped band runs around the hat's base. Pearl imagines a young woman like herself in some humid workshop, carefully sewing that band so the striped pattern aligns without interruption at the seam.

The old lady puts down the book and dissolves into a coughing fit that she attempts to soothe with sips of soda water. All wrong, Pearl thinks. The bubbles tickle your chest, stimulate shallow, fruitless coughing. Take a glass of hot water with a slice of lemon to massage the throat, and lemon draws out the phlegm for more productive coughs. But Pearl keeps quiet. For now, this woman is the boss.

Rather than reserve an expensive private day cabin, Pearl and Mrs. Friedman are economizing by sitting in the lounge, which still feels plenty luxurious to Pearl. Waiters serve coffee in white china marked with "P & O" in blue lettering. The chairs are crushed red velvet, a darker, handsomer shade of the color of Pearl's dress.

Pearl asks if Mrs. Friedman wants to go on deck, or if she'd like some food. "No, thank you, dear," she says, unpacking a hard-boiled egg, which she sprinkles with black pepper. She's on a special diet recommended by a Cuban woman, a local healer. No red meat or fried food. Lots of garlic, and milk with black pepper.

Pearl picks up the American magazine she's pretending to read, titled unimaginatively *The American*. She stares over the edge of the pages until Mrs. Friedman plucks the magazine out of her hand and turns it right side up.

Mrs. Friedman finishes her egg and hands Pearl the shell to put in a slop pail.

How much longer until Key West? Pearl's about to ask Mrs. Friedman when a steward in a dark-blue jacket speaks to Pearl.

She doesn't understand him. So many English words aren't in her phrasebook—how do the Americans remember them all? Also, this man speaks so fast. She giggles like an idiot, then nudges Mrs. Friedman. Staring at Pearl, the man repeats himself to Mrs. Friedman, who answers easily, quickly.

"What did he want?" Pearl asks after the man walks away.

"To know if we're enjoying our trip," she says.

"Is that all?" Pearl says, her voice trembling. She buries her face in her magazine. What will she do in America? Pretend to be a deaf-mute?

○

AROUND FOUR O'CLOCK that afternoon, Pearl presses her face to the window of the lounge and catches her first glimpse of Key West, a band of white, brown, and green along the horizon. As they get closer, the colors break up into shapes of houses, land, and trees. America, she whispers, then feels a chill. Did anyone hear? Did her accent betray her? Thankfully, no one's listening. Three wireless telegraph towers poke out above the landscape, like ladders reaching to the sky—and falling laughably short of their goal.

So she's made it to Key West.

Pearl has been sweating so much she smells, and the rip under her arm is growing. She wishes she had a needle and thread and a place to hide, so she could remove the dress and fix the hole. Oh, who cares? Tomorrow night she'll be in New York hugging her sisters.

As their ship rounds the tip of the island, the water turns jade green. A flock of gulls plunge nose first toward the water's surface, strike it with their beaks, then pull up short and fly upward again.

Further on, a black bird with an orange bill balances on a piece of driftwood. Their ship draws near, and the bird flies away.

Pearl admires the sailboats lined up neatly at the wooden docks. Americans in rough blue pants jump between the boats and the docks, cheerfully tossing lines of wet rope. A man gutting fish pauses his work to wave to their ship with both arms, one hand clutching his clasp knife. She waves back, but he doesn't notice.

Where's the train to Miami the eye doctor had promised? And why is the ship sailing past the harbor? Maybe they've found her out and are going back to Cuba.

She returns to her seat. Mrs. Friedman is reading her book. Are there any other passengers smuggling too? They seem like unremarkable American tourists, laughing, tightening their baggage straps, and pointing to shore.

"Why aren't we stopping here?" Pearl asks the old woman.

"We must cross the harbor, with the other commercial boats, the big ships," Mrs. Friedman replies. "We'll arrive shortly."

"Good," says Pearl, exhaling.

Mrs. Friedman puts down her book. "Could I ask . . . is it possible to have the balance of the money now?" she says in a shaky voice.

"Oh!" Pearl was planning to pay Mrs. Friedman once they'd made it onto dry land, but they're so close. She opens the tiny beige suitcase she'd brought and extracts twenty dollars. The old woman snatches the money out of Pearl's hands before Pearl has opened her fingers. "And the other twenty?" she says.

Pearl would rather wait until they're on the train to Miami. However, Mrs. Friedman coughs again, shaking so terribly that Pearl gives her the rest anyway. She's a feeble old woman, Pearl thinks, not some slick charlatan. Now that I'm in America, I have to stop being so suspicious. This is an honest country. I have to stop lying.

"Don't you worry, dear," says Mrs. Friedman, folding the paper bills into a worn beaded change purse. "It will go swimmingly. And if it doesn't, remember you're Polish. You're perfectly within your rights."

Pearl doubts that's true, but why argue? Polish, Russian, or Chinese, she's not supposed to be here. Yet she is here, and she's doing this. Breathe, she thinks. Though it's awfully hard to breathe in this dress.

They reach the other side of the harbor, and Pearl sees that the eye doctor in Havana told the truth. There are the beautiful ugly black train tracks, laid on a bridge directly across the pier from where they're docking. And there's a train, its smokestack chuffing gray smoke. Passengers from Key West are already boarding.

Imagine: a bridge over an ocean, all the way to the Florida mainland. How could men build such a thing? Maybe America really is a magical land.

A loud blast of the ship's horn announces their arrival. Men scurry below to prop the gangplanks up against the boat. For several minutes that feel like hours, she waits beside Mrs. Friedman until a steward announces they may disembark.

The two women descend a flight of stairs, then emerge through an oval-shaped hole into the hot light. They step cautiously onto the wobbling gangplank, arm in arm. The train waits across the pier. Even old Mrs. Friedman wouldn't need a minute to reach it. Frieda must have taken this same walk with the Meyers. She probably did it easily.

I can do this, Pearl thinks. Their bags are too small and light to smuggle anything to arouse the customs officials' attention. If they do get stopped, Mrs. Friedman will present her landing card and say Pearl is her daughter, Ann, her trusty traveling companion and apple of her eye. It's a credible story. Much likelier than the notion that an old woman would travel to Havana and back on her own.

Here at the port, it's all dried dirt and gravel, and the train yards, and three giant gray metal vats. A bit of sea scrub grows by the water. Next to a green picket fence, horse-drawn carriages and automobiles wait to take tourists into town.

Walk with confidence, Pearl tells herself. Like those proud beautiful Cuban women strutting on the Paseo, confident that trails of admirers are following behind.

She thinks, I wish I had a Spanish shawl. If I had a shawl to cover my shoulders, I could easily carry this off.

At the bottom of the gangplank waits a man in a black uniform with a black hat riding atop his blond hair, combed and set with pomade so it looks brown. The gold badge on his hat glints in the sun. His stern lantern-jawed face is interrupted by a dirty-blond mustache like a shaving brush. No beard. Americans don't seem to like beards. Except maybe Abraham Lincoln. The man stands beside a steward from the boat—the steward who'd asked Pearl about her journey, the one whose English she failed to understand. Don't look at him. Don't look at the man in the hat either . . . but the gleam of his badge demands her attention. The steward utters a few quiet words, and that old devil's voice whispers in her ear again, betraying her with bad advice. Go on, the voice says. Stare at those two men.

"You!" the officer points to her, and Pearl feels Mrs. Friedman's arm loosen from hers with surprising dexterity. "You," he repeats as they step off the gangplank. Mrs. Friedman continues toward the train, stepping primly along, pretending Pearl's a stranger she'd used as a human crutch. "Stay here. You've got something on you."

"H-h-here?" Pearl asks, her little beige suitcase swinging from her hand. Her chest tightens, and her legs go weak. Another passenger, eager to pass by, says, "Excuse me," in an annoyed voice and makes a show of stepping around her. Mrs. Friedman slips away. Wait, help, Pearl thinks, but her voice is gone. So is her money.

The officer points to his left, while the other tourists board the train or march into town, having enjoyed their Cuba weekend getaways. A few turn their heads, briefly curious about the petty drama involving a dumpy woman in a raspberry-colored dress. Mrs. Friedman has reached the train, and a young man helps her up the steps onto the third-class carriage. Pearl is relieved to see him take care of the old woman. Then she remembers, I'm the one in trouble. That lady is leaving with all my money. Stop, you!

Why didn't Mrs. Friedman argue, demand indignantly, "How dare you treat my daughter this way?" Or even, "She's Polish, so it's all right." Maybe Mrs. Friedman never believed that Polish business.

The ship's steward returns to the ship. Pearl wants to ask him, what harm could it have done to let her go. He must have no heart.

The customs officer performs his work in a brisk, businesslike manner. No scolding. He speaks to the passengers in a cool, dry voice while opening suitcases, crates of oranges, and a box of coconut candy containing a small bottle of rum. "I'll take this," he says, tucking the bottle and box under his arm.

Where does the liquor go? Where will she go?

Three more women are ordered to wait beside Pearl: a tiny Romanian and two sisters from Latvia. One cries softly into her sister's arm. Rivers of perspiration run down Pearl's neck. The strings of the bow on her dress sag down to her navel, and her once sprightly collar has wilted. Can't they stand in the shade? Pearl removes her hat to fan her face, flushed with heat and shame. I'm no criminal, she thinks. I'm a cantor's daughter. Help, help, but there's no help. Her mouth tastes like paper.

The last passengers have disembarked. Pearl and the other women wait as the customs officer confers with his colleagues. Men from the SS *Cobb* are unloading boxes of fruit from Cuba, sacks of sugar, and a pile of sea sponges. A sailor jogs down the dock toward the town. No one asks for his papers. Across the dock, the conductor blows his whistle and the train pulls away, to America.

Dark water sloshes against the pilings, making a soft swooshing sound. Pearl briefly considers jumping in. She can't swim.

In Havana, she heard that others in her current situation were sent back to Cuba. Maybe she'll be sent back too, never to return, to die alone in a Cuban sweatshop, listening to Spanish voices from the street. And Frieda will marry the wrong man in front of strangers. She'll live in a house of fighting and tears, raising liars and cheats for children. That's if Mendel keeps his word rather than breaking off their relationship with lies that could ruin her reputation.

The officer returns with two more men in uniform. "Okay, ladies," he says, not unkindly. "Come with us." The Romanian woman starts to speak, but he puts his finger to his lips. They march down the dock, past a freight depot where towers of steamer trunks await further instructions, a café with streaked windows, and a Western Union office—whom could she wire for help? They step off the pier, and Pearl sets foot in America, the Golden Land, which is just a street. The dirt is still dirt. The air is still air, and it smells of salt and grease.

Their party is divided between two boxy black cars. The sisters go with the blond officer in one car, while Pearl and the Romanian ride in the back of the other car with the two officers in front. The windows are rolled down, but Pearl wants to roll them up. She doesn't need the breeze, just an end to her humiliation.

The town of Key West is surprisingly small, even smaller than Turya but better organized. The streets, quiet for a weekday afternoon, are laid out in a simple grid. Cars, like the one Pearl's riding in, new and clean, utilitarian and black, are parked along the curbs. They all face the same direction, unlike in Havana, where drivers leave their gleaming cream and silver coupes wherever strikes their fancy.

The wooden buildings, one or two stories high, are framed by shady verandas. Their front yards are bordered by white fences, and the houses are set far enough apart to let in sunlight, though the view of the sky is interrupted by a network of electricity lines. Closer to the town center, more people are out on the sidewalks, sailors and men returning home from work. Many have brown faces, and some are speaking Spanish. Maybe this is a dream and she hasn't left Havana?

They turn right, then left toward their destination, which casts a long shadow over the end of the road. It's a red brick building with arches over the entrance, set off from the street by a flight of cement steps. Like a castle or fortress. They park in front. Pearl follows the officers and the other women up the steps. I've made a terrible start, Pearl thinks, lying in this land of honest people. Now they'll write my name in a book, using dark ink that can never be erased. Perhaps I'll never be allowed to leave this building.

Just in case, she inhales a deep, final breath of fresh air.

The main hall, with tall ceilings and a marble floor, is cool and dark. To the right is a post office, now closed. Two women coming out of it watch their little parade ascend a grand, steep staircase to the second floor. Pearl shades her face with her left hand.

Upstairs feels stuffy and warm. Pearl and the women wait on a bench outside a suite of offices where whirling ceiling fans rustle skirts, papers. She listens to the clickety-clack of typing, and her fingers tap her thighs nervously to the rhythm of it. A man in uniform checks on them, and Pearl, whose throat is parched, asks, "*Wasser?*" He doesn't understand, so she leads him to an office and points to a glass. "Can I drink?"

Thinking she wants an alcoholic drink, they start laughing. Red-faced, Pearl slumps back down on the bench. More waiting. She's glad no one she knows can see her like this, being detained by the police. Are they police? Police aren't supposed to be as terrible here as they were in the rest of the world, but how can she know for sure?

After an hour, they're approached by an odd figure: a tall, slender man with a pointy face and a trim mustache. He wears a straw hat with a wine-red bow tie and two-toned shoes, brown and white, with frenetic stitching at the toes.

The man removes his hat, revealing a yarmulke. "Good day, ladies," he says in Yiddish. "I'm Rabbi Singer, here to translate." He's wearing three gold rings, and there's a gold watch on his wrist. Pearl's confused. Rabbis are poor and their clothes smell dusty like old books. This one looks as if he could lead a circus.

The officers call them one by one for questioning, and Pearl has the awful luck of going first. In the office, a nervous-looking woman sits at a transcription machine, next to a large black desk belonging to the officer who nabbed her at the dock. His name is Anderson. Behind him stands a young man with a prominent Adam's apple. He appears uneasy, as though he'd like to sit, but suspects he shouldn't.

Pearl sits with her knees locked, her arms crossed, and her hands clenched in fists. Her chair is hard, and the floor is hard too. The warm air in the room, swirling from the ceiling fan, stirs the tips of her hair, as if there are flies swarming around her head. There's a telephone on his desk and she wishes she could pick it up and call Basha for help right now, but she cannot implicate her sisters in her own trouble.

The man who calls himself a rabbi says something in English. Evidently, he finds his chair uncomfortable, so they send for another, more to his liking, and bring him a drink: dark and sparkling, with ice. She realizes it's Coca-Cola. Though Pearl's dying of thirst, this black liquid looks vile.

The stenographer moves a blotter on Anderson's desk to make room for the soda. Such deference these goyim show to a rabbi. Pearl's not yet sure he really is one.

"Don't be afraid," the rabbi reminds Pearl in Yiddish. "Just answer honestly." Pearl nods, though she's not convinced she should be honest with these men.

The interview begins with a string of simple questions.

"What is your correct name?"

"Have you ever been known by another name?"

"Your age?"

"Of what country are you a citizen and where were you born?"

After Pearl answers these questions truthfully, they want to know: "Is it true that your politics are of the Bolshevik type?"

Pearl asks the rabbi to repeat that last question. "Don't they understand?" she says. "We're running away from the Bolsheviks."

The police say something and the rabbi translates: "We?" he asks. "You mean you're in league with these ladies here?"

Her heart gives an extra squeeze. "I never met these ladies before."

The questions quickly become more detailed.

"What is the address of your last permanent residence?"

"By what vessel did you arrive in Havana?"

At first, she faces Anderson, who runs his thumbs along the edge of his desk as he asks questions in English and she answers in Yiddish. Is she saying what she should? Gradually she shifts her focus to the rabbi, relaxed in his chair, long legs crossed knee over knee. He finishes his Coca-Cola and asks for a coffee.

"Could I also have something?" Pearl asks. They give her cloudy-looking water in a smudged glass. She gulps it down and asks for more, which they bring. Outside, the sun sinks lower in the sky. As the questions continue, she wants to say, I'm an ant you can squish between your fingers, a piece of driftwood washed up on your shore, an accident of history. Do with me what you will, and no one will protest. But get it over with.

"How long did you remain in Havana, Cuba?"

"Are you married or single?"

"What is your race?"

"What is your occupation, if any?"

She says in English, "I am a dressmaker," hoping her use of their language will impress them.

"How long have you been a dressmaker?"

"What kind of work did you do before you were a dressmaker?"

"Can you demonstrate your trade for us now?"

Thus far, she's answered truthfully. So she's surprised when the rabbi tells her in Yiddish, "Consider your answers carefully. They don't believe you."

"If they don't believe my words, let them look with their eyes. Tell them I made this dress I'm wearing," she says.

The rabbi touches her chair. "They think you were brought here as a white slave." She doesn't understand what this means, so he explains it, to her horror.

"Absolutely not!" she says.

"What's she saying?" asks Anderson. "What's going on?"

"I am a dressmaker," she repeats in English, tapping his desk with each word. She's exhausted, hungry, hot, and she needs the toilet. By what right do these men accuse her like this? She tells the rabbi in Yiddish, "A woman who leaves home to preserve her life and her virtue is accused of selling herself? How can they talk to me this way?"

The rabbi pats her sleeve. "Lower your voice," he says. "Let me help you."

She supposes he really is a rabbi. She wants to believe it because if so, maybe he can help. "Tell them I'm an honest girl from a good family. A hard worker. They want me to go back to the Old Country to be starved, beaten, or shot? You're a man of God. What would God want me to do in this situation?"

"God would say it won't do any good to argue with them," says the rabbi, speaking so quietly she has to sit forward to hear. "I have friends here. Key West is a small town. I can help you in my own way if you'll follow my guidance."

She slumps back in her chair. All these men, the world over, controlling her fate. The past really is repeating itself. The unfair questioning resumes.

"Is it not a fact that you boarded the SS *Cobb* at Havana, Cuba?"

"Yes," she sighs after the rabbi translates. The stenographer takes a quick break to stretch her fingers before resuming her duties.

"And is it not a fact that you paid a smuggler money to bring you from Havana, Cuba, and land you in the United States?"

She hesitates. She doesn't want to get Mrs. Friedman in trouble with these stern men, even if she did take all that money. Finally, Pearl says yes again.

The questions come more quickly. This Anderson isn't satisfied. The man behind him stifles a yawn, then straightens his posture, tries to look stern.

"How much money did you pay to travel from Cuba to the United States?"

"One hundred dollars. In American—United States money," she says in English.

"To whom did you give this money?"

She describes the eye doctor in Havana, puts him on board the ship in Mrs. Friedman's place. In this instance, it doesn't matter if she lies. They don't believe when she tells the truth. "I lost him on the boat," she says.

"We'll check his name on the passenger manifest," says Anderson. "When and where did you pay him to bring you from Havana and land you in the United States?"

"In the Anglo-American Optical Company store at 98 Obispo Street, Havana, Cuba. It is his store."

"Is it not a fact that he brought you here to make a living by illegal means?"

She shakes her head. They're stubborn, aren't they? And lacking imagination. They can't fathom a woman supporting herself on her own.

"And these women here? Did he make similar promises to them?"

Again she says no.

"Have you any other connections in the United States? Any relatives?"

Pearl shakes her head. She doesn't want to mention Basha. And as far as the United States Government is concerned, Frieda is a ghost, does not exist.

"For what purpose did you come here?"

A better life, she says. A safer life.

"Are you sure of your answer?"

Who do they think she is? Rosa Luxemburg? She hates this calm Anderson with his blond mustache and kind eyes that disguise his black purpose, to entrap her into confessing crimes of which she's innocent. When can she use the toilet?

"Have you any further statement which you wish to make as to why you think you should not be deported?"

"No," she tells the rabbi. "I know I am here illegally."

○

PEARL IS FINALLY allowed to go to the ladies' room. After using the toilet, she lingers over the sink, splashes her face with cold water. Dear God, she thinks, why have you forsaken me again? If I've done wrong, haven't I paid for my sin, double, triple? But God doesn't work like a bookkeeper balancing accounts.

"I don't understand," she whispers to no one.

Pearl returns to the bench to wait. Her nerves are worn out.

She's given a cold meat sandwich, and though she's so achingly hungry, she can't even pick off the bread because she won't put something that has touched nonkosher meat into her mouth. Leaning against the wall, she closes her eyes and thinks of warm brown bread slathered in golden goose fat, or a Polish fried dough cookie called Angel Wings that she used to buy in Warsaw. Or papaya chunks squirted with lime juice.

She thinks of *Shabbes* dinner in Turya, with roast chicken and a crowd singing psalms after their meal. Her lips mouth the opening verses of Psalm 118:

> *From the depths of my distress, I called on the Lord.*
> *He answered me and brought me relief.*

As a girl, she was confused by this prayer. Why was it necessary to call on God? Couldn't he just come when needed? Her father said the prayer's true meaning was "He answered me, saying you are already free." The act of calling on the divine is its own redemption. "Your willingness to see the possibility of a miracle is salvation."

Pearl has never understood that explanation. What if I'm willing to see a miracle and it never comes? How am I better off than if I hadn't been willing? But no one cared what a girl thought about prayer.

Pearl is alone. The other girls have been taken for their own interrogations, and she wonders how long she'll be kept here. She knows of people incarcerated for decades for committing crimes against the tsar. Some were never heard from again.

○

PEARL'S DETENTION LASTS only hours, not decades. The rabbi is taking her away.

"Our community has an arrangement with the magistrate, to host young Jewesses in your situation, for a small fee," Rabbi Singer explains as he leads her down the front steps. "We used to come here bringing kosher food. But then I said to Wendell, he's the magistrate, I said, 'Wendell, why not let us take care of these women ourselves? After all, it's an island. Where could they go? In the ocean?'"

The sun has set hours ago, and the leafy square across the street from the courthouse is deep in shadow. The darkness feels soft and fresh on her skin. One of the trees gives off a heady fragrant smell, like a lilac, only sweeter.

"So," the rabbi says, "you are my responsibility, until they send you back."

Then they are sending her back. At least she won't have to go to jail.

"But I have no money," says Pearl. "How can I go back?"

"The shipping company is responsible. You won't have to pay."

"Where are the other girls?" asks Pearl. "In jail?"

"No, they're going to different homes, other Jewish families."

"Why are we waiting? Why don't they send us all back now?" She rubs the back of her neck, flexes her wrists. This strange man has an answer for everything. His good looks and good clothes are unsettling. His face and manners are too smooth.

"They believe you're here as part of a plot, to bring in girls for prostitution. You understand? They want to investigate your case."

"But I'm innocent," she says. "How can I make them believe me?"

"You can't," he says. "They have to learn it themselves."

NINE

PEARL FOLLOWS THE RABBI DOWN SHADY RESIDENTIAL streets littered with dried leaves, shaggy coconut husks, and long branches, tough and rigid like rifle barrels. His blond straw hat bobs ahead, intermittently catching the moonlight through gaps in the tree cover. He seems strangely cheerful, as if he regularly escorts strange women to his home.

Pearl trips over the trunk of a young palm that's fallen across her path. After the rabbi helps her up, they step carefully around the tree's withering fronds, massed like a head of unwashed hair. He lets go of her arm, and she resolves not to trip again.

Her suitcase was confiscated at the customs house, so her hands are as empty as her stomach, though her mind is full with anger. Anger at Anderson and his fellow race of bureaucrats who ruin lives with government forms and edicts that spill blood. Anger at Mrs. Friedman and her false friendship. Pearl feels angry enough to rage like a Cossack through this town of Key West.

The evil spirit always tugging at her heart murmurs softly: What about God?

No, she decides, leave God out of this. God does not force any human being to behave as a beast or a cold snake. To be angry with God above means absolving the guilty on earth.

A short walk brings them to the synagogue, her first American synagogue. She's unimpressed. It's a modest white building, the same footprint as its neighbors at the foundations, but taller at the roofline. About half the size of Turya's smallest synagogue, nicknamed Rich Man's Shul because they had the poorest congregants.

The rabbi's living quarters are attached to the sanctuary. He leads her into the parlor, which is cluttered with chairs, lamps with silk shades, and a box piano. Behind the parlor is a small dining room and a kitchen, where the rabbi's wife sets down the book she's reading to greet them with a loud yawn. She scoots upstairs, waving at Pearl to follow.

On the second floor are three bedrooms, one for the parents and one for each of their two girls. The older girl is moving in with the younger so Pearl can occupy her tiny room with its single bed, a doll-sized chair with a pink teddy bear, and a shelf shared by picture books and hairless china dolls with cold blue eyes. Pearl stands against the wall as the girls troop between the bedrooms, carrying neat piles of blankets, schoolbooks, and clothes. They appear to be used to this arrangement.

The rabbi's wife rubs her eyes, then gives Pearl a simple white nightgown and a loose, washed-out blue cotton dress to wear in the day. It's ugly but cooler than her raspberry crepe. No matter, Pearl thinks. I deserve to wear ugly things.

In bed, she lies awake, listening to the high-pitched whine of insects outside, while shadows from the trees shift on the ceiling. Her grandmother used to scare Pearl and her sisters by moving her knobby hands in front of the hearth to make shadows of fiendish animals dancing on the floorboards. Don't look too long, Grandmother warned. The devil lives in shadows. He wants to get into your dreams.

Pearl never played such tricks on her little sister. If anyone tried to tease Frieda, Pearl gave them such a tongue-lashing they never attempted it again.

Pearl's gaudy raspberry-colored dress lies in a heap on the floor. A disastrous failure of design. She wants to burn it. How foolish to think she might transform herself into a bubbly American ingénue. That's for someone like Frieda. Pearl is a working drudge, dull and solid as a potato, with a figure to match.

In Havana, she'll have to hope the Steinbergs will accept her again. She'll need months to work off that advance on her salary.

A few steps more and she could have boarded that train. She'd be riding to New York this very second.

For now, she's trapped here, until she proves her innocence. She could wire Basha in New York to vouch for her. Basha's in America legally. But a wire costs money, and the little pocket money she had is in her suitcase, currently captive at the Customs House.

○

JUST PAST SEVEN in the morning, Pearl wakes to the sounds of dogs scuffling in the road, growling and kicking up dust clouds like the wild dogs who fought over scraps behind Father's butcher shop. It takes her a moment to remember she's in America. She gets out of bed and looks out the window, but a tree blocks her view, and in one of its branches crouches the strangest animal, something from a nightmare: a lizard the size of a cat, glowing yellow-orange among the leaves.

Pearl screams, covers her eyes, then peeks again. This thing's head is crowned by spikes, and its toes are topped with curling claws. The sun lights up its skin as if it's on fire. Can it fly? Does it bite, and is it poisonous? She slams the window shut.

Afraid to make the rabbi's family wait, Pearl runs to the washroom. She makes the bed, puts on her new dress, and sits, listening to the sounds of the house.

Will someone bring food? Perhaps starvation is part of her punishment.

The rabbi's wife knocks on the door. Her sleeveless yellow dress barely covers her knees. American women must constantly catch colds, walking around so exposed.

"You're dressed already!" she says in Yiddish. "I thought you were sleeping. Aren't you hungry? Come down to the kitchen."

The *rebbetzin*'s name is Alma. Though her Yiddish is not as fluent as her husband's, it is good. Pearl follows her, stepping cautiously down the creaking stairs. The kitchen faces the garden, and it's baking in the full heat of the morning sun. With that and the heat of the stove, the room feels like a steamy bathhouse.

The two Singer girls dry their plates beside the sink. They speak no Yiddish, and as Pearl sits at the small table, the girls stare with their mouths open. Pearl finds their manners off-putting.

Alma brings coffee, sliced peaches, tomatoes, lukewarm fried cod cakes, and a grainy corn porridge called grits. Pearl avoids the tomatoes—she's heard they're poisonous like death cap mushrooms. There's butter, but it's too yellow. The sugar she stirs into her coffee tastes suspiciously sweet. Unsure of how to eat the grits, she spreads them on the cod cakes and the peaches, whose color and flavor reminds her of mangoes. The girls are giggling. Did she do it wrong?

Pearl wipes the perspiration on her forehead and her neck. However, the heat in that kitchen doesn't affect her appetite. She quickly finishes her meal.

"Will the rabbi take his breakfast with us?" asks Pearl.

"Of course not. He's gone already," says Alma.

Pearl is crestfallen. With the rabbi gone, there's no hope for her to plead her case today. "I need his help."

Alma looks at her curiously and says, "He'll be back. You'll see."

She checks the girls' dresses, straightens a hair bow, and inspects their hands and behind their ears. Pearl thinks they look fine, but Alma reproves the younger girl for wearing dark stockings and sends her upstairs to change into white ones. Pearl admires how she manages the girls easily. It takes effort to get a girl ready for school.

Pearl finishes her meal and suppresses a burp. "The breakfast is good," she says.

"Grace does it the night before and leaves it in the icebox," says Alma. "I warm it in the oven. I'm not much of a cook, I'm afraid. Or a housekeeper. As a child, I wasn't taught these things. My family expected me to marry a wealthy man."

Pearl knits her eyebrows. "Who is Grace?"

"Grace is our maid," says Alma.

A rabbi who wears gold and can afford a maid? He sounds plenty wealthy to Pearl. She offers to help with the dishes, but Alma insists she leave everything. "Grace will do it." Grace seems to do everything. So what does Alma do, Pearl wonders. As if to answer her question, Alma says, "I'm going upstairs to write. Help yourself to more coffee. No, Pearl, sit back down and leave those plates where they lie. Now please excuse me." She heads up the stairs, and soon Pearl hears the bedroom door click shut.

Pearl wonders what kind of writing Alma is doing. Maybe synagogue business. She drinks the last of her lukewarm coffee as a fan buzzes fitfully by the open window. The kitchen is small but handsome, with metal handles on the cabinets, shelves crowded with bowls, serving trays, wicker baskets. So many things for a small family. Pearl admires the large white oven. She could bake a fine loaf of bread in there, show them who she really is, not some unfortunate prisoner, but a woman of skill.

Americans are oddly trusting of strangers. Pearl could walk right out of this house, and who'd stop her? However, she'd only get lost and draw more suspicion to her case.

She leaves her plate, but washes out her cup—after all, Alma said nothing about not washing the cup—then returns to her room. Pearl opens the window; the horrible golden lizard has moved, thank God. The chair is small for a grown woman, so she sits on the edge of her neatly made bed, trying not to muss the covers.

A wire to her sisters would cost fifty, maybe sixty cents. Pearl looks for something to sell, what might not be missed. But she's no thief, she wouldn't really . . . unless she was desperate. She could mail her sisters a letter. No one could begrudge her the cost of a stamp.

Pearl stretches out on her bed. Perhaps Anderson will grill her further, accuse her again of being a *zonah*. Her fingers feel itchy, restless. She isn't used to idleness. At least her cotton dress is comfortable. Ugly, but loose and ample. What will happen to her? Her head is aching.

At lunchtime, Alma knocks again. She's holding a small leather notebook and a pencil. "This isn't a jail," she says with her hand on her hip. It's strange for Pearl to hear such an American-looking woman speaking Yiddish. "It gets so hot up here, especially when the sun shifts to the front of the house. Why not go for a walk?"

Pearl's confused. Isn't she a prisoner? "Do you want me to walk?" she asks.

"What do you want to do?"

What's the right answer? "I'll wait for the rabbi to come home," says Pearl.

Alma hesitates, then says, "All right. Come get lunch."

As Alma goes to her room to prepare for a Sisterhood luncheon, Pearl is served in the kitchen by Grace, the maid, a slender woman with straw-colored hair who wears a white apron and a lacy white headpiece to match. Pearl has little hope for the meal. Someone so thin can't be a good cook.

Grace's voice is kind and cheerful, though she speaks in the thick accent of the region, which Pearl can't understand. Lunch is a white-bread sandwich filled with chopped eggs mixed with mayonnaise, celery, and green onion. The sandwich is cut into triangles. Pearl inspects them for nonkosher meat and finds none. The soft bread compresses under her fingers and tastes like paper. The creamy filling oozes out, falling onto her plate in soft puddles. Unlike in Havana, no fruit is served after the meal.

While Pearl's eating, Grace sets the dining-room table for dinner. Pearl wishes she could join in, maybe earn some money. Alma stops in the kitchen to say farewell, wearing a lovely off-the-rack dress. A shocking thought occurs to Pearl: What if Alma can't sew? In any case, it's a fine dress, cool and slim, and it complements her short hair. Funny how Alma looks as if at any moment she could go dancing.

Pearl asks, "Aren't there any chores I could help with? Or sewing? I could make the breakfast in the morning, so Grace doesn't have to do it the night before."

"Don't bother," says Alma, fussing with a glove. "I waste a good part of my day kibbitzing at silly Sisterhood luncheons. That's time when I could be writing."

What a lot of writing Alma does, thinks Pearl.

"Now it's too hot to stay in your room," says Alma. "Try the porch. Grace will give you lemonade." She sounds impatient. Pearl's sorry she's such trouble to her.

As instructed, Pearl goes to the front porch. There are rocking chairs, but she's afraid to sit in them. She leans against the railing and watches the street, empty except for a crowing rooster chasing away a gray gull—and a small band of children who take turns riding the back of a goat. This idleness, the waiting, they infuriate her.

Grace brings the lemonade. Pearl has heard of this drink but never tried it before. The liquid gleams yellow in its cool glass, beaded with moisture, and is served with a chip of ice and a thin slice of lemon. The ice and lemon brush against Pearl's lip as she takes her first sunny taste of the drink, sweet and tart, cool, crisp. She holds it up to admire the color, then takes a second, longer drink. It's marvelous, lemonade. She laughs in her deep appreciation of it. Setting down her drink, she pulls up a rocking chair and braces it with her hands. She sits down carefully and begins to rock, slowly at first, then with vigor. It's lovely! She grabs her lemonade, presses it to her cheek to feel its coolness, then drinks and rocks, which makes her sleepy.

Pearl goes upstairs and naps. She's woken up by the two Singer girls, who barge in arguing over a silk bag of clicking marbles. The children seem very independent. Maybe the parents raised them to be this way. The older girl, Hannah, shows Pearl her doll collection. One of the dolls wears a diaper, and Pearl is given the task of changing it. She does it expertly, as she used to for Frieda. Hannah's English sounds slower and clearer than what the adults speak, and Pearl can understand it better.

Rebecca, the younger girl, dark-haired and dark-eyed, sits on the floor and leans on her chubby elbows as Hannah talks. Apropos of nothing, Rebecca asks Pearl, "Where's your mama?"

Pearl finishes changing the diaper and returns the doll to Hannah. "I have no mama," she says slowly, thinking out each English word. "Mama is died."

"Dead," says Hannah, tugging out her doll's hair. "Mama is dead, not died."

"Dead," Pearl repeats and feels the weight of the word. Mama is dead.

Rebecca tugs on Pearl's wrist, and the girl's touch feels startling, intimate. She asks, "How old are you? I'm six."

"I have twenty-seven years," says Pearl, though she's actually twenty-eight.

Rebecca shrugs. "I'm six," she repeats.

They hear the front door open downstairs. "Girls?" It's Alma, home from her luncheon. Soon she appears in the doorway, fanning her neck and face with a rumpled pink hat. "Quit bothering our guest," she says in English. She then switches to Yiddish for

Pearl. "I'm afraid my daughters are wild as Indians. It's their father. He indulges them."

So in America, Indians are called wild, Pearl thinks. Where I'm from, it's the Cossacks who are called wild.

Hannah drags her feet toward the hall, but Rebecca stays where she is on the floor and asks Pearl, "Why are you wearing Mama's old housedress?"

"Hush, you!" says Alma. "I'm sorry," she says in English, shakes her head, then apologizes in Yiddish.

"It's nothing," says Pearl.

"You've been here all day?" Alma asks. She pulls Rebecca into the hall. "Your choice. Supper's promptly at six." She pauses at the doorstep. "The last one who slept in this room, only it was a man in this case, he was also afraid at first to go out, but then he'd walk for hours. Once, we thought he drowned in the Gulf. It was a shame he had to go back. He spoke English so beautifully."

"There have been many others here?" Pearl asked.

"Oh, yes," says Alma. "My husband's always bringing in strays. Thankfully, he doesn't care for animals or we'd be overrun."

"What happened to them? The others?"

Alma pauses. "They were sent back to Cuba. Mostly. I can't remember all the details. Ask my husband later. But they were very nice people, all of them."

Pearl absorbs this information, then asks, "Could I ask, is it possible . . ."

"Yes?" Alma's eyes widen with interest. "Tell me, please."

"May I see the shul?"

"Right now? Well, I suppose." She switches to English again. "Girls, what did I tell you about stomping in the house? Go play in the garden or something." Then she invites Pearl to follow her downstairs.

Pearl and Alma exit the house and walk to the front door of the sanctuary, which swings open with a screech.

The large, plain room has wooden floors and pews, as well as wood-lined walls that give way to stucco. The left side wall is slit with tall windows that face the street, letting in the glaring tropical light. Donors' names are carved into the ark's wooden frame, above which, an eternal light hangs, unlit.

"That bulb's out again," says Alma.

She sits in the front pew and Pearl sits there also. It's a proper shul, she thinks.

"Our shul in Memphis, where we used to live, was far grander," says Alma, her voice echoing in the empty room. "But there Ezekiel was only the junior rabbi."

"Ezekiel?" Pearl repeats doubtfully.

"My husband. That's his first name. Ezekiel Singer." Alma dabs the corner of her eye with her pinky. "I miss Memphis. The girls seem happy enough, but the people here! Oh, they're friendly, but they don't read or know anything about the arts. I'll bet they all voted for that dull old Warren and his 'Return to Normalcy' promises. In this town, I stick out like a sore thumb, Wilsonian that I am."

Pearl hasn't been listening too closely. "Who is Warren?"

"Only the president, my dear, of these United States. Warren Harding."

"And you call him by his first name?" says Pearl.

"I've called him far worse, believe me."

"You think if I wrote to him, he might help a girl like me?"

"That crook?" says Alma. "He's too busy lining his own pockets."

Though Pearl knows people here are allowed to talk this way about the government, it feels unnatural, dangerous, especially for a woman. She remembers rushing to hang the little Russian flags on their door for the tsar's birthday. Otherwise you'd be arrested.

Now look where the tsar is, and where Pearl is. Who's luckier?

"What does your husband think of this president?" Pearl asks.

"We share exactly the same values. Otherwise I wouldn't have married the man."

An interesting response. Pearl makes a note to watch the two Singers together, to see if she can observe their same values.

She and Alma sit for a while in the quiet, shady synagogue, which feels eerie without people. "Is there a service tonight?" Pearl asks in a soft voice.

"No, only on *Shabbes*. Try rounding up ten men to do anything in this town, even build a fence. Everyone here's so busy looking after their own interests."

"And what does the rabbi do when it's not *Shabbes*?"

"Oh, lots of things." Alma picks at one of her cuticles. "I wish I had an ounce of his energy. He goes around, you know, helping, giving advice. He travels to Cuba too. To lead services. Or advise on Jewish laws. And he can slaughter meat and perform a bris."

"Could he help me?" says Pearl.

Alma looks at her as if for the first time. "Can I ask you something?" she says. "In Havana, was your life . . . I mean, it can't be easy down there."

"It wasn't easy. I had to work hard to earn my living." Then she adds, "Not the bad thing they accuse me of doing. I made hats."

"Yes, yes, of course," says Alma. "I wasn't suggesting something awful."

"I worked hard. Just like you, you work too," says Pearl, "as a secretary."

"What makes you think I work as a secretary?"

"With your writing. For the synagogue."

Alma laughs. "No, no. I write for myself. I mean, I'm a poet. I write poems."

"Religious poems?" Pearl asks.

"Not in the traditional sense. But I write about beauty, nature, the ocean. There's more than one way to worship God. There's Ezekiel's way and my way. They complement each other. You can pray or you can honor the glory of what God has created for us here on earth. You see?"

Pearl's intrigued. A way to believe without doubt. These modern women, like Alma and Mrs. Steinberg, they certainly feel very free to tailor their religion to their personal tastes. But if you can dictate to God, then what is God for?

"And you earn money for these poems?" Pearl asks.

"No," says Alma. "But two of them were published in the *Key West Citizen*."

"They should pay you," says Pearl. "It's your work; you should be paid for it."

"You don't understand. It's my art." Alma looks confused, though she says Pearl's the one who doesn't understand. "Maybe you're tired. Do you want to go back to your room to rest?"

"No, I don't," says Pearl. "I want to stay here longer."

So Alma leaves her the key, tells her to lock up when she's finished. When she's gone, Pearl feels more at ease. She curls up in her pew, watching the dust motes dance in the rays now streaming through the windows. This place is much plainer than their shul in Turya, which had beautifully carved wood-framed windows, and a Holy Ark painted with the symbols of Israel's twelve tribes. Sometimes on *Shabbes*, Pearl would let her mind wander, staring at that ark from the women's balcony.

Before the war, everyone lived for *Shabbes*. Friday mornings, the air filled with the yeasty scent of challah baking. In the afternoon there were the earthy smells of bean stew, or chickens roasting in their own fat. The synagogue sexton walked down the street, singing in a raspy voice, "Come, my beloved, to greet the Sabbath bride" and rapping a stick against people's windows to announce the arrival of sunset.

Rivka and Elka, wearing white shawls over their heads, came over early to help with the food. Their table sagged with the weight of it: stuffed cabbage, poppy seed cake, gooseberry jam, warm schmaltz, and cold pickled horseradish, everything made as Mother taught them to do. Looking at it all, Pearl felt thrilled and exhausted.

Avram came in, tripping over the threshold with Father behind him, mocking his clumsiness. Their non-Jewish neighbor stopped by to feed the fire so it would last the night. They gave him a square of noodle pudding and a heel of challah, which he called Christmas bread.

They sang the prayers after meals at the top of their voices, Father's voice loudest of all. The beauty of his singing made her ashamed of her own voice, which she can barely remember using. She remembers more of what they ate than what she sang.

Maybe Alma is right, and there is more than one way to worship God. Prayers are one way, Father's way. The making and hosting of a Shabbat dinner, that's another way, Pearl's way. Perhaps a better way. Because prayers were made up of words, and words could be twisted by the spirit of evil, used against you.

All those Friday nights, she thinks, I was worshipping and never realized.

○

THAT EVENING, RABBI Singer sits at the head of the table, a tight fit in the small dining room. Pearl is careful not to scratch the wall when she pushes her chair back. Grace serves them quickly, anxious for them to finish so she can wash the dishes and go home to her own family. Pearl wishes she understood, what exactly is left for Alma to do?

Today is not *Shabbes*, yet the table is covered in a linen cloth and they light candles. To drink, they have delicious lemonade, and to eat there's a real roast chicken, its skin beautifully speckled with golden brown spots. The rabbi assures Pearl it's kosher. She sinks her teeth into a chicken leg, savoring the taste, the fleshy texture. She hasn't had meat in a year, and she sucks every bit off the bone. Hannah and Rebecca watch, fascinated. They fail to finish their food, but no one scolds them.

"Go on, have more," says the rabbi, smiling at her enjoyment in a way that Pearl dislikes. However, she can't turn down chicken. She takes two more pieces, and by the end of the meal, her stomach is aching. Let it ache. This is heaven.

"This tablecloth was my mother's," says Alma, smoothing out the linen.

Pearl squeezes the cloth. "Beautiful. The material has a good body to it."

"Growing up, our home was always filled with the loveliest things," says Alma.

"So you keep reminding me," says the rabbi, teasing her. "Maybe you'd rather have married an oil tycoon."

"What do I need with an oil tycoon?" Alma says. "He'd probably leave greasy, oily footprints all over my living room rug. I'm happy with my Ezekiel."

"That's my girl," says the rabbi and blows her a kiss, which Alma pretends to catch and cradle to her cheek. Pearl smiles shyly, enjoying the company and the feeling of a full belly. They seem like a happy family, she decides. This is a good life.

After dinner, Alma takes the girls out onto the porch, and Pearl asks to speak to the rabbi. He invites her into the parlor, where he settles into a velvet chair and crosses his legs, revealing his bright red socks. Pearl sits on a loveseat with a low cushion, probably where the girls sit when the family convenes in this room. An electric chandelier shines overhead, its glass bowl filled with dead insects. The chicken from dinner sits heavy in her stomach.

"I'm no bad girl," says Pearl. "I can prove it to you, and to the magistrate."

The rabbi waves his hand. "Unnecessary. I paid a call on the magistrate today. He's a friend." He waits for Pearl to take in this information, as if he wants her to be impressed. "Justice moves slowly in Key West. Everything moves slowly here. In short, you'll be our guest a bit longer, maybe another week. Hard to say. So settle in. Alma says you're afraid to leave your room. Don't be. It's a small island. You can't get lost."

Oh, yes I can, thinks Pearl. I can get lost crossing the street.

"Since you have to stay in Key West, why not have a look around, get to know the place?"

Pearl frowns. She doesn't want a tour, just to get on with her life, be free to go her own way, make her own decisions about how she works, where she sleeps, when and what she eats. "Could I have more lemonade?" she asks.

"Surely," says the rabbi, yet remains seated instead of getting it for her. "You know, Pearl, if you truly want to immigrate to this country, there are ways."

"How?" she asks.

He searches her eyes, holds the moment. Is it a test? He opens his mouth, pauses, then asks, "What about miracles, prayer? Don't you believe in God?"

Pearl thinks, why do people in the Americas keep asking me this question?

Rabbi Singer rises, indicating their meeting is over, then takes Pearl to the kitchen and pours her a glass of lemonade. He smiles as she gulps it all down in one go. Under his gaze, she feels like a trained dancing bear.

"Let me show you something," he tells Pearl. "Follow me."

He leads her out to the garden, where it's so dark she can hardly see her own hands. The dirt under her feet feels gritty and unsteady; she might fall at any second. Why are they here? He stops at a tree with a rough thatchy bark. "Look," he says, plunging his hand into the leaves. "Do you see?"

In the darkness, she can't see anything, not at first. But then she makes out a white flower glowing in the dark, its pointed petals extended like grasping fingers. "They only bloom at night," Rabbi Singer says. "In the morning, the flower will be gone." He reaches across her body for one.

"Don't pick it," she says, but he plucks the bloom anyway, and gives it to her to smell. The fragrance is faint, like a shy cousin of jasmine.

"If you want to live in America, there are ways," he says in a low voice, his lips uncomfortably close to her ear. The hairs on her neck bristle as she senses the presence of his body creep nearer. The chicken from dinner is moving in her stomach, threatening to rise back up her throat. What's happening? Maybe he's being friendly. Please let it be so. He is a rabbi. A rabbi in a fancy modern hat, with a fashionably thin mustache, and those red socks. His fingers brush her arm. Possibly by accident. Or if on purpose, perhaps not to harm. Some men are like this. They don't do anything, only want their masculine presence to be felt. But there are other men who always look to press their advantage. Like the Polish soldier. When he saw an opportunity, he took it.

The rabbi murmurs softly, "Pearl, you're a handsome girl. You know that? The kind of girl men want to do favors for."

She smells his breath, feels it warm her cheek. Maybe he expects her to be flattered? Why won't he say clearly what he means? Wishing she had a stick or something heavy to throw, she folds her arms over her chest. They're alone in this yard. Alma's on the other side of the house, where Pearl's screams would only sound like one of these seagulls crying all the time. She could run. Where to? Her ears are flushed. Her heart's beating harder. The rabbi murmurs something else, but she's too distracted to listen. What can she do to stop it from happening again? What can she do now that she was unable to do with the Polish soldier? If he is trying to do what that soldier did.

Maybe he's going to offer her a deal. If she does what he wants, he'll help her. That soldier who took what he wanted gave her nothing. If she gives the rabbi her body, he might give her America. But if she agrees, then she'd enter America as a victim, his victim. On those terms, she'd rather stay in Cuba.

"My father is also a singer," Pearl blurts out, so loud she's shouting.

"What?" he asks.

She looks over her shoulder, hoping Alma might come and interrupt them. "Your name is Singer," she says quickly, panting. "My father, he's a singer too, a cantor. I am a cantor's daughter. He can write you, to prove who I am."

Her eyes are adjusting more fully to the dark, and she sees the mercurial expression on his face as he watches her, waiting before he answers. She knows now: What happened before will not repeat itself. He won't force her. She's stopped him.

"Oh, I have no doubt of who you are. You've made that quite clear," he says in a wry voice, then steps aside so they can return to the house.

TEN

IN THE MORNING, WHILE SEARCHING FOR A HAIRBRUSH, Pearl opens a drawer and a tiny brown lizard crawls out, looks up in terror, and darts away. A day earlier, she might have recoiled in fear, but today she stands her ground, watches the lizard dissolve under a door jamb. She takes out the brush and closes the drawer.

The animals might just be the ones who are really in charge of Key West. The gulls with their anguished cries, chickens pecking dirt, lizards slinking up telephone poles, dogs roaming at will across invisible property lines drawn by men.

But people are also animals. Pearl's had a rotten sleep, thinking of the rabbi in the garden. How lucky that she'd mentioned her father being a singer. What if she hadn't thought of saying those words?

She goes down to the kitchen, where that dreadful flower the rabbi picked shrivels in a water glass. Blushing, she sits with the girls and Alma, who's reading a book. Put down your reading, Alma, thinks Pearl. Look around you.

Or do you know already? Has he done this before with other young women and you pretend not to know?

"Is there anyone who needs work done?" Pearl asks while stirring salt and butter into her grits. She's learned how to eat them by watching the girls. "Maybe help with cleaning, or sewing, or minding children. Someone in your congregation?"

Alma lowers her book. "You need money, Pearl?"

Pearl looks down at her cereal, which she's still stirring. "I'm not used to sitting all day like a queen. I like to work."

"How much do you need?" Alma asks.

"Only enough for a telegram to New York."

"Who do you know in New York?"

Pearl lets go of her spoon, falls silent.

Alma tells Hannah to fetch her purse. She gives Pearl a whole dollar. "I wish you'd trust me," she says, handing over the heavy coin. "If there's something you need, just ask. How can I know what you need if you don't tell me?"

"Thank you." Pearl puts the money in her pocket.

Alma gives Pearl directions to the telegraph office on Greene Street. "Shall I show you on a map? Or I could walk you there."

"I haven't decided when I will go, and I don't want to interfere with your day," Pearl says. "It's no emergency." She looks Alma in the eye, trying to read what's in this woman's heart, but it's impossible. Pearl tries to imagine being married to such a man as the rabbi. She might never know what such a husband was doing. How could she trust him, or any man?

And here she thought they were so happy together.

Pearl waits until breakfast is finished, the girls are sent to school, and Alma goes upstairs to do something, Pearl's not sure what, but doesn't care. She hurries out the back door, almost knocking into Grace.

The back alley is littered with loose boards, twisted blackened vines dangling from trees, and stinking trash barrels. A large insect with transparent wings buzzes in Pearl's face. She waves it away, then faces down a hissing gray cat with its back arched. Pearl backs up against a fence, grabs a broken fishing pole on the ground, and pokes it at the cat, who scampers off, squeezes under a fence. Feeling stronger, Pearl grips the pole until she reaches the end of the alley. She's saved herself again. Now and last night.

Pearl tosses aside the pole she's been carrying. She doesn't need it anymore.

The houses in Key West strike her as unfriendly looking, with their sharp right angles, the symmetry of their doors and windows, and closed shutters. The gardens smell of rotting honeysuckle and are cluttered with coconut husks and dried palms.

What's wrong with the people here, who hide in their dark parlors instead of sweeping away the leaves in front of their homes? Don't they have any pride?

She repeats the directions to herself several times, and in a few minutes she arrives at Duval Street. So there, she thinks. That wasn't hard.

After the rabbi's sleepy street, Duval seems cosmopolitan, busy with sailors and housewives carrying glossy black-leather purses. These women seem bland, with flat, pale faces, especially compared to the heavily made up and perfumed women in Havana. Even the flowers printed on their dresses don't appear fully bloomed. Pearl can't imagine becoming friends with these women, or becoming one herself. They look as if they keep too many secrets. The women in Havana always let you know what they're thinking—to a fault. And as for Turya, well, Turya's too small for anyone to keep secrets.

How naïve I was to trust that I kept my secret, Pearl thinks. It's quite possible that Frieda has known for a while the truth of what that soldier did. Frieda and who else?

Pearl shuts this unhappy question out of her mind and stays on the shady side of the street, eyeing with equal hunger a shop window displaying chocolates and another with smart-looking dresses at reduced prices. She finds the International Ocean Telegraph and Cable Office on that street called Greene, which like so many English words has a mysteriously unpronounced "e" at the end. Further down the block is the towering red roofline of the Customs House. Perhaps Anderson is there now torturing other women.

The telegram to New York costs forty-five cents, cheaper than she'd expected. Pearl keeps her message brief:

> IN KEY VEST STOP MUST RETURN CUBA
> STOP DONT GO NEW YORK STOP WILL
> SEND LETER STOP

As Pearl leaves the office, Alma's change clinks in her pocket. She could buy a snack, but she's spent enough of other people's money today. To avoid temptation, she passes Duval and heads east, the direction of the port and the train station. She might go there, sneak aboard a boat or the train, or walk on the tracks all the way to America.

Sneaking onto a train or a boat? What nonsense. She'd be caught in two seconds. No, she needs a real plan, not some silly dream.

Then she spots Rabbi Singer standing outside a grocery, talking and laughing with the owner, a Chinaman in a grocer's apron. Hiding behind a tree, Pearl watches the grocer take a stack of dollar bills from his pocket and hand them to the rabbi. What in the world? The two men go into the grocery, and she creeps closer. Through the window, she watches the rabbi follow the owner into the back. Maybe she shouldn't, but her curiosity gets the better of her, so she approaches the entrance, peers into the empty store, all those shelves lined with cans. You'd never go hungry here—unless you lacked a can opener. A basket of red-cheeked apples sits next to the register. She imagines biting into their crisp white flesh. Go on, Pearl, take one.

She's in enough trouble. Why borrow more?

Backing away, she almost runs into a policeman patrolling the block. She rushes past him, turns down a street she doesn't recognize. Oddly, it happens to be the one where the synagogue is located. Stepping onto the porch, she lets out a deep, relieved sigh.

That evening, Alma's busy with Grace in the kitchen. Pearl offers yet again to help, but Alma ushers her out to the sitting room, where she's waiting for dinner when the rabbi comes in. "Well, there," he says as he shuffles through a few bits of mail Alma left for him, "did you have a fine day?"

"I walked," she says in a small voice. It's the first time they've spoken since their encounter in the garden, and she feels stronger, not just because of her resistance last night but also because she possesses this bit of knowledge of his whereabouts today.

"That's good. Walking's good," he says, staring down his nose at one of his letters. He tosses it aside and reads another.

"I thought I saw you," she adds and watches his reaction. "At a grocery."

He puts down his mail and faces her with a puzzled look. "What would I do in a grocery?" he says, his nose wrinkled as if she's farted. "Grace does our shopping."

Rabbi Singer must be lying. What is he hiding? What was all that money for?

"I thought it was you," she says.

"Obviously not." He squeezes past her to go upstairs. "Now pray excuse me while I wash up before supper."

His face, his voice, they seemed impressively calm. But what was he doing in that grocery store? Who is this man? What's his scheme? What does he want from her?

Maybe it's better not to know the answer, to keep her distance.

○

IN ALL HER travels, Pearl's learned the importance of establishing a routine and sticking to it with a religious fervor. After breakfast, Pearl follows Grace around the house, using a mix of sign language and broken English to communicate her desire to help with the chores, as if good behavior can earn her some kind of reprieve.

Thankfully the egg sandwiches do not make a return appearance at lunch. Afternoons she spends on the porch practicing English with a children's book, until the girls get home and pull her into their games.

Those girls don't realize how easy their lives are.

One afternoon, the girls are giving Pearl a spelling lesson on the bedroom floor—they love to play school. They're the teachers, and Pearl is their underachieving student. For Pearl it's no game. She's hungry to learn English, not to waste her time in Key West, so she works hard at her spelling. Too bad the girls' lessons aren't always practical. As Pearl struggles to write "chrysanthemum," she sees Rabbi Singer in the doorway, studying her. She thinks of him laughing outside the grocery store, and in the garden, holding that sickening night-blooming flower.

"Any news?" she asks, as always.

He pauses, then says, "No, nothing new."

Pearl resolves never to be alone with him. After eating dinner with the family, she stays at Alma's side, sitting with the children. She asks Alma to read aloud her poems, to keep her close until it's time for bed.

Alma asks why she's interested, says she wouldn't understand the English.

"I just like the sound," says Pearl. It's true, she appreciates the sound of it, like a song, this woman making music with words. I will never have this easy a life, Pearl thinks. But such a life, or at least Alma's life, comes at a cost.

Rabbi Singer watches them with his enigmatic curled-lip smiles. His words and actions are unfailingly polite, and Pearl wants to believe she's misremembered that night in the garden, that it was a dream. In Turya, she might make herself believe it, but after Havana, and after Key West, she can no longer swallow fairy tales.

On *Shabbes*, they attend services. As in Cuba and Russia, the women stand in back, including Alma, singing with a beatific, contented expression on her face. Occasionally, she winks or clasps hands with an acquaintance. Just the opposite of Mrs. Steinberg and her grumbling about why women must be safely hidden from view.

Pearl avoids looking at the rabbi by focusing on the prayer book, printed with the same Hebrew prayers she recited in Turya, sung to the same melodies Father sang. Here, the devil and his doubts seem feeble, and fate's randomness is impossible.

The service ends and with it the welcome sense of surety it briefly brought. The congregants spill out onto the front steps, where Alma greets them with outstretched hands. They speak a flat kind of English, swallowing their vowels and consonants. Grace doles out paper cups of wine made from a brick of mashed grape pulp soaked in water, government-approved for religious rituals. You could drink it by the barrel and feel nothing. So far, Pearl thinks, America is like this wine I'm sipping.

She's approached by an old woman who was born in a town upriver from Turya. "The rabbi told me about you," the woman says. "Isn't he marvelous? Everyone is his friend and he's everyone's friend."

Could he be *my* friend, Pearl thinks. "His wife is very kind," she says.

"As are their two sweet girls. Maybe next they'll have a boy."

"Aha," says Pearl. "So she is in the family way? I didn't know."

The woman smiles wisely. "She hides everything, that one. If she played cards, she'd be a life master."

"And the rabbi? What kind of card player would he be?"

The woman squints at Pearl. "*Gut Shabbes*," she says, drifting away.

○

THE NEXT AFTERNOON, Rabbi Singer makes a shiva call while Alma and the girls attend a birthday picnic for a classmate, so Pearl goes out, walking the grid of streets that in every direction end at the water, trapping her on all sides.

Sunday afternoon strolling is a popular pastime. Pearl sees families, old men, sailors, and a lone attractive girl wearing a bathing costume, a blue sleeveless outfit that exposes her arms and legs. She has on a bathing cap, and she's slung a towel over one of her tanned shoulders, lightly dotted with freckles, like flower buds in a spring field.

Pearl follows the slender young woman, hurrying to keep up with her long, confident strides. The woman's arms swing freely to match the swing in her hips and long legs. As if it's normal to walk in public in her bathing costume. She occasionally dabs her damp cheeks with the ends of her towel.

The woman turns sharply and walks up the steps of a one-story white house with a broken swing on its front porch. After removing her cap, she shakes out her sandy blond hair, goes inside, and closes the front door behind her with a loud slam.

Pearl looks around. She's on her own, in an unfamiliar neighborhood. She searches for some landmark to guide her and finds none. Even the streets, which in Key West all look alike, seem to be following a different direction.

Then it starts to rain.

She walks for an hour, turning around and around in the wet, with rain in her eyes, her hair, dripping inside her collar—that's what she gets for following that pretty girl in her bathing costume. When Pearl reaches the synagogue, her dress is so drenched, she can wring water out of the hem.

The girls rub her hair and skin with towels. Alma offers Pearl several dresses, but none fit. "Do you have anything else?" Pearl asks, shivering in her underclothing.

"Just Ezekiel's clothes."

She shrugs. "I'll try it." So while her dress is drying, they give her one of the Rabbi's white shirts and a pair of dark pants. The clothes fit perfectly, and the girls laugh.

"Oh, Pearl," says Alma, also laughing. "You're a handsome man. I'm going to take your picture. Here, let's give her a tie too." They do, and then bring a mirror to show Pearl the disappointing, depressing truth: She really is a handsome man.

But I want to be beautiful, she thinks. Or if not, then handsome might do.

○

ON PEARL'S ELEVENTH day in Key West, the rabbi comes home with her travel bag and news: The magistrate's investigation has concluded. She'll be sent back to Havana.

Everyone seems sorry about it. The girls pout through the meal as though their favorite new toy has been confiscated. Grace prepares a small parcel of food for Pearl to take on the trip. After dinner, Alma touches Pearl's shoulder, says, "God bless you," and gives her the photo in the shirt and tie on that rainy day. On the back, Alma has written a poem in English:

She marches forward, determined to make her way
Her head of pitch-black curls held manly high
Come what tribulations and vexing troubles may
This proud daughter of Esther will someday fly

No one has written a poem about Pearl before, and it makes her dizzy, being the heroine of someone's writing. She stares into her own eyes in the photo, and she's surprised by the haunted expression she finds there.

The rabbi asks Pearl for a word in the parlor. She looks at

Alma, silently inviting her to join them, but Alma follows the girls outside, to the porch. At least they're close enough to hear if Pearl calls for help.

Pearl sits on the red velvet divan. The rabbi, in the hard chair opposite, says, "You're a million miles away. A girl with the worries of an old woman."

"A girl?" cries Pearl. "I'm not a girl, or even a young woman." Her face is hard. Her hands are dry, worn out. Her neck and hips and middle are thick.

"One day, when you have a family of your own, you'll see things differently."

Pearl shakes her head. She scratches a mosquito bite on her hand, then digs at the red welt with her nail to stop the itching, but only succeeds in hurting herself badly.

"You have your whole life ahead of you." He offers a handkerchief from his pocket. The fabric droops teasingly from his fingers. She shakes her head, sniffs a few times, blinks back tears. "Pearl?"

"No, I have nothing ahead of me, only bad luck. Something must be wrong with me, something broken that can't be repaired," she says in a hoarse voice, forgetting she's speaking to a rabbi, though with this one, it's easy to forget. She's fighting to avoid making a scene in front of him, to avoid making her meaning too clear.

"Pearl, don't give into despair. That's the devil's voice speaking," says the rabbi. "God is powerful enough to bless anyone. But He desires that first we ask for what we want. You see, I believe our material reality reflects our spiritual state. If we don't have what we want, something is wrong in our hearts."

"You're saying I deserve to suffer?"

"I wouldn't say it in that way. But if it teaches us something, then what you call suffering is only a temporary setback. Like Jonah in the belly of the whale."

"Or you and me in your dark garden," she bursts out, not meaning to. It just happened.

"Oh, Pearl," says the rabbi in a sad voice. "I've only been trying to help you."

"Have you?" Pearl fingers the seat cushion, tries to calm her anxious breathing. Why would he want to help her?

The rabbi gets up, goes over to close the door, and then the window, through which she can see Alma and the girls on the porch pointing at the stars. He sits down again and lowers his voice. "I invited you to the garden that night to tell you that I travel to Cuba and I have friends there who can help you, give you advice about getting to America. Even without papers. Are you interested?"

"Of course I am. But what do I have to do?"

He sits forward in his chair. "First, I must clear up any mis-understandings about that night. Did I touch or harm you in any way?" Before she can answer, he continues, "No, I did not. Oh, don't apologize. I couldn't blame you for thinking otherwise. I know how women like you have suffered. You might imagine all sorts of things."

"Maybe you're right." Pearl knows he's not, but men get angry if you correct them. And she wants his help. If he's willing to provide it.

"You're likely wondering why I took you to the garden to tell you this, so I'll explain. It's because what I had to say, what I'm saying now, these are secrets. Things not for Alma to get mixed up with. I would have explained this to you at the time, but I sensed you were feeling upset, so I stopped the conversation. But since you're calmer now, I can tell you more. Listen closely." He tells her an address in Havana. "Don't write it, just remember it." He repeats the address. "And you'll need money."

"I haven't got a penny," Pearl says.

"Can't someone lend it to you? Some family back in the Old Country?"

"They gave me all they could to get me here," she says.

"Anyone else you could ask?"

She pauses. At this point, why not tell him? "I have sisters in New York."

"Do they have a telephone? If so, you can use my phone to call them."

"That's at least two dollars," she says.

"More like four," he says. "Let me worry about the cost. You go on. Call them."

She eyes him suspiciously. He sounds kind tonight. Is he helping her to make up for his behavior in the garden? Because she saw him accept money from a Chinese grocer? Or simply to be nice? She's afraid to ask him directly about his motive. Maybe he is being nice. As a rabbi should be. It's true that since that episode in the garden, nothing else has happened. Didn't that woman from the shul say he was everyone's friend?

Pearl's father says when you're everyone's friend, you're no one's friend.

Ultimately, the prospect of hearing her sisters' voices, it's too much to resist.

"When could I telephone?" she asks.

"Would right now be amenable?" He points her to the phone, resting lifeless on a table beside the piano, next to a framed picture of the rabbi and Alma in a loving pose. She stares down the black phone as if it's a small dog.

"Can you tell the operator the number?" she asks. "My English is not so good."

He picks up the receiver, tells the operator the exchange, plus the number in New York, then hands Pearl the telephone. "Speak into this part."

"I know." She bends over it to get close.

"You can sit down," says the rabbi.

"Oh, yes." She sits on the edge of a chair and straightens her dress, which seems shabby for a long-distance telephone call. Rabbi Singer sits too, puts on a pair of spectacles, and picks up the *Key West Citizen*. Pearl shifts her chair around, with her back to the rabbi. The line rings several times before a woman answers.

"Basha?" Pearl says. "Frieda? Where are you?"

The woman says something in English, and Pearl's confused. She asks again, and then there's a long silence. "I don't understand," she tells the rabbi.

"Wait," he advises. "Maybe they're looking for her."

Another woman comes on. This one speaks Yiddish. Pearl explains she's looking for her sister, and the woman says to wait a moment. What kind of a house is this? How many women live there?

She waits several costly seconds, maybe a minute, before she hears Basha's precise, reedy voice for the first time in years through the earpiece. "Pearl, where are you? Are you in trouble?" It's Basha all right. She sounds so far away.

"Basha?" says Pearl, though of course it's her, and she starts crying.

"We got your telegram. We were so worried," says Basha.

"I'm fine. I'm in Florida now. But I have to go back to Havana tomorrow."

"What? Pearl, you have to speak loud."

"They're sending me back to Havana. I'll write you from there." The rabbi's watching her over his glasses, perched on the end of his nose. "I can't talk for very long."

"Wait a minute, Pearl. I have Frieda next to me."

After a pause, Frieda comes on. "Pearl? I don't know what to say."

"Say nothing," says Pearl, choking out the words through more tears. The earpiece feels hard and cold in her hands. "Or something. Anything."

Frieda pauses before answering. "Listen, do you need money?"

Pearl is about to say no, sister, your money is no good with me. But instead what comes out is, "Well, do you have any?"

"No . . . but Mendel might. Or he could ask his brother, Ben. Ben has a good job in a grocery and he promises to get Mendel to work there too."

Pearl can't resist a crack. "He has a good job? Maybe you should marry him."

"Ben the Oak? He's only a thousand years old." Frieda sounds worn out. Has she been working too hard? "So is that what you called all the way from Florida to ask me? If I'm going to marry Mendel?"

"No," says Pearl, though she would like to know.

Frieda breathes heavily into the telephone. "Mendel's looking for a better job, to support us both. Also, his aunt and uncle live in Detroit, and he says I could live with them until the wedding. If I did, it would be completely proper."

"An aunt and uncle," Pearl repeats. "That's okay. If you do go to Detroit, stay with them. And if you don't like it, you can always go back to New York."

The rabbi's newspaper rustles between his fingers.

"I can't talk for long," says Pearl. "This call is so expensive. Just don't be in a rush to do anything, Frieda. You're very young."

"Not as young as you think," says Frieda. "You want me to talk to Mendel, to ask him for your money? Or his brother?"

The answer is painful, yet Pearl gives it. "Yes."

The rabbi rises from his chair. Pearl fears he'll take the phone out of her hands, but he's just reaching for some cigarettes.

"Listen, Frieda, I have to go. This call is expensive. Wait for me. I'll find some way to join you. I'll write you from Havana, once I'm settled somewhere. For now, I miss you and I love you. Be well."

"Yes, yes, I miss you too. I love you," says Frieda.

Pearl puts down the receiver and keeps her hands on the black metal stand for a moment, doesn't want to let go. The rabbi tosses the newspaper on a side table. He relaxes in his chair, legs crossed, foot tapping. She feels an urge to grab his foot, grab his whole leg, pull him to the floor, and force him to tell the truth. There's something she's still missing. What does he want from her? "Was it a good talk?" he asks.

"Yes," she says. "A wonderful talk."

"Glad to hear it." He stands up and stretches. "I wish you a good night. You're making an early start tomorrow morning."

She marches upstairs, the voices of her sisters in her ears. Tomorrow she'll leave this house, and then this country. But she won't give up hope.

America, she vows, this is not the last of me.

ELEVEN

WALKING AWAY FROM THE PORT OF HAVANA, PEARL IS struck by how different the city seems since she left, only two weeks ago.

As the American tourists wait for taxis behind her, street musicians compete for change, singing Cuban love songs badly but with gusto. A girl with her hair done up in a crown of braids is selling bouquets of white ginger flowers, Cuban orchids, and yellow morning glories. She runs up to Pearl, repeating "*Fisens, fisens,* flowers, *fisens.*"

"Sorry, I don't have even one cent," says Pearl.

The girl gives her a strange look, then plucks a wilted orchid from a bouquet and hands it to Pearl. For luck, she says. Inhaling the cloying, slightly putrid smell, Pearl continues into the Old Town, passing an old man on the sidewalk, playing a guitar for change. The curving streets shaded by European-style buildings are comforting after the stiff grid of Key West, which feels like some strange dream, not America.

The crossing back from Florida went smoothly. The shipping company, which had to bear the cost of her fare, assigned her a seat in the drawing room and served her a lunch and two cups of tea besides. Now her belly is full, and she feels oddly relaxed, more than she has in weeks. Here in Old Havana, no one is trying to catch her in a lie. In this city of outcasts and desperate people, she fits in. Though she has nothing, the choice of where to go, what to do, it's entirely hers. She's as free as, no, maybe more free than any woman she's known, Mrs. Steinberg, Julieta, even Alma Singer.

The scent of the orchid nauseates her. Pearl tosses it away and heads to the Steinbergs' flat. Where else? She tries to think up an excuse for running out on them. She was sick. She was kidnapped by a white slaver.

No, the best course is honesty. This was her chance at freedom, so she took it, and it didn't work. She betrayed their trust and she's very sorry.

It's a short walk to the Steinbergs' bright yellow building on Muralla Street. Holding her breath, Pearl knocks on that familiar old door and rehearses her lines of apology. But when the door opens and it's Mrs. Steinberg, Pearl has no words.

Mrs. Steinberg draws back in surprise. She stares at Pearl through her glasses, then quickly reaches out her hand, as if Pearl were a friend paying an unexpected social call. "Come in," she says. "We're having an early supper. Won't you stay?"

Flooded with relief, Pearl gives a quick nod.

Mr. Steinberg, frowning at the *Havana Post* at the dinner table, brightens as Pearl walks in. His collar is unbuttoned, and his hair needs combing and more dye at the roots. He's the kind of man whose hair looks unnatural when it isn't dyed. "Look who's back!" he says, draping his newspaper over a chair. "So, Pearl, it didn't work out up north?"

Pearl says in a bitter voice, "They didn't want me."

"Impossible!" says Mr. Steinberg. "Maybe you didn't try hard enough."

Mrs. Steinberg says, "Of course she's trying hard to get to America. Her sister's there, isn't she?"

"No, no," says Mr. Steinberg. "I didn't mean . . ."

"He never means anything. Excuse him, Pearl. He can't help being a man."

As Mrs. Steinberg brings out bowls of bean soup, Mr. Steinberg pulls out a chair for Pearl, who thinks, *This is what kindness is.*

No meat tonight, not even for Mr. Steinberg. With his habitual cheer, he says there's been no replacement for Pearl, not enough work. Maybe things will change when the tourist season picks up again. However, Pearl's welcome to stay in the workshop, now empty. Shortly after Pearl's departure, Julieta left too, to marry a peddler and move to the provinces. "A Jew?" Pearl asks doubtfully. She's relieved to hear that he is.

Mr. Steinberg briefly leaves the room, and Pearl apologizes to Mrs. Steinberg for the advance on her salary, swears she'd planned to pay her back from New York.

"It's nothing," says Mrs. Steinberg. "You must have needed the money badly."

"Thank you," says Pearl. "And thanks to Mr. Steinberg too."

Mrs. Steinberg waves away her thanks. "I never told him. Sometimes in a marriage it's healthier to keep a few secrets." Pearl's still pondering these words when Mrs. Steinberg offers the soup tureen. "More beans? We always have plenty of beans."

Suddenly Pearl breaks out laughing, loudly, freely, and can't stop. Mrs. Steinberg looks confused, then laughs too, in sympathy.

○

SAME OLD WORKSHOP. Same rough tweed curtain, worktables, twin beds. On the washstand, same pitcher with its broken handle. The pitcher is so heavy, maybe it's better that the handle is broken, a good reminder to pick it up with two hands. Remarkable how familiar it all is. This Cuba isn't a home, yet it's more than a hotel. Outside, a teenager teaches her younger sister to dance without music. Pearl leans against the window and exhales deeply as she watches them go around and around.

○

THE OLD DRESSES that Pearl had left behind in the workshop now seem wrong to her, too plain and earnest, the uniform of a scullery maid. She chooses the least offensive of the lot, pairs it with a jacket, then sews on a smart belt and adds a bright ladies' bow tie for a pop of color. She applies some of Julieta's old lipstick to her lips and smudges a bit on her cheeks. Thus attired, she sets forth to find a job.

For several days, she makes a futile circuit of the tailor shops. Her reception is polite, yet always the same. It's the end of November, the low season for tourism, not exactly fall, yet not quite winter, so there's no work. She calls on Mrs. Steinberg's friends, for whom she used to make slacks or do minor alterations, but they're not home, at least not to her. At the last house, she kicks the front gate and bruises her big toe.

On a Tuesday morning, she takes a break from job searching to seek out the address Rabbi Singer gave her, in the Colon neighborhood. Pearl's been warned repeatedly by the Steinbergs, the ladies of the Ezra Society, Julieta, pretty much everyone, to avoid the Colon, especially at night or on weekends, when the streets are packed with American tourists of the seedier sort and Cuban factory workers, who get paid on Fridays and are flush with cash to waste.

In the Colon, cement and dirt crowd out anything green or fresh. A noisy truck pumps petroleum into a sewer to combat mosquitoes. The buildings are plastered with ads for Heinz Soup and Borden's Milk. Also, there's a poster featuring a beaming man saying: "The Doctor gave me scientific treatment for syphilis. Now I'm well—what joy!" Next to him, a sad-looking fellow moans: "A folk healer gave me a home remedy. What a disgrace! I'm paralyzed! If only I went to the doctor."

The address from the rabbi belongs to an aqua-blue building, a cabaret called Gold Dollar with a gold coin painted on the door. It's closed, locked. The windows, covered in metal grilles, are dark. Did Pearl remember the number wrong? Is it a trick? She doesn't think so. Because she's seen the worst of Rabbi Singer, she trusts his word.

A man with a wrinkled, tanned face asks in Spanish what she wants. Pearl says nada, nada, but he persists. "You want narcotic? I know where you can find narcotics." Pearl says nada again, and the man goes on. "No one's there now. They're asleep." He puts his hands under his cheek, closes his eyes. "Why wait for them? I'll help you now."

"People like you only help themselves," says Pearl. "Leave me in peace."

"One minute, señora. No need to feel ashamed," he says, but she hurries away, grabbing the loose folds of her skirt to walk faster.

Pearl's glad to emerge from the Colon at the Prado Avenue, with its pruned palm trees, curled streetlamps, and electric trolleys. She continues walking into Old Havana toward the Women's Home, to eat free soup with strangers. Though she'd prefer to buy her own lunch, to eat alone, she can't afford it. Isidro offers her peanuts without charge, but his charity embarrasses her. She tries to avoid him.

At the Home, a woman from the Ezra Society is giving a tour to a delegation from the Ladies' Lyceum Lawn and Tennis Club. "Here is one of our unfortunate sisters," she says, and the group turns on their bootheels to stare at Pearl. "Without our help, what choice do these women have but to sell their own bodies?"

These bored tradesmen's wives are calling me, a cantor's daughter, unfortunate? Pearl thinks. Maybe she is unfortunate, but not the way they're thinking. "You want to take my picture?" she snaps in Yiddish and brushes past their stunned faces to the dining hall. Today's soup is a salty chicken broth thickened with flour instead of bone marrow. The woman sitting next to her is Hungarian, and like most Hungarians, has rotten breath.

At least she's no longer like these greenhorns sweating in their woolen stockings, sniffing suspiciously at mangoes and chatting excitedly about their plans to get to America, only ninety miles away. Let someone else disappoint them with the truth. As Father says, never give unsolicited advice. People resent it and they don't listen anyway.

Pearl deposits her half-full soup bowl in the kitchen, then walks to the American consulate as she does every day to join the line that never moves, just lengthens as the day progresses. Today, there's a mob at the door, men with dark hair and flowing white tunics. They resemble Cubans from the provinces, but on closer inspection she realizes they're Hindoos. How did they get here? The Hindoos indignantly wave their British passports, demand to be respected as subjects of King George.

Pearl touches the back of her wrist to her sweating cheeks and forehead. She's tired of coming here so often for nothing.

A young man tries to push through the crowd. Pearl guesses he's American because he's wearing a summer suit. At the end of autumn, despite the heat, all Cuban men switch to dark winter suits with stiff collars. Tall and thin, this man towers over these Hindoos shouting for their rights. The Hindoos, perhaps guessing he's a consular official, wave their passports in his face.

Without warning, the door to the consulate opens, and the crowd surges forward. The man in the suit stands aside, then loses his balance, teetering in the open plaza as if drunk. His eyes rolling upward, he reaches out his hand, then trips over his own feet. Pearl rushes to help. Though she isn't strong enough to catch him, she manages to break his fall. Kneeling beside him, she props up his head with the crook of her arm.

"Let me help you," she says, speaking Yiddish on instinct.

Pearl's trying to translate her words into Spanish when the man's eyes flutter open. To her surprise, he speaks Yiddish. "Please, help me go there." He gestures weakly to the portico across the square. "In the shade."

A Jew? she wonders, searching his face. "Can you walk? If I help you?"

It takes him a few painfully slow seconds to answer, "Yes, I think so."

Still amazed to hear an aristocrat like him speak Yiddish, she places his arm around her shoulders and they shuffle to the portico, where she sets him gently against a pillar. "Agua," she calls to a sweaty-cheeked boy skipping by. Immediately, he rushes to a nearby café. Even for a stranger, Cubans will drop whatever they're doing to help.

Pearl fans the man's forehead and flushed cheeks with his hat, an expensive hat lined with silk. Also the fabric of his light summer suit is cut to fit his body, by a skilled tailor. The man's expression strikes her as earnest, kind, and now that she considers it, yes, Jewish. She sees it in the hint of an aquiline nose, the slight fullness of his lips.

He blinks a few times, then looks at her. "What's your name, sweetheart? I couldn't believe it when you spoke to me in Yiddish just now. The last person who spoke to me in Yiddish was my mother." He smirks. "You're not she, are you?"

"Shh," she says. "Just rest."

"Please, I want to know your name." She tells him and he repeats it back to her. "Pearl," he says. "You're a lifesaver. My name's Alexander."

The boy comes back with a waiter in a bow tie, who brings water in a glass. Alexander reaches for it, to gulp it down, but Pearl holds it to his lips, tilting the glass slightly, and says, "Slowly." He obeys. When he's finished half the glass, he thanks the waiter and the boy in Spanish. He tells Pearl in Yiddish, "I've lived here five years. I know how to manage hot weather. But today the heat, it just got to me. I feel foolish."

"You shouldn't," she said. "Your body did this, not you."

The waiter invites them to his café, where it's cool, so they walk there together. Pearl and Alexander sit at a table, under the breeze of an electric fan, while the waiter fetches more water. The boy sits with them. His legs, which don't quite touch the ground, are swinging rapidly. If he were her son, she'd tell him to quit it. The three of them could be an odd sort of family, like three mismatched socks: the smiling brown boy; this tall, fair gentleman; and Pearl, with her dark, intense eyes and her mop of black curls.

"I feel so foolish," Alexander says again in Yiddish. "I had urgent business at the consulate, and I ran there before taking my lunch, but then those men from India were blocking the way in. You know, I've never seen an actual Hindoo before."

"So you don't work in the consulate," says Pearl, disappointed.

"No, I'm in import-export," he says quickly. "And here comes our reward."

The waiter brings them pastries filled with guava preserves, saying, "The sugar is good for the gentleman." He won't accept Alexander's money. The boy devours his pastry in three bites, then runs away, leaving her alone with Alexander. Pearl's grandmother used to warn her never to sit alone next to a strange man, that's how you got pregnant. She laughs at the thought and Alexander asks what's so funny.

"Nothing," she says. "The foolishness of human beings."

Pearl, who's starving, eats her pastry quickly. Alexander, who is more delicate, holds his pastry by his fingertips and nibbles at the edge, as if he'd prefer to use a knife and fork. Pearl feels self-conscious about the crumbs on her lips and cheeks. Blushing, she wipes them away with her fingers before remembering the cloth napkin.

Alexander's neatly combed hair is thinning on top, though his face looks young, smooth, and fresh. He tells Pearl that his parents immigrated from Germany. So that accounts for his fluent Yiddish and elegant Central European demeanor. Between his middle and index fingers, he extends his card, printed with the name Alexander B. Lewis, which hardly sounds like a Jewish name or a German one for that matter. He says he's been in Havana for five years, since America joined the war. "I could not in good conscience kill another man because my country tells me he is evil."

"But the war is over," she says. "You can return home."

"Not me. They'd put me in jail."

"I didn't know they could do that in America." If what he's saying is true, then what is the point of America, if the government there can treat its citizens the same as the tsar did to his subjects in Russia?

"I feel proud," he says, "to have my beliefs tested and know I'm willing to defend them."

Without knowing a thing about it, she's on his side. "Won't you ever go back?"

"It isn't for me to decide. The question is whether they'll have me. For now, I'm comfortable here." He relaxes in his chair. "Tell me your story."

Pearl tells him a version of it, starting with the miserable journey from Danzig and stopping short of Key West. As she recounts her adventures, they hardly seem real, as if she's a character in a book written by someone else.

"So you're trying to get to America," he says. "How sad for Havana."

Sad for Havana? she thinks, then realizes Mr. Alexander Lewis means to pay her a compliment. "Oh. Well, thank you."

"You're most welcome, Pearl." He sits up in his chair, exhibiting marvelous posture. "You've been an angel to me, and I feel much better now, but I'm afraid I have an appointment." He stares at her, thinking for a minute. "May I ask, before you go to America, could

I prevail upon you to remain in Havana just long enough to meet me again, so I may thank you properly for your assistance? And as added incentive, I know a few chaps at the consulate. I could talk to them, see what's what."

"Really? You can?" She isn't sure how she feels about this Alexander, but if he could help her at the consulate . . .

"Yes, I could really. And when we meet again, I could tell you what they say."

The elegant way he talks mixes up her thoughts. Is he mocking her? "But are you healthy enough to go now?" she asks.

"Please don't insult me by thinking twice about it," he says. "I feel as strong as an ox. Now, will you meet me again?"

He's so insistent. Just to say thank you? Whatever his reasons, she's in no position to refuse. "Yes, sure."

"We'll meet here, then? For a proper dinner, not just pastry. Tomorrow night?"

"So soon?" she says and wishes she hadn't. "I mean, yes, it's fine."

"We'll say eight o'clock. And you promise you'll come?"

"Of course." As he stands, she adds, "You're sure you're well again?"

Alexander Lewis laughs. "Just to please you, I'll call for a taxi." He tries again to pay the waiter, who declines his money. Outside, Alexander raises his arm gracefully, and a taxi arrives in an instant. She watches him slip easily into the car the way she might tuck an artificial flower into a silken hatband.

o

THE NEXT DAY, Pearl sleeps late, wakes up feeling dizzy, happy, and nervous. Now she has two prospects to get to America. Later this afternoon, she'll try the Colon again, and afterward she'll see this Alexander Lewis.

Rather than go on her usual fruitless job search, she stays in the workshop, leafing through Julieta's old movie magazines, writing a letter to Frieda and giving it up. She holds Alexander's ivory-colored business card up to the light. Though it's been in her pocket all day, the card remains crisp and clean. The city center address must be his office. Someone who dresses and speaks as beautifully as an Alexander B. Lewis should have a refined suburban address to match his manners. And a distinguished lady to run his household. He didn't say he was married. But he also didn't say he wasn't.

She runs her finger across the card, feeling the good paper, the exquisite printing of the words in raised type that doesn't smudge. The property of a real aristocrat. A Jewish aristocrat—is such a thing possible?

By late afternoon, Pearl's anxious and bored. She coats a slice of bread with a thick spackle of butter, then gulps it down. It tastes so good, she has a second piece.

Though her meeting with Alexander isn't for hours, she washes and brushes her hair and considers her outfit. She chooses a sand-colored dress, fixing it up with a bow at the neckline. To go with it, she finds a purple hat with a wide brim and a dark silken band. Unfortunately, she's stuck with her same old pair of shoes.

Alexander B. Lewis. Such a grand name. Maybe he's some evil spirit in disguise.

Tired of waiting, Pearl grabs her handbag and goes to the Colon.

December evenings in Havana are not as hot as summer evenings but are plenty warm. After an entire year with so little change of seasons, she feels anxious, waiting for the cold that never comes. If only it would snow.

Pearl waits for a jitney to pass, and the conductor calls out, "Hop on board, only a nickel!" She continues walking, as if out for a stroll. A woman walking alone in the evening would be a rare sight in Turya, but in Havana, Pearl has seen far stranger things.

The streetlights flash on along the Calle San Rafael, where Chinese vendors are frying up batches of greasy Cuban snacks like fried pork skins or malanga fritters. The smell of burning fat mixes with the humid air and cigar smoke and scratchy recordings of American songs floating out of the bars. Julieta used to love those fritters. They smell nice and they're cheap, but Pearl suspects the vendors mix pork fat with the food.

She clutches her handbag tightly as she reaches the heart of the Colon, crammed with bars and theaters and a movie house; Pearl sees the orchestra members filing inside with shabby-looking instruments to play the musical scores. There are also nickelodeons showing pornographic scenes, gambling parlors, and shooting galleries. One place, called Babylon, advertises in English: "Live Show Nightly."

Like a scene from the wedding of Lilith and Asmodeus, King of the Demons.

Open taxis putter along, bearing American tourists who point out the local color on their way to order overpriced daiquiris at La Floridita. It's early for the area's regular customers. The men out at this hour are here only to gawk, not to buy. Children dart around them, fingers extended, calling out, "One dollar! One dollar!"

Pearl passes a man urinating in a doorway. She quickens her steps, averts her eyes, then turns her head again to avoid the searching stares of working women wearing slinky red and black dresses and doused in perfume. They pinch the men walking by, including a policeman, who smiles and continues on his beat. A few women rudely bump Pearl's shoulders. God forbid they mistake her for competition, invading their turf. But she realizes quickly they don't care about her. She's just in their way.

Finally Pearl reaches the Gold Dollar, where tonight the doors are thrown open. There's nothing to stop her besides her own fear. She inhales deeply, straightens her hat, plucks at her dress, then steps inside. The sticky floor is littered with peanut shells that crunch under her boots. Or roaches? No, must be peanuts. Pearl wills herself forward, squeezing between the tables and splintered wooden chairs. Four American sailors sitting by the door are getting drunk on Cuban Hatuey beers, laughing as they loudly practice Spanish phrases from those cards for tourists that are handed out at the souvenir shops.

Give me a kiss. *Dame un beso.*

I want to buy a good cigar. *Quiero comprar un buen tabaco.*

You're very charming. *Es usted muy simpático.*

We want to have fun. *Queremos pasar un rato divertido.*

She dislikes their smug Spanish, as if it isn't worth their time to learn the language correctly. You're guests in this country, she thinks. Show respect.

A rumba band of women in silver dresses are setting up chairs on a low stage lit by strings of harsh electric bulbs that pulse and snap. Beside the bar, two African waiters talk in animated voices. Their bow ties hang untied around the collars of their dress shirts, unbuttoned halfway down their chests, revealing pink silk undershirts. The shorter waiter titters, stands on tiptoe, and plants a quick teasing kiss on his friend's lips.

Pearl now realizes the waiters are inverts, little birdies. Her oldest sister Rivka had two classmates whose husbands were that way. They ran off together before the Great War. The rabbi at the Poor Man's Shul kindly initiated proceedings to declare the two husbands dead, so the wives could remarry.

One of the American sailors, a real Yankee with a round chest and a pasty complexion, yells something at the Cuban waiters that makes his friends snicker. The shorter waiter shouts a snappy reply, miming an obscene sexual gesture with his hands.

Everyone in the room laughs: the musicians onstage, the sailors, a man drinking alone at the bar. Everyone except Pearl, who presses herself against the wall, and the Yankee sailor, who charges at the waiter like a bandit on a horse.

Before the sailor can reach his target, the taller, darker waiter steps in his path and lands a solid punch to the jaw. The sailor tumbles backward to the ground, blood dribbling from his nostrils, down his lips. His friends gape in amazement, then grab their beefy mate by his armpits and feet and haul him outside. Meanwhile, the waiter and his friend saunter away arm in arm, into a back room.

A musician onstage shakes her hips and calls to the onlookers outside, "Come in! Don't be shy! Or are you afraid?"

Coming here was madness, Pearl thinks, hugging the wall. But she must see this through. She might lack the courage to return.

Squaring her shoulders, she approaches the stage, where one of the musicians hikes up her skirt and brazenly straddles her cello so her knees and the insides of her thighs are showing. If she drops that cello, what else might be revealed?

Pearl asks, "Where can I find a Señora Martin?" That's the name Rabbi Singer mentioned. The shameless cellist points her bow at a heavyset man at the bar. Pearl must have used the wrong word in Spanish. "No, no, Señora Martin," she says.

Hearing that name, the man spins around on his stool—revealing himself to be a woman. A woman with short hair parted down the middle and sculpted around her forehead. A woman in a white dress shirt with decorative stitching and a vest with silver buttons. A woman in pants with a metal-studded belt and a shiny gun holster containing a revolver, its grip inlaid with mother of pearl. The comfort she shows wearing these clothes tells Pearl that they're not a costume or for play, or even like when she dressed up in Rabbi Singer's clothes and posed for a picture. For this woman, Señora Martin, they are her everyday wardrobe.

Pearl walks slowly to the bar. "You are Señora Martin?"

"I'm Martin. What do you want?" she replies in the English of an American. She shifts in her seat, and in the light Pearl sees a penciled-in mustache above her top lip. And that gun—Pearl's never seen a woman carry a gun.

Pearl stammers out her explanation, that Rabbi Singer told her to come, and Martin cuts her off. "So you're one of his projects. He never sent me no woman. What's your name?"

"Pearl," she says in a low voice. Pearl finds it hard to choose her words properly if she doesn't know whether she's addressing a man or a woman.

"Pearl? As in oyster fruit?" Martin laughs, a deep belly laugh that echoes in the room. "Tell me, Pearl, weren't you scared to come here alone, a single gal like you?"

"No," Pearl lies. Since Key West, Pearl's English has improved, yet she often comes up short with native speakers. Her fallback strategy is to brusquely yank the conversation around to her own terms. "Please, can you help me? I don't have papers."

"You must want to go to America real bad. Why? To get rich? Or for a fella?"

"No fella," she says. "I want to be free."

"Bah! In America, you can't be free. You have to be square all the time." Martin salutes Pearl with a shot glass. "If you want to be free, my advice is stay here."

Pearl struggles to absorb this Martin's words. She's distracted by the penciled-in mustache and the man's suit.

"I can see you won't take my advice. You folks never do. You got any money?" Martin asks.

"Now, I don't have," says Pearl. "But I can get. How much I need?"

"Singer didn't tell you our price?" She downs her shot of liquor in one go as if it's water, doesn't even wince. "What if I told you a hundred bucks?"

Another false path. Pearl should be used to it now. Perhaps God wants her to say on this island. She's almost glad for the excuse to get away from Martin and her frightening confidence. "I must find different way. Thank you . . . Señora Martin. Goodbye."

Martin grabs her sleeve. "You say you're a friend of Singer?"

"Yes," says Pearl, trying not to hope.

"Just how much of a friend?"

Pearl shakes her arm free of Martin's grasp. "I am friend of Singer and I am a friend of his wife," she says, raising her chin. "And you? You are a friend of Singer? Maybe you are Jewish?"

Martin lets out a bitter laugh. "No one's asked me that in a long time." She taps the bar for another drink. "I used to be a lot of things. That's why I came here, so I could be none of them." She circles around Pearl, runs a finger down her sleeve. This Martin is nothing if not confident. Pearl's reminded of Talia, the crass matchmaker in Turya who used to make Pearl open her mouth to inspect her teeth. "Okay," says Martin, "for a friend of the rabbi, that's almost a religious thing. I'd lower it to seventy."

Seventy? Some bargain. At least it's less than a hundred. "Maybe," says Pearl. "But I cannot go by Florida. Or New York. Too strict."

"You can sail to Baltimore or New Orleans, maybe."

"Agree," says Pearl. "I return when I have the money. Good evening."

"Hold on. You're planning to hoof it? In this part of town at this time of night?" Again Pearl doesn't understand. "Let me offer you a ride."

"I can walk," Pearl insists.

"I'm sure you can. I bet you got a nice pair of legs under that plain-Jane dress. But around here, in the dark, you'd better let me take you."

My dress isn't so bad, thinks Pearl. Who are you to criticize fashion? "You walk here alone in the dark, no, Señora Martin? So can I."

"Yeah, but you're not me. And dry up with that Señora bull-shit. The name is Martin, just Martin. My driver and I will take you wherever you want. Except America. That's extra." She clicks her teeth and slaps Pearl's behind. Pearl jumps, covers her backside with her hand. She thinks, I bet Rabbi Singer never invited this Martin to his garden.

Onstage, a woman with a flute asks where Martin is going. "Out," says Martin, then tells Pearl, "That's my old lady. A real nag. The pretty ones are always trouble, but they're my weakness. Now let's find the Queen of England."

Old lady? Queen? What's she talking about? Pearl's feeling increasingly lost, and she doesn't care to be found.

The tall Black waiter comes in from the back, and Martin yells, "Hey, Queenie, meet Oyster Fruit." He looks at her quizzically. "He doesn't get the joke. His English ain't so hot." Martin shouts louder as if he's hard of hearing. "Pearl! Oyster Fruit."

There's a loud smash. The flute player has grabbed a bottle of rum off the bar and thrown it against the wall. The rum now drips down to the floor, pooling around a nest of broken glass. The few customers are laughing, as if it's all for show.

"She's jealous because I'm talking with you for so long. I told you she's a nag," says Martin. "And that was a good bottle of rum."

As the flute player runs off the stage, the rumba band quickly launches into a lively song that hurts Pearl's ears. Why would Singer send her to this topsy-turvy place, where one woman claims another as her "old lady"?

"You go on with the Queen," insists Martin. "You'll be safe with him. He's got the nastiest uppercut in all Havana." She puts an arm around the flute player's shoulders, speaks to her softly. It's an odd sight, this woman in pants soothing her jealous lover, but the way Martin carries herself, no one in the room dares laugh at her.

TWELVE

THE QUEEN OF ENGLAND—PEARL ASKS FOR HIS REAL NAME, but he won't tell—escorts her through an empty kitchen and out the back door to where his extraordinary Ford is parked. The front grille is decorated with artificial flowers, while Cuban and American flags are draped around the sides and trunk. "I don't like the color black," the Queen says, opening the passenger door for her. "Too boring."

After she tells him where she lives, he jumps into the driver's seat, bounces up and down a few times, and starts the engine. They whiz along the coastline, as the waves shoot up against the seawall. Pearl grips the doorframe. This car is going at a dizzying rate: thirty miles per hour on the car's speedometer. Thirty miles. She calculates in her head—that's about fifty versts.

Equally dizzying are thoughts of Martin and her flute-playing friend, her "old lady." If the friend is the lady, then Martin must be the man. How can she . . . do what men do? Wincing, Pearl forces herself to think of something else, like surviving this car ride.

They reach the harbor, where taxis parked at haphazard angles compete for tourists. The Queen slams the brake to avoid hitting a caravan of donkey carts crossing their path. The tourists and taxi drivers point to their car and laugh. Pearl, mortified, digs her chin into her chest.

Impatient with waiting, the Queen of England lurches the car onto the sidewalk, shifts into reverse, and zooms backward, causing several tourists to jump against the buildings and clear out of his path. Now it's Pearl's turn to laugh at them, skittering like mice until the Queen jerks to a stop and shifts direction, careening down a narrow side street, and Pearl loses her balance, slides across the seat into his white silk shirt, which smells like coconut and rose water. If a man has to have a smell, Pearl would prefer it to be musky-earthy, like a fall forest.

"You all right?" he asks.

"Yes." She's strangely moved by his concern. It occurs to her that because he is an invert, she's as safe with him as she'd be with a woman.

Thankfully, the narrow streets of Old Havana oblige the Queen to bump along at a more reasonable speed. Pearl loosens her grip on the edge of her seat and inhales slowly. The night is humid, perfumed with rotting fruit and human sweat. The Queen is humming a little song. She'd like to talk to this man, to learn more about him, so she asks what the song is about, and he says sadness. Everyone's life needs sadness to make it interesting.

Really? she thinks. Mine is too interesting.

Then he asks her in English. "You a friend of that famous Rabbi Singer?"

Pearl says, "Why do you ask? He is very famous?"

He lets go of the steering wheel to make the hand gesture for "so-so," and she begs him with her eyes to grab the wheel again, which he does. "What's so great about America? Weather, we got much better over here. Better music. Better food. Lot better drinks. Better men. Better women too, if that what you like. You think you gonna get rich in America? Over there, rich people like Vanderbilts, Rockefellers use people like you to work for they. They keep all the real money they-selves. You don't got no chance."

"How do you know? You've been there?"

"No, but I hear plenty. I hear everything. I'm good at listening."

She sees a deep mark on his cheek, a scar, and gestures toward it. "Who did this?"

"This? My ma. She the only person I let touch me. Understand? Anyone else, I do to him like I did that American in the bar, you know?"

"I am sorry. It hurts?"

"I don't think about it much."

"Why she did this to you?" Pearl asks.

"She don't like how I live my life." He laughs. "My ma, she crazy."

No mother should do this to her child, Pearl thinks. She'd like to touch his cheek or pat his shoulder to comfort him, but it feels presumptuous. "You live your life as you want," she says. "And don't be ashamed for nothing."

"I'm not ashamed. You talking about me or you talking about you?" he says.

Before she can answer, Pearl notices the time on an oversized clock, with rum bottles for hands, hanging above the entrance to a bar. She's late for her meeting with Alexander, so she asks to be let off at the café rather than at home.

He laughs. "You don't want the people you live with to see me, right?"

"Not true, I live alone," she says. Perhaps she shouldn't have admitted it. "I go to this café because I must meet someone there."

But she is embarrassed when she spots Alex, Alexander, Mr. Lewis—she's unsure what to call him—standing near the café, wearing a dark suit and a fedora. His lovely clothes bring out the dowdiness of her simple frock.

Alexander, she decides. That's the right name for someone so elegant.

Seeing her, Alexander touches his hat. He doesn't seem upset that she's late, though he does look surprised to see her arrive in the way that she has. Pearl struggles to appear at ease, sitting up tall, pretending to adjust her collar, which needs no adjusting.

"He's your meeting?" says the Queen. "Good work, sister. He's beautiful."

"No, no, it's not like that. You don't understand."

"You don't want him? I take him from you, no problem."

"Please," she begs him, "not so loud. He'll hear you."

He comes to a stop and holds her hand, helping her get down from the car. She blushes at his touch, feels Alexander's eyes on the two of them. "Be a good girl, okay?" says the Queen. "You don't want to become a mama before you get to America."

"Quiet," Pearl says, but he laughs uproariously, then drives away.

She slowly approaches Alexander, wonders what he'll say about her extraordinary arrival. Imagine what he'd think of Martin and the Gold Dollar.

He smiles politely and extends his hand for her to shake, as if to close a business deal. His palms are soft, like he's never pulled a weed in his life. She's not sure she likes such a feeling in a man's hands, too slippery. It's a different feeling, that's for sure. "What a colorful taxi," says Alexander, to her deep embarrassment. "The Cubans are nothing if not a creative people. Even the taxi drivers."

He takes her for the type who rides in taxis!

"Who's getting married?" she asks, glad to speak Yiddish again after so much English. He doesn't get the joke, so she says, "You're dressed like a million dollars."

"You're embarrassing me," he says.

"You're embarrassing me. The man shouldn't look prettier than the woman."

He could offer her a compliment. Instead he says, "As my mother would say, is that the eleventh commandment? Isn't that the expression?"

"Now you're mocking me."

"I promise I'm not," he says. "But I apologize if I offended you."

She dislikes hearing others accurately name her emotions aloud. "How is your health?" Pearl asks, changing the subject.

"Marvelously well. I'm drinking water by the bucketful. Say, do you really want to eat here? I know a better place on the square. Very special, unique to Havana."

"Is it expensive?"

"You needn't consider the cost. I'm paying."

She hesitates. "I—I wouldn't want to take advantage."

"But I wish you would take advantage. I'd love to be of use to someone."

Maybe he's right, she shouldn't be so formal, like a modest shtetl girl. People aren't that way here. "Fine," she says. "I'll take advantage."

"That's the spirit!" Alexander lends her his arm. She finds it awkward to fit her arm through his, so he arranges it for her. What if the Steinbergs happen to pass by and see? Oh, well, people will think what they want. Thoughts are worth nothing.

The lightly humid air feels like a warm bath on her skin. She takes in the noises of Havana at night echoing against the buildings: cars sputtering, a woman singing in Spanish, a drunk American kicking a bottle. She hopes Alexander has remembered his promise to help her, and that his way costs less than Martin's seventy dollars, which might as well be seven hundred dollars. Who has seventy dollars?

As if to answer that question, a Cuban woman offers them a lottery ticket, pleading, "It is sure to win a prize."

"Really?" says Alexander. "Then keep it yourself and enjoy the prize." He tells Pearl, "Every unemployed soul in this town sells fraudulent lottery tickets."

"Your Spanish is excellent," Pearl marvels.

"Mine? Merely passable, which for an American is admirable. Most Americans compel the natives to speak our language badly, to confirm our sense of superiority."

"If you say so," says Pearl.

"Do be careful of swindlers. Havana's full of them," Alexander tells Pearl. "I've seen every scam imaginable."

"I'm not an innocent child. I know a few things," she says. Why is she being so brusque? Whatever the reason, her gruff mood seems to please him.

"Of course you know things. But even Rashi himself might be fooled by these types," says Alexander. "They're clever and ruthless. One of my friends at the consulate told me about a case involving a pair of coolies—"

She interrupts him. "Coolies? I don't know this word." Another English slang term. Will there ever be an end to them?

"What's the word for it in Yiddish . . . Chinamen."

"If that's what you mean, then why don't you say Chinamen?"

He hesitates, looks embarrassed, falters before he goes on. "Anyway, these two men paid some sailors fifty dollars to go to Florida, and once they were offshore, the sailors dumped the coolies—the Chinamen—into the water to drown."

Pearl imagines herself in such a situation. She'd kick, scratch, and scream, threaten to tip the whole thing over so they'd all drown. But perhaps his story is an opportunity for her to ask what's really on her mind. "This friend of yours at the consulate, did you talk to him about me? Can he help me?"

"I don't know yet," says Alexander, his voice dropping.

"That means no."

"No, it means I haven't talked to him yet. But I promise to."

Pearl unhooks her arm from his. "People like me, we get plenty of duties but we get no favors." If Frieda had asked for help, she'd have gotten it already.

"I'm sorry, it slipped my mind," says Alexander. "I promise to look into it."

Look into it, how? What does he mean?

"If you didn't talk to him, then why did you want to meet me tonight?" she asks.

Alexander stops walking. "Because I enjoy your companionship, Pearl," he says in a gentle voice. "I thought perhaps you also enjoyed mine."

No man has ever spoken to Pearl in such a tender way. She's not sure whether to trust it. "Yes, okay," she replies, not knowing what else to say. "Fine."

The restaurant entrance is framed by two bare male torsos carved into the building facade. Inside is a large noisy dining hall where fans blow furiously. Pearl feels tongue-tied in such a grand place and is glad to let Alexander take the lead. The walls are smooth and white while the floors are paved in a striking orange-and-blue tile pattern; it might make a pretty blouse. They're shown a table by the door, but Alexander rejects it, and she's struck by the host's deference as he finds them a table in the center of the room.

A gramophone by the bar is playing the popular Irving Berlin song, "I'll See You in C-U-B-A," which trills constantly out of bars and shops for tourists. She asks Alexander to translate the lyrics.

"In short, the song says that since alcohol is banned in the U.S., Americans ought to go to Cuba to get drunk," says Alexander. "Does that shock you terribly?"

"Not at all," Pearl says, still annoyed that he forgot his promise to talk to his friend in the consulate. "I've seen plenty of Americans drunk before."

He laughs. "Oh, Pearl, when I'm with you, I feel"—he lets out a deep breath—"I feel at home. As though I'd gotten back something I'd lost."

"I hope something good."

"Yes." He looks at her intently, resting his chin on his right hand. "Very good."

He genuinely likes her. Why? She's not educated enough to make witty conversation as he must be used to with his American friends. As for tempting him sexually, she feels too old, too short, and, though she often goes hungry, too plump. Yet his interest is unmistakable.

Pearl squares her shoulders and says, "I'm very hungry."

"Tell me about your day. I'd tell you about mine, but it's boring."

Should she tell him that only an hour before, she was cavorting with inverts and hussies at the Gold Dollar? "Nothing so interesting," she says. "I hope the food here is good. What do you recommend?"

"Plantains," he says. "Have you tried plantains?"

"Is it a kind of meat?"

"No, they're like a banana, only not as sweet. Delicious with beans and rice."

"I don't like black beans. They're like mud."

He laughs so hard that she laughs too. "Then no black beans, I promise."

His life seems very light, with lots of laughter.

Over their meal, he describes his family in America and explains the mystery of his American-sounding last name, which he changed from Levin to Lewis. "It makes things easier," says Alexander. His father has a thoughtfully curated library of books in English, German, Yiddish, and French. His mother paints watercolors of flowers and plays the piano expertly with long, delicate fingers. To reach the farthest, most difficult keys, she can play them with the backs of her hands. "She taught me to love music," he says. "You'd really like her. I believe she'd like you too."

Pearl stabs her food with her fork or pushes it with her thumb, which she licks clean when no one's looking. Alexander, however, holds his fork in his left hand and lightly guides his food toward it with his butter knife, held in his right hand. His manners are as beautiful as his suit. Determined to eat as gracefully as he does, she studies the dance of his hands.

He asks about her family, so she lists them all: Father, Mother may her memory be a blessing, her four sisters in descending order of age, and Avram.

"I have no siblings," he says. "But I've always wanted one. Which of them do you feel closest to? Isn't there one you'd confide in, tell your secrets?"

What secrets? She has only the one, a terrible one. Sometimes she fears strangers can see it in her eyes. "I don't keep secrets from my family," she says slowly.

"I've upset you," he says.

"I'm not upset. Don't tell me how I feel." Something about his fine manners brings out an urge in her to speak with her true voice, to cut through his lovely words with hard truths. After all she's been through, pretty language sounds wasteful.

And yet her plain speech doesn't offend him. He actually seems to enjoy it, and he gives her a mock salute. "Yes, ma'am."

"If you must know," says Pearl, "I am closest with my sister in America. She's mixed up in a bad love match."

"What's bad about it?" he says.

"She and this man are not married yet, not even living in the same city, and already they're constantly fighting in their letters."

"Some couples enjoy a good scrap."

"Would you enjoy that kind of marriage?"

"I'm hardly an authority on the subject. I've never been married."

Pearl's embarrassed. She's genuinely enjoying their conversation and doesn't want him to think it's all been some kind of ruse to entice him. "My sister is young, and she's bright," she says. "If you met her, you would like her far more than me."

"I doubt it." Alexander takes a flower from the vase on their table and gives it to Pearl. Unsure what to do with it, she sniffs the blossom, then shoves it back in the vase.

"No, I promise you," she says. "Everyone loves her."

"Perhaps they love you too, but are too intimidated to show it," he says.

"No, they don't," she says firmly. Has she become intimidating? She doesn't see it, but then maybe she only sees herself as she once was. He sees her as she is now, even if she can't. "Tell me," says Pearl, "if it was your sister, what would you do?"

"Try to interest her in a hobby, to distract her mind from the gentleman in question. You know how distractible women are."

"And men aren't?"

Alexander laughs. "You've got me there, Pearl. Once again, you're a truth teller."

Is that what I am, Pearl thinks, a truth teller? She resumes eating, forcing herself to hold her fork in her left hand. If he can do it, so can she. With some effort, she succeeds.

After the main course, he orders for them both without asking what she wants: coffee and flan. He tells her more about America, the grand concert halls of New York, Chicago, or smaller towns like Miami. This is news to Pearl, who sees America as a place of work and money, not culture.

"Maybe in the future you will be allowed to return to America," she says. "Many men in our shtetl ran away to Poland during the Great War. Then came Revolution, no more tsar, and they came home."

"Even if a revolution were to occur in America, hardly likely, there's another problem," he says. "I'd be branded a coward, for standing up for my convictions."

"Don't listen!" she says, suddenly angry on his behalf. "Anyone who would say such things doesn't know what war is. You were being true to your faith."

"Not faith, exactly. I want to be clear. Though we are technically coreligionists, I can't pretend to be a believer in the traditional sense."

What other sense can there be? "What do you believe?" she asks.

"I believe in tolerance. Personal relations. Consideration for others. The unseen forces of love and goodness that help us avoid cruelty. I suppose some call that God." He digs his fork into their flan. "Anyway, who says I want to go back to the States? I like this place, and you might too if you gave it a real chance."

She's thinking over his fine words when a man in a tuxedo claps for attention a few tables away, in a space that's been cleared out among the tables. "Honored guests," he announces, "we have a special surprise tonight."

Alexander murmurs in her ear, "It's the same special surprise every night. Anyway, it's a good one."

Surprise? But they've already had their dessert.

The man in the tuxedo continues: "Some friends have come to welcome you."

Pearl hears these "friends" before she sees them: a line of African men in white robes. They slap at drums suspended around their necks, wrapped in colorful yarn nets decorated with tiny silver bells, shells, and beads. The drummers are followed by three gaunt bearded men, also with black skin and wearing white robes. They chant in nasal tones that remind Pearl of a violin that's out of tune.

A wave of Black female dancers runs in, chests rolling, hips shaking, heads jerking, arms and elbows flinging vigorously in all directions. The women shake maracas and bend over to kiss the drums as the men bang them harder, with wide, twitchy fingers.

When the dancing stops, the audience, thinking the performance is over, begins to applaud, but one of the chanting men holds out his hand.

"That one's the high priest," Alexander whispers to Pearl.

"A priest?" she says. "This is a religious ceremony?"

"It's Santeria," says Alexander.

Julieta used to mention Santeria, though Pearl hadn't paid much attention. She was under the impression it had to do with the lottery.

The priest says several words in his language, then points to a pretty woman seated a few tables from Pearl and Alexander, dressed in a demure flower-print blouse with a ruffled collar. The woman's skin is tanned, like a golden piece of toast, and her bright yellow hair, which looks dyed, is curled into tight finger waves. "Lovely girl," Pearl whispers, though she hadn't meant to say so aloud.

"Tolerable," says Alexander. "But then, I have little interest in Cuban women."

The high priest in his white robe beckons her forward, and the woman rises slowly from her seat and marches stiffly toward his open hands, her face frigid and expressionless, eyes blank and hollow. The drummers tap their drums softly, and with each tap, the woman jerks a different body part, a shoulder, a hip, a hand. The dancers shake their maracas to the drumbeat, and Pearl's foot taps too. She presses her knee to keep her leg from moving, but it wants to wriggle free.

At the blond woman's table, a man jumps up to wake her from her trance, but his friends hold him back. Meanwhile, the priest barks out an order in his native tongue, and in response, the woman kicks off her left shoe, a ballet slipper. He speaks again, and the woman kicks off her right shoe. Next, her hands move to the buttons of her flowery blouse. She methodically undoes each one.

Look away, Pearl tells herself, but she can't stop staring at this lovely woman, the soft neck, the ecstatic expression on her face, like a promise of something. Her blouse is open, revealing her deeply tanned shoulders, her delicate collarbone, her lacy brassiere. Now she's loosening her skirt. Pearl breathes through her mouth and clenches the sides of her chair, in case the high priest calls her on stage too.

"What's going to happen?" she asks Alexander. "Can't you stop it?"

"The show's almost over," he says, his eyes on the woman.

What does he mean? But Pearl loses her breath to ask because the woman's blouse and skirt fall to the floor, and she's standing in her brassiere and bloomers, showing off her ample figure, round and firm at the hips and in the bosom. A seduction.

The whispers in the audience grow into full-throated voices. Pearl wants to rush to help the bewitched woman, cover her nakedness from greedy eyes with a warm, tight, protective embrace, but she stays in her seat. A woman at the table next to Pearl and Alexander is crying. Another woman shouts to her husband in angry English.

The male performers bang their drums, bringing the chatter in the room to a halt. Then the drumming stops, and the high priest hurls out a strange-sounding noise, as if he'd been punched in the gut, and claps twice.

The entranced woman blinks rapidly, wipes her eyes, looks

down at herself, and screams. She grabs her clothes, presses them to her chest, and runs outside, screaming louder. The man at her table picks up her shoes and runs after her.

The priest, the drummers, and the dancers are bowing, and the audience is applauding. Alexander smirks and applauds too. What's so funny?

"I want to leave," Pearl says, so Alexander pitches a few dollars on the table for the waiter. She's tempted to swipe a dollar or two, but she can't take what's not hers.

On the street, Pearl keeps an eye out for the undressed woman, in case she needs help. Alexander says, "You're awfully quiet. You didn't believe that was real, did you?"

"Real?" she repeats.

He passes under a streetlamp that lights up his pale cheeks. "That woman was a plant. That whole Santeria ceremony, it was staged for tourists."

"Staged?" she says in a dazed voice. "Why would they do that?"

"Pearl, you're amazing. Unlike anyone I've ever met, man or woman." He puts his arm around her shoulders. This is another part of what he wants from her, not just the companionship. She must admit, she too has imagined this kind of moment with him. Now that it arrives, it feels warm, comforting, and she fears that if he should press further, she might not push him away. Perhaps noticing her discomfort, he lets go.

"I can manage the rest of the way," she says, still feeling the pressure of his arm.

"I'm sorry. Have I offended you?"

Even now, he exhibits such thoughtfulness, such careful manners. She hardly knows how to react to them. "I'm not offended," she says. "I just want to go home."

"In that case, dear Pearl, when can I see you again?"

"Why? What exactly do you want from me?"

He takes her hand. "Please don't embarrass me by making me say it aloud."

Alexander is staring, waiting, and Pearl's feeling light-headed. What does she want from him? A visa to America or a warm embrace?

"I have to go home." Pearl pulls back her hand. "Good night."

"Wait! How will I find you?" he asks.

She gives him the address of the workshop, tells him good night a third time, then runs away before he can get it into his head to chase her.

○

AFTER CHANGING INTO her nightdress, Pearl opens the windows to air out the stuffy workshop and hears a guitar playing, a street vendor hawking hot empanadas, the syncopated rumble of car tires rolling over cobblestones. Day and night, someone in Havana is always making noise. A strange city, constantly changing forms like an evil spirit. But Alexander says she should give it a chance. Alexander admires her. Alexander wants to be her friend, and her lover.

Pearl examines herself in the mirror. Yes, she decides, some people might consider me a looker. Not like Frieda, but in my own way.

She liked the feeling of him holding her shoulders, her hand, maybe liked it too well. In time she might be able to love him, or anyway marry him. He could provide her an easy life without work. She'd be a mistress of the tropics, lying on a reclining chair in the shade, no more mud or snow, plenty of food, and she wouldn't be a burden for her family. From time to time, he might let her have some money to send them.

Or she could continue as she has, somehow scrape together Martin's seventy dollars, which Alexander could probably lend her, though she could never ask him. Who else could help? She's taken enough from the Steinbergs. Her family in Turya has only what Basha sends from New York, and Pearl cannot divert any of that for herself. Though Frieda promised to ask Mendel for a loan, he probably doesn't have two coins in his pocket to rub together. He'd have to borrow it from his brother, Ben the Oak.

Ben the Oak. Now, he's something different. Honest, serious, a man with a fine reputation. After the war, he threw himself into work, running the store six days a week. Even when the bandits came to town, followed by the Reds and the Whites, his store stayed open, served a loyal stream of customers. She heard a story that he once saved the town by bribing a Cossack with his own watch.

Frieda said Ben was doing well in America. . . .

She doesn't have many memories of Ben, who rarely attended their Friday night dinners. When he did, he barely talked, while Mendel monopolized the conversation. If she tries, she can picture his face vaguely. Round, solidly shaped, like a potato. Fair skin, the color of potato flesh. And blue eyes.

Pearl takes out pen and paper. What words should she use for such a crazy request? To a man who's almost a stranger? She's never been much for writing, especially in a situation this delicate. She really should have worked harder in school.

Look, either Ben's going to help her or he isn't. What does she have to lose? She might as well find out. If she offends a stranger, who cares?

So she writes:

Dear Benjamin,

This is Pearl, Frieda's sister, writing to you from
Cuba. Can you lend me some money? Twenty-five dol-
lars, or fifty if you can spare it. When I get to America,
I'll earn the money to pay you back.
Don't wait too long to answer.

Sincerely, Pearl

THIRTEEN

As NOVEMBER TURNS INTO DECEMBER, AND 1922 DRAWS to its end, there's no word from the Ben the Oak, but then mail travels slowly.

Pearl does receive a brief and welcome letter from Frieda:

> All over with that mamzer Mendel. Never mention his name to me again.

Let's hope for good this time, Pearl thinks, though she doubts it.

> . . . My life is for myself now. I'm in America, and I intend to make the most of it. I'm taking a night class to improve my English. I want to work in an office someday.

That last sentence floods Pearl with hope. She lets her mind run wild with dreams: Frieda wearing a white silk blouse with a lady's necktie, sitting at a polished oak desk and assisting some great man. Or continuing her education, perhaps at a ladies' college. She's young, with more life ahead of her than behind.

More good luck. Pearl has found a job sewing zippers. Anyone can sew a button or a hem, but zippers require a special mix of patience and perfectionism, the kind she has. Her new boss, a Jew from Baltimore, closes on *Shabbes*, yet he doesn't mind if Pearl takes a stack of garments home to earn extra pennies. Actually, he expects it.

Determined to save, Pearl trims every expense she can. She fills a hole in her shoe with cardboard. She cuts her soap into pieces, which she adds to boiling water to extend its life, dousing her clothes, body, and hair in this same runny soapy liquid. When the tailor brings leftovers cooked by his wife, Pearl divides them into smaller portions to stretch over several meals.

She also fills up during periodic outings with Alexander Lewis, supper in regular restaurants. He continues claiming that he'll speak to his friend at the consulate about her and will have news soon. Pearl doubts it will ever happen. He seems more bent on convincing her to stay here than helping her leave. Anyway, she's been hesitant to press him. In Alexander's company, she likes to forget her planning, working, and saving. Being with him feels like a welcome vacation from her life. She sometimes worries she's enjoying that vacation all too well, that she'll never want it to end.

For Alexander too, life in Cuba is just an extended vacation, though it's supposed to be his punishment, an exile. He hardly seems to be suffering.

At dinner, Pearl will order a plate of tiny smelts, fried Cuban-style until they're dried and brittle, or a cheese sandwich, which she inspects rigorously for ham with her fork before taking a bite. He asks her to teach him the blessing before meals, explaining that his parents weren't people of faith. So she recites it and he repeats after her. "Such simple words," he marvels, "yet so profound. Like a poem."

That's not right. Prayers aren't poetry, any more than recipes or sewing patterns are poetry. (Then again, maybe there could be poetry in a sewing pattern.) No, prayers are confirmations of God's place above, and ours below. Or else they are cries for help. In all his life, hasn't Alexander ever needed to cry for help? She guesses not.

Alexander peppers his Yiddish with American slang like "giggle water" and "on a toot." She asks him to teach her more American words, to show her again how he holds his knife and fork. In return, he requests stories of shtetl life. A fair trade.

"I'll teach you something else," Alexander says one evening. "See that man at the bar, the one nursing a whiskey? He's a smuggler."

"How do you know?"

He shrugs. "One of my few talents, sniffing out criminals. I get plenty of practice in Havana. When Americans come here to live, it's generally because they've failed at something back home. That also goes for the women." He puts the back of his hand to his forehead in mock horror. "Mostly silly, fancy-free flappers."

"Maybe you're a criminal too." She's only half joking.

"Anything's possible," he says. "Maybe you're one."

"Seriously, what exactly is your job?" When he answers with his usual "import-export," she demands to know what he imports or exports.

"Many things. Like cigarettes." He extends a packet of French cigarettes and she takes one. "I smoke only French cigarettes. The others are stinkeroos."

She can't tell the difference between a French cigarette or any other, but Alexander often notices fine distinctions between things that don't matter to her.

Perhaps the real reason he can't return to America is that he's doing something wrong, like rum-running. But rumrunners wear flashy ties. Their faces are unshaven and their breath constantly reeks of alcohol mixed with Sen-Sen to disguise it. When Alexander kisses her cheek good night, she smells only his aftershave, like lavender and cedarwood. He asks her permission before offering the kiss, and she gives it. His soft lips press delicately on her skin in a way that feels respectful, kind, and very safe. She catches a faint whiff of his breath, sweet like a ripe strawberry. "Good night, Pearl," he says. "The next time we meet, I promise, I'll have a terrific surprise for you."

Like all people with money, he enjoys surprises. Pearl tries to imagine leading a life where the unexpected is welcome, a delight.

She walks home slowly, thinks of Alexander kissing her, perhaps as his wife, a grand lady in a mansion with high ceilings and gauzy curtains floating in tall windows, open to the garden. Every morning, she'd wake up late, feeling well rested, yawning lazily as he brings her cold green coconut milk on a tray. He'd be wearing one of his pretty suits, and as she takes the glass, he'd bid her farewell and go to work in the city.

A silly fantasy. As she's told Alexander many times, Havana doesn't feel like a real place to her, only a playground for tourists or a sweatshop for poor people like herself. A way station to join her sisters in America, where she can be truly safe, truly free. Alexander listens politely, but she suspects he can't really understand how she feels about Cuba and America. He chose to run away from his country, from war and its attendant horrors, and now he enjoys his life here. He had the freedom and the ability to choose. She did not. She came here with nothing but nightmares of what she was forced to witness and experience, things he could only imagine, and his life is too agreeable for him to want to imagine them.

A small crowd is listening to a band of street performers singing a love ballad, and Pearl stops to listen. If Alexander were with her now, he might enjoy it. He appreciates good music. And so does she—there's one thing they share—though he likes to spend time analyzing it afterward while she savors the feeling it stirs inside, in the moment she hears the music. When it's over, it's done.

The ballad ends. The Cubans in the crowd applaud and whistle while the Americans toss change into the plate at the musicians' feet. Pearl, who's in a melancholy mood, strolls home to her workshop. She now feels safe walking alone at night. How different she has become from that nervous girl stepping tentatively down the gangplank of the SS *Hudson*, or that terrified teenager hiding at home during the war and the Revolution, listening for soldiers, afraid to move or turn on a light or cry.

Her life has changed so fast, she could use a minute to catch her breath.

At the workshop, she's surprised to run into the Steinbergs, who have come to drop off boxes of hats in need of adornment. Mr. Steinberg has a special commission for her, a season's worth of hats for an American lady whose husband runs a big sugar mill. She's glad, for her and them. Lately Mr. Steinberg's handsome suits have looked rumpled, and the generosity with which he extends smiles and free candy or cigars seems more anxious than good-natured.

Tonight, he's positively giddy, even mentions reopening the workshop full time. Mrs. Steinberg seems happy too. Good for her.

"By the by," says Mr. Steinberg, "the funniest-looking person was just here looking for you. A woman dressed in a man's suit. With a driver waiting outside in a Ford, all decked out in flags and flowers, like a carnival tent on wheels."

"Must be some mistake," says Pearl, forcing a laugh. Inwardly, she panics. Martin's expecting her seventy dollars, which she doesn't yet have. And what about Alexander, with that lovely kiss that mixes up all her ideas of what she wants? Still, disappointing Martin doesn't seem like a good idea.

○

PEARL MAKES HERSELF crazy between sewing zippers for the tailor and decorating hats for Mr. Steinberg, taking breaks only to visit the water closet, grab a meal, or accidentally doze off at her worktable. She needs to earn more, much more.

She's at home when Martin drives up with the Queen of England in the funny-looking car. Pearl hears them come to a screeching stop on the sidewalk, narrowly missing a boy chasing a baseball.

They enter the workshop with an air of possession, as if they're buying the place. The Queen sifts through a box of buttons, holds a few to his chest. Martin sticks her thumbs in her belt and plants her feet in the middle of the room. Her thick-soled boots add to her height, and the revolver with the mother-of-pearl handle glints in its holster. Pearl can't stop staring at the gun. Does she actually use it?

"May I?" Martin asks, taking out a cigar and a lighter. "Besides the company of a good-looking woman, there's nothing so absolutely satisfying as a nice cigar."

The novelty of Martin's mannish act no longer intimidates Pearl, and she wants to make that known. "Not inside, please," she says, pointing to the cigar. "It hurts my eyes."

"Anything for you, my dear." Martin puts the cigar away.

"I don't have all your money yet. But I work hard." Pearl gestures to her worktable, covered in hats, pants, and jackets. "You see how much I work, no?"

"It's okay, my dear anxious Oyster Fruit. I'm not here to scold." Martin removes the man's hat she's wearing and tries on a ladies' green felt cloche from the stack on Pearl's table. The penciled-in mustache is missing today. "I guess I don't make much of a lady, to my mother's eternal disappointment. She was always lecturing me on how to be one." She raises the pitch of her voice, like a bird's. "A lady should walk with a light step, an easy smile. She should never wear yellow gloves, drink more than a glass of champagne, or be so vulgar as to raise her dress with both hands when stepping over a mud puddle." Martin tosses the green hat aside.

"Your mother also lives in Cuba?" asks Pearl.

"Heck, I'm not sure if she lives anywhere. I left home at fifteen and never looked back." Martin taps the floor with her boot. "This is some dump."

You're coming here to insult my housekeeping? Pearl thinks. I sweep this floor every day and mop with soapy water so the cockroaches and ants can't find their footing.

"Now Pearl," Martin says, "who's this young man the Queen says you're running around with? I thought you didn't have a fella."

"This man is not my fella." She shoots a glare at the Queen, feeling hurt that he'd betrayed her privacy. "Why do you tell stories on me?"

"Sorry," he says.

"You didn't mention our arrangement to him, did you?" Martin asks.

"No, nothing," says Pearl.

"Okay. Just checking. You can't trust no one in this crazy town."

It sounds like a warning. Pearl thinks of those Chinamen that Alexander described, lost in the sea, limbs flailing, heads sinking below the waterline. However, she believes she can trust Martin. Call it an instinct. "I will get your money, I promise."

Martin jabs her finger into Pearl's shoulder. "Maybe you don't want to go to America anymore. Maybe you want to stay here with your fella."

"No, no, I want to go to America." Yet her voice sounds flat as she says it.

"As you wish. But I warn you, the laws are changing. The ports, the coastlines, everything's getting tighter. If you want to go, you have to go soon, or I might not be able to get you there at all. Understand?"

Pearl swallows hard. "I understand. But I don't yet have the money."

"Seventy bucks is a bargain, even if it means a bit less for me, and for your friend Rabbi Singer, who was none too pleased to hear about it. He expects me to make up the loss on his end with my share. How do you like that? I'm doing all the work here on the ground, and he thinks I should take the whole thing on the chin!"

Rabbi Singer's making money from this deal, Pearl realizes. She feels embarrassed not to have guessed it earlier. Maybe all he ever wanted from her was money, not her body. Or was it both? She'll never know.

Martin sidles up to Pearl, then says to her, directly into her ear, "At the Gold Dollar, we got some rooms upstairs no one's using.

You can have one for free, save up your seventy bucks faster. We could become good friends, you and me."

Friends? What friends? "But I don't pay nothing to live here," explains Pearl. She dislikes the direction this conversation is taking.

"You have remarkable hair." Martin pats a lock of Pearl's frizz. "It's so, so . . ."

"Big!" says the Queen, then accidentally tips over a bottle of buttons, scattering a few on the floor. "Sorry," he says and scoops them up.

Pearl shrinks from Martin's hand. She must know I'd give her anything, Pearl thinks. But I have nothing, just my own two hands. Unless she wants me to be her mistress, or as she calls it, her "old lady."

Though Pearl fears losing her connection to the States, she has to be clear on this point. She folds her arms and says, "I must speak, Señora Martin."

"Please, just Martin." Her face has a strangely tender look. "I'm not trying to press any advantage. Just tell me what you do want and what you don't want."

Right now, though Pearl wants sleep, she must stay awake, alert. "Martin," she says in a slow, calm voice, "I don't say to other people what's right or wrong. But I can't live in your place. Your place, it's not my kind of place." It feels good to say so clearly.

Martin throws back her head and laughs. "You're a real pip, Oyster Fruit."

"You finished, Martin?" asks the Queen of England. He scoops up the last of the spilled buttons and deposits them in their box.

"Apparently so." Martin pats Pearl on the behind and says, "Farewell, my dear. And don't worry. You get the money, I'll get you to America. Only don't take too long."

Pearl rubs her behind, as if to wipe away the touch. "One more question," she says. "Your gun? Is it for protection? Why do you have it?"

"Want to hold it?" Martin draws it out of her holster, grabs it by the barrel, and extends the handle to Pearl, who shakes her head. "Suit yourself," says Martin, putting it back in the holster. "Every woman ought to have one, I say. It would be a better world."

○

PEARL FINISHES HER day's work near dawn, then collapses, fully dressed, on her narrow bed. She wakes at noon, barely enough time to change into her good dress, dab on her lipstick-rouge, and meet Alexander at the Plaza de Armas. He's wearing his beautiful white suit with white shoes. In Turya, a man only wears white when they put on his burial shroud.

Alexander has a taxi waiting. Pearl asks if he's heard about new laws in America to tighten the borders. He says, "Not a word, I promise you. Now get in so I can take you to your surprise."

As they head west from the city center, Pearl forgets her worries about America and enjoys driving through the open space, the sunlight. Alexander gleefully refuses to explain where they're going. It's lovely, putting herself in his care. Maybe he'll kiss her cheek again. Or her lips. Pearl takes off her headscarf, letting the wind have its way with her hair. She falls asleep, and when he nudges her awake, she feels foolish.

They're rolling up a long driveway bordered by beds of red and purple flowers and dwarf palm trees with the bottom halves of their trunks painted white, a few of them tied with red bows left over from Christmas. Their destination is a caramel-colored mansion with a red-tile roof and a line of cars out front discharging their passengers.

Alexander explains they're going to the Jockey Club to observe the afternoon horse races. Isn't she pleased?

"Horses smell," Pearl says, thinking of the Whites on horseback, waving swords and screaming like wild boars. She'd be much more pleased if the surprise were an American visa. Why does she feel so cross today? Or maybe she isn't cross, just speaking her own mind, and she's confusing that with anger.

Alexander laughs, as he often does when Pearl says something serious. It's a vexing habit. "Well," he says, "at least it's an honest, earthy smell."

"Spoken like a city dandy," she says, and he laughs again. What would he know of the earth and its smells? You want to smell the earth? Come to Turya after a summer rain when the mud gets in your hair and eyes, and everywhere stinks like a stray dog.

The mansion appears more beautiful up close, and so are the people descending from the taxis: elegant women in sheer silk dresses that must cost several times the fare of a boat trip to the United States, or husky men in light gabardine coats and silly safari hats smoking cigars and complaining in loud voices about lazy waiters. "You should have told me we were going somewhere fancy," she says, patting her hair into shape. Her dress is embarrassingly shabby.

"You look just fine," he says. "You look real."

He doesn't understand. She's fine with looking real, if that's by choice. But first she needs to know what's expected, to have the opportunity to make the choice.

Alexander wants a closer view of the horses, so they walk to the side of the mansion, along a bamboo hedge thick with long knobby branches. In a fenced paddock, horses paw at the red mud. Some wear fancy leather saddles and white leggings. Those animals are better dressed than I am, Pearl thinks. They fit in better with these fine ladies than I do.

A group of spectators read newspaper clippings and point at a board with the horses' names and their position in the starting line. Pearl moves away from the crowd and looks out over the field. In the distance, a factory chimney puffs out white clouds toward the sea. Beyond that lies America.

Alexander joins her. "That factory is responsible for sweetening half the coffees in Havana," he says. Everything to him is an opportunity to show off his intelligence, or his impressive wit, which Pearl must admit is worth showing off. "Shall we see if we can root up some luncheon in this place?"

"How do you know it's not horsemeat?" This time she intends for him to laugh. He does, and she laughs too, good and hearty.

Back at the mansion, they pass through the marble lobby with fringed velvet curtains. In a side room, Americans cluster around a roulette wheel. Music drifts in from the shaded veranda overlooking the racetrack, where a string quartet serenades guests eating at wrought-iron tables painted white. Alexander requests a table for four, as if he expects another couple. Pearl hopes not. She feels embarrassed in this impossibly lovely place. Climbing tea roses, Chinese hibiscus, and royal *poincianas* are planted between statues of Greek goddesses with exposed breasts. Americans with binoculars hanging from their necks chew cigars or swill rum cocktails, while attendants in fitted green uniforms walk around taking bets and holding dollar bills between their fingers.

Pearl pulls her hat more tightly around her head and shrinks into her chair. Alexander gives a casual wave—it's as if he were born knowing how to signal waiters—and an attendant rushes over to take his bet. "Pearl, care to place a wager?" Alexander asks, but she declines. "Then how about a drink?"

He says it like a dare. So she can get drunk and make a fool of herself? She's about to refuse, but then she thinks, if all these people enjoy it, I can too. Maybe it will relax my nerves. "What do you recommend?" she asks.

"That's a good girl. One drink wouldn't kill you. I know just the thing." He orders a Mary Pickford, fresh pineapple juice, rum, and a splash of what looks like red ink. Though Pearl generally dislikes the smell of alcohol, this drink is sweet and refreshing. She finishes it quickly. Alexander claims it's healthy—the pineapple juice is excellent for digestion. He orders her another and something called deviled eggs.

Deviled? Does that mean with ham? Alexander says no. She asks if he'd like to recite the blessing before meals, as she's taught him. Usually he likes practicing it with her when they eat out alone, but he glances at the fine people at the neighboring tables, then says, "Let's skip it for today, shall we?"

Next comes a salad with baked beans, cold veal (which she won't touch but Alexander eats with relish), potato cakes, and sautéed carrots. She expertly wields her silverware in the American style. Alexander talks about the race, but she's preoccupied noting the flavors and textures of each bite. She keeps looking to see what's coming next, like the next chapter of a story. You don't just eat this kind of food. You savor it.

"I wish Frieda could taste this," Pearl says, interrupting his horse chatter. Her head is buzzing pleasantly, her lips feel loose, and she's hit with a powerful wave of nostalgia for her sister. "Frieda's always saying if she could take a pill and fill herself up for the day, she would. Let her taste a meal like this and see what she'd say." She takes a deep sip of the pineapple drink. With Alexander, she could eat like this all the time. Though so much rich food might make her stomach hurt.

"Frieda's not here," Alexander reminds her. "Forget her for a minute and tell me about you, what you're enjoying today."

"Everything." She waves her fork, then lets it droop between her fingers with a girlish giggle. Frieda vanishes from her mind. Work is a distant memory. America is a rumor. Russia is a crumb from her roll that's fallen to the ground.

He leans forward and says, "Then I'm happy." There's a funny fluttering in her throat, heart, and stomach.

For dessert there are orange marmalade cookies and little lemon cakes decorated with Christmas trees in piped frosting. Though the holiday was two weeks ago, Pearl has noticed that Gentiles hold on to it as long as possible. I'm not worshipping Christ, she tells herself. I just want to eat this cake. She scrapes off the Christmas design with her butter knife and bites into the cake, a burst of citrus and rich butter punctuated by a high note of sugar. If only all of Cuba were like this, she thinks, luxuriating in the sweetness, though she knows full well that places like this club are beautiful because people like Pearl work like packhorses to produce the beauty. She's no socialist, but maybe it's better to have a bit less beauty in the world and a lot more fairness.

A bell rings and the spectators rush to the fence along the racetrack, though they have a perfectly fine view from their tables. Pearl reluctantly joins Alexander, who's found a choice place to stand. The horses and jockeys amble out onto the dirty track. She hears shouting in the open stands on either side of the veranda, where factory workers and Chinese immigrants pack the cheaper seats—I belong there, not here, Pearl thinks. "I'm thirsty," she says, but Alexander is studying the horses through his field glasses.

On the track, a man raises a pistol and sets it off with a vicious snap that makes Pearl jump. The horses kick up clouds of dust while the jockeys whip their sides. All around, people shout: "Come on, Chestnut!" "Let's go, Starry Night. Hurry now!" The horses' noses flare as they go around a second time. A gong sounds, and the race is finished. The whole thing takes five minutes.

Back at their table, they await the posting of results. Waiting, always waiting. The string quartet plays a new waltz, and Alexander asks if she'd like another drink. Pearl says okay, and maybe more cake? Alexander nods to the waiter and wiggles his finger.

The results are posted on a giant board, and there's a loud chorus of sighs and groans as the winning jockey skips forward to receive a green wreath around his neck. Meanwhile, the people on the veranda rip up their betting slips or toss their hats into the air in celebration. What if they lose them and have to buy new ones?

Alexander instructs an attendant to collect his winnings, then tells Pearl, "See, you should have bet. What happened to your drink?"

She taps her empty glass. "I was thirsty." Her head hurts.

"My dear, I do believe you're tipsy."

Before she can answer, a male voice calls out, "Alex, you old swell!" The voice belongs to a slender middle-aged man holding a rum cocktail and an unlit cigar. Behind him, a small group of men in summer suits flirt with a middle-aged woman with a sparkling headband. The woman frowns at Pearl.

Alexander stands up, moves in front of Pearl's chair as if to block her view, and yelps in an impossibly cheerful voice, "Carleton! Any luck today?"

The man called Carleton sets his drink down to shake his hand. Get that glass away from me, thinks Pearl, feeling a burning sensation behind her eyes.

Carleton wears a straw hat, a light-gray three-piece suit, and pince-nez. He has a puff of gray hair atop his forehead and thick black eyebrows that arch in the middle, as if he's on the verge of asking a question. "No luck at all," he says. "How about you, you old sheik? Wait, don't answer. Your people always come out ahead. Aren't I right?"

Alexander winces briefly, then says with an awkward laugh, "Touché!" and puts his hand on his heart. The two of them kid around like father and son.

"Who's this pretty gal you're hiding? Penny for your thoughts," says Carleton.

Realizing he's talking to her, Pearl looks up. Her head is buzzing terribly.

The man shakes his head, raises those dark, arched eyebrows. "Another lovely Cuban woman with no English."

"I hate to contradict you, Carl, but she's not Cuban," says Alexander.

"No? She has the right coloring. Where is she from?"

Alexander hesitates, then waves his hand in a circle, "Oh, around."

Carleton leans over, peers into her eyes, and Pearl lets out an inopportune hiccup. "You're pickled!" he says and raises his drink. "You may be ahead of me now, but I'll catch up."

"I speak," Pearl says indignantly. Her mouth feels fuzzy.

"Excellent, excellent." The man points at Alexander with his unlit cigar. "If these Cubans worked harder at their English, they'd have happier lives."

"Come now, that's bosh. Many Cubans speak fine English," says Alexander.

"Which just proves my point. If more made the effort, you'd see a blessed change on this island," he says. "But sadly, your average Cuban whiles away his days picking food from trees, walking half naked through sugarcane. All he wants are a few coins to buy a lottery ticket or wager in a cockfight, and he's in paradise."

"Yes, I know. You want to turn them all into proper Yankees."

"And you want to keep them barefoot and poor, yet pure. Noble savages. That's how all you well-bred elites think. But I know a thing or two about poverty, personally. As a boy, I worked for years sorting rotten potatoes in a grocery store. It didn't demean me. It benefited me, financially and other ways. It helped me grow up, become a man."

"Horatio Alger couldn't have said it better," says Alexander.

"I'll never convince you. But enough of this blah-blah. Alex, you're being terribly rude. You haven't told me the name of your pretty friend."

Alexander hesitates, then says, "Only if you promise not to steal her from me," and introduces them.

"May I borrow your fella for a moment?" Carleton asks Pearl as they shake hands. His skin feels even smoother than Alexander's.

Pearl says, "Okay," an all-purpose word that serves a variety of situations.

"I won't be long," Alexander says in English, then whispers it in Yiddish.

"I'm not feeling well," she whispers, but he doesn't hear.

"Are you sure she's not Cuban?" Carleton asks as they walk away. "She's certainly striking. Especially those dark piercing eyes. Where'd you pick her up?"

Alexander belts out another fake laugh as they join a few other men at the bar. Meanwhile, Pearl holds her head. If this is being drunk, she dislikes it. It's like riding in a Ford going too fast. She wants to put her head down for a minute. Alexander's not even looking her way anymore; he's focused intently on some stuffy old man's jokes.

The woman in the sparkling headband stops at Pearl's table and asks, "Haven't we met? Miami? Newport? Somewhere."

"I don't understand," says Pearl.

The woman touches her own rouged cheek. "Sorry! I thought you were . . . Oh, well, no matter. But aren't you a lucky girl? Hobnobbing with the American consul."

"Consul," Pearl repeats slowly. This woman talks so fast, maybe on purpose to confuse her. "Who is consul?"

"Don't you know? Carl. Of course he's the American consul."

Pearl's stunned. Never has she been so close to a man with such power over her life. This is Alexander's friend? Maybe meeting him is the real surprise Alexander promised her. When she stands up, she stumbles forward, like the woman at the Santeria performance. But she can't miss this chance.

Alexander, still in conversation with some of the men, notices her and, as if already sensing disaster, waves his hand no. Why, thinks Pearl. Are you ashamed of me?

"Mr. Carl," Pearl says in a clear, strong voice, louder than she'd intended. She grips the back of a chair to steady herself. "I want to say something to you."

The consul needs a moment to recognize her. "Ah, Alex's friend. *Mi encanta*. Well, whatever a bewitching little señorita like you has to say, I'm all ears."

Pearl begins with "I . . ." and then falters. Until now, the American consul has been a man hiding behind a title, a man offering taunting advice to immigrants that she's read in the Yiddish newspapers. Go back where you came from. Your own rotten luck to be born on the wrong soil. Stay far away from us.

"Don't be frightened," Carleton says genially. "Talk to Uncle Carl."

Alexander, looking concerned, is trying in vain to get away politely from a man telling a long, involved yarn.

Pearl's head is humming. The consul is no longer a story in a newspaper, but a real flesh-and-blood man, holding a cool, intoxicating drink with pale fingers. If she could take away that drink and replace it with a pen, he could sign forms to reunite her with Frieda. She could ask him, here and now. She could beg for mercy.

She blinks a few times, focuses her thoughts. "You are a great man," she says.

He laughs. "Am I?" He thinks she's flirting.

"You have power to do good things for many people." She's shouting again. "To help their problems. The immigrants."

The amused expression on his face hardens.

"But you don't help us," she says. "You laugh at us. Like we are animals."

"I'm sorry, Carl," says Alexander, inserting himself between them.

"This person is your friend?" asks the consul. "Or is this some kind of put-on?"

"Please, I'd like to explain," says Alexander, but Pearl interrupts.

"You, you . . ." Pearl lacks the words she needs, but she can't stop. People nearby are watching, and she points to them. "Where is your heart? Why don't you help us? We leave everything, our families, our homes. We have nothing. You have everything."

"Perhaps she has had a few too many," says Alexander with a pained expression. This time, he's unable to force a phony laugh to diffuse the tension.

"Always a pleasure to meet any friend of Alex's," says Carleton. "Enjoy the races." He wanders inside the mansion, toward the room with the roulette tables. She wants to follow, but Alex grips her arm. His fingers are tight and they hurt.

"Help us!" she shouts, losing her balance, but Alex holds her up. The nearby chatter halts. After a brief, humiliating silence, the string quartet musicians resume their playing.

"Come with me," Alex whispers fiercely in Yiddish and guides her back to their table. Why isn't he on her side? Whose side is he on? "Sit for a while. You're not well." Alexander pulls out her chair, but she doesn't sit.

"You let him get away without answering me."

"You're doing yourself and your cause no good. Particularly in your current state. Just sit for now. I'll bring coffee."

"My cause? Isn't it your cause too? You're a Jew, remember?"

"How could I forget with you here?"

Stunned by his awful words, she sinks into a chair. How dare he tell her to be quiet? "Don't you know what he says about immigrants? It's in the newspapers."

"I'm sorry for being so cross. But the way to influence people like Carl isn't by shouting like someone in a shtetl marketplace. Try to understand. Carl is simply ignorant of your plight, as are most people in his position." He looks around, seems satisfied that the others are losing interest in the little scene she's caused. "Though even if he wanted to help, his hands are tied by the law."

She's made a fool of herself. Fine, she doesn't care. These people enjoying themselves, they don't appreciate what all this pleasure costs. "Why are you defending that man?" Pearl asks. "You have some business with him?"

"I'm merely stating facts. Carl's not a bad guy, not really. He knows I'm Jewish and he has virtually no problem with it. He considers us friends."

"Okay, so it's not a problem, but you think he likes it?"

"Besides," Alexander goes on, "he can't just disobey the policy dictated by his government back home. Imagine if you were he. What would you do?"

"I would do what is right."

"And that's why you're not the consul."

No, she thinks, that's not why. There are so many reasons.

○

WHEN PEARL GETS home, Alexander advises her to drink plenty of water and apologizes for the way their outing ended. Shockingly, he says he'd like to see her again. She says that's fine, but later she thinks about all the things he said, and worst of all, how he fawns over men like Carl. In that light, Alexander's fine clothing and manners now seem like a carefully curated costume, worn to ensure that he isn't mistaken for one of his coreligionists with their dark hats and loud voices and rough beards.

She harbors no regret for her outburst, which lost her nothing, not even Alexander's friendship. If anything, she's gained something, an understanding of who he is and where his loyalties lie.

Just as she originally suspected, a man cannot be both a Jew and an aristocrat.

Alexander's wife wouldn't be a great lady in a mansion, but another part of the disguise of a hanger-on, a neutered flatterer dependent on others for status. Here in Havana, where riches are concentrated in a closed circle, a man like Alexander probably has to behave as he does if he wants to maintain his position. And that's not freedom.

Marrying Alexander would be a compromise, like Father becoming a butcher. At least Father had a reason to settle: History got in the way of his dreams. She won't give up so easily.

○

MAYBE IT'S TRUE, what Martin said about the laws changing, about America tightening its borders. Lately, she notices that the lines at the American consulate are growing longer, and she hears people talk of trying Mexico or Argentina.

Meanwhile, she receives a letter from Basha. After a lengthy description of a new book she's been studying, she delivers bad news. Mendel has telephoned Frieda, and their engagement is back on. "I can't tell her anything," writes Basha. "Frieda has a special, fragile soul."

No, she's tougher than you think, Pearl thinks bitterly.

That same day, Pearl hears from Ben the Oak. He has wired her the money she requested. No additional message. He could have thrown in a friendly word or two. Oh, well, she doesn't need his message, just his money.

Putting on a dress to go out, she notices how loose it fits now, practically dripping from shoulders. She's been working so hard and eating so infrequently that she's lost weight. She'll have to take in her clothes.

As Pearl waits in the post office to cash the money order, she pictures Ben the Oak taking the dollars out of the bank or a sock or under the bed, then going to the post office to fill out the forms. What must he think of her, scheming this way?

Perhaps soon, she can ask him face-to-face.

○

"NO!" SAYS ALEXANDER.

They're sitting outside San Cristobal Cathedral with its pock-marked facade. Alexander argues that the only way to appreciate the architecture is to go in, but she won't because Jews should not enter a church. Nearby, an old man plays a wooden flute for change, then stops because no one's listening. Alexander is talking about the building, another glorious highlight of this city she wants to escape. Finally, she confesses her plans.

"Wait a bit longer, I could secure you a proper visa," he says. "If you had a proper visa, no one could deny you."

"And if they refuse me?" Pearl says. Maybe they'd have her name from when she tried to get in before. Alexander's friend Carl has taught her the law is not on her side. "I can't wait. I hear they're closing the borders. Soon no one will be able to get in."

The man with the flute strolls up to them. "Leave us in peace!" Alexander growls in Spanish, and the man hurries away. "If you're caught entering illegally, you might be banned forever from America."

"Like you are?"

"Yes, Pearl, as I am." He scowls, shoves his hands in his pockets.

She's surprised at his vehemence, his profound disappointment. Has she misjudged him? His intentions always seemed wafer thin, like those of a flapper, if a man could be a flapper. What's the slang for a man flapper?

"It's too late," says Pearl. "I already paid some money."

"I'll get it back for you," he says.

She's tempted by his earnest voice, the eager look in his eyes. "I still don't understand how you can help me get a visa. From your friend Carl who I offended? What exactly is your connection with him?"

"It's complicated."

"You think I wouldn't understand because I don't have your education?"

"That's rot, Pearl. You're the smartest girl I know."

"Even if you could find me a visa, how long would it take?"

"I don't know for sure. But I can talk to Carl. Or perhaps another chap there."

He'll be talking forever, she thinks. Martin's a sure thing, though not for long. If I don't go now, I might waste my chance. Alexander's way means more waiting. And if he's wrong, I'm stuck here. Sure, Alexander would be very sorry and apologize for his bad advice. He'd apologize beautifully, like an aristocrat.

"I'm sorry to disappoint you," Pearl says, "that is, if you thought maybe you and I might, you know"—she can barely say it—"Get married."

"I'd be of no help to you in that way," says Alexander bitterly, crossing his long legs. "You'd better find some other American to marry."

She wishes she had something to hit him with. "There are other reasons to get married, besides immigration."

"I know there are." He stares at his pretty shoes. She can't face him, so she stares at the shoes too. Bad enough that she as a woman is talking so directly. Can't he offer some reply? Or does he lack the basic gallantry to be frank, to tell her she's mistaken his intentions? "You caught me by surprise," he says. "I didn't think you'd leave so soon. Perhaps I hoped, irrationally, in time you might change your mind. About Cuba. And maybe about me." He pouts, digs his hands deeper into his pockets, like a little boy. She wants to pat his cheek, which is a problem. She's fond of him, but his advances stir nothing in her heart, inspire no real desire. The pretty way he talks now reminds her of the little quips he makes to impress his influential friends.

"As you say," Pearl says, "people come to this country because they've failed somewhere else. I don't want to be like that. There's no opportunity for someone like me in Havana. Here there are only a few rich people, and many more who are poor."

Alexander pauses, then says, "I may not be wealthy, but I'm not a poor man, Pearl. I have a comfortable life here. You could have it too."

Another problem. He'd do anything to preserve his comfort. He can't survive without French cigarettes, horse races, or fine suits. He hasn't been deprived, tested as she has been, so she doesn't know what he's made of, down deep. Maybe if he'd gone to the war . . . Of course, she admires him for not going, though it's kept him soft.

"I must go to America and you must stay in Cuba," she says. "How could I stay here with you and risk never seeing my sister again? I would never agree to that."

"I know." He gives her a helpless smile. "If it's America you want, I'm of no help to you. Not unless things change and there's some kind of amnesty for men like me."

"Could that happen?"

"I don't know, Pearl. And it would be false if I pretended that I did."

The wealthy, the privileged, they don't need to know things, she thinks. But poor people can't afford that luxury. We have to make choices. We have to be sure.

"Forget about me," he says. "We'll find another way to get you to America. But you must not do this risky thing. The people who smuggle immigrants, they're greedy enough to stoop to anything. You mustn't trust them."

"How do you know?" she asks. "Are you one of them too?" He turns to her, looks appalled. She says, "Is that your big secret? Your real profession?"

Alexander pauses, then lowers his voice. "I'm not one of those men, but some of them think I am. They share information with me that I pass on to men like Carl. It's my strategy to get to America. To earn my way back. Do you see now?"

"Yes," she says. "You made a deal. You're like a spy."

He digs at the cement with the tip of his lovely shoe. "The rotten part is I'm awfully good at my work. It's the one occupation I'm suited for. They're quite happy to keep me here. But Pearl, these smugglers are dangerous. Promise you won't go with them. I can get your money back if that's what's concerning you."

Maybe he's right. Pearl stops for a moment to consider it, searches the earnest expression on Alexander's fine face. Is she crazy to leave him? In some other neutral place or time, they might make a good match. But she could never imagine away what he said and did during that awful day at the country club, though she wishes she could, just as she wishes she believed that Martin was lying about the changing laws, the tighter borders. Wouldn't that be nice?

"Don't bother," she says. "I will talk to them, say I changed my mind. Women are famous for changing their minds, after all."

He seems to believe her, asks if she wants to hear more about this church and its architecture, and she says yes. How easily he accepts all her false words. If women are the weaker sex, then why are men so easy to fool?

FOURTEEN

At MIDNIGHT, PEARL STANDS UNDER THE COLONNADE OF the U.S. Consulate, its windows shuttered, its mahogany front doors bolted. Cloaking herself in the shadows, Pearl watches the Plaza de Armas, silent and deserted.

Or not quite deserted. A man is pacing only meters away, by the famous ceiba tree where Cubans make their desperate wishes. A cop, criminal, or tourist looking for a whore? If she called for help, who'd respond? Maybe this man is Alexander, following her to make sure she's safe. No, this one has too much hair.

The man continues pacing, and Pearl retreats deeper into the shadows with her wicker suitcase, packed with clothes, letters, and photos, her English-Yiddish book, a sewing kit, a small black velvet hat she'd made. And six packets of biscuits, enough for the week's journey to New Orleans. She gave the workshop a thorough dusting and mopping, and left a note for the Steinbergs saying she'd finished their last order without payment, to make up for her earlier debt.

This may be her last best chance to get off this island. America, America. She's thought, said, and dreamed that word for so long, she's sick of its sound.

The air weighs on Pearl's skin and smells sweet in a bitter way, like raw sugar burning on a stove. It's February—isn't that supposed to be winter? A full year in Havana has taught her that all months feel the same here, slight variations of intolerable heat.

The man pacing by the tree notices her, but says nothing. She spots a small traveling case at his feet. Are they waiting for the same reason?

She hears a car engine. It belongs to the Queen of England, chugging into the square. His Ford is stripped of its flags and fripperies, but the Queen drives as recklessly as ever, stopping short of a stone hitching post for horse-drawn carriages.

Pearl and the man by the ceiba tree simultaneously cross the square. In the light of a lamppost, she sees his full head of curly red hair.

Three men already sit in the back seat of the Ford as if arranged by size, starting with a baby-faced teenager crammed against one end. In the middle sits a wide-faced man wearing a tweed newsboy cap. At the other end is a portly middle-aged fellow with one bag on his lap and another tucked between his legs. Hugging his luggage, he eyes the other men. "Watch your feet," he says in Yiddish as the redhead squeezes in beside him. "These are new shoes I'm wearing. One scratch on this leather, and you'll pay."

"Listen to this one," the redhead says in Yiddish. "His roof is on fire and he worries about his challah burning in the oven." The others snicker. So they're all Jews.

Pearl feels them watching her, the only woman. At least they're Jews, so they might behave properly. If not, she can remind them how in the language of their mothers and sisters. She climbs up front beside the Queen and pats her thirty American dollars in a hidden pocket she's sewn in the lining.

That afternoon, she deposited her payment for the journey at a grocery on a street called Amarguesa—she'll always remember the name, which means "bitterness" in Spanish. In return, she was issued a receipt to give to the men who bring her to America so they can take it back to Havana to be paid. If she's deported back to Cuba, she can go to this store and present the receipt for a refund, less a fee of twenty dollars.

She's reassured to see the Queen, though he seems unusually tight-lipped tonight. He grimly inspects their receipts, which they hold up with tight fists.

"You promise it's safe, yes?" asks Pearl, hoping he won't lie to her.

"Yes, yes. Here." He slaps something hard and cold into her hand. "Martin say me to give it to you, to remember your old friend Martin, a souvenir."

She turns it upside down, unsure what it is—a comb? "Careful," says the Queen, showing her how it works. It's a silver switchblade, the handle engraved with leaves and vines. Pearl holds it by her fingertips, afraid the blade might pop out if she touches it the wrong way. Does Martin think she'll need it? Maybe it will be useful for cutting fruit.

As the Queen starts up the motor, Pearl scans the Plaza de

Armas. No Alexander. Why would he be there? Still, she looks over her shoulder once more as they speed away.

During their short ride to the port, the smell of rotting leaves gives way to a salty breeze blowing in from the water. The Queen parks beside a bakery with shuttered windows. They grab their bags, exit the car, and walk behind the Queen, who gestures for them to stay quiet and keep a slight distance.

Most of the businesses are closed for the night: dry dock repair shops, souvenir stands that cater to sailors, and penny groceries where in daytime fruit vendors polish their wares with a light coat of melted wax to make them shine. The bars are loud with jazz music and drunken sailors standing on tables and singing. Tourists line up to board a ship that's been impounded for smuggling alcohol to the States. A sign says VIEW AN ACTUAL CONTRABAND-ISTA! DAY OR NIGHT! ADMISSION 10 CENTS!

The road ends at a large open warehouse, where a sailboat with a rotted bottom is propped on a metal rack. The Queen guides them around the building to a narrow inlet, where he kneels beside a motorboat hitched to a wooden piling. Pearl watches closely, shivering in the night air. The Queen's fingers work quickly, untying the ropes as the water makes soft slurping sounds against the wood.

The portly man pushes ahead and throws his bags into the boat. "Ladies first," hisses the redhead, but the plump fellow gets on, claims a seat in the bow. The man in the cap and the Queen hold the boat steady. "Here," he says, grabbing Pearl's suitcase and offering his hand. She takes it and gets on the boat, settling in back near the motor.

"Quickly," whispers the Queen, and the rest of them scramble into the boat. The Queen jumps in back with Pearl and pushes away from shore. He passes the oars up to the ginger and the guy in the cap, and they row away from land, splashing loudly until the Queen says, "Quiet, quiet," moving his arms in slow circles.

When they're a sufficient distance from shore, the men pull up the wet oars, spattering Pearl's cheek with cool droplets of water that make her shiver. A breeze off the water blows out her hair, already plumping up from the humidity. The Queen turns on the motor and they speed toward one of the steamships that have dropped anchor in the middle of the harbor. The dock is filled with ships waiting for weeks to get paid for their cargo. Another side effect of plummeting sugar prices: Cubans can no longer afford to pay for all the goods they've ordered from abroad.

Their destination is a ship flying an Italian flag. Its massive black hull dwarfs their tiny craft. Pearl is astounded that such monstrous ships, big as castles, can float on water. The Queen takes out a whistle and blows three sharp blasts, and a man whistles back from the deck high above, then tosses down a rope ladder. The redhead catches it, and the Queen scrambles over and ties the ends of the ladder to their boat.

"How will we get our suitcases up there?" demands the pudgy man as if he's expecting a valet. Pearl's wondering about this too. The man tries to squeeze his bags under his armpit and pull himself up the ladder one-handed, but a bag slips out, hits the boat's edge, and tips into the water. The other men help him grab the bag before it sinks.

The Queen giggles, then yells up to the deck, high as a cathedral above their heads. A sailor appears, his face too dark in the shadows for Pearl to make out his features. He lowers a second rope for pulling up their luggage.

It's slow work getting them and all their baggage on board.

When it's Pearl's turn, she grips the rope ladder and pauses at the first rung. Inhaling deeply, she takes the first step, then marches steadily up the swinging ladder and doesn't dare look down. She wishes she'd worn pants for this. Also, she wishes she knew how to swim.

She climbs over the ship's railing and her boots hit the deck, a mess of tangled ropes, cigarette butts, a mix of dirt, sawdust, sand, and shards of broken wine bottles that glitter in the Italian sailor's lantern.

Pearl has never met an Italian, and she'd find it hard to distinguish between this one and a Cuban. He has dark curls, a long unshaven face, and knobby hands like an old man. His angular body juts out of a dirty striped shirt, and around his neck, he wears a red scarf, a decorative touch that gives Pearl hope.

The Italian takes frequent breaks from the work to slouch against the railing and sucks long drags from a hand-rolled cigarette. He knows very little English and no Spanish, but his language is close enough to the Queen's that they understand each other. His voice sounds deep and raspy, and when he talks, he swings the lantern he's carrying in an animated way that makes Pearl nervous.

Fortunately, the man in the newsboy cap—David, from a new country called Yugoslavia—knows the sailor's language and acts as interpreter.

"His name is Alberto," says David. "He'll be in charge of us."

Alberto isn't interested in their names. He says the rest of the crew is in Havana for the night. Pearl and the men must hide before they return. Only Alberto and the cook know of their presence, and the cook's getting a bonus to keep quiet.

"Good luck, my children," says the Queen. He turns to Pearl. "You sure you don't want stay in Cuba? We got much better weather over here. What they got in America? Nothing but sad people work all the time. No fun. No drink."

"I must go to America," she says, embarrassed by his special attention to her in front of the others.

"Then I must say you good-bye."

After saluting them all with two fingers to his forehead, the Queen scrambles over the railing, down the ladder. Pearl hears the motor buzz to life, and then his boat zips back to Havana. She'll never see this man again, and she feels sorry about it.

Alberto leads them through an oval-shaped metal door into the main cabin and down the companionway past the crew's berths. They stop at another oval-shaped door, which Alberto unlocks. He flips on a light.

They're in a large, square room that looks like a grocery, stocked with provisions loaded onto floor-to-ceiling wooden shelves tilted upward and edged in slats to prevent their contents from falling out. There are several barrels nailed to the floor, filled with potatoes, beer, and vinegar.

This room will be their home for a week, when they reach New Orleans.

Alberto explains it's his job to keep the ship supplied with water, wine, and food, much of it "spaghetti," as he calls the dried noodles that are a staple of his country's cooking. Also, he must bake the bread every morning. To prevent filching, the crew is not allowed in this room; only Alberto possesses the key. Just in case, they should sleep in the back, hidden behind two large cases of those spaghetti noodles and several tap barrels of red wine.

"No drink," he says in English, pointing to the barrels. He smiles for the first time, not in a friendly way. More like a warning.

In addition to the electric bulb, the room is lit by two portholes, which they can leave open for ventilation. Beneath these holes sits a bucket, whose function Pearl realizes with a shudder. There's a towel to cover the bucket when not in use.

The Italian speaks so quickly, David has to stop him occasionally to catch up. Though he doesn't always understand Alberto's accent, he teases out the significant points. During the day, Alberto will bring food, replenish their water supply, and empty their bucket. In short, he'll keep them alive.

Before leaving, he switches off the light and says not to turn it on again.

For mattresses, they have flour sacks stuffed with packing straw, which they arrange in the space behind the storage shelves, a tight fit for five people. The heavy man claims the most private spot, a corner by the wall. The redhead and David lay their sacks side by side at a perpendicular angle to his feet and head, leaving Pearl and the baby-faced kid to sleep beside each other, like mother and child.

She'll have to sleep with these strange men, now taking off their shoes, their jackets, even their pants. By the filmy moonlight seeping through the portholes, Pearl sits on her flour sack and pats down bits of straw that poke through the burlap. Clutching Martin's knife, she listens to the men talk, tries to guess whether any of them might be trouble.

There's Sholem, a puny gray-faced boy masquerading as a man. Pearl could easily flatten him in a fight. He's a student from St. Petersburg and a socialist, but the wrong kind for the Bolshies, who've put a price on his head.

The stout, self-important gentleman is named Avram, like her brother, though there the similarity ends. She nicknames him Skinny Avram in her mind, as a joke. He's more interested in his precious luggage than in her.

David, whom she dubs "the Italian" because of his language skills, seems like a gentleman with a calm voice and plain speech. She doesn't worry about him.

The most concerning one is the redhead. He's Yossi and he comes from Warsaw, which she counts as a bad omen right there. Also, he's constantly making little cracks. It's probably nothing, but she's watching this one.

Pearl removes her shoes, just her shoes, and rubs her aching feet.

They stop talking when they hear the buzz of motorboats, then the sailors climbing aboard, singing in deep voices, out of tune. "They're drunk as Polish soldiers," Yossi jokes, and Pearl's heart gives an extra squeeze.

"Quiet, imbeciles!" Skinny Avram says in a loud whisper. "They'll hear us."

The men lie low on their flour sacks. Pearl grips Martin's knife more tightly. She could use Martin's strength for the next few days.

Beside her, Sholem the Socialist dozes off, sucking his thumb in his sleep.

○

IN THE MORNING, she wakes up alarmed to see the boat moving toward the shore. They take turns checking the portholes, hoping for the port to disappear as it keeps coming closer. Is this a trick?

Pearl's invested every cent she has in this journey, plus what she borrowed from Ben the Oak. If she fails this time, what will she do? There's no one left to borrow from. And she can't go back to the Steinbergs a third time. She just can't ask their charity to stretch that far. She'll have to sleep on the street.

The mystery clears up when Alberto brings their morning

bread. He explains they're docking temporarily to load up on food and fuel before sailing to America tomorrow. Pearl says a silent prayer of thanks, then tears into her bread. It's surprisingly tasty, with a satisfying brittle crust. For all his surliness, Alberto has real skill at baking.

Their day is long and boring. Pearl's head hurts and her stomach is burbling, from gas or hunger. Skinny Avram keeps going through his bags, unpacking and repacking his possessions, then cracks his knuckles, one at a time. He's given up telling everyone to be quiet. Anyway, there's so much noise on the boat, they're unlikely to be overheard.

A key scratches at the door lock and Alberto enters with two Cuban deliverymen in blue uniforms hauling in crates of rum, whiskey, and gin, way more than even this thirsty crew could drink. The Cubans ignore them as they dump their crates, then leave.

"Look at it all," marvels Yossi Ginger. "We could open a bar."

They're left alone until Alberto brings dinner: long Italian noodles coated in a sweet red sauce dotted with a few—very few—bits of ground meat. David believes the meat is beef, not pork, but either way, it's definitely not kosher. Pearl tries cleaning off the meat from each noodle with her fork. She pushes it away and takes out her dry biscuits. Maybe she can work on the Sabbath, but unclean food she can never eat.

"You won't eat because of religious superstition?" asks Sholem the Socialist.

"No," she says. "I won't eat because I know who I am."

The men pause before resuming their dinners in silence.

Avram asks Pearl, "Can I have yours?" She hands him her plate. "My father always said, if you're going to eat pork, eat until the juice drips down your beard."

O

EARLY THE NEXT morning they hear the high-pitched ship's whistle declaring their right-of-way through the harbor. Pearl crouches behind a wine barrel and changes out of her skirt into her slacks, carefully placing her American money in the hidden inside pocket. Already she feels more relaxed, more powerful.

They take turns looking out the portholes. It's thrilling to watch Cuba's coastline disappear. Pearl thinks of the Steinbergs, Julieta, Isidro the peanut vendor, Martin and the Queen, and yes, Alexander. They're disappearing too.

Alberto comes in, his hands, forearms, shirt, and stubbled cheeks dusted in flour. He delivers their bread, butter, and water, then goes out and returns with several bags of straw and a stack of small burlap bags folded over his arm. Whistling a tune, he pries open a crate of alcohol and tells David that they're going to make hams.

Jews making hams?

Just watch. Alberto stuffs a burlap sack with straw, five quarts of rum, more straw, then ties off the end. See? he says. That's a ham.

It really does look like a haunch of meat.

Okay? says Alberto. You understand? Now, get started.

They exchange curious glances. Sholem the Socialist asks if they'll be fairly compensated for their work, and David tells him to shut up, this isn't a meeting of the Jewish Labor Bund. He stuffs a few bottles and straw into a sack. The others gradually do it too. Skinny Avram's the last to join in. He wonders aloud what the Italian wants all this money for. David asks and finds out that Alberto hates the sea. He has rheumatism, which is worsened by the ocean air, and he wants to earn enough to return to the poor village in the south of Italy where his family lives.

To their shock, they learn he's nineteen. Pearl had guessed about forty.

○

THEY FINISH THEIR "hams," and Pearl's sorry because the work helped pass the time. She sits on her flour sack and practices opening and closing Martin's knife.

Pearl keenly feels her lack of privacy. Alberto barges in without warning for supplies. The other men are being as nice as they can, but they burp and fart constantly. She stitches together a curtain out of burlap sacks, which Yossi and David string up so she can move the bucket behind it to do her business. Even so, it's difficult, especially when the ship rolls unexpectedly on the waves.

All day, noises drift in through the portholes, the sounds of men at work, heavy objects dropping on the deck, tools banging against pipes, shovels scraping coal. When the crew is bored, they line up empty bottles on deck and hit them with rocks, then cheer and shout in rapid-fire Italian. Pearl's father's choir sounded lovely singing arias from Italian operas, but Italian as spoken by real Italians sounds much harsher, like war cries.

Pearl's tired of their noise, as well as Yossi and David's constant debates, ranging from whether an unopened bottle of beer left out in the sun would explode in the heat, to philosophical questions about religion and the world to come. Or sometimes they recount the strange things they've witnessed in Havana, trying to top each other. Peddlers selling magic dried snakeskin, or Jews hawking Virgin Mary statues at the train station.

Hoping to impress them, Pearl describes Martin and her "old lady."

"You mean they're daughters of Lilith," says Yossi.

"A vice of capitalism, of unplanned economies," says Sholem. "If everyone behaved this way, there would be no more workers born."

Pearl's disappointed at their nonchalant reaction. Perhaps such relationships are more common than she'd realized.

In the evening, after a meal of the Italian noodles slick with garlicky oil, she settles on her own sack, rubbing an old ache out of her fingers and thinking about seeing her sisters. Once a comforting thought, the idea now makes Pearl nervous. Basha, whom she hasn't seen in years, may be a totally different person. Frieda too, now that she's been on her own, may no longer tolerate Pearl's oversight.

God in Heaven, she thinks, who will they see when they see me?

○

THREE DAYS INTO their journey, they wake up to a patch of rough weather. The whole room is shaking as the ship lists on roaring waves.

Bottles and jars of pickled vegetables slide and roll around on their shelves. Yossi, Danny, and Pearl try stuffing boxes, sacks of sugar, metal cans between the bottles to keep them still. Two of the wooden supports for the wine barrels crack and hit the floor, followed by the barrels, which roll down the middle of the room. Avram screams, while Pearl and the others chase the barrels, attempting to turn them upright.

Alberto runs in, forgetting to close the door. He inspects the barrels, which are all intact, no cracks, but the crew will need to come in to fix the wooden supports. Alberto takes the five of them to hide in his narrow room, which has no window and smells of mildew. His dirty clothes lie scattered on the floor, twisted inside out.

Avram, Yossi, and Sholem are crammed on the bed. David's on the floor. Pearl sits on a trunk. They wait silently without food, though no one's hungry; their stomachs have turned too many times as their boat tosses in the storm. Alberto left them a wine bottle filled with water, which they pass around.

A couple of hours pass. Sholem whispers meekly that he has to relieve himself. Pearl has to go too, but she's forcing herself to hold it. The bucket now seems a luxury.

Yossi and David find an empty tin lunch pail with a lid. They all look at Pearl. "Go ahead," she says, turns away, and covers her eyes. She hears the noise of Sholem's water hitting the metal, followed by similar noises as the rest of the men take their turns. Yossi says, "Pearl? We won't look." She declines, so they clamp the lid onto the pail.

A year ago, she couldn't imagine such a thing. Now this is her life, meeting strangers, sizing them up quickly, forming sudden intimacies, depending on their kindness, and then never seeing them again. It's surprising how many good people there are in the world. More than she'd hoped for.

The storm calms as the day toils on. While the sailors are at dinner, Alberto returns and leads them back to their room, which smells of fresh sawdust. The wine barrels are firmly fastened to the repaired supports. As the men admire the sailors' handiwork, Pearl crouches over the bucket. She doesn't care who hears or sees.

○

SIX DAYS INTO their journey, the ship cruises up a wide, snake-like river to the Port of New Orleans. The air is gray and smoky and smells of ash and dead fish. They peer at the city through the portholes, though their view is blocked by other boats like theirs, docked at the long, flat wharves. Cranes and conveyor belts unload coal, bananas, coffee, and tobacco. Further off are the rooflines of New Orleans against a gray sky: a puzzle of brick and concrete rectangles, dark red, brown, and white. The only color comes from the flags of different countries flying on steamships like theirs, and the currents in the water, some of them pink, some purple. Havana was far more beautiful.

Alberto comes in and out to stash the hams in the meat locker, mingling them with real legs of ham to confuse the customs inspectors. Tonight, a man with a small boat will ferry this contraband to shore. Pearl and the others will ride along.

They sit and wait for hours, too anxious to talk. Around noon, the sun pierces the clouds and bakes their room like an oven. Hoping for a breeze, Pearl sticks her face next to the porthole, but the air stays flat. Outside, a sailor plays a game, running up and down the gangplank and yelling the same refrain. David translates the sailor's cries: "Now I'm in America! Now I'm in Italy!"

Avram stands next to her. "You think Alberto's lying to us?" he asks.

"I don't know," Pearl says. "I've given up knowing anything anymore."

As if to answer Avram's question, Alberto rushes in, carrying sailor's hats, blue shirts, and dungarees.

"We have to put these on," David tells them. "Alberto says the customs inspectors are coming on board." They all talk at once, but David holds up his hand. "They're searching for booze, not us. But while they're looking, if they find us, then it's back to Hotel Cuba. Come on, we've got no time."

Pearl pulls the men's dungarees over her slacks and tightens the waist with some twine threaded through the belt loops. She tugs the blue cotton sailor shirt over her blouse, winds up her dark curls, and tucks them into the soft black cap.

"Pearl, you're a very convincing man," says Yossi.

"Thanks a lot," she says.

"See for yourself." He hands her the small mirror they've been using when they wash in the mornings. She's depressed to find that she really does look like a man, one who's worked all his life. Her face is firm and fierce, with heavy brows and a bold jaw. She's a far more convincing sailor than the ingenue she tried to portray in Key West.

"What about our suitcases?" Avram asks.

"Don't worry about them now," says David. But Pearl grabs her knife and a few photos from her case, which she stuffs into her pockets. She has her money with her all the time, stashed in that pocket she's sewn inside her slacks. If they catch me . . . she thinks. No, don't think that way. Don't think at all. Just breathe.

Alberto utters a few sharp-sounding phrases, and David says, "The inspectors are coming here. He wants us to walk around, lose ourselves among the other sailors."

"Won't the other sailors know we aren't one of them?" Yossi asks.

"Yeah," says Pearl. "And what about me?"

"He says to keep our heads down and no one will pay us attention. We should walk separately, and after a while, go to the mess hall. Alberto will find us there."

"It's a terrible idea. I'm not moving," says Avram, but they go and so does he.

Fearful she'll be recognized as a woman, Pearl lingers in the shadowy companionway until she sees the customs officers coming.

They wear the same dark-blue uniforms as the officers in Key West, and they carry long flashlights, like clubs. Pearl exits onto the deck, busy with sailors who shout out cheerfully to their friends down on the docks. For the fun of it, they heckle strangers walking by.

So these are the faces belonging to those booming voices Pearl has heard for six days. The faces look even less attractive than the voices sounded. One sailor asks her something in rapid-fire Italian. Alberto taught them to say "Bo" and put up their hands, meaning "I don't know." She does, and miraculously it works! The sailor moves on.

A few feet away, Yossi leans against the railing—she recognizes his bright hair—so she wanders in the other direction, almost tripping over a coil rope. A pair of sailors chatting in Italian walk by. She can never tell whether Italians are angry or happy.

She walks close behind them, as if she's their pal. The duo walks to the gangplank and off the ship, skipping easily down the wooden boards. Her hands trembling, she follows them. The boards sway under her footsteps, but she does not grab on to the rope railings because the sailors don't. What if she falls into the water? Her sailor's cap feels tight, squeezing her forehead as her foot touches the dock, American territory.

Another sailor salutes them, shouts something, and the two sailors laugh, shout back, wave, then walk on. Pearl waves too, passes a customs officer who pays her no notice, continues walking behind the two men down the length of the dock. Her cheeks and the back of her neck feel hot and flushed, and her stomach fills with foul air, grumbles. She shoves her hands deep into her pockets and clenches them to stop them from shaking. But all she's doing is walking, eyes fixed forward.

They step onto the sidewalk, an American sidewalk. No one

stops her. No one cares about a few sailors stretching their legs in port. Yossi and David must wonder where she is. She can't worry about them now. They'll have to look after themselves.

Pearl maintains a slight distance behind the sailors, until they stop at a dry goods store, attracted by fresh bananas. Pearl goes on walking, past cars, warehouses, an old Black man passing out handbills for a concert, buildings, and concrete. The sea is far behind her. She's waiting for a stroke of bad luck, for God to extend a hand to punish her, keep her in line, but nothing happens, and she continues walking into the heart of this city, New Orleans, with its heat and the smells of banana trees, cigarettes, and melted butter, the sounds of streetcars and flying cockroaches.

She has no direction in mind, and no one can tell her where she can or cannot go. She dares to look over her shoulder. No one's following her. To make sure, she stops abruptly, turns left at one corner, right at the next, and left again. Breathing heavily, she risks looking one more time. Still, no one's following her.

She can't risk thinking, just goes on walking. Can't risk stopping. There must be a place where she can take off this hat, these clothes, change back into a woman. There must be a station somewhere, with trains that will take her deep into the heart of this new and young country. Again she looks over her shoulder, and again no one's there, so she continues walking and walking . . .

And then she's free.

FIFTEEN

PEARL FEELS LIKE A MOUSE, A GRAY MOUSE IN A CHEAP GRAY dress and tight gray hat, in the New York train station, perversely named Pennsylvania, as if to confuse her. The soaring glass ceiling, braced by crisscrossing ribs of black steel, traps the noise of engines and hollering conductors, as well as the fumes of burning coal. Disembarking passengers push past her, swiveling abruptly on their shoe heels to weave in all directions.

Pearl straightens her hat, says a quick short prayer for luck, and then marches up the platform beside women in furs complaining about the cold, men in long thick overcoats, and porters balancing suitcases under their arms. All she's carrying is a newly purchased handbag, gray like her dress. Pearl wishes she looked nicer for her first day in New York, but the outfit was the most decent thing she could afford in New Orleans.

A worker in a blue uniform bumps past Pearl and yells an insult that startles her—not so much the words as his uniform.

Men in uniform are trouble. During the trip from New Orleans, she held her breath whenever a conductor asked for her ticket. Luckily, no one asked to see a passport. For once, she had the right piece of paper.

Here in America, she's ready for her new life to begin, for her new self to take shape. She hopes to be strong like Martin, graceful like Alexander, creative like Alma, kind and just like Mrs. Steinberg. Every person she's met has taught her something. Even the evil ones, who've taught her to always carry a good sharp knife.

Pearl's caught in the crowds pushing upstairs from the tracks and through the station, their voices echoing against the domed ceiling above and the pink marble floors below. The station interior is as large and lofty as a temple, yet it feels profoundly earthly, smelling of ink, leather, and urine.

For so long, she tried to imagine this moment, to prepare herself. Yet all the places she's been are so unlike each other, there's no way to prepare. Look at me, Pearl thinks, a girl who never went anywhere for the first twenty-seven years of her life. Now she rides boats and trains like nothing.

She sees Basha first, looking stately with her hair up, wearing a smart green American dress with a natural sash waist. Pearl, in her gray dress, must seem positively frumpy by comparison.

Frieda's waving frantically at Basha's side. She cries out Pearl's name, then flings herself into her sister's arms.

Pearl utters a tiny, high-pitched cry. Frieda, she thinks, is it really you? As they embrace, she presses her sister's limbs to ensure they're real, and to test their thickness. Is she eating enough?

Pearl lets her sister go to have a good look at her. She recognizes the tips of Frieda's tender ears, her tiny pink nose. But her hair is shorter, darker, straighter, blunter. She wears dark lipstick and pale powder on her cheeks. Also, her jaw, her arms, her hips have a new roundness, and her figure has filled out. Yes, Pearl decides, Frieda must be eating good in America. It's becoming on her.

She gives Frieda another hug. After all this time apart, it feels strangely normal to hug her sister, as if yesterday they'd woken up together in their Havana workshop.

"You look tired," Frieda shouts above the crowd.

Pearl clears her throat, finds her voice. "A rough journey." She sniffles twice to keep from crying. "Let's forget about it. Thank God, we're back together."

Basha's watching them, no longer a bookish teenage girl who exists only in memory and letters. She's now a woman in her thirties with rough hands and a fretful expression on her painted face, which resembles Father's in the brow, the hawkish nose, and the gray eyes. So this is Basha, Pearl thinks. They exchange quick kisses.

"Well," says Basha, adjusting her glasses. "You've changed."

"I hope so!" Pearl says. "The last time you saw me I wore my hair in braids."

"No, I mean something else," says Basha.

"She's right," says Frieda. "Pearl, you've lost weight." It's as if they've exchanged bodies; Pearl's the skinny one now. "And you've got muscles," Frieda adds, squeezing Pearl's arm.

"So watch out when I punch you." Pearl jabs her sister lightly, and they laugh.

Basha has brought Pearl a heavy coat that smells of another woman's perfume. She puts it on and they step out into the street, which is even dirtier than inside the station. The very air floats with garbage: ash, soot, papers, droplets Pearl cannot identify. The sidewalks, excavated between mounds of dirty snow, feel slick and rough.

But snow! Winter again! The weather has finally righted itself after being on an eerie hiatus in Havana. "I haven't seen snow in I don't know how long," says Pearl. "I want to taste some."

"I wouldn't," said Basha. "Not in New York."

"Pearl, what's with you?" says Frieda. "You're positively chatty!"

"Maybe I'm just happy to see you," says Pearl, squeezing her hand.

The avenue is clogged with cars, their horns sounding like sick geese. Buildings tall as mountains extend in every direction. As the people shove past from all sides, Pearl's cheer fades. A stranger flicks the end of a lit cigarette at her feet, as if she's the gutter. She's reminded of those peasants in Russia, darting for cigarette butts, and then to her shock she sees a shabby-looking person grab the butt and smoke it. In America?

They board a crowded streetcar, with barely enough room for them to stand squeezed between other passengers shivering in their coats and mufflers. The fringes of a stranger's scarf tickle Pearl's nose. Basha dispenses advice so Pearl won't look like such a greenhorn. Don't stare at people. Don't point at the tall buildings. If a man looks you in the eye, look away quickly if he seems strange. In America, women should behave nicely and appear modest, retiring. No yelling or pushy manners.

There's too much to take in—the screeching of the streetcar, more buildings flashing by, extending upward and outward. Do they ever end? Imagine spending your whole life hemmed in by buildings. Looking up at their highest floors makes Pearl dizzy. So do all the signs vying for her attention, and the jolt of seeing Basha after almost ten years. Frieda, between her two sisters, smiles at the ads in the streetcar. She's like a flower that's sprouted between two weeds.

When they reach the Lower East Side, the three sisters beg their pardons to push through the crowd toward the exits. Pearl notices that for all this time Basha has been in America, her English, though technically correct, comes out stiffly from her lips. By contrast, Frieda's speech sounds like singing. Pearl compliments her English, and Frieda says, "Oh, I love this language. Everything should be in English."

Pearl disagrees. She finds English clumsy, with its slang and strange sounds like *th* and *j* and *w*. She can get around, buy food, ask for basic things. Could she ever dream in such a language?

The sidewalk is covered in wrinkled newspapers, bottle caps, and bits of food. All this distraction and stimulation jumbles her thoughts, and the cold burns her nose and cheeks. Though it's evening, the lampposts and illuminated signs light up the street like day. Pushcart vendors sell copper pots, stockings, and baked potatoes puffing out white steam. Acrobats and organ grinders perform for spare coins. In Havana, Cubans burst into a dance or song when the spirit moves them. Here, people only dance and sing in public for money, and their music melts into the street noise: the whistling, wailing, and honking, the regular thunder of trains on overhead tracks, pigeons warbling, jazz records squealing, sheets of wax paper rattling in the wind, and Italians, Poles, and Jews hollering about hot bread and fresh fish.

"Who are all these aristocrats putting on airs?" Pearl asks, pointing out all the stylishly dressed people with their fur-collared coats.

Frieda laughs and Basha replies impatiently, "That's just how people dress here."

Basha and Frieda live on a block of brick buildings called dumbbells because they bulge in front and back and shrink in the middle for the airshafts. Their two-room flat, with the toilet in the hall, is up three shadowy flights of stairs that stink of stewed onions, body odor. Nowhere in Havana was there a stink this pungent. Basha says the housekeeper tries valiantly to keep the hallways clean, but with so many people sharing, it's like trying to part the Red Sea on a daily basis.

"Things are different in America," Basha and Frieda say again and again, like a prayer, or an apology.

Though they're inside, Pearl can see her breath in the cold air. Basha steps expertly over some boys playing on the steps and explains this is considered a good living situation. "The first family I boarded with made me help with the children and complained I ate too much. When Frieda came, we moved to another place where we slept in the kitchen, on a cot by the stove."

"The gas fumes gave me headaches," says Frieda.

"Why are you complaining?" Basha asks. "I always gave you the side closer to the wall, and in the morning, I ended up on the floor."

"Oh, Pearl, we're home!" says Frieda. "Welcome!"

Basha unlocks the door and lights a kerosene lamp. Frieda leads Pearl to the freezing back room, which has just enough space for two iron folding beds. "Here's where we store our clothes," says Frieda, pulling out two wooden crates from under a bed. "We'll find you a crate too." Her cheery tone sounds freakish in this dismal room, its walls covered in mustard-colored paper and streaked with the dried tracks of some dripping brownish liquid. The one small window, a smudged square pane of glass, is hidden by a thin patched curtain. Pearl nudges the curtain with her finger and sees crisscrossing lines of laundry in the airshaft.

This is America? she thinks. This place is a perfect hell. Please, God, don't let me die here.

The small front room has three wooden chairs, a table with a wobbly leg, and a two-burner gas plate on an oilcloth-covered box. Basha uses it to heat soup from cans. Frieda sets out three chipped bowls and crooked spoons. "Sorry," says Basha, "Frieda and I have been so busy working, we had no time to shop and cook you a proper meal."

Not that they'd know how, Pearl thinks. I was always the *balabusta*, cooking and cleaning while Basha studied and Frieda was busy being Frieda. The two of them could barely boil water to make kasha.

How can anywhere be so ugly? Pearl wishes she were back in Russia or Havana, anywhere but here. Then she feels guilty for the wish, like those ungrateful Israelites in the desert whining to Moses that they were happier as slaves in Egypt, where at least they had melons and cucumbers.

"You'll get used to eating food from cans," says Basha, scraping her spoon against the bottom of her bowl like a Russian farmer's wife. Her American makeover seems to have stopped at her dress.

"Basha, you'll scare her away," says Frieda and takes out a white bag. "Pearl, try one of these sweet buns. They're addicting, and so cheap. I'll show you where I buy them. We'll take you to the movies. And shopping. I'll teach you everything you need to know. Won't that be fun? Me teaching you for a change."

"It might not be so gloomy in here," says Pearl, "if we painted, or hung pictures."

"What for? It's not ours," says Basha. "If we dolled up the place, our landlord might raise our rent, say it's now worth more." She takes a loud slurp of soup.

All that money Basha sent from New York, Pearl thinks. I imagined she lived like a princess.

Wearing their winter coats, they finish eating, holding the steaming bowls close to their faces. Pearl's yearning for some fruit, something sunny and lightly sour-sweet, like the yellow-green bananas in Cuba. She doesn't care for the bun Frieda shares with her, too sugary. Pearl can't admit how depressed she feels. It's cost too much effort and money to get to America. How could all her struggling have been for this?

When they go to the back room to sleep, Frieda trips over one of Basha's books. "Why do you need so many?" Frieda snaps, kicking it across the floor. "We should sell a few."

"Don't you dare!" Basha dives for the book and takes it to bed. She falls asleep quickly, snoring just like their father.

Shivering under a flimsy blanket, Pearl listens to the sounds coming through the walls: families fighting in various languages, dishes clanking, an old man calling out the name of his dead wife. God help me, she thinks.

"I'm so glad you're here," Frieda whispers, shifting around in the bed she and Pearl share. "Basha can be tough to live with. It's like she's angry always."

"What's she angry about?" Pearl whispers back.

"Plenty of reasons," says Frieda. "She thinks she has the wrong life."

"And your life?"

Frieda pauses. "Mendel promises he'll send for me soon."

"Still singing that same old song? Soon as in days, weeks, months?"

"We don't like to put a number on it. He's busy getting settled, working, saving to find us a suitable place to live, and I think . . ."

"You think? Thoughts are worth the same as they cost, nothing. Don't they have Jewish boys here in New York?"

"Yeah. Like they have everywhere, even Cuba. Not that you noticed."

Shows what you know, thinks Pearl. She's not telling her sister about Alexander. Frieda might misunderstand and tease for months, accuse her of being sentimental.

"I'm sick of cleaning other people's floors, rich people's floors," says Frieda. "If I have to take care of anyone's floors, let them be Mendel's and mine." She draws her portion of the blanket around her shoulders. "New York is so dark these days, so cold and dreary. Let's pretend we're in Cuba, in the sunshine."

Briefly, Pearl permits herself to imagine being with Alexander, laughing over a meal in a busy restaurant. With music playing. And fans stirring the warm air.

"I don't like to pretend," Pearl says, blowing on her hands to warm them. Her fingers feel sticky. When was the last time these sheets were washed? She'll take care of that tomorrow. "I'm going to sleep."

○

PEARL HOPES HER second day in New York will be more cheerful than her first. Her sisters take her shopping for American clothes at the so-called "pig market," which has this dreadful nickname because they sell everything imaginable except pork. Pearl says she can go on her own, but her sisters insist on accompanying her, saying that as a newcomer she'd be cheated by the peddlers.

On the way, Basha points out the shuls. "I'm sure you'll want to go on *Shabbes*," she says. "We've fallen out of the habit, but if you want, we can go every week."

"Maybe," says Pearl. "For now, I want to get settled."

Today feels warmer because the sun's out, though it's veiled in a white mist. Pearl buys a bright yellow blouse with red buttons, holding out stubbornly for the price she wants, without her sisters' help. The blouse is such a vibrant color, it makes Basha blush. Pearl also buys some pantry basics: flour, salt (how can they live without salt?), and a sprig of coriander, limp but pungent. Mrs. Steinberg used it sometimes to flavor her food.

"What is it?" Basha asks, sniffing the leaves suspiciously.

"Put this in the canned soup and it will taste better," Pearl says.

They tell her in America you must wash at least twice a week. They buy tooth powder and promise to show her how to apply it to the toothbrush that Basha and Frieda share; now Pearl can share too. Pearl asks about washing the sheets. They say she can do laundry in the kitchen, in the iron bathtub, then hang the wet clothes in the air shaft to dry. Only a greenhorn takes the laundry to the river, which is probably against the law. There are so many laws here, and Basha says you have to obey them.

"Of course I wouldn't take my laundry to the river," says Pearl. "What do you think I am, a pig farmer?"

In Havana, women walk with more freedom. Here, the women march in a tight line, eyes on the ground, cheeks covered in scarves. The children dart in packs with uncombed hair and pants with ragged cuffs, and they curse and make farting noises. "Uch," says Frieda as a sooty-cheeked girl steps on her toes. "Where are the parents?"

"Working," says Basha, leafing through a new book she found at the pig market.

"When I have children, they'll learn some manners."

But the children have nowhere to play. People sit on stoops or hang out of windows and yell at fruit or clothing peddlers below. As in Havana, the buildings are crammed close together, but here they're much taller and there are few public squares. The sun and sky are rumors. There's no hint of the sea in the air, no plants or flowers, not even weeds. Pearl sees a vendor selling fistfuls of pretty purple violets and feels insulted by their beauty, so out of place in this city.

And this is supposed to be a Promised Land.

Maybe there is no Promised Land for people like her. What if she has to fight to survive for all her life? It's an awful thought, enough to break a weaker spirit than Pearl's.

Basha gets in line at a vendor cart for some hot knishes, and Frieda tells Pearl, "You see what I mean about Basha? She's impossible."

Pearl disagrees. "It's our living situation," she says. "We might be happier in a different part of town, with more space, more light, more air."

"Sure," says Frieda. "And why not a bedroom for each of us, so we don't have to share, and a view of a park, and marble floors. Meat for dinner every night, and new shoes every month. Honestly, Pearl, sometimes I think you don't want to understand."

Maybe I understand you better than you understand yourself, Pearl thinks.

Basha brings their knishes, pale brown and fat with filling. The flavor is pleasantly starchy as Pearl bites into the warm soft potato. She chews slowly to make the flavor last, to appreciate the feeling of fullness in her mouth.

Frieda finishes hers in two bites, chewing with her mouth open. "Aren't you going to finish yours?" she asks Pearl. "If you don't, I'll have yours. What happened to your famous appetite? You're all skin and bones these days."

"I'll finish it," says Pearl. "I'm just taking my time to appreciate it, that's all."

○

BASHA SAYS, "I won't let you work at a factory," and takes Pearl to where she works, a dress shop in the Garment District serving wealthy clients. Before they leave, she gets dressed up, as if for a holiday. "In America, you have to look your best when you go out," she explains.

Frieda puts on a simple black dress for her job as a maid for a wealthy Jewess on the East Side, in what Basha calls the "forties." It's the latest in a series of posts that Frieda inevitably loses. Not a surprise. As a girl, Frieda was always spilling well water or getting a splinter while sweeping the floor with a birch broom. Pearl spared her the worst chores because Frieda never knew a mother. Also, she burst into tears if you pointed out her mistakes.

Dressed in her machine-made American clothes, with their stiff, impersonal factory stitching, Pearl rides the noisy, crowded streetcar with Basha up Broadway. She wears that coat they gave her, still smelling of the other woman's perfume. And a new pair of sturdy American shoes that fit her feet as if they'd been molded to them. There's nothing like American shoes. Pearl has also powdered her face lightly. Thank God she no longer has to use Julieta's old lipstick for makeup.

"I hope you can help with Frieda," says Basha. "She's so heedless, always forgetting to turn off the hot plate or put out the lamp." Pearl asks her opinion of Mendel, and Basha says, "They've been apart so long, they'll naturally lose interest. Leave them to quarrel, and it won't look like we put our finger on the scale."

Pearl isn't yet used to Basha's company. Luckily, Basha doesn't expect a chat; she reads her book during the journey as Pearl sits with her thoughts. This doesn't seem the way sisters should be.

Pearl has so many questions. Why is a dime worth more than a penny when a dime is smaller? Why do people say "Bless you!" when a stranger sneezes? Why do Americans chew gum all the time? They look as if they've got something caught in their back teeth, and they're trying to work it free with their tongues.

And what happened to Basha's education? There must be some other work she'd rather do than make dresses. Basha, what about your dreams? But such questions feel invasive, intimate. Anyway, Pearl can already imagine the answer: "It's different here in America." Poor Basha, whose poor English must be like a prison. All those brilliant ideas and bits of knowledge swimming in her brain, without language to get them out. Meanwhile, Frieda can form the most complicated sentences you like, though her ideas are generally as simple and frivolous as a Purim carnival play.

They get off at Forty-Seventh Street, walking between hulking hotels and department stores standing shoulder to shoulder. The dress shop is on the ground floor of a low brick building with a dirty facade but impeccably clean windows, through which Pearl sees silk draperies, silver mirrors, and a soft carpet.

Basha ushers Pearl through the peach-colored showroom to meet the boss, a middle-aged widow from Vilna with a solid compact body like a tree trunk and a severe gray bob. Her name is Safaya Gluck, and she has a reputation for being strict but fair. Because she and much of her clientele are Jewish, the shop is closed on Saturdays.

Gluck's a lucky name, thinks Pearl. Hopefully I'll have good luck in her place.

"If you vouch for her, let's see what she can do," Safaya says in a raspy voice like a man's. Pearl suspects she smokes too much.

Basha leads Pearl upstairs, which smells of sewing machine oil and glue. Nine women, all Jewish immigrants, sit at three long tables with black sewing machines bolted into them, all clicking away, wheels spinning. At a station off to the side, the only male employee is entrusted with the important task of cutting the material.

Pearl chooses one of the wooden spindle chairs and snaps on the electric lamp above her machine. Okay, she thinks, something familiar. She launches into her work, stopping once to use the toilet, and again at lunchtime, when she goes out to get cheese sandwiches with Basha and a chatty girl named Batya, who goes by Betty and has pretty gray-green eyes. "So Basha has a sister," she says.

"That's what they tell me," says Pearl.

Betty laughs. "You'll fit right in here." She loosens the pale-green scarf she uses to tie up her hair, which falls to her shoulders in a smooth wave. How wonderful to have such lovely flowing hair, thinks Pearl, keenly aware of her own intractable curls. "It's a fair shop. You can talk or sing while you work. The clocks are real clocks that keep the right time. And no fines for missed stitches or staying too long in the toilet."

"I don't spend long in the toilet anyway," says Pearl.

Betty laughs again. "Basha," she says, "your sister's a riot!" But Pearl doesn't know what joke she made.

When Pearl returns to her station, she finds gray-haired Safaya holding up the hem of the dress she'd been sewing, examining it with a magnifying glass as wide as a tea saucer. Pearl coolly takes a seat, thinking, if you don't like my work, you don't know what good is, and there's nothing I can do for you.

But Safaya rests her firm squarish hand on Pearl's shoulder.

She announces, "Not too bad. Maybe a bit crowded just here. But you're okay."

"Sure, I'm okay," says Pearl. "This isn't my first time doing a seam. And I don't see where it's crowded. These stitches are perfectly even." She points to where Safaya criticized, knowing she's right. She wouldn't have dared talk this way to Mr. Steinberg, though because of him, she knows what she's worth. "Seams, zippers, pleats, puffed sleeves, I've got experience with everything. And I'm not afraid of hard work."

"I can see that," says Safaya. She pulls Pearl's shoulders back slightly. "If you sit this way, relax your posture, you'll get more done and you won't kill your back."

"I was born knowing how to sit by a sewing machine," Pearl mutters, and the girl next to her giggles.

"What was that?" Safaya asks.

"I said, may I please get back to work now? I want to finish these seams."

Betty and another girl are craning their necks to hear more. Safaya purses her lips. "Your sister's a spirited one," she says to Basha, who starts apologizing. "No, it's all right," says Safaya. "Let her prove she's as good as she says."

"Don't worry," Pearl tells Basha after Safaya goes away. "She'll see who I am."

○

EACH MORNING, PEARL takes the trolley with Basha to the shop, where she hangs her coat and hat on a peg to keep them clean. She gets used to the clack-clack-clack of the sewing machines in her ears, and the heat from the clothes press, which the women also use to warm their lunch. That heat is welcome in winter, though Pearl can only imagine how awful it will feel in summer.

The women take turns singing while they work. The ones at one table will start:

Working woman, working woman, endless days of toil and pain
But when my darling true love comes, my life will be my own again.

Inevitably, the others sing back, at the top of their voices:

Suffering is a woman's lot in the home or in a shop.
A husband's just another boss, so either way, our freedom's lost.

Betty goads Pearl to sing too, so she warbles a few scandalous lyrics from "I'll See You in C-U-B-A," and the women laugh and laugh. They laugh all the time, over jokes or newspaper comic strips like *Gasoline Alley*, or while teasing painfully shy Jacob, their cutter, always in need of a new shirt or a haircut. They dream of finding a man to marry and take them away from the shop—at the very least it would be a change of scenery—but poor pokey Jacob would never do, because of his personality.

In America, you're expected to have a personality, and Pearl learns that she's considered a jokester. Though at first she wasn't trying to be funny, she likes her new role, so she plays it up. "Stop waiting for some man to save you, ladies," she'll say. "Go out and look for some man to save instead."

That line always sets them shrieking with laughter.

Pearl hopes she can earn enough so she and her sisters can move, but there are so many unexpected expenses, like paying ten cents into a fund for buying coffee and tea. As the women sip their drinks, they crowd around copies of *True Story*, with its romantic tales, or *Ladies' Home Journal*, with pictures of proper American homes with sprawling lawns. Basha sits on her own with a book she's using to improve her English, though occasionally she looks up from her reading and listens to the conversation.

Pearl's favorite girl is Betty, who teaches her how to use a Marcel iron to tame her curls into stylish waves. How wonderful, that one invention could solve a lifetime of struggle. There at least is one good thing about this country.

Betty lives on coffee and tea, doctoring it with plenty of milk and sugar so it feels like a meal. She's saving her lunch money to stay at some fine hotel upstate and meet a rich man. "Say, Pearl, you got a fella yet?" Betty keeps asking.

"No, what for?" says Pearl, sipping her tea without sugar. "How about you?"

This usually prompts Betty to complain about her latest steady, another in a string of dewdroppers, meaning lazybones. More American slang for Pearl to learn. Also, a steady is a boyfriend. There are many rules about choosing a steady. Like, if a boy takes you uptown and treats, it's okay if he tries something, just not too much.

"If a boy tried something on me, watch out," says Pearl and shows off the knife Martin gave her. The girls crowd around as Pearl opens and closes it.

"Oh, Pearl, you're terrific!" Betty marvels.

"Ladies," says Safaya, interrupting their conclave, and they hurry back to their tables. "Back to work." She beckons Pearl with her finger. "And you, follow me. I've got something for you." Pearl sticks out her tongue at Safaya's back to make the other girls laugh, then follows her downstairs to meet a customer, a wealthy widow who has asked to meet Pearl, whom she wants to work on all her clothes in the future.

"Of course," says Safaya. "She'd be glad to."

"Yes, ma'am," says Pearl.

Safaya gives Pearl more and more work, especially the dresses needing the most delicate, complicated stitching. Occasionally Safaya gives Pearl tiny suggestions, which Pearl usually ignores, but there are no additional criticisms about crowded seams. And when Jacob the cutter is out sick, Safaya entrusts Pearl with the scissors.

A woman cutter? It's unheard of. "Just watch me," says Pearl and attacks the material with the determination of any man. When the day ends, the other girls applaud for her. Even Safaya joins in. Elated, Pearl and Basha go home to share the news with Frieda, who's sulking in bed, nibbling a sweet bun.

"You're lucky to have other girls your own age to talk to," she says. "The other servants at Mrs. Rosenbaum's are a thousand years old. They talk about me when I leave the room." She looks at Pearl. "I've got to get married. Don't you see?"

Basha picks up a book and drifts into the front room. "No, I don't see," says Pearl, irritated with Frieda for changing the subject.

"Look at the women I work for, or the women who come to your shop for fine dresses. Do they work as secretaries? I'm certainly as pretty as they are. Why don't I deserve what they have? I'm no good for anything else. I'm not like you."

"What did you mean, you're not like me?" Pearl asks. "Not like me how?"

"Oh, you know," Frieda says. "Lately, you've become this aggressive person. Of course you've always been that way with me, but now you're like this with everyone. Next, you'll be taking over that dress shop."

"Maybe I will," says Pearl, surprising herself. For now, all she wants is for the three of them to get along, which is impossible in such tight quarters. She must make more money so they can move, have space to breathe so they don't kill each other.

She decides to ask Safaya for a raise.

Basha cautions her not to. Safaya's a tough cookie, and Pearl's barely been there a month. What if Safaya fires her? But Pearl says too bad, her mind's made up. If Safaya doesn't like it, there are other dressmakers in Manhattan. In the morning, however, she has second thoughts as they leave for work and pass an evicted family on their stoop, with all their furniture and a plate for strangers to drop coins. It feels like a bad omen. But Pearl isn't sure she believes in omens anymore. Better to believe in herself.

Pearl waits until the others leave. On her way out, Betty pinches her arm for good luck. "See you at home," Basha whispers and follows Betty out to the street. It's dark outside and inside the shop too. Safaya sits at her slim mahogany desk with its brass claw feet, filling out order slips in the showroom by the light of a tiny green lamp. This desk is a flimsy, impractical piece of furniture. Pearl would have chosen a solid man's desk with fat legs and plenty of drawers. All her nerve fails her. Jokey Pearl vanishes, and the old Pearl, shy and meek, comes to reclaim rightful ownership of her soul.

Without looking up from her order slips, Safaya asks, "Yes?" Up close, at the end of a workday, Safaya appears less intimidating, her eyes more tired, her shoulders gently curved, her hair grayer.

Pearl says, "Well, it's like this. I got to earn more money."

Safaya removes her narrow reading glasses and sets them on the desk. She looks carefully at Pearl as if sizing her up for a dress.

Pearl continues: "I need it for myself and my family. And you're giving me more work all the time. You like my work? You've got to pay for it."

Safaya's lips are pressed together—in anger? Amusement? She says, "Why don't we discuss it? Are you hungry?"

"I want a rise," says Pearl, using the English word, then adds, "or I'm leaving."

Safaya laughs. "It's raise, Pearl, not rise."

"Oh," says Pearl, ashamed. She hates making English mistakes, particularly at a time like this. One day, she thinks, I'll speak such good English, I'll throw my dictionary into the East River. How many English words can there be to learn?

"Let's grab a bite," says Safaya, "and we'll talk."

They walk to a real restaurant, not a dairy bar where people eat at a counter, but a restaurant with starchy tablecloths and stiff, printed menus. Bewildered by all the options, Pearl stares blankly at her menu. Safaya laughs and says, "Leave it to me. I know what's good here." Safaya does all the ordering, talking, and paying. Usually so terse and quiet at work, she talks and talks, about her late husband, her only daughter, now in California, and the ache in her fingers she can never massage away.

First, they're served a salad, American style. Americans love eating vegetables with their meals: lettuce leaves, spinach, and green beans. Pearl finds them tasteless and sour, but she's not one to leave food on her plate.

"Where did you learn such beautiful table manners?" Safaya asks. "You don't eat like a factory girl."

Blushing, Pearl silently thanks Alexander. He's taught her well.

"You're different from these other girls," Safaya says. "You've got quality."

"My father was a cantor. He was born in Lithuania."

"I'm not talking about your father. I'm talking about you, Pearl." Safaya taps the table with her knobby index finger. "These other girls, all they think about is getting married. But it's 1923, not 1823. These are modern times. You have an eye, a feel for the material. I bet you could become a designer someday if you wanted."

"Really?" Pearl knows she has talent, but has never imagined someone like Safaya might recognize it so quickly. How much more per hour does a designer make compared to a seamstress?

"Yes. If you'll permit me to guide you. Take my suggestions sometimes instead of disregarding them. You know a lot, Pearl, but not everything. You haven't lived as long as I have. I can share with you what I learned from hard experience. I can save you time and difficulty, if you're open to it."

Pearl feels so happy, she stares down at her plate to hide it. This restaurant serves food on beautiful white plates, and at every place an ironed napkin. They must trust the customers not to steal them.

Safaya pats her mouth with her fine cloth napkin. "Or maybe you're like the other girls. Waiting for a man to say I love you, so you can wait on him hand and foot all your life. And then you'll go away from me. Is that what you want?"

"Don't worry. I'm not the marrying type," says Pearl.

Safaya drops her napkin. Leaning over to grab it, she asks, "Why not?"

Pearl wishes she hadn't said that. "I just know myself," she says. "That's why I have to earn more, so I'll never have to depend on anyone. Maybe I'm not as pretty as some girls, or as smart as Basha, but I work hard."

"You don't think you're as smart as your sister?" says Safaya.

"Basha's a very smart girl," says Pearl. "She went to gymnasium."

"And so are you smart. But are you smart enough to accept my help?"

Pearl feels embarrassed again. Talking this way with Safaya is like talking to a friend. Certainly she has far more in common with Safaya than man-crazy Betty. However, Pearl can't forget her mission. "Anyway," she says, "my rise?"

That evening, when she gets home, Pearl announces to her sisters' astonishment that all her demands have been met.

"How did you get her to agree?" Basha asks in awe. She's rubbing the wrinkles out of her cheeks with cold cream, her one extravagance, a rare nod to vanity. The cream works for a while, at night. But each morning, the wrinkles return.

"I said what's fair is fair. I said to her, you like my work? Pay me for it."

"And what did she say?" Basha asks.

"Nothing. What could she argue? She said okay."

Basha lets out a low whistle and screws the lid shut on her jar of cold cream. "I'm there a year, and nothing. You come in and after what, four, five weeks, you're the hero of all the girls on the floor and you've got a raise."

"You exaggerate. It's not exactly like that," Pearl says.

"Yes, it is exactly like that."

Pearl wants to argue, but then enough people are saying what Basha is saying about her. To pretend otherwise would be a lie.

"Good for you, Pearl," Frieda says, stretching out her hands near the stove to warm her fingers. "People used to say I had the loveliest hands. Now with all the scrubbing I do for Mrs. Rosenbaum, I have the hands of a goatherd. Fat and rough."

"I told Safaya what I wanted and she said okay," Pearl repeats, annoyed that Frieda is once again turning the conversation back to herself.

"I tell you, I'm sick of Mrs. Rosenbaum. And all the Mrs. Rosenbaums," Frieda says. "I didn't come to America to be a maid. I look like a wreck. I can't go on like this anymore. I've got to do something else, change my life."

She has more to say, but Pearl turns away, goes into their sleeping room, and punches the mattress on the bed they share. She wants me to join her misery, but I refuse.

Pay attention, Frieda, won't you? Safaya said I could be a designer someday.

SIXTEEN

SAFAYA REWARDS PEARL WITH HER FIRST RAISE THE VERY next week, and another raise two weeks after that. The newspapers say the economy is good lately. Maybe it's true because orders keep coming in for fancy dresses, adorned with expensive beading, lace, fringes, and bows. Pearl stays later at work, eating dinners paid for by Safaya, bringing home magazines and patterns supplied by Safaya. Together they visit suppliers, storerooms crowded with bolts of cloth, poky storefronts filled only with buttons or ribbons or lace.

Safaya gives Pearl some material and allows her to come up with her own design. Pearl is thrilled. Her brain is full of clothing and patterns. She wakes in the middle of the night, thinking of new ideas. Each morning, she feels inspired to work on the dress, and when it's finished, she stands back from the dummy and takes satisfaction in knowing what she's done is good.

Pearl has made a daring navy-blue V-neck with a lime-green

sash, a bolt of lightning in this sober urban landscape. Lately, she craves accent pieces in tropical Caribbean colors: lime greens, cobalt blues, and bold yellows. She needs these shots of color in drab New York, stubbornly gray all March and into early April.

"Outstanding work," says Safaya, "but no."

"What's wrong with it?"

"Only that I could never sell such a thing. It's too loud for the modern woman."

"If it's good, you teach the customers what to like," says Pearl. "You lead them."

"That's a sure way to go out of business," says Safaya. "It's a nice start, Pearl. Just keep refining your ideas. Go see what's in the stores. It's all right to get out in front of the fashions by a step or two, but not a mile."

Pearl, fuming, disagrees, but she has no choice; she's not her own boss. So she goes back to working on Safaya's dresses and designs. A day later, she takes out the V-neck again and begs Safaya to try to interest a customer with it. It's no use.

Then she visits a department store and sees what Safaya's talking about. The dresses, blouses, and skirts are all in a muted palette of colors: pistachio green, cadet blue, parchment yellow, dusty pink. Touching the sunny orange scarf she has on, Pearl feels like a lost tropical bird who's been blown into this city on a trade wind. Yet she doesn't remove the scarf. She likes the color anyway.

Meanwhile at work, Safaya keeps saying, "Someday you'll start your own shop and leave me. Or you'll get married. Everything I value I lose. It's my lot in life."

"I tell you, I won't go anywhere," says Pearl. "I'm plenty happy here."

"No you're not," says Safaya. "You want to make Joseph's coat of many colors. You resent me because I won't let you."

How should I answer, Pearl thinks. You wouldn't let me do what I want, and I followed your orders. Now you want me to lie, say I'm happy for it?

Later she tells Basha about what Safaya said, and Basha explains that Safaya's husband died very early in their marriage, and her daughter in California rarely writes or calls. "We in this shop are like her family," Basha says.

"I don't think so," says Pearl. "Safaya is a strong woman."

○

MAY FINALLY ARRIVES, and Pearl's spirits lift with the warm weather.

Once, while she's getting off the streetcar, a pack of Italian boys taunt her with the chant, "Greenhorn, foreign-born, make her cry! Fly, fly, go to hell and die!"

Pearl faces the boys with her angriest glare. "No, you will die," she says, aiming two fingers at each of their foreheads. "And your souls will enter a cat, and a mad dog will bite it." They look surprised, even scared. She laughs, then resumes her walk home.

Anyway, this name-calling happens only the one time. Her current attitude about her new home can be summed in a single word of American slang: okay. She's grown used to the dull ache in her eyes and back, her frayed nerves, and New York itself, the dirt, the crowds, the constant smell—only the nature of the stink varies from neighborhood to neighborhood. At least she's making decent money, and she knows her way around.

Here, even a factory worker or a poor seamstress can afford white bread. On occasion, she and her sisters eat kosher meat, and every day, they have real coffee with cream and sugar, though Pearl is losing her taste for sweets. The food has so much sugar: candy, doughnuts, cookies, ice cream, soda, and ice cream mixed with the soda. In Cuba they had plenty of sugar too, but they didn't put it in the food so much.

Each month she earns more, though with their expenses and the money she sends Father, it's not enough to move. Maybe the girls in the shop are right: The only way out is marriage, which is also a trap if you pick wrong. Anyway, no one's lining up to ask Pearl, so she'd better get used to being poor. But then, when was she not poor?

She fixes up their place to make it more cheerful, scrubbing the floors with baking soda, dusting the bureau top and chair backs, and hanging colorful fabric and pretty magazine ads to hide dirty patches on the walls. "So much color," Basha complains. "Makes me dizzy."

"You should have seen the colors in Cuba," says Frieda. "The flowers, the fruit, the sunlight. Remember how beautiful it was, Pearl? All those lovely long walks in the sunlight."

"You did all the walking in the sunlight," Pearl says. "I was in the shop doing your work and mine."

"I see you still enjoy playing the martyr," says Frieda.

"Ladies, please, peace in the household," says Basha, removing her glasses to wipe the lenses with a rag. "I stay out of the sun. It's bad for the eyes. And it dries the skin, adds years to the face."

Sometimes Pearl agrees with Frieda: Basha can be a pill, especially when she tries to play the older, wiser sister. But unlike Frieda, Basha lets Pearl teach her how to make a simple soup and lightly fry eggs so they don't taste tired. Frieda cares only about frivolous diversions like the movies or dance halls or letters from Mendel.

One evening after work, Pearl is strolling home, enjoying the pleasant warm air of late May. Near the apartment, she notices a forlorn-looking woman buying a nonkosher hot dog from a peddler. Then she realizes the woman taking a savage bite of her hot dog is Frieda. She's never appeared quite so miserable, so lost. The way Pearl felt so often in Havana. Maybe she's had another bad day at Mrs. Rosenbaum's. Being in this city has been tough on Frieda, who has no special skills, only her looks. And there are already plenty of pretty girls in New York.

Pearl goes over and says, "Hello, Frieda."

"Oh." Frieda shoves the rest of the hot dog into her mouth as if afraid Pearl will make her throw it away. When she finishes, she asks, "You're not going to scold me?"

"No," says Pearl. Surprisingly, seeing Frieda consume *treyf* doesn't bother her. As if her sister is a stranger whose behavior isn't Pearl's responsibility. "None of us is so perfect all the time."

○

PEARL'S ENGLISH IS slow to improve, likely because at work and at home she speaks Yiddish. In the markets, at the baker's and the butcher's, it's all Yiddish. She reads Yiddish newspapers, eats in Yiddish dairy bars, and when tickets are cheap or when Safaya pays as a treat, she attends Yiddish theater, where the air is warm, the floors and walls are clean, and the seats comfortable. Pearl's favorite play is *The Jewish King Lear*, which reimagines Lear as an immigrant on the Lower East Side. He has two religious daughters who keep kosher and observe the Sabbath but treat him cruelly, as well as a gentle atheist daughter who marries a goy and hasn't gone to shul in years. The atheist is the heroine.

Basha asked once why Pearl spends more time at the theater than in shul. It's not that Pearl has become an atheist like the daughter in the play. She's simply tired from work and needs her Saturdays to rest. Anyway, her faith is modern, the kind she doesn't have to prove by standing with the women at the back of a shul every week.

Determined to improve at English, Pearl reads the papers but finds them boring. She asks Frieda to teach her, but Frieda's always tired or busy. Pearl registers for night classes, where the instructor makes the students recite poetry by Longfellow. I don't need that, Pearl thinks. I need words like *invoice, baste,* or *no meat on my sandwich*. She drops out after a month.

She spends most nights alone, while her sisters go out almost constantly. Basha attends a women's discussion club, though she complains the meetings devolve into gossip about movies and romance novels. Sometimes she puts on her best green dress, which makes her look like a schoolmarm, and goes to free lectures at the Settlement House on topics like "The Life of Louis XIV" or "Scenes of an African Village." Though she doesn't understand half of what is said, she feels it's a way to continue her education.

Frieda laughs at her. "How will you meet a man at a lecture?"

"There are nice men at the lectures," says Basha. "American men. Not these Yiddish types who smell like herring or the factory floor."

"Let's see her bring one home," Frieda tells Pearl later.

Frieda spends her evenings with new friends, often at the dance halls. Her English is so proficient that at these dances she's sometimes mistaken for native born.

One Sunday evening in June, Frieda drags Pearl along, after combing her hair and powdering her cheeks. "If you don't dress well or wear face powder, you won't get asked to dance," she says.

This dance, sponsored by a Jewish culture club, is held in a hall on Grand Street. Entry is free for women, twenty cents for men. The polished marble floor is slippery under Pearl's new shoes, which Safaya helped her choose. They have pointy toes and rickety heels, and Pearl dislikes their gloomy dark color, but sometimes it's easier to go along with Safaya and fume in silence than argue.

Colorful banners float above the mirror-lined walls. A sign over the refreshment table reminds guests to observe the rules of proper deportment at all times. There's a band on a platform led by a "professor." In a corner, an American dance instructor gives lessons to girls who don't know the moves. Frieda tells Pearl not to bother. "I'll teach you. We will dance together until a man comes and 'breaks' us."

"And if I don't like the man?" says Pearl.

"Stop arguing and let's begin," says Frieda. So Pearl takes Frieda's hand and waist, spinning her around. "Pearl," Frieda hisses, "not like that!"

"Not like what?"

"You know, with so much rhythm and shaking. This isn't a Cuban street festival. It's a proper dance hall." Frieda's demonstrating a simple two-step when a man in a brown suit asks her to dance. "I?" says Frieda in her lovely English. "Well, I suppose."

Pearl, glad for the break, serves herself some syrupy punch and an American-style cookie, like a biscuit, but sweeter. Her face is flushed from the hot room, which smells of dime-store perfume and bitter aftershave.

Frieda's partner asks for another dance, and Pearl loses sight of them. The ragtime music isn't to her liking, and neither are the men in their sweat-stained shirts. A few men ask Pearl to dance, but she's not interested in these no-good dewdroppers. She roams the perimeter of the room, then spots Frieda, who's trying to pull away from her partner. He's kissing her and squeezing her tight. As Pearl rushes over, she hears him say, "Come on, my sweet little dumpling, be a darling."

"Keep your hands off, please," Frieda says, squirming in his arms.

"I know you fresh-off-the-boat Yids pretend you're innocent, but you want it all the time, don't you? You're a bad little girl, right?" he huffs.

Her head swirling with fury, Pearl punches him in the back, hard. Stunned, he lets go of Frieda long enough for Pearl to pull her outside. They run down the block and turn onto busy Allen Street, where they stop to catch their breath in the humid summer air. At least here is cooler than in that crowded hall. Pearl's feet are throbbing in her new shoes.

"Where did you learn to hit like that?" Frieda asks, panting.

"It's nothing." Pearl's recalling the Queen of England and his mean left hook. She slows her breathing. She's fine now, in control. "You okay?"

"No, I'm not." Frieda yanks off her hat and fluffs the back of her hair. "Did you hear him call me a Yid?"

"Sometimes I think there are more anti-Semites here than in Russia," says Pearl. Definitely more than in Cuba. No one there called her a name for being Jewish.

Frieda lets out a bitter little laugh. "I thought I was really becoming an American. Men like him think I'm some stupid greenhorn they can play with."

"When you try to be someone you're not, it's a crime against yourself."

"I know, I know. You and Basha think I don't, but I do know myself. And now you'll tell me I live in dreams and I should give them up."

"Maybe not all of them." Pearl smooths out an errant lock of Frieda's hair. "What's life without a dream or two?"

○

AT THE END of summer, Betty at the shop gets engaged to her latest steady. Not her true love, just the guy who happens to be around now that she's tired of working. The women celebrate, decorating the sewing machines with ribbons and pooling their money to buy Betty an American-style cast-iron skillet.

As the women exchange toasts of seltzer water, Pearl stares glumly at the skillet. Safaya comes over, says, "Watch, you'll get married next."

"I tell you, I won't," says Pearl. "I've got a chance to make something of myself. I wouldn't waste it marrying some factory worker."

"That's my good girl," says Safaya.

Afterward, Basha goes to her English club and Pearl trudges home, reflecting on Safaya's words. Good girl. Am I her good girl? I'm tired of always being someone's good girl. She hasn't given up her dream of opening her own shop, but it seems like she can never save enough. Plus, all her contacts come from Safaya. What existence does she have of her own? She is Safaya's good girl.

Opening the door to their rooms, Pearl is greeted by a pot of boiling water that's almost evaporated steaming on their hot plate.

She quickly removes the pot, turns off the plate, then runs into the bedroom, where Frieda has spread her clothes across both beds, along with a suitcase.

"I have news," Frieda says. She holds up a train ticket to Detroit. It's real. Mendel wants her. "I told him if he didn't send for me now, I'd break with him forever and this time I meant it. And look, here's the ticket! Pearl, we're going to be married."

So this is it. Frieda's really leaving. Somehow Pearl had imagined that she and Frieda wouldn't be separated again, even if Frieda did marry Mendel. Maybe she hadn't quite understood the distance between Detroit and New York.

"Don't," Pearl says, removing a dress from the suitcase.

"Pearl, no. You can't stop me."

"But you're wrinkling it horribly," says Pearl. She unfurls the garment, a beige tailored silk-blend crepe, Frieda's nicest dress. Feeling sad for the way it's been treated, Pearl tenderly pats the material back into shape.

"Pearl, you knew it would eventually happen," says Frieda.

"Because of a promise you made to some boy years ago in Turya? He may have changed since then. You may have changed."

"Aren't you always saying I should accept myself as I really am?"

"But what if being Mendel's wife, or anyone's wife, is not who you really are?"

"I know that it is. And stop running down Mendel."

"Forget Mendel. Why marry anyone right now? Frieda, give things more time. Don't get married because you haven't found your place yet here."

"Where is that, working as a maid? No, my place is at Mendel's side."

"Father will be furious. And I'll..." But Pearl can't think what she'll do. She's tried everything, arguing, pressing. And she's tired. "I'll be lonely," she admits. Though they haven't gotten along well lately, the thought of Frieda's absence is shattering.

"You can visit."

"Visit," Pearl repeats. "When? And with what money?"

"I can't stay here to stop you from being lonely," Frieda says.

In Turya, Pearl could have appealed to family honor, maybe locked her sister in a cupboard or something. But here, where there is free will, people do as they wish. Pearl likes that way for her own life. The price is that Frieda too must have her free will.

"After we fold these clothes properly, I'll fix you something for dinner," says Pearl. "So you don't burn the house down."

○

FRIEDA GOES TO stay with Mendel's uncle and aunt for a few weeks before the wedding, weeks that become a month, which turns into two months, then three. Finally, the marriage is set for the Christmas holiday, the only time Mendel can spare from work.

Unlike after their first separation, Pearl feels more numb than depressed. The weather turns gray and cold again, miserable. She buries herself in her work, her fabric. I feel okay, she tells herself. Better than okay. I feel lighter. Frieda's a worry off my mind.

But these thoughts are lies. Pearl has a hole in her heart. She feels it every day.

At work, Safaya stops by Pearl's table. "You're quiet lately."

"Eh, it's nothing," says Pearl. "I've been on my own more recently. I've gotten out of the habit of conversation."

Safaya sits on the edge of the table. "I belong to a group of single women who meet socially on occasion. Would you like to come, make some friends?"

So Sunday afternoon, Pearl attends a coffee klatsch at Safaya's apartment. She wears a new dress she's made, a flowing lavender-colored number with a flashy yellow collar of which she's quite proud. She brings a bouquet of violets as an offering.

It's her first time at Safaya's flat, surprisingly small and crammed with pretty furniture, tall chairs with tiny feet, dainty tables with glass tops resting on thin brass legs. If you move wrong, you might break something. "Very nice," says Safaya, accepting the flowers, then leads Pearl to the sitting room. The women, who are mostly middle-aged or older, are having a political discussion, throwing out names of people Pearl never bothers about, like Calvin Coolidge, who's now the president (as if such a thing could affect her life), and Margaret Sanger. The women toss around words like "shit," "libido," and "birth control," arguing nonstop, pausing only when there's a knock at the apartment door, and they crane their heads to see who's coming in.

Pearl asks Safaya for water. "Yes, yes, in the kitchen," says Safaya, then rejoins the discussion, eager to offer her opinion about Governor Smith.

In the kitchen, Pearl ignores a contraband bottle of dry sherry and fills a glass with water from the sink. She hears someone at the door. Funny, these guests all knock the same way: three sharp raps, followed by a quick double-knock. Maybe it's a new fashion. Returning to the living room, she squeezes past a young woman with greased-back hair who wears a man's shirt with rolled-up sleeves, revealing a star-shaped tattoo on her forearm. She flexes her bicep to the cheers of two admirers, performing with the bravado that Pearl hasn't seen since her conversations with Martin in Cuba.

And now it's clear to Pearl what kind of party this is.

She's puzzled. Safaya once had a husband. Is it possible to change? Watching her boss talking with these women, Pearl wonders: Is this how Safaya thinks I am? What have I said or done to give that impression?

Safaya lets out a loud ringing laugh like Pearl never hears in the shop. She comes over to see how Pearl's doing. A lock of her hair has loosened itself from her tight bun, and she lets it hang there.

"I should go," Pearl says. "I don't know anyone. My English is terrible."

"Stop it, Pearl," says Safaya. "I mean it." She presses her hand. "Don't put yourself down this way. I won't let you. You're as good as anyone here. Okay?"

"O-o-okay," says Pearl. Safaya thinks I feel inferior, to these women?

"That's a good girl. Now let me show you around."

Safaya introduces Pearl to a woman who smells of powdered soap and works all week in a stationery store, where she's terrified of losing her job. "Even when they force me to take a day off, I stop by to make sure they don't give my post to a younger girl."

"Yes," Pearl says in a noncommittal voice. She sits primly on her chair, presses her knees together, folds her arms tightly across her chest.

An auburn-haired young woman sits beside Pearl, holds up a mug of dark, sharp-smelling liquid. "This so-called sherry's making me woozy. Tastes more like cough medicine." The woman wears an emerald-green blouse that sets off her ruddy hair and fair complexion. She seems nice enough.

"I don't like alcohol so much," says Pearl.

"That's wise of you," she says. "Are you a friend of Safaya's?"

"I work for her."

"Oh, yes, she mentioned you were coming. Said you're an absolute treasure."

"She talks about me?" This woman has glittering green eyes, a rare color, like a dark jade. Pearl could stare at those eyes for a while. Any man would be proud to have her on his arm. No one would guess just by looking what she's like.

They're interrupted by that funny knock again—clearly it's a signal—and then a great cheer. Here is the bootlegger, a woman in a man's suit and a black bowler. She's brought gin, dyed pink with a splash of grenadine. As it begins to flow, Safaya puts on a record, and the ladies pair up to dance.

"How about it?" the woman asks Pearl, offering a long white hand.

Pearl considers it. This woman seems plenty nice. Of all the guests here, she'd be the one Pearl would choose.

Two women rush to the window to pull the curtains so no one can look in. All this listening for signals at the door, hiding behind curtains. It's too much like Pearl's life in the Old Country, living behind closed shutters, turning off the lights, hiding in the dark.

What are you doing? Pearl thinks. Stop this nonsense.

She gives the lovely woman a shy smile and shakes her head no. You're a sweet girl, Pearl thinks. You deserve good things. But not from me. I came to this country to be free, to live out in the open.

"Suit yourself." She rises from her chair and approaches another woman. Soon, they're dancing. Pearl watches the two women holding each other and thinks of that woman in Cuba, the one with the cigar and the artificial bird on her head who tried to teach her to tango. The way these women dance is different. It has tenderness.

She wonders, Will I always live my life without any love?

"Excuse me," Pearl says to no one and slips out of the flat. She trots downstairs to the lobby, bangs open the front door, and inhales deep lungfuls of fresh-dirty air. Which way will she go? It all depends on the choices she makes now.

SEVENTEEN

CHRISTMAS EVE, PEARL BOARDS A NEARLY EMPTY TRAIN bound for Detroit. If Frieda must get married, at least Pearl can watch, make sure it's proper. Basha's staying behind, ostensibly because Safaya can't spare them both for so long. "The ticket is so expensive, and what would I say to all those people I don't know?" says Basha. "You're closer to Frieda anyway. You practically raised her. I'll stay here, get some reading done."

After the conductor checks her ticket, Pearl leans back, closes her eyes, and broods about Frieda's upcoming marriage. When a woman gets married, her life is with her husband, her new family. It's natural. And yet it's terrible.

Occasionally she interrupts her worrying to dip into her food supply: dark bread, hard-boiled eggs, fruit, and dark chocolate bars, her new American addiction. She glances through the *Forward* and an issue of *Elite Styles*, a gift from Safaya, who told Pearl, "Don't forget to come back. I need you."

Maybe Mendel has changed his character, or maybe it isn't as bad as she remembers. She can hope. Father is punishing the young couple by refusing his blessing. Frieda asked for her help, so Pearl wrote him to say she was sorry she couldn't fulfill her promise, but that no one could or should fulfill such a promise. In this country, people make their own choices. She caught herself using her sisters' expression: "It's different in America."

There's been no response.

Because of the Christian holiday, it's a lonely day-and-a-half train ride from New York to Michigan Central Station. Going through Canada would have been quicker, but even after nearly a year in the US, Pearl's afraid to risk crossing the border.

All this time alone, with only the train noise for company. Her few fellow passengers stretch out on the seats or sleep as their train hurtles across not–New-York America. Towns with space between the houses and space between the people. Fields of dried brown grass that give way to forests like the ones near Turya where she used to play as a girl and then hide during the war and the chaos that came after.

○

WHEN THEY ROLL into Detroit, Pearl's yearning for human interaction. She wants to hug her sister tightly, walk arm and arm and share all their news. No one—no boss, coworker, no friend—is like family.

In the station there's no Frieda, just Mendel's Aunt Rochel, a square-jawed woman with dyed black hair that rises in wings on the sides of her head. Her long cloth coat with its oversized belt makes her resemble a soldier. Hiding in her shadow is an asthmatic-looking woman with the tiny build and diffident affect of a girl. This must be Deborah, the daughter from Rochel's first marriage, whom Frieda described as "sweet, maybe a bit shy."

A *bit*? Pearl thinks. If she's a bit shy, then I'm a bit of a beauty queen.

"Frieda didn't tell me how stylish you were," Aunt Rochel says. "What a fine coat you're wearing. Luxury."

Pearl recently finished the coat: red velvet with a Persian lamb fur collar. Underneath, she wore a silk blouse and flowing gray slacks, the legs cut with extra material to pass as a dress under the cursory glances of strangers.

"You're teasing me," Pearl says.

"I'm complimenting you," says Rochel. "You must be rich to wear a fur collar."

If it's a genuine compliment, Pearl thinks, you shouldn't have to explain. "A remnant," lies Pearl. "From a friend in the fur business." Actually, the fur collar is another of Safaya's gifts. "Frieda didn't come?"

"She's on an errand," Aunt Rochel explains. "But here is Deborah. Don't you want to say hello?"

"Sure I do," says Pearl, confused. Why isn't Frieda here? "Hello, Deborah." Deborah offers a limp palm and a pained smile. No one offers to take Pearl's bag, which Pearl is plenty capable of carrying. But they might at least chat as they walk to the exit, their trio gloomy as a funeral procession.

The station is marvelously empty of people, airy and clean with sparkling marble columns leading up to a brick vaulted ceiling and glistening smooth floors that look freshly mopped. If you dropped an orange by accident, you wouldn't be afraid to pick it up again and eat it. Outside, Pearl is impressed by the sweeping lawns around the entrance, the vast unused space and open stretches of sky. She feels the habitual tightness in her chest unclench. Aunt Rochel leads them to the side of the building where a handsome black car is parked, its coat of paint smooth and sleek.

"This is yours? Or did you borrow it?" Pearl asks.

"Of course it's ours. You think we're paupers?"

"Not at all," says Pearl.

"Sure you do. All New Yorkers think like this about the rest of the world. But we live well in Detroit. You'll see."

Pearl has never been in so nice a car, with a mechanical heater to keep the inside warm. No need to cover up with a motor robe. Relaxing against the cushions, she inhales the woody smell of new fabric, a blue gabardine with a zigzag pattern. Aunt Rochel starts the engine in seconds, and the car drives smoothly over the city's freshly laid roads with hardly a bump. The avenues are lined with trees and trimmed grass rectangles dotted in patches of bright snow. Just as she'd imagined America: big, comfortable, and clean.

The stores and homes they pass are decorated for Christmas, hung with silvery-green pine wreaths and fat plaid bows, pretty as poisoned berries. In America, they go crazy for Christmas, worse than anywhere. Pearl's glad to arrive in Aunt Rochel's neighborhood, where Jews live and there's no sign of Christmas.

Rochel has a trim brick house fronted by a white square of snowy front yard and a neatly swept front walk, but inside, no Frieda.

Aunt Rochel says Frieda will arrive soon, then invites Pearl into the kitchen for a simple luncheon of those egg sandwiches of which Americans are so fond. Irritated by her sister's absence, Pearl eats her sandwich, then retires to the room they'll share. Frieda's clothes are flung over a chair, the bed, the nightstand. She'll have to learn to be neater once she's married. Pearl picks up the clothes and puts them away before unpacking her own things, draping them carefully over hangers.

This room once belonged to Uncle Irving and Aunt Rochel's son, a boy of nineteen who works in a bank and now lives on his own. Though Frieda's been here a month, the room still has a man's rough, metallic smell.

Pearl's hanging a silk blouse when Frieda rushes in and throws her arms around her sister. Pearl squeezes her back. My sister, she thinks. We're together again.

"Pearl, he's awful," Frieda says, her voice muffled by Pearl's shoulder.

"Who, Mendel?" Pearl tries not to sound too hopeful.

Frieda lets go of her sister. "Of course not." Her cheeks look bloated and her eyes seem tired. Even her hair looks flat and dull-colored. "I mean the rabbi who Mendel chose for the wedding. He has no beard and he prays in the German style."

"Where were you today at the station?" Pearl asks. "I haven't seen you in four months, and I travel all this way, and you weren't there."

"That's what I'm trying to tell you," says Frieda. "I was stuck with Mendel, to meet the goyish rabbi he chose to marry us."

"Stuck, how? They locked you in a room?"

Frieda collapses on the bed. "This rabbi's a nightmare. I look at him, and I see a priest. He's probably afraid of women. I need a bite of something. I'm starving!"

"So?" Pearl asks. "You don't go to shul much here in America."

"But when I do go, I want a proper rabbi. With a beard. Who speaks Hebrew."

"Mendel's going to be your husband," says Pearl. "You ought to believe as he does. If he believes in the German style, then you should too." She can't resist adding, "Or marry someone else who believes the way you do."

"Mendel doesn't believe in the German style. He chose this rabbi because he's cheaper. But I want a good rabbi. Otherwise it won't be a good marriage. It won't start the right way."

Pearl takes out a metal candy box from her suitcase. "I have a hundred and thirty-five dollars. They must have other kinds of rabbis here. This isn't Cuba. Get whatever kind of rabbi you want, and I'll pay the extra."

Frieda shakes her head. "Mendel wouldn't like it."

"He can learn to like it. You can teach him. Husbands must be trained." Where was that from? Pearl wonders. Maybe Betty read it aloud from *Ladies' Home Journal*.

"I can't touch your money, Pearl," says Frieda. "I'm fine. I feel better already."

Then what do you want from me, besides talk? Pearl thinks. In her opinion, what good is talk without action? But for Frieda, talk is as great a need as action.

Another odd thing: Frieda prefers not to wear a white dress. She makes this clear when they go shopping for the material, which Pearl is expected to transform into a bridal masterpiece in two days. A blue wedding dress masterpiece.

"You didn't tell me before?" Pearl asks. "I could have brought the material from New York. Now I'll have to do it at the last minute."

"I thought we could work on it together. It would mean so much to me."

Sure, Pearl thinks. When Frieda says "together," she means me.

Pearl unfurls a bolt of blue silk on a worktable at the back of the store, then uses her arm to measure what she needs. The store is a large, open space, especially compared to those cramped stalls in New York, where the rolls of fabric are jammed in together, so the material can't breathe.

"What's wrong with white? You used to wear that pretty white dress in Cuba," says Pearl, trying to imagine a blue wedding gown.

"White looks good in a tropical climate, where the sun darkens your skin, but here in the cold, you blend in with the snow. It puffs you up like a snowman."

Convinced she's hiding something, Pearl says, "Is it because you and Mendel already . . . because you aren't . . . ?"

"No, no," says Frieda quickly.

"You can tell me if the answer is yes. I won't be shocked."

"I said no, didn't I? I want to look modern. Not like some poky Yiddish bride."

What's with Frieda's unusually sharp tongue? Prewedding nerves? Her thoughtless chatter, which sounded delightful from a young person, now from an older woman comes off as panicked and unattractive.

Or maybe Frieda is the same and it's Pearl who's changed.

Pearl looks around the store. The clerk at the counter is busy with a customer. "There are ways to stop a baby before it truly gets started," she says. "And not those herbal teas from the Old Country. Modern medicine, I'm talking."

"Pearl, stop talking about dirty things. You of all people."

"What are you implying?" Pearl asks, feeling a hollowness in her throat.

"Nothing." Frieda casually pats the blue silk, mussing the fabric that Pearl's so carefully measured out.

Pearl grabs Frieda by the wrist. "No, you meant something.

Something you heard about me in New York?" But she fears Frieda is referring to something further back in their history—an unfinished conversation in that shabby hotel room in Havana, with that Meyers couple lurking outside the door. "Something in the Old Country?"

"Forget the Old Country," says Frieda. "We were different there."

"Not so different," Pearl says. "You've been saying little words, hinting at this and that for a while. If you want to tell me something, say it."

"I have nothing to say."

"I think you do. I'm not afraid. Tell me what you saw, what you know."

"Please, enough! Don't say anymore!" Frieda cries out, her cheeks red, her dark eyes terrified. Her voice, sharp and loud, echoes in the store. The other customers and the clerk at the counter turn their heads.

"It's nothing," Pearl tells them. "She's getting married soon. Just nervous."

The clerk smiles knowingly and returns to her business, but one of the customers stares curiously as Frieda softly whimpers.

"Okay," Pearl says, rubbing her sister's shoulders. "The subject is closed." Yes, because she's closing it. Letting go of Frieda, she sees herself in one of the fitting mirrors: a stylish woman in a dark blue bell-shaped hat with dark good looks that over time might turn surly or handsome. Nothing like that other Pearl from the Old Country.

"The wedding is in two days," Frieda says. "You shouldn't upset me this way."

"I'm sorry," says Pearl. I should be the one who's upset, she thinks, but here I am handing Frieda a handkerchief to dry her eyes. "Everything will be fine."

After another minute, Frieda feels calm enough to allow Pearl to buy her the material for her wedding dress: a shimmery pale blue silk that ripples like a stream in moonlight. It will make a fine dress, but Pearl's mind and eye are on her sister, who will never confess the full extent of what she saw or heard back in Turya, whether she knows the truth or just senses it. Either way, knowledge or a feeling, it's enough to inspire fear.

Is that why Frieda's so eager to marry, Pearl wonders, for protection? I'm the one this happened to, but I'm not afraid. You don't see me running after a husband.

She's hit by the full force of this thought: I'm not afraid.

○

AS PEARL PREDICTED, Frieda leaves her alone to make the dress. Actually, Pearl enjoys the work, cutting, folding, and running her needle through the supple material. It's like falling into a soothing trance, especially in a quiet space without so many noisy machines and noisier girls around—and without Safaya to offer unwelcome suggestions. Frieda occasionally stops in for a fitting, and they try different looks and folds, an asymmetrical neckline, exposing more shoulder. They laugh together as they have not done since Havana. In New York, Frieda was so often depressed that Pearl's forgotten how much fun her sister can be.

The dress is progressing nicely, so when Mendel comes over on Friday night, Pearl wishes she didn't have to put down her work and eat with the others. She'd be fine with a sandwich, but Aunt Rochel has invited Mendel and Ben the Oak, who share an apartment by their new store, though now Mendel is renting another place for himself and Frieda.

Since Pearl last saw him, Mendel's dark curly hair has grown thick and full, and he brushes it back with pomade that exudes a warm spicy scent, like Christmas spices. His body is thin as ever, yet his face is round and plump like a well-fed belly. He wears a thick, luxurious-looking cloth coat, which he tosses at Deborah.

"Careful with that," he says. "It cost more than your daddy makes in a month." Ben taps his arm, speaks softly in his ear. "Why, what did I say?" says Mendel. "Can't a guy kid around here?" He rubs his hands and advances into the middle of the room, maybe to size it up, see if there's anyone here he can use to gain some advantage. Seeing only Deborah and Pearl, he shrugs and resigns himself to a useless evening.

After greeting him and Ben politely, Pearl has nothing to say. She wants to get along with Mendel, but like Father, she can't stand the man. Then again, few men in Turya met Father's demanding expectations. Maybe she shouldn't be as rigid as he is.

Mendel says, "Well, Pearl, you've become a real New York swell. But a word to the wise, you'll never catch a man wearing those pants. Like they say. 'When the wife wears the pants, the husband washes the floor.'" As he laughs at his own joke, Ben leans against the wall beside the front door with a pained look on his face.

"Now you're an expert on ladies' fashion?" Pearl replies.

Deborah, who's shrinking quietly against the wall as if she hopes to melt into it, astonishes them all by letting out a high-pitched cackle.

Aunt Rochel breezes in from the kitchen and removes her apron. As always, her wings of dark hair stand up stiffly in place.

"Hello, Mendel. Frieda's just getting the soup," she says. "Where's your brother? How mean you are to leave him at home."

"No, he's here," says Mendel, nodding over his shoulder at Ben, still standing awkwardly near the door, holding his coat. Pearl makes a mental note to pull him aside at the right time to thank him and repay her debt. Happily, he seems too polite to mention it in front of everyone.

Ben looks as though he's grown in America. He seems bigger, tall and broad-shouldered, with thick, capable hands and a powerful frame that's straining to fit into his ugly suit jacket. The opposite of Mendel, whose beautiful clothes conceal his body's slightness and stooped posture, as if he's constantly about to lean over and share a secret.

"Benjamin!" trills Aunt Rochel. "Deborah, you're letting him stand like a stranger? Maybe you could pay your gentleman caller a nice compliment, take his coat? Show him to the table and then let's get the candles lit before my chicken catches a cold."

In the dining room, Mendel grabs Frieda like a rag doll and plants a long kiss on her lips, not caring who sees. Frieda places her hands on his waist, her fingers dangerously close to his hips. Like a modern American couple, Pearl thinks.

Aunt Rochel sets a gorgeous table, like a picture, with flowers and a delicate white cloth. They hush as she puts on a lace head covering and lights the candles, waving her hands over the flames. Then she leads them in a psalm, singing in her pretty voice that makes Pearl jealous. Though Pearl enjoys singing, she's tone-deaf, as is Frieda. Ironic for cantor's daughters.

"Doesn't Ben look handsome in his good suit?" Aunt Rochel prods Deborah.

"Yes, handsome," Deborah agrees.

No, not handsome, Pearl thinks as they sit. Ben looks ridiculous in his expensive suit that's a size too small and rides up his wrists and ankles. With mismatched socks and shoes that needed replacing long ago. A man like Ben needs a simpler, more relaxed cut to show his body to its natural advantage. Why didn't Mendel tell him? Maybe people in Detroit don't know much about style, but natty Mendel seems to know something, in his blue serge suit with fine stitching on the lapels and a puckered silk handkerchief sprouting from his breast pocket.

If Mendel can afford such clothes, surely Frieda won't go hungry—unless Ben becomes a regular dinner guest. How that man tucks into his food, smacking his lips, sucking chicken cartilage off the bone, licking his fingers. Pearl's enjoying the chicken too, but you don't see her spraying bits of flesh all over the good tablecloth.

Rochel encourages Deborah, seated next to Ben, to make conversation. It's a hopeless cause. As Pearl notes to her private amusement, Ben seems more interested in the food than Deborah's obviously coached attempts to spark chatter.

"It's very cold out."

"It's a nice tie you're wearing."

"It's lovely to see you again."

To each of these, Ben the Oak replies with a wooden "Yes," "Thank you," and "You too," then resumes attacking his challah, chicken, and after-dinner stewed prunes. Frieda presides at the end of the table, as if to practice for her future, and reviews the wedding menu with Aunt Rochel, who clearly enjoys playing the role of Frieda's mentor. Without Pearl around to stand up for her sister, she can imagine Frieda being steamrolled by Aunt Rochel and her "advice."

What Frieda needs is an ally, but she's unlikely to find one here, not in cousin Deborah, nor in Uncle Irving, now trading crass jokes across the table with Mendel. Irving, who isn't wearing shoes and despite Rochel's hectoring refuses to put them on, was called Michoyl Feldsteyn in Russia. But then he fled to the States to escape the draft during the war with Japan and changed his name to Irving Field, in case the tsar came looking for him. As the rest of the family trickled over, they changed their last names to match his.

Ben says nothing and, once he finishes eating, dozes off in his chair. Pearl and Frieda exchange looks, then dissolve into giggling. Mendel joins in too. It's nice to share a moment with him, yet his disloyalty to his brother bothers her. Mendel ought to nudge Ben awake, rather than let him be laughed at. Deborah peers curiously at them all, then at her mother, as if to gauge whether she too should laugh, but Rochel isn't looking. In the end, Deborah compromises on a half smile, like she's suppressing a fart.

Enough already, thinks Pearl, who gives Ben a good kick.

He wakes up with a start. "Sorry," he says and knocks over a teacup, spilling lukewarm coffee on the tablecloth. "I've been working late in the store."

"Never mind, that's what tablecloths are for, to get stained and ruined," says Aunt Rochel, sounding peeved.

"You see my bride?" says Mendel. "The prettiest thing in the room. Except of course for my new suit—just kidding! Can't a fellow make a joke?"

Pearl used to hear this kind of bragging and pointed teasing between men in the Old Country. In America, she understands it better and resents it less. It's a way for Jews to spite their enemies, to show that in the face of so much tragedy, laughter is still possible.

"Have more cake," Aunt Rochel commands Deborah. "You're too skinny. Rich people are fat. Poor people are skinny. Look at your cousin Frieda. She eats good and has a fine full figure." Frieda looks upset, and Pearl wants to tell her not to be so self-conscious if she's gained a few pounds in America. But Frieda might mistake such words of comfort for criticism.

"How's that new store of yours?" Uncle Irving asks Ben. "This greenhorn buys himself a store on Clay Avenue. A grocery yet. On Clay Avenue!"

"I had a cushy job stocking shelves at Heller's," says Mendel. "Then my brother tells me, I'm counting on you. I can't run the store by myself. That's how Ben operates. Makes you feel guilty for living."

"Why didn't you consult your family before buying this store?" says Uncle Irving. "No one ever did anything in that location."

Ben shrugs. "I don't know what's wrong with it. There's plenty of foot traffic. And that new automobile factory is opening nearby."

Stick to your plan, Pearl thinks. Don't let them bully you into giving it up.

"Tell me how much you paid for that store," Uncle Irving says.

"Fifteen hundred," says Ben.

Impressive. Pearl supposes he must not miss the twenty-five he lent her.

"You hear that?" Mendel says. "I could buy a nice car with fifteen hundred. Instead of slaving away in a grocery store."

"You're going to lose that money," says Uncle Irving. "You worked hard for it."

"Well," says Ben, "I don't think so." Then he lets out a short burp.

"You're all my witnesses," Uncle Irving announces. "I warned him. Now he can't claim any different when it goes belly-up and he needs a hand. I earned my own way to where I am, with no help from nobody. Some of these kids who come over now, they expect the ones who came before to do everything for them. But I'm not that way, see?"

"No one expects you to do nothing," says Ben.

Thank God, at least one person here doesn't put on airs, Pearl thinks.

"A little success here, a little failure there, it makes a man out of you," says Irving. "Aren't I right, Mendel?"

"Sure," says Mendel, busy brushing crumbs off his chest.

"Advice, of course, I'm always happy to give," Uncle Irving adds. "But money, once you start doling it out, that's a bad road for everyone."

Pearl had always heard that Irving was a ne'er-do-well in Turya. Yet here he's making a nice living in the junk business. It reminds her of Alexander Lewis's saying about Cuba: Everyone who comes here failed somewhere else. The difference is that in America you have a chance to make something of yourself. In Cuba, it's hopeless.

After dinner Pearl helps in the kitchen, and Aunt Rochel says, "Wow, the fancy New Yorker doing dishes!"

"Oh, yes," says Pearl, "we also have dishes in New York."

Aunt Rochel looks at her funny, thrusts a plate for drying at Pearl's gut.

"Tell me," says Pearl, "what's your honest opinion of Ben the Oak?"

"I wouldn't bet against him. A hard worker. He's got plans. He and Deborah make a nice pair, no? She's a planner too. As a girl, she'd make up stories about her dollies, marry them off, give them babies. She still has her dollies, can you believe?"

"And Mendel? He doesn't have plans?" Pearl asks.

"Him? He's confused," says Aunt Rochel, scrubbing the dishes so hard she's spraying water all over the kitchen. "He thinks dreams are the same as plans."

EIGHTEEN

On Frieda's wedding day, Pearl pulls up the Persian lamb collar of her coat, presses it close around her neck so the silver curls of fur tickle her chin. A scrap of protection against the winter wind billowing through the broad streets of Detroit.

Here, wherever she is, she can see the sky. There's room to breathe.

She's only been in this city six days, but already she can tell she likes it. Detroit is prettier than she'd imagined, and in warmer weather, she'd enjoy this walk. Compared to the foul-smelling streets of the Lower East Side, the air is cool and bracing, with a crisp taste. The traffic is calm, moves in an orderly way. New cars with freshly painted bodies are parked along the wide, empty roads. The curbs are free of garbage and don't stink, and the sidewalks give you room to swing your arms freely as you go, without fear of knocking into a strange man who could misinterpret your mistake as an invitation.

This city is a real America, she thinks.

For most people this is a peaceful Sunday morning. But Pearl is busy searching for a mango because Frieda says she's queasy with nerves and the only thing her stomach might tolerate is a mango. It's her wedding day, so perhaps she ought to be indulged.

Pearl hasn't had much luck. Most of the greengrocers are closed. Ben and Mendel's store is closed too, because of the wedding. At the groceries that are open, the storekeepers do not sell mangoes, cannot think where to find one, don't know what a mango is, and Pearl trips over her tongue trying to explain.

Frieda couldn't have asked for something simpler, like the tsar's wedding ring? Pearl hasn't thought of mangoes in forever. Now she recalls their taste and texture, the slippery flesh mashed against the roof of her mouth and sliding down her tongue.

In America they don't eat mangoes. They do eat bananas, though they're not as flavorful as the bananas in Cuba. They also eat apples, the finest Pearl has ever tasted, plump with rosy skin and juicy flesh. And they eat shriveled oranges that remind her of old women's skin. Best of all, they eat pineapples from Hawaii, out of cans. Aunt Rochel served some after dinner one night. The pineapples, cut into rings, were soaked in a delicious sweet and heavy syrup that Pearl scraped from her dish with a spoon.

Waiting for a traffic light to change, Pearl presses her wool mittens to her cold cheeks. She's not sure why, but she's thinking of Safaya. She hears her saying, "I need you." Safaya needs me, Pearl thinks. Who do I need?

A policeman patrolling his beat tips his hat, then whistles his appreciation of her figure. Quickening her pace, Pearl almost slips on a patch of ice. She collects herself and continues walking, aiming to project confidence . . . don't stop me, please don't stop me. Will she ever lose her fear of men in uniform?

To save time and warm up, she pays to ride the streetcar home. She no longer fears getting on the wrong line. After navigating the New York subways and the winding lanes of Old Havana, she can find her way by streetcar pretty easily. Pearl sits beside a woman who gathers her skirt to make room and utters a few friendly words. The Americans of Detroit are unnervingly cheerful. When the woman sneezes, Pearl smiles quickly, but cannot bring herself to say, "Bless you." It's too odd, this chumminess with strangers. To avoid the woman's gaze, Pearl looks out the window.

Pearl has heard Detroit is the city for cars, but she didn't realize it was also such a city for building things. Downtown is all office towers and hotels, like the Book-Cadillac Hotel, which Uncle Irving boasts will be the tallest hotel in the world. Here too, in this Jewish neighborhood north of downtown, they're building plenty: new stores on the main streets, and on the side streets bungalows of wood or brick for young families.

"They call this city the Paris of the West," Irving said at dinner last night, in a grand voice like a carnival barker. "After the war, times were tough, but now everyone in the world wants a car, and this is the only place that knows how to make good ones. Whoever wants work in this town, he can find it. A worker in a car factory has his pick of any girl he wants to marry. And if you don't know how to make a car, you can serve the people who make the cars. They need doctors, tailors, grocers, and junkmen."

"What about dressmakers?" Pearl asked, to tease him.

"Sure, dressmakers too." He leaned in closer, offered a conspiratorial smile. "Or if you don't care to work on the level, you do what they call night work, smuggling liquor from Canada in fishing boats across the Detroit River, to deliver to the speakeasies. Those delivery men always have thick wads of cash in their pockets."

"How do you know so much about it?" Aunt Rochel asked. "Stop kidding these girls. Deborah, ignore your father. Big talker. He knows nothing."

"Oh, I know everything," said Uncle Irving. "I have friends. Smart friends. Lucky friends. Friends who are getting rich."

Pearl's still thinking about Uncle Irving's assurances about dressmakers. He must be right. If there's money in this town, then there are women with money who need dresses. It's probably like in Havana: you find one of these women, and they introduce you to their friends if you're good, which Pearl knows she is.

This is idle speculation. She's returning to New York after the wedding.

Uncle Irving and Aunt Rochel's home is just off the avenue, close to the streetcar. Though Pearl has the key, she hasn't yet needed it; the front door is always left open. Inside, the house feels warm with the steam sizzling off the radiators. She smells chicken soup simmering in the kitchen, and sweet homemade wine, which has fermented in the basement for weeks. Uncle Irving claims he knows the secret of making good wine, which he will not divulge. Yesterday, Pearl tasted a sample, too vinegary.

Pearl knocks twice, then opens the door to the room she and her sister share. Frieda, wearing the light-blue dress Pearl made, has tucked a flower behind her ear and is inspecting its effect in a mirror. "Pearl, you're late. Did you find my mango?"

"No, it was impossible," says Pearl.

Frieda spins around. "Oh, Pearl, I was counting on you."

Pearl silently counts to three in English, which takes longer than it would in Yiddish, giving her time to marshal her powers of patience. "They don't have mangoes here," Pearl says slowly, firmly. She straightens the flower behind her sister's ear.

"Maybe you're right." Frieda sighs theatrically and returns to the mirror, futzing with the flower some more. "I wish I could taste one again. Don't you? Remember what good times we had in Cuba? Havana must be the prettiest city in the world."

What do you know about Cuba, Pearl thinks, you were there for a baby's breath. This constant chatter about Cuba is meaningless, just one of Frieda's many odd behaviors and sayings in the days and now hours before her wedding. "Yes," Pearl says. "I remember the good times. Now let's finish getting ready."

Once Frieda's hair is done and her dress is zipped, Pearl puts on her own outfit, a distinguished gray jacket with a matching skirt, and a blazing pink chiffon blouse. She combs out her hair with the aid of her Marcel iron, lightly dusts her face with powder, and dabs her lips with brick red lipstick, just enough to give her mouth personality.

Deborah comes in wearing an ivory dress that's too long and washes out her complexion. "Oh, Pearl, what a lovely blouse. I've never seen such a color," she says in her soft voice. "What's it called?"

"Pink, I guess," Pearl lies. "No special name."

Bougainvillea. Like a bougainvillea vine dripping over a garden wall. But who here in Detroit would know what bougainvillea is? Maybe Frieda. Yes, she'd remember.

Before they leave, Pearl hands Frieda a soft packet wrapped in green tissue. Frieda unwraps the package and takes out a white crocheted head covering, in a snowflake pattern. From the Old Country. Basha brought it over. It belonged to their mother, whom Frieda does not remember.

Frieda handles the head covering gingerly, then brings it to her nose and lips. She and Pearl exchange kisses. "Use it well," says

Pearl as Deborah watches them. Poor thing, Pearl thinks, growing up without sisters.

It's time to drive to synagogue. As they carefully insert their arms into the sleeves of their winter coats so as not to muss the dresses underneath, Frieda asks Pearl, "Shouldn't we write the Steinbergs?"

The Steinbergs? Why involve them? "What for?" Pearl asks.

"Surely they'd want to hear I'm getting married."

"They've probably forgotten us."

Frieda shakes her head. "You don't know them as I do. I'll write them tonight. Or tomorrow, after the wedding. You remind me."

"Fine," says Pearl. But she'll forget to remind her, and it will never happen.

o

AUNT ROCHEL AND the three girls ride to shul. Even in New York, it would be a striking structure, with its three arched entrances, a row of painted striped columns on the second floor, and a stained-glass window with a Jewish star above. Extraordinary, Pearl thinks, spending so much on that window without fear some Jew-hater would throw rocks through it. Going into the shul, she feels proud, as if she'd built the place herself.

The rabbi's wife invites them into a room off the sanctuary, where she brushes Frieda's hair, adds more powder to her cheeks and paint to her lips. Pearl dislikes the artificiality of the look. New York women are more judicious in their use of cosmetics.

Then it's time. Pearl clasps Frieda's hands. "You sure?" she asks, one final chance to stop this madness. Frieda nods quickly. They proceed.

She thinks of all the dreams she had for Frieda—working as a private secretary to a distinguished gentleman. How ridiculous this idea now seems.

The German-style beardless rabbi addresses the crowd in English. "Welcome, Jews and Jewesses." He conducts the traditional service just fine, so perhaps Mendel was right to get a bargain there.

The scene is all their family could have wished for Frieda, aside from their absence and this particular groom's presence. Beneath the chuppah, Ben stands next to Mendel while Pearl stands beside her sister, pretty and happy in her blue dress. Frieda walks around Mendel seven times, and Pearl is moved by the familiarity of the old ritual, how it ushers a sense of holiness in the room. She notices Ben staring at her. Because of her blouse? He probably thinks the color's too showy.

Mendel breaks a glass under his shoe, and it's over. As Uncle Irving takes pictures after the ceremony with his Brownie box camera, Pearl looks on, thinks of her own future life as a spinster, the butt of jokes for children and rude people with loose tongues who'll look at her sideways and whisper, "Why did she never marry?"

Perhaps Alexander has married a brown Cuban woman. If Pearl had married him, they could have had children, deeply tanned, fluent in Spanish, English, and Yiddish.

Like having a child is an accomplishment. Any starving, flea-bitten cat can have a litter of kittens.

Even if she had stayed in Cuba, she doubts she'd have married Alexander. She never loved him. Of that she's surer than ever. What if she isn't capable of that kind of feeling for anyone? Maybe it's no accident she's alone.

The family returns to the house, which is suffocatingly

crowded, stuffed and hot like a boiled meat bun. The guests bump elbows and knees. There's plenty of food, and the sour homemade wine flows plentifully. Gifts of things pile up beside the fireplace: linens, pans, silver kiddush cups, and a garish brass menorah. Gifts of money are delivered to Mendel, who shoves them into his pockets.

Pearl looks on as Frieda greets the guests with her sparkling smile and enchanting voice. They say how lovely she looks in her robin's-egg blue dress that Pearl made. Blue, not white, of course! Blue is perfect! Frieda gracefully accepts their compliments, looks each guest in the eye and listens intently as if she's been waiting expressly for their good wishes. Pearl also takes in their praise. Too bad Safaya's not there to hear. You see, Pearl thinks, my designs aren't so crazy. These people never saw such a wonderful dress.

She shakes hands with Irving and Rochel's son, a skinny man-boy with dark, hollowed-out eye sockets and a gloomy stare. Funny to think she's sleeping in his room. He congratulates Frieda in the formal language of a member of the Hebrew Burial Society, then looks Pearl up and down before going to stand next to his father. When he thinks no one's looking, he scratches his armpits.

Across the room, Mendel stands with friends and collects handshakes, cigars, and more envelopes with money. They're discussing how to get rich, some scheme involving scrap metal. He'll be scheming and dreaming like this forever, she thinks. He'd better not blame my sister when he comes up short.

"Excuse me," she tells Frieda and goes over to her new brother-in-law.

"Well, well, Pearl," says Mendel. "Nice to see you in a skirt for a change. Help yourself to some wine. It's a wedding. You're supposed to celebrate."

The other men laugh. Not that what he says is so funny, but these days it's expected to laugh when alcohol is mentioned in conversation.

She moves in close to Mendel, and says in a plain voice, right into his ear, "I just want to tell you, I know who you are."

"Of course," he says, giggling. "And I know who you are. You're Pearl."

"No," says Pearl. "I know who you are. And I'll be watching. Even from New York. So take good care of my sister. Because if you don't, I'll know."

Mendel takes a step back, his face ashen.

Pearl turns away. Now it's up to Frieda to make her own story, she thinks. I've helped all I can, yet maybe it hasn't been enough. How can I leave her now?

She wanders among the unfamiliar people, then sits on the arm of a sofa to watch the dancing, which seems boorish and boxy compared to the dancing in Cuba, or that sleazy New York dance hall. The music is old-fashioned, yet sweet. Aunt Rochel finds Ben the Oak, dressed in his small suit, and drags him to Deborah, who keeps stepping on the hem of her too-long dress. They dance, or rather glumly march in a circle, like a pair of greenhorns looking for a seat on a crowded trolley. Uncle Irving grabs Rochel, and she tries to slap him away, but Irving's like a bear when he sees something he wants. Plus he's drunk. Soon he's twirling his wife like a dreidel. Frieda and Mendel are dancing too. Their movements fit together, as if each person knows what the other will do next.

Pearl feels alone and out of place among these people who are supposed to be hers. Where does she belong? Aunt Rochel's son looks hopefully in her direction, so she retreats to the kitchen, for a break from the guests and their drunken nonsense. Filling a glass with water, Pearl recalls how Alexander Lewis used to say she didn't know how to have fun, to relax and give herself over to being silly. Back then, his observation sounded true, which bothered her. Now she thinks maybe it is true but also not a problem.

My God, she realizes, that was a year ago already.

This glass she's holding reminds her of Alexander: tall, thin, and elegant, pretty but impractical. Can't hold much.

Ben the Oak comes in with an empty tray. "They need more cookies," he says, sounding strangely forlorn about it. Right then, he looks so much like the orphan he is, she feels sorry for him. "Aunt Rochel sent me."

Pearl brings down a tin box of the goose-feet cookies she'd baked. She and Ben fill the tray without talking. His strong, fleshy fingers are too clumsy for the dainty art of arranging cookies, and he piles up great bunches of them in a hurry. She shows him how to place them in concentric rings so people will want to take one.

The tray is filled, but he leaves it on the table. Maybe he came here to escape the crowd, and finding her, he's disappointed. She's always thought of Ben as such a solid man, yet up close, his body has a pleasing hint of fragility. His blue eyes are gentle, almost sleepy, and his hair, a delicate shade of nut brown, is thin on top. A few strands float up in wisps, as if he'd walked in a wind. She's tempted to pat them back in place.

"I wrote my grandmother about the wedding," he says. "She'd want to be here, to see Mendel marry a cantor's daughter."

"Yes, of course she would," says Pearl.

"Frieda says New York's not so nice," says Ben. "What do you think?"

"New York is fine," she says. "I have a very good job."

"I was in New York about ten days. At Ellis Island. We stayed there longer than we had to. The first day, they called our name, but they said Feld-stain, instead of Feldsteyn. I didn't know it was me."

Pearl laughs. Her feet are tired, so she settles into one of Rochel's kitchen chairs. Rochel is very proud of these chairs, which she bought new at a store. She calls them French Empire chairs, but they're just wooden chairs with curved backs and padded seats. What's so imperial? Detroiters like to put on airs about not very much.

Ben sits too. "I hear you made your sister's dress," he says.

"Who told you?" She sounds harsher than she means, like an interrogator.

"To be honest, no one. I just figured. You wouldn't find such a dress in this city. No one here would know how to do it. Frieda's always bragging about what a talent you have." He's looking at her intently. "You're different from how you were back home."

"To me, that's not home anymore," says Pearl.

"Yeah? So where's home now?"

Pearl shrugs, a painful admission that she has no answer. "You say I seem different. How so?"

"I don't know if I can explain. It's how you dress, how you walk in a room, sit in a chair. Like you wouldn't be afraid of anything."

"Maybe so, maybe no," says Pearl. "But when I am afraid, I have learned better not to show it." When Ben knew her in Turya, she wasn't so good at putting emotions into words, especially in public. Lately, she feels easier about sharing her opinions.

He smiles. "You weren't afraid to ask me for that twenty-five dollars."

Oy, thinks Pearl, I forgot. Maybe he thinks I'm such a skinflint I need reminding. "You want the money? Is that what you're asking?"

"I never expected you to pay me back. My grandmother taught me never to make a loan of money, only a gift. If you get paid back, it's a miracle."

"Shows what you know," Pearl says. "I got the money in my room. I'll go right now." She rises, but he reaches over the table as if to press her wrist or touch her hand, though he doesn't quite get there.

"Not now," he says in his gentle voice, so she settles back in her chair.

She says, "Tell me, your store, you think you and Mendel can make a go of it?"

"Sure. About stores, I know plenty."

"Maybe in the Old Country. Business here runs different."

"Here, too, I know things. This is a city of opportunity, even more than your New York. You could open your own business right here, making clothes."

"I told you, I have a good job in New York. Every day, I get more responsibility."

"But you're working for someone else," says Ben. "In America, to make something of yourself, you have to go out on your own."

Ben takes off his tight jacket—he looks better without it. His strong arms are visible through his shirt, damp with perspiration. The two of them nibble on cookies from the tray as Ben describes his first job in Detroit, washing celery and lettuce in ice water in a damp cold basement. He was the only Jew, and his boss told him, if they laugh at you for being a greenhorn, pay no attention. He started part-time and did so well that he was hired for more days, until his fingers swelled up and grew itchy. The doctor gave him a salve, which didn't help. Finally, Ben quit. For weeks, he couldn't find work, until he saw a notice in the Yiddish newspaper: A guy named Heller with a grocery needed a boy.

"Heller said no," says Ben as Pearl fixes him a glass of hot tea in a metal holder, with a sugar cube. She's enjoying hearing him talk. "He wanted a boy. I'm a man. I told him, I need a job, I don't care what. Take me on trial for a week." Within a month, Ben was managing the store on his own. "Business was so good, the owner didn't want me to go away for lunch for an hour, so his wife made me lunch. Also, some of our clientele wanted delivery, but I couldn't leave the store, and I don't know how to drive a car. So I called Mendel, because he knows how to drive, see? I loaded the truck, and he dropped off all the orders. He liked that. You know, talking to people, making friends. In our new store, we have no delivery yet, but we will, and he can go back to driving and be happy."

"You think that's all he needs to be happy?" she asks.

"Yeah, sure." He places the sugar cube between his teeth and then gulps down the hot tea, letting it pass through the sugar. When he's done, he lets out a burp and says, "Pardon," with an expectant look on his face, as if she should congratulate his manners. She doesn't mind the burp. It's an honest sound.

"I wanted to tell you earlier," Pearl says, "good for you, opening your own store."

"Yeah?" says Ben. "Why don't you do the same? You know, we have an extra space, next to our store. I could rent it to you for cheap. New York rent must be expensive. You could set up your own dress shop right here. And be close to your sister."

"No thank you," she says. "My life is in New York."

"Why? I see how good you are. You'd have customers lining up down the block."

How can she make him understand it's impossible? Though at the moment she's having trouble understanding why herself. To change the subject, she asks, "Tell me, at your store, do you carry mangoes?"

Ben asks what mangoes are, and she describes them. He seems interested, so she tells him about her Cuban adventures, the music, the dancing, the strange yet delicious food, the tall, flimsy trees and angry sun, the drunken tourists, and the Queen of England. She enjoys talking about it with someone from her old home, someone who's now family. The stories make her feel like a grand adventurer. "This Queen of England could take out any man with one punch," she says. "I saw with my own eyes."

"You don't mind," he asks, "that your younger sister got married before you?"

"Your younger brother just got married before you. You don't mind?"

They both laugh. How silly these shtetl questions sound here. How glad they are after all they went through to be alive and safe. "You're an unusual girl, Pearl," he says.

"Not such a girl anymore."

"No? How old are you now?"

"Twenty-six," she lies. Why did she bother? Oh, well, who's going to check?

The kitchen door swings open. "I need more cookies. Where are my cookies?" Rochel asks. Ben and Pearl smile guiltily at the half-filled tray—have they really eaten so many? Aunt Rochel stares at them, puzzled, then says, "Isn't that just like a man, to eat them all. Come on now." She waves Ben to her feet. "Deborah's waiting for her dancing partner. She's had several requests, but she's saving her dances for you."

"Here," says Pearl. She spreads the cookies so the tray doesn't look so empty, then hands it over. Ben hesitates before accepting it.

"And you," Aunt Rochel orders Pearl, "stay here and rest. You look tired." She and Ben return to the living room, leaving Pearl alone in the kitchen.

NINETEEN

THE NEXT DAY IS NEW YEAR'S EVE. RATHER THAN RUSH back to New York, Pearl remains in Detroit over the holiday and the rest of that week. She'll help Frieda set up housekeeping, then return to work, always work.

Mendel has chosen a small L-shaped apartment above a five-and-dime, facing an alley. Pearl wouldn't open the windows in summer, to admit the garbage fumes wafting up from below. There's no hallway, just two rooms and a bath, and the kitchen is tucked into an alcove. But it's all theirs.

During Pearl's first visit, she looks on as Mendel and Frieda share a lengthy good-bye kiss. No one has ever kissed Pearl this way. As she waits for them to finish, she imagines the home she'd choose for herself, with lots of windows, and a space for her sewing machine. A better kitchen, and somewhere to plant a garden, so she'd always have something to cook.

She's sleeping at Aunt Rochel's to give the newlyweds privacy—

that's the excuse she tells everyone. Actually, Pearl would rather avoid moody Mendel's company. Even when he's friendly, he's too casual with his friendliness. She mistrusts it.

Aunt Rochel's house is hardly a refuge, especially now without Frieda there as an ally. After work, Uncle Irving comes home to bury his nose in the classified ads, seeking out used furniture, or what he calls "business opportunities." Deborah has a cough, which she tries to suppress so as not to annoy her mother. Since the wedding, Aunt Rochel treats Pearl with the frostiness of an ice witch, removing Pearl's plate from the breakfast table before she's finished, swishing by with a curt nod. Yes, a perfect witch, a *machashefa*. That's what Pearl thinks, but she says nothing. There's little point in starting up with her. In a few days, Pearl will be breathing dirty air in New York. Her ears will fill with sewing machine noise. Safaya will bury her in piles of orders, making Safaya's clothes according to Safaya's specifications, sitting hunched over a sewing table for hours, until Pearl will forget what it's like to straighten her back.

For now, she enjoys the work of setting up Frieda's apartment, which keeps her plenty busy but in a quiet, soothing way. Sometimes Pearl imagines she's setting up housekeeping in her own apartment. She tries not to laugh at Frieda's fancy "housewife" outfit, like something a starlet would wear to portray a housewife in a moving picture.

To be fair, Frieda makes progress with the washing, ironing, and folding, the dusting, sweeping, and mopping. Pearl helps her sew cheerful yellow-and-white striped curtains to hang over the bedroom windows. They make the bed and, as is the new fashion, set a china doll between the two pillows.

Cooking, however, remains a disaster. While making a cake,

Frieda adds a cup of powdered sugar instead of flour to the wet batter, where it dissolves into nothing. In a potato soup, Frieda accidentally adds cubes of horseradish. "Horseradish, potato, they look the same," she says. "Both white."

"Can't you taste the difference?" Pearl asks.

Frieda bows her head. She dislikes tasting as she goes, fearing she'll become too fat. Maybe so, but all good cooks are fat, at least a little.

It's as if Frieda doesn't want to learn. What kind of home can she make for her husband if she can't cook?

Mendel and Ben take advantage of the store being closed for New Year's to take inventory. Then they'll both come home for dinner. Pearl's glad. She was wondering if she'd see Ben again. She decides it's a good time to show Frieda how to make kreplach. Though Pearl hasn't done it in years, she recalls exactly how to roll their mother's pillowy, tricornered, meat-filled kreplach, to float in chicken soup. You have to put your whole body into rolling out the sticky, elastic dough so that it doesn't retract. Pinch hard around the filling, and don't overfill. As they work, she hears Mother's voice, almost absurdly high-pitched, but warm. Also, Pearl imagines Ben, with his good appetite, biting into those kreplach. He probably hasn't tasted anything so good in years.

Frieda must not have paid attention; her dumplings explode in the soup.

"There's so little scope for the imagination in chicken soup," says Frieda in a dreary voice. "Can't we make a delicious black bean stew like we ate in Cuba?"

Pearl, busy fishing out the wreckage of Frieda's dumpling casings and bits of meat, says, "Their dirty bean soup probably had *treyf* in it."

"No! The Steinbergs would never."

"They would too," says Pearl with confidence, though she doubts it's true. "Bits of bacon. I'm sure I tasted it at the time, but I didn't want to alarm you." She thrusts a bowl into Frieda's hands. "Let's salvage what we can from our kreplach so we have something to serve your husband for dinner tonight."

They eat the broken kreplach for lunch, and for dinner they serve the intact kreplach—the ones Pearl made—in a soup thickened with the marrow of chicken bones and stewed onion. The sweet meaty aroma spreads through the apartment, intoxicating like wine. It was their mother's favorite perfume.

As soon as the brothers come home, Mendel locks himself in the bedroom. Already keeping secrets, Pearl thinks, with the marriage barely four days old. While Frieda pleads through the door for him to come out, Pearl watches Ben sit at the table, nervously rubbing his fingers. Something must have happened between them at the store, but it's not her place to ask. Whatever it is, she's on Ben's side. "Here," she says, handing him a glass of orange juice and touching his shoulder. "Drink."

"Thank you," he says and drains it all in one go.

After twenty minutes, Mendel emerges in a rotten mood and they sit down to dinner. "Frieda made these kreplach herself," Pearl announces at the table, which Frieda has set with an American-style cloth and new dishes from the wedding.

Ben catches Pearl's eye, and she drops her spoon into her nearly empty soup bowl, splattering droplets of golden salty liquid on the table. He knows she's lying.

Mendel looks up from the soup he's slurping absent-mindedly, first at Pearl, then Frieda, who's waiting for his reaction. "So, you want a Victory Medal?"

"Oh, Mendel," says Frieda, throwing her napkin at him playfully. "How can you pretend to be so awful? In front of company too."

No, no, Pearl thinks. Flirting's not the way. You have to be strong with him.

"What company?" Mendel points with his elbow at Ben while spooning up soup. "It's just your sister and my brother."

"Why isn't that company?"

Mendel shrugs, then resumes working at his soup, hardly noticing the flavor. But as Pearl suspects, Ben appreciates the meal. She watches him bite into a dumpling, chew the onion-flavored meat, then eagerly dig his spoon into the bowl for more. He knows what good is, and she's glad to feed someone who appreciates her work.

"Frieda, your soup is delicious," says Ben. "Maybe you got some more?"

"That's right," says Mendel. "Work me like a dog all day long, then eat all my food. I had it so easy at Heller's. Heller, there's a guy who treats a man with respect. But my own brother orders me around like Pharaoh."

Seething in silence, Pearl squeezes her soup spoon. Someone should tell Mendel to shut his big mouth, but Frieda's too timid, Ben's too passive, and Pearl, well, it's certainly not Pearl's place. Here's what none of them understand: like a whiny child who needs discipline, Mendel wants to hear a parent tell him no. When he doesn't hear it, he cries harder, not knowing why or what he really wants.

"You're tired, or not in your right head," says Ben, but Mendel ignores him.

"Here, Ben, I'll give you some more," Pearl says and fills his bowl. Meanwhile Frieda watches for a sign of contrition from her husband, who's quiet for the rest of the meal. After dinner, Frieda smiles prettily at Ben and Pearl, but her eyes look worn out. She says she'll take care of the dishes, so they might as well go home. They need no second urging. Pearl grabs her coat and is outside so fast she forgets to put it on until they're already in the cold. Ben holds it up for her to slip her arms into the sleeves.

He volunteers to walk her back to Aunt Rochel's place. As usual, she's carrying Martin's knife, so Ben's protection isn't necessary, but after that awful dinner, she's glad not to be alone. Frieda has to learn not to let her husband rule her. If only Pearl were here longer, she could teach Frieda how to talk to him.

They walk silently until Ben says, "You made that soup, not Frieda. Am I right?"

"I suppose." Pearl shrugs. "But why do you let Mendel talk to you that way?"

"Ach, it's nothing," says Ben, his breath visible in the cold night air. "He thinks the world doesn't respect him enough. He wants people to think he's big *macher*."

"And you?" Pearl says. "You want to be a big *macher*?"

Ben bends over, grabs two fistfuls of snow, packs them into a ball, and flings it up in the air, as high as he can, trying to reach the highest branches of a pine tree. "Me?" he says. "I'm already a big *macher*. Can't you tell?" Out in the fresh air, he moves his body freely, beautifully. But when he's inside a house or a room, it's as if he's constrained by the tightness of the space, the four walls.

Pearl laughs, pretends to consider her answer. "Not in those shoes."

"What's wrong with my shoes?"

"They're only ten years out of style and look like they've walked off to a war and then come home, that's all. Why don't you get yourself a new pair?"

"I haven't got the time," he says.

"Tomorrow, you stop by Mendel and Frieda's and leave me one of your old shoes. I'll take it to the store and find you a new pair, same size."

"Yes, ma'am."

He submits to her bossing nicely. Other men wouldn't take it so well.

They've arrived at Aunt Rochel's house. Again, Uncle Irving has forgotten to shovel the front walk, and they crunch through the snow to the porch. "You'd do that for me?" Ben asks, steadying her elbow as they pick their way up the path. Though his hand is heavy, the touch is tender. On instinct, she jerks her arm away, then wishes she hadn't because he's staring dejectedly at his empty hand. Sorry, she thinks, I was surprised. You could put the hand back, try again.

"Sure," she says. "You're a good man and no one's taking care of you." They pause at the door. His teeth are chattering in the cold, which is a different kind of cold than in Russia. This cold has a dampness to it. "You probably want to get home."

He shrugs. "Not much of a home. I sleep in that empty space next to the store I told you about. What's there? A bed, that's all. Anyone who wants to rent it, I could clear out in two seconds and they could set up shop no problem. Come sometime and see."

"You're really offering me?"

"Sure. Maybe it's an opportunity. New York's an old town. All the good chances have been used up by the people who are already there. Here, everything is new, good for greenhorns like us. And you could be near your sister."

"You don't have to tell me where my sister lives," she says.

"So come by the store, have a look at the space. To look costs nothing."

Before she can answer, they hear a noise from the house, on the other side of the door. "Aunt Rochel," says Pearl. "We're being spied on by that *machashefa*."

He laughs. "She'll hear you calling her bad things."

Pearl's standing in his shadow, and it feels comfortable there. "I don't care who hears. This is a free country. Whoever doesn't like my words can tell me to my face. Now go home. It's freezing."

"Yes, ma'am." He bows to her.

"And don't forget to bring me that shoe tomorrow."

○

IN THE MORNING, Pearl puts on a fine dress, suitable to wear to a department store. Maybe Ben won't do it. He might treat her offer as a joke. But at Frieda's apartment, she finds one of his dress shoes, what he'd save to wear for shul, and a five-dollar bill. She ignores the money and tells Frieda to clean the silver after breakfast so it won't stain. Then she takes Ben's shoe downtown. It feels intimate, riding this streetcar among strangers and holding his shoe. She slips her fingers under the tongue, in that space once inhabited by his large foot.

The store is called Hudson's, like that boat in which Pearl and Frieda crossed the Atlantic. A couple of years ago she'd have chalked up this strange coincidence to a sign from God rather than a quirk of fate.

Inside, Hudson's is even more magnificent than Macy's, with barrel-vault ceilings, stained-glass lantern lights, and black-and-white tile floors. The walls are lined in warm-toned wood. On every counter is a tiny Christmas tree, its blinking lights reflecting in the glass countertops. She steps past each tree cautiously, for fear of bad luck.

The men's department is on the second floor, up a grand set of stairs that seem to float in the middle of the room. Today the store is mostly empty of customers, since it's after Christmas. A solicitous clerk stops Pearl, who explains her errand, and he asks if she's shopping for her husband.

"I don't have no husband," she says, though a part of her enjoys the idea, which would make Ben her husband.

"Well, you're not shopping for yourself," he says. "Or are you?"

Pearl wants to yank the knot of this man's satin puff tie tight enough to choke. Does he think she's like a man-woman, like Martin from Cuba, like Safaya's friends? In this pretty chiffon dress she has on? She shakes Ben's shoe at the clerk. "You think my feet are this big? Stop asking silly questions and show me what you got."

"Right this way," he says insolently. He tries to show her an expensive pair that's out of style, but she's too smart for such tricks and chooses a good pair on her own. At the cashier desk, she lies and says no one helped her, to deprive him of his commission.

Finished with her business, she lingers in the ladies' department, inspecting the dresses. They're nicer than she'd expected. In the corner, a customer stands before a three-way mirror to be fitted by a young woman with pins in her mouth, who's taking forever just to mark off a simple hem. Pearl's tempted to push her away and grab the chalk and pins herself, just to get it over with. If I did set up shop in this town, she thinks, I'd do fine with this as my competition.

A clerk interrupts her thoughts, asks if Pearl needs help.

"No, no help," she says, backing away.

Back at the apartment, Pearl finds the silver sitting in the sink ready to tarnish while Frieda daydreams at the kitchen table with a department store catalogue. Pearl drops her shopping bag with a thud, and Frieda straightens her posture. "Oh, there you are," Frieda says. Her bottom lip trembles like a girl's. "I've been feeling so hopeless this morning."

"How do you think the silverware feels?" Pearl says.

"Is this why I worked so hard to get to America? To be my husband's servant?"

Now she's waking up? "What did you expect?" Pearl asks.

Frieda thumbs the edges of her catalogue. "At least in Cuba, everything was new and interesting. Then New York was so awful, all I wanted was to escape. But here, it's not interesting or awful, just bland like milk. Like we picked up our shtetl and plopped it down in America. And Mendel, he used to know how to have a good time. But now that we're married, it's like he forgot. Or he wants to have a good time, but he doesn't care if I do." She grabs the dustpan, flings it against the wall, where it leaves a mark. "Mazel tov. You were right. Marrying him was a mistake."

It's a long-awaited admission that gives Pearl precious little satisfaction. She sits down across from her pouting sister. "Forget right or wrong. All this time, you wanted to be Mendel's wife. Now that you are, barely a week, and already you don't want it. But Mendel isn't a new doll to put in the cupboard when you're tired of playing. He's your husband, the future father of your children."

"I know." Frieda stares at her fingernails. "I'm no idiot."

"Listen, I've only got a couple days before I go back to New York. In that short time, I can listen to you complain, or I can help you make life here better, easier, more comfortable." Frieda starts

crying. Pearl takes her hand, strokes it. "When will you stop playing the little girl? You're a woman now."

"I'm sorry," Frieda says through tears, "to keep visiting my
troubles on you."

"I'm your sister. There's no need to apologize."

"Yes, you're my sister." Frieda wipes her eye with her fist. "But
you got stuck with the job of being my mother. And for that I
apologize."

You see me, Pearl thinks, maybe for the first time. She squeezes
Frieda's hand, then gets up to put on her apron.

"Do you really have to go back to New York?" Frieda asks. "I
think I could make it with you here, but otherwise, I don't know
what I'll do."

Pearl has been wondering the same thing. All alone here,
how will she manage? And then another thought comes to mind:
Without her, how will I manage?

"You'll be fine," Pearl says. "Mendel's not so terrible."

Lies, but what else can she say?

"Pearl, you and I were always together, until I left Cuba, then
when I came here," says Frieda. "If you leave now, when will we see
each other again?"

Her question hurts because there's no clear answer. "What
about Basha? It's okay for us to leave her alone?"

"She was before. She'd probably be happier. She only needs
books for company."

You don't know Basha as well as you believe, Pearl thinks.
Still, it's true that she's not as fragile as Frieda. "And my job?" Pearl
says. "Safaya's teaching me all there is to know about the business.
What would I do here?"

Frieda nods at the shopping bag containing Ben's new shoes.

"Such nonsense." Pearl ties her apron strings extra tight behind her back, gives them an unnecessarily vicious tug.

"Is it nonsense?" Frieda asks. "I see how you two look at each other."

Pearl takes a deep breath. "I feel sorry for him, that's all. He's a good man."

"A good man? That's all? Pearl, you're lying to me or yourself."

"More than good," she admits. "A hard worker, and I respect him. He's practically all alone in this world, and I'm doing him a favor."

"He may not see it the same way."

Unable to face her sister, Pearl folds her arms, inspects the floorboards for dust, crumbs, and stray chicken feathers. "And that Deborah?" she asks.

"Pearl, be serious. You think he cares for her?"

She knows he doesn't and feels an irrational sense of pride to hear it confirmed. "Why are we talking and talking about things that will never be? Let's get to work."

Frieda's probably right, Pearl thinks. With encouragement, Ben might be willing. He's a good man. If she did want a husband, what better offer could there be, here or in New York? And to have Frieda close by again, that would be something.

She thinks of Ben holding her tight in his strong arms, shielding her from harm. That's also something.

All this talk about marriage throws Pearl off her natural rhythm. She bangs Frieda's dustpan extra loud while emptying it into the waste pail and spills half the dust back onto the floor. As she sweeps it up again, she wonders if Ben will like his new shoes. Will he even notice the difference?

Pearl hasn't done this many household chores since Mother died and she took over the home, though she was barely taller than the door handle. Every day while Frieda trooped off to the Jewish girls' school with its dreary lessons about how to form curving Hebrew letters or observe the rules of bodily purity, Pearl cleaned dishes, swept the pale-red wood floor, and set the copper samovar to heat on the stove, its steam rising up to the low ceiling beams of their house, where she hung bundles of fresh herbs to dry.

Pearl liked working alone. She was good company for herself.

She used to spread breadcrumbs for the hens, cradling their warm eggs in her apron, and milk the cow, with her constant mournful stare and round hairy stomach. Afterward, she'd pull the sheets taut over straw tick mattresses that she bullied into shape with her fists, then boil mushroom soup and listen to the sound. That's how you knew if it was cooking right, by the sound. She can hear it now, and the sound of Father and Avram kicking their boots on the doorstep, coming home from the butcher shop, expecting dinner. And after dinner, the pleasure of no sounds, as she sewed by the kerosene lamp, or sometimes did nothing, just sat, basking in a few stolen moments of stillness.

In New York, there's never any peace like that, only work without end, without a future. Sure, Safaya talks big, but would she really turn over the shop to Pearl, who's no blood relation? No, Safaya would want to sell it for a good price, to give the proceeds to her daughter. She'd want to get the kind of money Pearl could never earn. Pearl would have to find another job, maybe for less money. Maybe in a sweatshop.

With Ben, she could have a home of her own, children of her own. A little tribe to dress and feed and guide as she sees fit, according to her own design.

For the cost of her freedom, she can finally be her own boss.

○

AT DINNER, PEARL presents Ben with the stylish new shoes, with fancy stitching on the edges, a low heel, and a narrow toe. Inside the left shoe, she put the five-dollar bill he left her and another twenty-five bucks besides, to repay her debt.

"I told you, I never figured on you paying me back," Ben says, fingering the money. "Keep it. Use this money for something useful."

"What useful? I got everything I want." You're the one who needs my help, she thinks, but it might wound a man's pride to say so.

"Put it toward starting your own shop," he says.

"If I wanted to do that, I wouldn't need any man's charity," she snaps, startled by how touchy she sounds.

He pouts as he accepts the money, then takes off his old shoes and puts on the new ones. Pearl's appalled by his threadbare socks.

Mendel, who's in a good mood tonight, teases Ben, "You're a fashion plate."

"I don't know about that," he says. "But these look like plenty nice shoes."

They are nice shoes. Already he looks like such a gentleman in them. Imagine, Pearl thinks, how handsome he'd look if he'd let her pick out all his clothes.

Later as he walks her home, they're both a bit pensive, quiet. Pearl's glad. It's so cold, she'd rather conserve her breath. Also, the silence gives her a chance to sort out her thoughts. It's nice being with a man who asks little of her, who seems to know her mind without asking too many questions, a man she pleases simply by being herself. A man who reminds her, in a good way, of the place she once called home. She bumps his arm accidentally, apologizes, and notes with embarrassment the bit of excitement it inspires.

As they turn onto Aunt Rochel's street, Ben talks about his store. Now she's sure he's courting her. "It's a safe business," he says. "People always need food. Even in the Old Country, during the worst times, our family store always did a good business."

Mendel, Frieda, and Ben must have been talking, conspiring to get her to move here. They feel sorry for her, Frieda's old maid sister. Like she needs their pity. In a few words, she could upset all their plans, then catch a night train to New York. So there! She smiles, imagining their surprise. Then her delight fades as she sees herself riding that train alone, leaving them behind, especially Ben, who's still talking about grocery stores.

"In the Old Country, we stayed open all the time," he goes on. "The Reds, the Whites, Polish, Germans, they all came through our store. The Polish were terrible."

"Yes," she says, spitting into the snow.

"But it was the Whites that almost killed me. They came in the store, acting up, saying things about Jews. Then they took me outside. I heard them talking about tying me up behind their horses and dragging me through town, see if I'll live or die. I thought that's the end of me." His voice and hands are shaking, and she knows exactly how he's feeling. Americans, like Safaya or Betty, or her old friend Alexander, wouldn't understand. Alexander has never seen people murdered for no reason other than to give a thrill to a bored and otherwise powerless, penniless soldier.

The worst punishment Alexander has experienced is exile, not death.

Ben continues with his story: "Then one guy asks me, what's in your pocket? It was cigarettes. I always kept a pack with me, not to smoke, just in case I needed something to trade. He took the pack and said, 'Yid, run as fast as you can.' Took pity on me I guess. I didn't wait for explanation. I ran into a field before they realized, and I hid there in the grass until sundown."

"It isn't right," Pearl says. This war, this revolution, the pogroms. It robbed them of their time to be young and foolish.

"No, it isn't," says Ben. "But here we are."

Yes, there they are, and they've found each other. At this moment, she feels very close to him, and the urge to speak rises in her throat. She wants desperately to trust him, and for him to know that she understands, she too has feared for her life. So she says, "I too had some troubles, a bad situation, with a soldier." It's hard to get out more words. But he should know, especially if he's considering asking for her hand. Maybe he'd change his mind. "Only I didn't end up as lucky as you," she blurts out. "You see?"

The wind picks up, shaking the snow from the branches of a tree overhead, startling them both.

"Yes, I see," says Ben, and his eyes grow wet, not just because of the cold. "I'm sorry to hear it. It's a cruel thing for a woman."

"Anyway, it was years ago, and I don't like to talk about it," she says quickly.

"Then we won't talk about it," he says in a soft voice, so caring and mild, it's hard to believe it comes from a man. Where would she find another like him?

She breathes easier, glad there's no need to say more. If she can help it, she'd rather not tell this story again to another human being. "I like to think that somewhere, in some way, someone is punishing them for what they did to us."

"I don't know," he says. "I think you got to leave it to God."

Yes, God, she thinks. Wise words. "Maybe," Pearl says. Her breathing eases and her stomach settles. Maybe she will leave it to God.

TWENTY

THE NEXT DAY, SHE FINDS IN HER COAT POCKET THE twenty-five dollars she'd given Ben. This is getting ridiculous, she thinks. So before going to Frieda's, she visits the store, named, unimaginatively, Grocery Stand. The man must have his money, and this time she's going to order him to keep it.

Approaching the entrance, her nerve falters. She feels embarrassed by what she revealed last night, which gives Ben a kind of power over her she'd rather he not have. Hopefully he's true to his word and will keep silent about it. It's all very confusing.

In front of the store, a couple of dozen bushels are lined up neatly, filled with ripe produce and marked with chalk signs. The large freshly washed windows admit plenty of light. The floors are swept clean, and the air smells of lemons and celery. Customers weigh fruit and vegetables on a scale, then hand money to Mendel and Ben, who tuck it in the pockets of their white aprons. Ben looks more natural in his apron than his brother, whose apron is gleaming white, as if he hasn't done a lick of work all day.

After Ben finishes waiting on a young American woman in a long green coat, Pearl claims she's come to see the extra space next to the store that he keeps talking about, because she wants to give him the money in private. Ben asks Mendel to mind the store for a minute, and Mendel says, "I get it. You want me to do all the work while you cavort with your girlfriends. Well, watch out. She's setting her cap for you."

"I work plenty around here," says Ben. "It wouldn't hurt you to do some too, get your hands dirty for a change. And show more respect for your sister-in-law."

"It's okay," Pearl interjects.

"No, it's not," says Ben. "Mendel, apologize to her."

"Okay, okay, brother," says Mendel. "I'm very sorry, Pearl. Only kidding. No harm done, right? Okay, go ahead, you two. But don't be too long,"

"Thank you," Pearl whispers to Ben as they leave.

"I wouldn't let anyone disrespect you, Pearl," he says, and she lets out a nervous laugh.

Ben gives her a tour of the whole building, the office, the storeroom, and then the empty storefront he was telling her about, a cramped dusty room with bare scuffed walls, lonelier than a coffin. "I sleep on that couch by the window," he says, pointing to a narrow sofa with a wrinkled quilt and a sunken pillow.

You poor man, Pearl thinks. She pats the pillow into shape and straightens the quilt, though he tells her don't bother. You need someone to take care of you, a manager.

"This room gets nice light in the morning," says Ben. "And in back, I could build a partition for your customers to try on their clothes in private. You'd be your own boss, not working for another. What's his name, the guy you work for in New York?"

"Her name is Safaya."

"Okay, you call this Safaya on the telephone and say I got a better prospect here and I'm staying. You can name this place yourself. What name would you choose?"

"I don't know." She's feeling winded. Everything's moving so fast.

"It's a busy street, good for business. When I first saw this space, I noticed all the foot traffic. A couple of factories not far. Yet four different groceries opened here, then closed. Why couldn't they make it? Made no sense. I knew I could do better."

"You seem to be doing well here," Pearl says, giving the quilt a final tug.

"Can't complain."

"Because of all your girlfriends." She's enjoying teasing him. "If you ever got married, they'd probably stop coming around to shop."

"No, I think they'd still come around," he says. Is he joking? She can't quite tell.

"Your grocery needs some decoration." Pearl thinks of Safaya's store, with its tasteful floral wallpaper. "And a woman at the counter to chat with the customers."

"Maybe you'd be interested in the job?"

"Me? I'm not much for chatting. I'm a dressmaker."

He's run out of talk, and she has nothing to say either. She feels comfortable being silent with him, but is that the basis for a good marriage? Her mother died so young, Pearl can't recall if she and

Father talked much together. As for other couples she's known, it's always a mystery what goes on in the houses of outsiders.

"Well," she says, pulling on her coat, "I don't know, I have to think about it." As they step outside, she adds, "It's colder than I thought. I should run back to Aunt Rochel's for my wool sweater before going to Frieda's."

"I could use some fresh air. I'll go with you."

It's a short, silent walk, maybe five minutes, but Pearl feels light-headed, out of breath at the end of it. When they reach Aunt Rochel's porch, she has an urge to see Ben's face once more, to turn his head toward hers and look into his pretty blue eyes, but she's embarrassed. Rochel stares at them through the living-room window. Deborah's watching too. When Ben and Pearl look at Deborah, she moves away from the window. But Rochel stays where she is, staring.

"You'd better get back to the store," says Pearl. "Mendel's waiting."

"Yeah, sure. See you tonight for dinner."

"You're coming?" she asks, though she knows he is. She just wants him to say it.

"If you're cooking, I'm coming," he says, which makes her happy.

Inside, she runs to the room, finds her sweater, and then realizes she never gave Ben his twenty-five dollars. Oh, well, she thinks, I'll repay him eventually.

As she's about to leave, Aunt Rochel moves in front of the door. "You're going out like that?" she asks, nodding at Pearl's slacks. "Okay for you. But I don't think such an outfit would appeal to Ben. You might consult Deborah to learn about his tastes."

Deborah waves meekly, as if to say, yes, of course, happy to help. Pearl tries not to laugh. "Who cares what Ben thinks?"

"You seem to care," says Aunt Rochel. "By the way, you got a telephone call from that boss of yours in New York. What's her name? Sonia?"

Pearl's cheeks and the back of her neck grow very warm. "Safaya."

"Yeah, Sonia. She asked when you're coming back this weekend. Or aren't you?"

"Of course I am."

Aunt Rochel raises an eyebrow. "I'm sure she'll be happy to hear that. She sounded pretty anxious to hear your answer."

"She likes my work." Pearl grips her sweater. "If I wasn't so busy with my sister, maybe I could teach your Deborah a few things."

"No, this was a different kind of call. Like someone in love." Aunt Rochel titters. "Maybe she saw those pants of yours and got confused." Now she's really laughing, a loud throaty laugh that draws Deborah from the other room.

You *machashefa*, Pearl thinks, twisting her sweater tightly in her hands as if to tie it into a noose. I see your true purpose, and your empty words won't move me an inch. She pushes her way outside. "I can't waste time on chitchat."

"Give Frieda my love." Aunt Rochel reaches over to fix Deborah's collar, which looks rumpled. "A new bride is a wonderful thing. Don't worry, when you're gone, I'll come by every day to make sure her apartment is in order."

"I already am making sure."

"Well, I'll make double sure."

No, you won't, Pearl thinks. On her way out, she slams the door behind her, so hard that a snow shovel leaning against the porch railing falls over. Why is she so angry? But then she realizes this is quite something else: She's happy.

○

BEFORE DINNER, BEN excuses himself to the toilet. While Frieda carves the roasted chicken, Mendel takes Pearl aside. "I wouldn't push it, Pearl, but you know my brother's a nice boy. What are you waiting for? An old maid is a terrible thing. Get married and stay in Detroit. Frieda would like it, and so would I."

"You would?" she says, deliberately playing innocent.

"Yeah, you're a much better cook than Frieda."

Go bother a goose, Pearl thinks. "Frieda's improving. Give her credit."

"You know how much I admire you. Why can't we be friends, Pearlie?"

"The name is Pearl," she says. "You admire me? It's the first I've heard of it."

"So I tease you plenty. I tease everyone. It's just my way. Okay?"

Pearl's exhausted of their banter. When he's like this, Mendel's not so bad, even has a kind of charm. Right now, they share the same goal, so they might as well get along. "Okay," she says.

With everyone pushing them together, Pearl figures now that she's decided, the rest will fall into place. But at dinner, Ben barely looks her way. Has she imagined his interest? Perhaps her story about her past turned his heart to ice.

Whatever the reason, Ben fails to do his part. Maybe it's hard for him to say the right words, I love you, or even I like you. Mendel and Frieda valiantly try to fill the silences. After the meal, while helping Frieda clear plates, Pearl makes it a point to mention she should check the timetables for the New York trains.

Finally Ben speaks up. "Why? Stay a *bissel*. See what's going on in Detroit. Tell you what, you can have that extra space of mine for nothing the first month."

Pearl slams the dirty plates down on the table. "Listen to me, Mr. Ben the Oak. Here or there. A job I can get here because there are not so many talented dressmakers like New York. And if I'm here, I can be near my sister. But I can't stay with that *machashefa* Rochel much longer and I sure can't stay here in Detroit no more without a good reason, and your extra space is not a good reason. So either I go to New York, or I stay here and we get married. What do you want?"

She's worked herself up into such a state, she hardly notices Frieda and Mendel sliding out of their chairs and tiptoeing out of the room together. "Thank God one of them spoke up," Mendel mutters on their way out. "It took long enough."

"Keep quiet for once," Frieda says in a fierce whisper, which Pearl is glad to hear. Frieda pulls Mendel into their bedroom and closes their door.

Ben is sitting there with a stupefied look on his face. A nice face, now that she's gotten to know it. Tonight he wears a baby-blue tie that brings out his eyes. He should wear blue more often. And avoid red. It doesn't match his coloring.

She was hoping this might work out, more than she first realized. Now it seems she's made a mistake, and she's so upset, she wants to hit him or hit herself or run away. That means it's back to New York, to make dresses for strangers. Fine, if that's what she has to do. But at least he could react. Say yes, no, something.

"So?" asks Pearl, standing over Ben. "You want to get married, don't you?"

Ben smiles nervously in her shadow. "I suppose I do."

Pearl, feeling weak in her ankles, grabs the back of a chair to steady herself. "Okay, we'll do it." She lets out a low sigh, then resumes bringing dishes to the sink. "Now I have to wash them all myself," she says. "Whenever there's work to do, Frieda disappears." Her hands tremble as she reaches for the soap. Did that even happen? Her eyes cloud with tears. Yes, she knows it's real. She's staying here in Detroit. With him. And she feels . . . well, she can't properly name her feelings. Until she senses Ben's presence behind her.

"Here," he says, handing her his dish. "You want some help?"

She's so touched by this simple, thoughtful gesture, from a man no less, that it takes her a second to get out the words. "No, this is for women."

"Where is it written?" he asks, so she lets him help. In the warm soapy water, his hand finds hers and kneads it gently.

○

FRIEDA'S OVERJOYED, TAKING turns hugging them both and crying. Mendel pumps his brother's hand several times and says, "Good on you, Pearl. Good on you."

As they leave, exchanging more hugs and kisses, Frieda reminds Pearl that she's promised to teach her to sew, really sew. Could they start tomorrow? Pearl agrees to bring over a dress pattern from one of her magazines, something simple.

"Just like the old days," Frieda says, "sewing hats together in Cuba."

"You two are lucky girls," Mendel says, then sings a line from "I'll See You in C-U-B-A." "I'd like to see Cuba sometime. What was it like there, really?"

Frieda's face lights up. "The most beautiful place in the world!"

"Don't listen to her," Pearl says. "It was a place to stay for a year. A poor city with no opportunities."

"I know what I'm talking about," said Frieda. "I lived there the same as you. Only I wasn't afraid like you were. I went out. I explored. I saw everything."

Okay, okay, don't be offended, Pearl thinks, though she herself feels offended at that moment. I saw plenty of Cuba, but what I saw was different, more complicated. You breezed through that place, but on me, Cuba left its mark. You wouldn't understand.

When Ben walks her home, he reaches for her hand and she grasps it firmly. They talk about practicalities, decide not to wait. They're not children. Also, the sooner they're married, the sooner she can move away from Aunt Rochel. Ben knows of a decent room they can rent near the store. It's a start. Until they have children.

She makes it clear she doesn't want a marriage and a home like Frieda's. If Ben wants to be king of his castle, fine, but Pearl must be queen. Also she says she will not take advantage. If she does use his space for a shop, she'll pay him rent for it regular.

"As you want," says Ben as they say good-bye on Aunt Rochel's porch. "Don't worry. I'm not my brother. I wouldn't want his wife or his style of marriage."

"I know," she says. "Dear Ben, of course I know."

He has this questioning look as if he's unsure whether to kiss her cheek, her lips, or anywhere. So she holds his face and brings it closer to hers. Their kiss is sweet, tentative at first, but then his lips press hers with vigor, prying them open with his tongue. Pearl opens her lips to match his. She's breathing heavily through her nose, and her heart is throbbing—she feels so much pleasure that it scares her. She pulls away, bids him a crisp good night, and runs into the house.

That evening she dreams of Cuba. She's lost again in Old Havana, and she's forgotten her Spanish so she can't ask the way. She's also forgotten the name of her boss and his wife. Frieda's there too, looking lovely in white, leaning on Mendel's arm and laughing. Pearl stands at the water's edge, the Malecon, where the waves crash and then recede into the bay, and she rides along with them, and now she has a vision of open sky and ocean, of blue spreading in all directions, and she's in the center, floating yet stable.

Pearl wakes up later than she has in a while, breathing heavily and her forehead damp with sweat. She remembers now, she's engaged to be married. After all the people she's met, the places she's been to, the things she's seen, now she's here, engaged to a man with holes in his socks.

A man with holes in his socks who loves me.

She doesn't feel ready to open her own store in a strange city, so she'll look for a job first, to establish herself. Perhaps that Hudson's store could use a skilled New York dressmaker. Eventually, on the side, she'll take orders, make clothes for family or their friends. She might start by making Ben a handsome gray suit for their wedding.

She must really have a feeling for this man, since she's fantasizing about making him a suit.

Closing her eyes, Pearl recalls standing on Aunt Rochel's porch with Ben, and that long kiss. Yes, she decides, I want more.

As she gets out of bed, Pearl thinks, I could pretend it was all a joke. Mendel practically goaded me into making the proposal. I could leave, take the train back to New York right now and resume my old life as a single woman carrying a knife for company. Safaya still my boss, Basha and other single women for friends, or dancing partners. Frieda far away and lost. When I get older, I'll run a shop that'll run me ragged with worry, or work for someone else, living in constant fear of losing my place, always a step from being cast into the street.

No, I've given Ben my word. It's 1924, a new year, and I'm ready for a new life.

Pearl pulls on her clothes, a slim green skirt and her pink blouse, then hunts for that magazine with the dress pattern she's promised her sister. Tonight I'll write Father, Pearl thinks, and I'll telephone Basha to break the news. I'll tell her it will be a small wedding, don't think of coming in for it, so as not to rub it too much in her face. Basha can visit in the summer. She could move here too if she wants. Or stay in New York.

Move or stay. Move? Or stay . . . Which one?

If there is a definitive answer to that question, Pearl suspects she's unlikely to find it. That kind of surety has disappeared from her life, like some object she once had and lost, maybe left behind in Cuba. Something she once valued greatly, and now she can't remember what it is. Maybe she never will.

Outside her bedroom window, the sky is gray, the trees are bare, the ground is covered in snow. A landscape stripped of all its color, Pearl thinks. I guess I'll be responsible for bringing the color to this place.

She can't find that magazine she's looking for—where is that pattern?—and the day is slipping away from her. Now Aunt Rochel is calling her to the telephone, saying it's from that woman in New York. She says she must speak with you immediately.

Pearl takes a long breath and accepts the phone. Without fanfare, she shares her news, then says nothing for a while, even though it's long distance.

Finally Safaya says, "I didn't think you wanted to be married."

"I didn't either," admits Pearl. "But I've changed my mind. I've found a decent man and with him I can make a home as I see fit, and I can be near my sister."

"I never pictured this kind of life for you. You could have been a designer."

Pearl shrugs. "And a cow flew over the roof and laid an egg."

"Don't mock me with your Old Country sayings. You're a talented woman."

"I know that," says Pearl. "I can be a designer in Detroit. In my own way."

"Tell me honestly," says Safaya, "you think you can be happy, settling there?"

Pearl lowers the earpiece for a minute. She finds such talk exhausting, especially over a telephone. She wants to say, yes I think so, but no I can't be sure. This is how life is, giving up some things to get others. You make these decisions one at a time, find the best way to push forward, and move to the next thing. It's the opposite of making a dress, where everything is planned out before you act. Only when you look back on your life do your choices create a line, a shape, yes, a pattern. Is this settling? Pearl won't know for sure until she's dead, when it's too late. Yet at least this way, she'll be free to make her own choices rather than live under someone else's direction.

"Yes," she says. "I think I'll be happy."

"But are you satisfied with this marriage? If you need help, Pearl..."

"No, I don't want help," Pearl says, interrupting. "I want to do this on my own."

"I see." Safaya pauses before she continues. "Maybe in my head, I wanted to see you as someone you weren't."

An image of the pretty woman from that party flashes through Pearl's mind, a lifetime of hiding in tight rooms with one eye on the door. No thanks. That's not freedom. She thinks of Alexander Lewis with his dainty salad forks and costly cigarettes. That's not freedom either. She remembers him telling her: *You'd better find some American to marry.* Well, now she has.

"This is me as I really am," says Pearl. "I choose this and I ask you to respect it."

"Of course I respect it, and you," Safaya says. "Pearl, as long as it's clean under your bed and on your bed, I wish you all the luck in the world."

Hanging up, Pearl feels dizzy from her small victory. She could take it all back, call Safaya right now and say she's changed her mind, but she will not. It's the end of something, she thinks, *a different future I'll never know.* At the same time, going back to New York would mean the end of other things, like this future that's about to be hers. Either way, emerging wholly unscathed is not an option.

She wants to finish getting ready, but Aunt Rochel stands up, moves into Pearl's path. Rochel's been sitting in the kitchen, waiting for Pearl to finish the call, and now she has something to say. "Wait a minute, young lady. Don't think I didn't suspect about you and Ben. You can't fool me so easy. And don't think I didn't hear you saying I'm a *machashefa.* Why do you have to talk about me that way?"

"And I know what you say about me. Don't start with me. I can do things too."

"Why, what did I say?" asked Aunt Rochel.

"It wasn't what you said, it was what you meant. All that cruel talk about my boss in New York, a fine woman who's been very generous to me. You had no right to talk about her like this."

Aunt Rochel lowers her head. "Maybe sometimes I speak too

direct. I'm sorry. There, I said it. You see? I'm not so bad. Aren't you ashamed to call me *machashefa*?"

"Why should I be ashamed?" says Pearl. "If I'm speaking what's true."

"Because you and I, we're family, which we don't have so much of in America."

For once, Pearl thinks, something we can agree upon.

"Also, now that I think of it, maybe your Ben wasn't right for my Deborah, after all. She's too refined for him. You're probably the better match."

"Too refined?" says Pearl. "What am I? A grater for horseradish?" She's tempted to add, Ben chose me, remember? Yet that's not right. Pearl asked him. Pearl chose him.

"There you go again," says Aunt Rochel, "twisting my words. I'm paying you a compliment."

"If it's really a compliment, you shouldn't have to tell me it's a compliment," says Pearl, "but I'll accept your word." She's anxious to get going and start her day. Anyway, she senses this is not the end of it with Aunt Rochel, just the end of this conversation. No matter, Pearl thinks. She'll see. I'll teach her who I am.

"Now was that so hard?" says Aunt Rochel. "I'm no *machashefa*. And to prove it, I'm going to make your wedding, just like I made for your sister."

"Don't bother, I got over a hundred dollars. I'll make my own wedding," Pearl insists, but Aunt Rochel won't listen.

"Just you try. Now stop with all this silly arguing. We're family." Aunt Rochel dances away into the kitchen, singing over her shoulder, "I'm making you a wedding. I'm making you a wedding!"

"Say what you want. Talk is free." Pearl goes to grab her coat. She'll have to give up looking for the pattern. She and Frieda can make a dress without a pattern, or make their own pattern. Then they'll set out a nice meal for Ben and Mendel: dark bread, smoked fish, potato soup, and fresh oranges. She'll try yet again to explain to Frieda the difference between a potato and parsnip, and she'll save the orange peels from their meal to mix with black tea, which she'll serve Ben, along with a sugar cube for him to suck. That's the way he likes it, with a sugar cube—she remembers.

As Pearl leaves Aunt Rochel's house behind, she remembers so many things, how on the SS *Hudson* she used to save those golden orange peels for her sister to smell, to keep her from getting sea-sick. She remembers—with a chill between her ears, in her heart, and down in her bowels—the horrors of their passage, storms on the open ocean, crying passengers and their terror. She remembers the war, the Revolution, the hunger and the cold, the hatred and violence, blood on the walls of a synagogue, and blood on her own muddy dress. And from earlier, lighter, kinder days, she remembers her mother's rough and busy hands, her father's sweet singing, ice melting in the river in spring, a dinner table on Friday night crowded with guests, heavy with warm food.

Over time, these memories will likely fade in color, like a piece of fabric, or the pages of an open book left out in the sun, but they will never leave her, never stop haunting her. She will always remember.

ACKNOWLEDGMENTS

THIS BOOK WAS INSPIRED BY THE IMMIGRATION STORIES OF my grandparents, Ethel ("Pearl") and Morris ("Ben the Oak"), who were in their eighties and nineties when I knew them.

I began the novel in 2017, after I went with a group of writers to Capitol Hill to advocate for progressive causes. While expressing my support for immigrants to Senator Debbie Stabenow of Michigan, I told her about my grandmother, who fled to the United States from persecution in Russia and was diverted to Cuba for a year. The senator replied, "You have to write your grandmother's story."

Having never written historical fiction, I was greatly helped by hearing historical novelist Dolen Perkins-Valdez describe her process, saying she wrote an initial draft of her story to figure out what she needed to research. That gave me the permission I needed to plunge ahead.

I could not have written *Hotel Cuba* without my family. My brothers Paul and Daniel recorded invaluable audio interviews with my grandparents. My brother Sheldon, a consummate genealogist, sent me this haunting image of my grandmother from Key West that sparked my conception of Pearl:

This story was also informed by anecdotes from my mother, aunts, and other family members, including my late cousin Melvin Fishman, son of "Frieda" in the book. He shared his mother's perspective and conveyed the horrors of shtetl life in the early 1900s. Sadly, he died in 2022. May his memory be a blessing.

While I was in Havana, a wonderful local guide named Maite mentioned that her grandmother used to stroll up the Paseo and peer into windows of the fancy stores to admire the latest fashions. I decided to have Pearl take that same walk.

An enormous thanks to Arlo Haskell, who wrote *The Jews of Key West: Smugglers, Cigar Makers, and Revolutionaries* and runs the Key West Literary Seminar, where I was a guest. Thanks also to Tom Hambright, a Key West historian.

Thank you to Margalit Bejarano, author of *The Jewish Community of Cuba: Memory and History*, who generously answered my questions about the Jewish Cuban community. And thank you to Libby Garland, author of *After They Closed the Gates: Jewish Illegal Immigration to the United States, 1921–1965*, for answering questions and for a line in her book about women dressing as male sailors, which inspired a major plot point of the novel.

In addition to those mentioned above, I read countless informative articles, websites, and books such as *The Chosen Island: Jews in Cuba* by Maritza Corrales; *Tropical Diaspora: The Jewish Experience in Cuba* by Robert M. Levine; *Pleasure Island: Tourism and*

Temptation in Cuba by Rosalie Schwartz; *On Becoming Cuban: Identity, Nationality, and Culture* by Louis A. Pérez; *Immigrant Women in the Land of Dollars: Life and Culture on the Lower East Side, 1890–1925* by Elizabeth Ewen; *The World of Our Mothers: The Lives of Jewish Immigrant Women* by Sydney Stahl Weinberg; and *Daughters of the Shtetl: Life and Labor in the Immigrant Generation* by Susan A. Glenn.

I studied photographs, advertisements, consumer products, popular songs, movies, ship timetables, and, of course, the fashions! I visited the Lower East Side Tenement Museum and the National Archives, where I read correspondence of government officers about undocumented immigrants from Cuba in the 1920s.

One note: In poring over primary and secondary sources, I encountered quite a bit of harsh language, often eerily reminiscent of the most bitter rhetoric of our contemporary politics. In this novel I tried to be as authentic as possible to the language of the time while bearing in mind the values of the present day.

Finally, some words about real life. In 1941 the Nazis, with the help of locals, horrifically murdered most of the five thousand Jewish inhabitants of my grandparents' shtetl of David-Horodok, including my grandparents' families.

My grandparents and their siblings operated a successful grocery in Detroit for years. During the Depression, they built a house on Webb Avenue—which still stands—where they lived together for about fifteen years. The family gradually grew apart, due to several small hurts and personality clashes, climaxing in a fight over the business in the 1950s. My grandmother and her sister cut off relations and never spoke again for the rest of their lives.

For their brilliant editorial feedback, thank you to Maureen Brady, Sally Bellerose, David McConnell, Carol Rosenfeld, Philip

Dean Walker, Mark Derenzo, Bruce Tracy, Genevieve Gagne-Hawes, and Abby Saul. A special thank you to both Avi Landes and Lesléa Newman—I am so blessed to have your friendship. Thanks to Wayne Hoffman at *Tablet* for publishing an early nonfiction version of this story.

Thank you to my writing community for their comradeship and support, including Stonecoast MFA, GWU, the Writer's Center, and Politics and Prose. Thank you to the DC Arts Commission for their support.

Profound thanks to Steven Chudney and Sarah Stein. Thanks to the whole team at Harper Perennial including Hayley Salmon, Jane Cavolina, and Stacey Fischkelta.

And thank you, Anthony, for so many things that I cannot begin to name.

ABOUT THE AUTHOR

AARON HAMBURGER IS THE AUTHOR OF THE STORY COLLEC-
tion *The View from Stalin's Head*, awarded the Rome Prize in Lit-
erature by the American Academy of Arts and Letters and the
American Academy in Rome, and the novels *Faith for Beginners*
and *Nirvana Is Here*, winner of a Bronze Medal from the Foreword
INDIES Book Awards. His writing has appeared in the *New York
Times*; *Washington Post*; *Chicago Tribune*; *Tin House*; *Subtropics*;
Crazyhorse; *Poets & Writers*; *Tablet*; *O, The Oprah Magazine*; and
The Forward. He has taught creative writing at Columbia Univer-
sity, the George Washington University, and the Stonecoast MFA
Program.